Vision Impossible

Vision Impossible

· ·
A Psychic Eye Mystery
· ·

Victoria Laurie

AN OBSIDIAN MYSTERY

OBSIDIAN
Published by New American Library, a division of
Penguin Group (USA) Inc., 375 Hudson Street,
New York, New York 10014, USA
Penguin Group (Canada), 90 Eglinton Avenue East, Suite 700, Toronto,
Ontario M4P 2Y3, Canada (a division of Pearson Penguin Canada Inc.)
Penguin Books Ltd., 80 Strand, London WC2R 0RL, England
Penguin Ireland, 25 St. Stephen's Green, Dublin 2,
Ireland (a division of Penguin Books Ltd.)
Penguin Group (Australia), 250 Camberwell Road, Camberwell, Victoria 3124,
Australia (a division of Pearson Australia Group Pty. Ltd.)
Penguin Books India Pvt. Ltd., 11 Community Centre, Panchsheel Park,
New Delhi - 110 017, India
Penguin Group (NZ), 67 Apollo Drive, Rosedale, Auckland 0632,
New Zealand (a division of Pearson New Zealand Ltd.)
Penguin Books (South Africa) (Pty.) Ltd., 24 Sturdee Avenue,
Rosebank, Johannesburg 2196, South Africa

Penguin Books Ltd., Registered Offices:
80 Strand, London WC2R 0RL, England

First published by Obsidian, an imprint of New American Library,
a division of Penguin Group (USA) Inc.

First Printing, July 2011
10 9 8 7 6 5 4 3 2 1

LIBRARY OF CONGRESS CATALOGING-IN-PUBLICATION DATA:

Laurie, Victoria.
Vision impossible: a psychic eye mystery/Victoria Laurie.
p. cm.
ISBN 978-0-451-23406-3
1. Criminal profilers—Fiction. 2. Women psychics—Fiction. 3. Women detectives—Fiction. I. Title.
PS3612.A94423V55 2011
813'.6—dc22   2011004011

Set in ITC Galliard STD
Designed by Alissa Amell

Printed in the United States of America

Acknowledgments

Acknowledgments are the ultimate FB status or Twitter post—they allow everyone to see all the special people in my life, and how amazingly supported I've been over the years. Were it not for the names listed below, there would be no Abby Cooper and certainly no M. J. Holliday, and for that, I am profoundly grateful.

To start: Allow me to humbly bow before my wonderful and amazing editor, Ms. Sandra Harding. Sandy is this incredibly talented and gifted editor who is so levelheaded, grounded, and sensible that I sometimes just call her for a girl chat. (Heh, heh . . . and I'm sure she *loves* that!) She's brought a wonderfully calm and reflective voice to bear in the process of creating the Abby and M.J. books, and I've come to consider her opinion, thoughts, and probing questions invaluable to my writing process. Thank you, Sandy. I think you've added the missing ingredient to the books, and I'm so, so, *so* grateful to have you in my corner.

Next: my agent, Jim McCarthy. You know, I gush about Jim at the beginning of every single book, and after sixteen of these puppies, I'm wondering what I haven't said that I might be able to say this time! In truth, Jim is every author's dream agent. He's personable, informed, a crackerjack negotiator, smart, witty, clever, and the best muse I could ever hope for. Plus, the guy speaks fluent "Victoria," which makes him invaluable just for that! Many a conversation has started with, "What's that guy who was in that thing?" I don't know how he always seems to know which guy and what thing, but he does, and I love him for that and so much more.

My *marvelous* copy editor, Michele Alpern, who somehow managed to squeeze this manuscript into her already overpacked schedule. You're always my first and only pick, Michele, so don't you ever quit copyediting, ya hear? ☺

My publisher, Claire Zion. Thank you for your continued support and unending enthusiasm. I'm SO blessed to be under the NAL umbrella, and your support has meant everything to me.

Also from the NAL team: editorial assistant Elizabeth Bistrow and publicist extraordinaire Kaitlyn Kennedy—you guys are simply fabulous, and you've provided such wonderful assistance and expertise. I'm equally grateful to have you in my corner!

Special thanks also to my own personal "Team Laurie," Katie Coppedge and Hilary Laurie—or my sistahs from other mistahs. Thank you for working so hard behind the scenes and for filling in the gaps for me. Also, thank you simply for being extraordinary women with unwavering enthusiasm to face the day and put a little sunshine into mine. I love you oodles and oodles, ladies.

I. J. Schecter, aka "Idgie Bibbles": Thank you for helping me with that tricky Canadian speak and for providing some navigation in and around the greater Toronto area. I'm grateful for that and for all the fabulous anecdotes you send me, which always bring with them an added laugh and a smile. ☺

Finally, extended thanks to my family and friends, with a few honorable mentions to those of you who have given extra special support to me and the books, and you are: Mary Jane Humphreys; Nora, Bob, and Mike Brosseau; Karen Ditmars; Leanne Tierney; Dr. Jennifer Casey; Tess Rodriguez; Shannon Dorn; Suzanne Parsons; Silas Hudson; Pippa and Betty Stocking; Juan Tamayo; Ric Michael; Drue Rowean; Thomas Robinson; and Neil and Kim Mahoney.

Hugs and love,
Victoria

Vision Impossible

Chapter One

. . .

For the record, burying a dead body is a *lot* more work than it looks like on TV.

Also for the record, burying a dead body while wearing a clingy cocktail dress and heels, and in the pouring rain—darn near impossible. Of course, I had help, which could be why we eventually got our dearly departed dude six feet under. (Okay, so maybe it was more like two feet under, but who's really measuring at that point?)

"I think that's good," said my oh-so-gorgeous fiancé as he patted down the mud, leaves, and scrub covering our dead guy.

"Thank God," I said, holding my hands palms up to let the rain wash some of the mud off. And that's when I realized my engagement ring had slipped off. "Son of a beast!" I gasped. (Yes, I'm still not swearing, which, at times, proves most inconvenient.)

"What?" asked my sweetie.

Before answering him, I dropped to all fours and began to feel around frantically in the mud. "My ring! I've lost my ring!"

My fiancé threw aside his shovel and came to squat down next to me. "When?"

Tears welled in my eyes and my heart raced with dread. "I'm not sure," I admitted, still scratching at the mud with my fingernails.

"Hey," he said gently, taking my wrists in his hands to stop my frenetic search. "If it's in the grave, we're not going to find it now. We've got to get out of here."

"But—" I began.

"No buts. Now come on. They'll catch on that we've killed the head of the guard any minute now, and they'll come looking for us. We have to put some distance between us and them."

I was still crying, however, and I couldn't get over losing the most precious thing I owned. "Please, Rick?" I begged, using the name easily now. "Just give me a minute to look; I promise if I don't find it in—"

And that's as far as I got before the woods all around us erupted in gunfire. Rick pulled me to him protectively. I stared into his deep brown eyes as he growled, *"Move!"*

He got no further argument from me; we surged forward and I stuck close to him as we darted through the underbrush. We ran for probably a quarter mile, and I tripped and slipped almost the entire way in my heels. The darn things had no traction, and if Rick hadn't been practically carrying me, I'm sure I wouldn't have made it that far that quickly.

We stopped to catch our breath and listen for signs of a chase behind us. I did my best not to quiver in fear while he scanned the area. In the distance I could hear the occasional pop of a gun, but nothing seemed close, and for that, I was grateful. I eyed my sore, muddied, blistered feet and wished that my black pumps were ruby red and I could click them together to go back home.

"You ready to move again?" Rick asked me.

"Yes," I said.

No, I thought.

"I can see a structure about twenty yards that way," he told me. "I think it might be a hunting lodge or a log cabin. We can make it there and hide out till they've finished looking for us. It'll also give us some shelter from this rain."

"Yippee," I said woodenly.

Rick smiled in sympathy and took my hand. "Come on, babe. It's not far."

Now, you're probably wondering what mess I'd gotten myself into this time—right? Let me take all that suspense out right now, and admit that it was a doozy!

It all began a few weeks prior to our mad dash through the forest, at a time when I was feeling . . . well . . . patriotic.

Of course, when you have three high-ranking members of the FBI, CIA, and armed forces telling you that your country needs you, it can be a powerfully convincing argument.

You see, several weeks before, there was a breach in our national security of epic proportions. Something was stolen that was so crucial to our country's safety that it left each and every one of us vulnerable.

What was it? you ask. Well, if I told you, I'd have to kill you.

Ha, ha, ha! *Kidding!* I'll divulge all; but let me at least start again at the beginning, which, for me, was on a beautiful late-April day in downtown Austin when I was called to a meeting at the FBI field office, where I was a civilian profiling consultant. That's really just a fancy way of saying that, as a professional psychic, I assisted the FBI by pulling warm clues out of the ether on cases that had long since gone cold.

At this particular meeting was my sweetheart—Assistant Special Agent in Charge Dutch Rivers—his boss Brice Harrison, *his* boss FBI regional director Bill Gaston, and a lieutenant colonel with the air force, along with some steely-looking dude from the CIA.

During the course of that meeting, it became evident that something of *great* importance had been stolen off a military base and was then summarily smuggled out of the country. The good news was that the item had been traced to Canada. The bad news was that everyone agreed it would not be there for long.

Now, naturally our government wanted its property back, and so they'd sent two CIA agents into Canada to retrieve it. Those agents' true identities were discovered, however, and I understand that their demise was swift and most unpleasant . . . something I'd rather not think about, actually.

Anyway, when it became evident that the task of retrieving the article in question was more formidable than first imagined, Bill Gaston thought of me.

I debated the idea of becoming a spy for about two whole minutes, something in hindsight I'm still sort of regretting, but I'd agreed, and Dutch and I had flown to Washington, D.C., the following week.

We'd been met at the airport by a lanky young agent with red hair and lots of freckles. He reminded me of Opie. "Agent Rivers and Ms. Cooper?" he asked, spotting us immediately from the faces in the crowd surrounding the luggage carousel.

Dutch extended his hand. "Agent Spencer?"

Opie shook Dutch's hand warmly. "Yes, sir," he said, offering me a nice smile too. "Our car is this way."

We trailed behind Spencer, toting our luggage to a waiting black sedan. I swear, if the FBI ever wants to blend in right, they'll need to add a few Priuses to the fleet.

Spencer loaded my bag into the trunk and we were on our way. "Are you taking us to headquarters?" Dutch inquired.

Spencer shook his head. "No, sir," he told us. "I've been told to bring you to the CIA central office."

I gulped. I grew up at the height of the cold war, so I still think of the CIA as an agency staffed with seriously scary people willing to do *anything* for the cause. But I held my nerves in check—I mean, I didn't want to appear all fidgety and nervous on my first day of spy school; how uncool would *that* be?

We arrived at the CIA central office and Opie handed us off to a female agent dressed in a smart black pantsuit, a crisp white shirt, and no emotion on her face whatsoever.

She took us through security before seeing us to a large conference room, where nearly a dozen men and one woman were already seated.

The woman stood when we entered, and I noticed she was at the head of the oval table. "Good morning," she said cordially. "Agent Rivers, Ms. Cooper, please come in and join us."

The agent who'd shown us in backed out of the room and closed the door. I felt Dutch's hand rest on my lower back as he guided me to the only two available seats left at the table. My mouth went dry as I took my chair, but when I saw FBI director Gaston sitting across from us and smiling warmly, I breathed a teensy bit easier.

It struck me then that the table was arranged somewhat by rank. The woman at the head of the table was obviously running the show, and she was flanked by two gentlemen who I'd guess were in their midfifties but seemed full of authority. The authority vein trickled down the table from there.

I also couldn't help noticing many steely eyes were focused my way. I could also see a little disappointment in a few of their expressions while they assessed me head to toe. Not the first time I'd experienced that reaction, and likely not the last.

"Welcome to Washington," the woman at the head of the table said into the silence that followed our sitting down. "I'm Christine Tanner, and I'm the CIA director of intelligence here in D.C."

I smiled and nodded to her, and Dutch did the same. And that was it for pleasantries, because Tanner promptly got down to brass tacks by clicking a button on a handheld remote, which caused the conference room to go dark except for the projection of a slide onto a screen at the other end of the room. "Ms. Cooper, as you have cleared our security background checks, we feel it wise to educate you on the nature of the security breach we encountered a few weeks ago."

I focused on the slide, which showed an aerial view of a large air force base. "This is a military outpost in southern Nevada. On the morning of April sixth, during a routine flight test, one of our military drones went missing." I heard a click and a new slide showed the image of an unmanned drone aircraft like I'd seen on the news used in air strikes against enemy militant fighters in Iraq and Afghanistan, although this one looked much smaller and sleeker in scale and on its top were mounted a small camera and what looked like a small rifle.

"The pilot claimed that midway through the test flight, the operating system on the drone failed, causing it to stop responding to his commands, and eventually crash somewhere out in the desert."

So far I was following. The air force lost a little drone. Got it.

"It is not unheard of for the operating systems on these aircraft to fail, especially since this model was a prototype."

"It's smaller than most of your regular drones, right?" I asked.

The colonel nodded. "It's also the latest in whisper technology. It's powered electrically from a lithium battery, and the drone is virtually silent, which allows it to get within a hundred feet or so of its target without being seen or heard. Because of its advanced technology, this model would be very expensive to replace, and this particular drone was carrying something of great importance, so an extensive search was immediately conducted to retrieve whatever remained of the drone and its cargo."

I looked at Dutch; he was focused on Tanner in a way that suggested there might be something more to this missing-drone story. "After combing through the area where the drone was believed to have crashed, no evidence of it could be found, which is why the military began to suspect the pilot's story."

A little way down from me and to the right, the lieutenant colonel who'd come with Gaston to recruit me in Austin shifted in his seat uncomfortably. Into the silence that followed Tanner's last statement, he said, "I personally requested the pilot come in for a polygraph. But when he failed to show up, we went looking for him. We found him on the floor of his shower, shot through the head at point-blank range."

"Suicide?" I asked, already knowing the answer.

"No," he told me.

"Any leads on who pulled the trigger?" Dutch asked.

"No again," said the military man.

"We hope to get Ms. Cooper's intuitive input on that later," Director Gaston said, with a meaningful look at me.

I nodded. I'd do what I could, especially if this was a case of national security.

Tanner spoke next. "Obviously, we no longer suspect there was an operational issue with the drone. We believe the pilot was coerced or bribed into delivering our drone into enemy hands."

I furrowed my brow. Why was one missing drone causing so much concern? I mean, when I looked back at the slide, the thing looked one step above a model airplane you could buy at any hobby shop.

Gaston seemed to read my mind, because he spoke next. "It's more than just a missing drone," he told me. "Agent Tanner, why don't we allow Professor Steckworth to explain?"

Gaston's eyes had settled on a slight man at the end of the table with salt-and-pepper hair and a nose much too big for his small square face. He cleared his throat when all eyes turned to him, and nodded to Tanner, who clicked her remote, and another slide projected onto the screen. It was a photo of a man young enough to be a college student, and somewhat unremarkable in appearance except for the fact that enveloping him on all sides was the most beautiful cloud of color I'd ever seen. "Oh, my God!" I gasped, already understanding what I was looking at.

"Do you know what you're seeing?" Professor Steckworth asked, eyeing me keenly.

I nodded. "You've captured the image of his aura." In my mind's eye when I focused only on the young man in the photo, I too saw a cloud of color, though it wasn't nearly as vivid or complete as what I was seeing on the screen.

Professor Steckworth smiled. "Yes, very good, Ms. Cooper. Your own abilities allow you to see auras, I take it?"

"Well . . ." I hesitated, not wanting everyone to assume my eyesight was clogged with images of color, color everywhere. "It's less that I *see* them and more that I sense them in my mind's eye. If I close my own eyes and focus, I can imagine, if you will, what someone's aura looks like. And in case you're wondering, Professor, yours is mostly deep blue with some wisps of yellow and olive green."

Professor Steckworth appeared surprised, and he reached for a folder and pulled out a printout of himself, surrounded by a blue bubble with traces of yellow and some olive green, which he held up for everyone to see.

I sat back in my chair and grinned at each person who'd given me a doubtful look when I'd walked in. Oh, yeah . . . I'm a badass psychic, people . . . uh-huh.

"I'm quite impressed," he said, and I relished the few knowing glances exchanged around the table before the professor motioned to Agent Tanner, and she clicked forward again . . . and again . . . and again. In every slide was the picture of another person wearing a different set of colors, varying in degrees of intensity and vibrancy. I knew why they were showing me the photos. "You've documented that each one is unique to the person," I said. "Like a fingerprint."

Professor Steckworth spoke again. "Indeed." He then seemed to want to talk at length and looked to Tanner, who nodded. "You see, twenty years ago I had the most astonishing encounter with a woman who claimed to be a psychic. I was working on my PhD at the time, and her abilities so impressed me that I made her the focus of my thesis.

"This woman was also an artist, and for a mere pittance she would paint your portrait and include your individual aura. Of the hundreds of portraits I viewed from her hand, no two were alike, and that began my quest to see if I could prove that auras really existed.

"What I discovered was that each and every human being emits a certain electromagnetic frequency made up of individual wave patterns that is unique to that person—no two frequency patterns are alike, not even with identical twins. I then worked with the psychic to match colors to each wavelength and was able to develop digital photography software that captured the frequencies and translated them into a signature color pattern. I called the system Intuit."

"Awesome," I whispered, completely fascinated by the photos and the professor's story.

The professor took a sip of water and continued. "As my research and applications turned increasingly promising, the air force learned of Intuit and became intrigued, requesting several demonstrations. They wanted to purchase my patent, but I didn't want to sell it outright. Still, when I needed funding to continue Intuit's development, they offered me a partnership and provided me all I needed in return for the exclusive use of the system. Even then I could see the far-reaching benefits of my research, and as a former marine, I readily agreed.

"Along the way, I made several key discoveries using the software, which could prove most useful to our national security. What my research team and I discovered was that when we scanned in a still photograph of test subjects, our software was unable to detect or produce an aura image; however, when we scanned in a *video* image, the software *was* able to capture the aura." The next slide showed a short clip of an infamous terrorist and it left me stunned. The United States' public enemy number one was surrounded by a bubble of color—mostly brown, black, and dark red—and then my own intuitive radar began to put the pieces together and it filled me with dread.

"The drone was carrying Intuit," I said softly.

In answer there was a click and the next slide revealed an aerial view of that same air base from before and on the ground were little blobs of vivid color.

I gasped.

"Holy shit!" Dutch hissed under his breath.

"The drone was carrying the only prototype of the technology," said Professor Steckworth. "We dubbed the prototype Intuit Tron, and it had reached its final testing phase on the morning it disappeared, which was right before it was set to be deployed. This is the last image it recorded, in fact."

The professor fell silent and in the room you could have heard a pin drop, but then Tanner clicked the remote again and a clip of the president's last State of the Union address began playing. Two seconds in I saw the man I'd voted for and fully supported, surrounded by a huge bubble of brilliant sky blue, emerald green, and deep purple. In that moment I believe my heart skipped several beats and my stomach felt like it fell all the way down to my toes. There was another click and the slide moved to a clip of the British prime minister, then the French president and on and on with each allied national leader's aura vividly portrayed.

It took me several seconds to realize I'd stopped breathing.

The lights came on then and I squinted in the brightness, while my mind raced with the possible horrible implications of having this particular technology in the wrong hands. "Now do you understand why your country so desperately needs someone with your talents, Ms. Cooper?" asked Tanner.

"Yes, ma'am," I said gravely. "Whatever you need me to do, I'll do it."

"Good," she said. "Then let's get started. . . ."

Dutch and I spent the next several hours being briefed on Intuit and its capabilities. I was somewhat relieved to hear that the original software was still with the good ol' U.S. of A., but the drone carried the actual working portable prototype, so if it was placed into the wrong geeky hands, it was only a matter of time before one of our enemies figured out how to reverse engineer it. The implications were beyond frightening.

"Imagine that you are a terrorist," said Professor Steckworth as if he'd been doing much of that lately. "You could easily sneak Intuit and the drone into any country, and fly it anywhere within fifty miles of your location. The battery on the drone is good for up to one hundred miles, or round-trip to your target and back. The software is programmed to look for whatever signature aura you input. If you are an enemy of Israel and you want to kill the Israeli prime minister, simply upload the PM's aura off of any film footage and send the drone over the border.

"Your only worry is that the drone will run out of battery life before it finds your target, but we know with certainty that there are some solar panel technologies being developed right now that are quite lightweight. One of the next improvements we were about to make to the drone was mounting some of these ourselves to extend the drone's range, and we've already calculated that it is possible to mount these on the top of the drone without compromising lift. As long as there are at least eight hours of sunlight available to charge the battery, your drone could run day and night. In theory, given the right climate, like, say, the Middle East, the drone could stay aloft for weeks and weeks."

"How good is the camera system on the drone that was stolen?" Dutch asked.

"Moderately sophisticated," Steckworth admitted. "But it doesn't need to be more than that. Again, Intuit itself is highly sensitive to the color patterns of the auras of your target. It does not need especially good camera quality to recognize the pattern and instruct the drone to fly lower to take a closer look. The software would need to be within five hundred feet or so to make a positive match, and the drone is quite small, only three and a half feet from tip to tail. It is also nearly completely silent. Anyone with a keen eye would think it a large bird gliding on air currents, not a man-made drone."

"Besides the obvious enemies of the U.S., who would want this technology?" I asked.

Steckworth leveled his eyes at me. "Who wouldn't, Ms. Cooper?"

It took me a minute to get the clear meaning of that. "You're telling me that even our allies would try to take the technology away from us?"

"Yes," he said flatly.

I opened my mouth to protest, but Steckworth cut me off. "Possibly not all of our allies will attempt to acquire the drone, but enough of them know about it that it gravely concerns us."

"You mean to tell me, countries like Canada, England, France, and Australia—countries that actually *like* us—might want to take it?"

"Quite possibly."

I sat there for a full minute with my mouth hanging open. I couldn't believe it. How had our world come to this?

"So the drone gets close, makes a positive ID . . . then what?" Dutch asked next.

Steckworth shifted uncomfortably. "We had the drone equipped with a nitro-piston gas-spring air rifle, able to shoot thirteen hundred fifty fps."

I turned to Dutch. "Huh?"

My fiancé's face was hard and not at all happy. "It's a nitro-gas-fueled gun able to shoot thirteen hundred fifty feet per second," he said.

Oh yeah, *that* was helpful. "Huh?" I repeated.

"It shoots darts, not bullets," he said.

I scowled. "Why didn't you guys just say *that*?" And then I thought about what Dutch had just said. "Hold on, it shoots *darts*?"

"Yes," said Steckworth. "But the gun was not loaded with any toxins at the time the drone went missing."

"Hold on," I said, putting up my hand. "It shoots *toxic* darts?"

"However," Steckworth continued, as if I hadn't spoken, "the actual darts outfitted for the gun were stolen from my office on the day the drone went missing."

"It shoots *toxic* darts which are currently *missing*?" Was I the only one just realizing we had one *mother* of a problem on our hands?

"What's the toxin?" Dutch asked in his usual calm style . . . which I found completely annoying.

Again Steckworth shifted uncomfortably, but he gave us the answer. "We created the trifecta of toxins: ricin, botulinum, and dieffenbachia."

"You created the *trifecta* of toxins?" I said, my voice rising in pitch. Seriously? Like, it wasn't lethal enough with just one or two?

"I'm familiar with ricin and botulinum," Dutch said, ignoring me again, "but what's the third one you mentioned?"

"Dieffenbachia," Steckworth repeated. "Highly effective. Works to swell the soft tissue and inhibit the ability to deliver an antidote for the ricin and botulinum."

"How quickly would death follow after the dart hit?" Dutch asked next while I just sat there with my mouth hanging open and a shudder running along my spine.

"In a strong healthy adult male of an average ninety kilograms . . ."

"Two hundred pounds," Dutch whispered to me.

"It would take approximately eight to ten minutes, during which time the subject would be in extreme agony until the convulsions and seizures took over."

"If one of our guys was hit with a dart, how quickly could an antidote be delivered?"

"It would need to be delivered in approximately ninety to one hundred and twenty seconds after exposure to the toxins."

I scribbled a note and passed it to Dutch. It read, *Steckworth must kill at parties. Literally!*

The corner of Dutch's mouth quirked, but he didn't write back. "You guys probably suspect the pilot for the toxin theft?"

"Yes," said Steckworth. "He had the appropriate clearance to be admitted to my laboratory and the area where the toxins were stored, although his ID badge was not used to gain entrance and by coincidence the security cameras were not working on the day of the theft. We believe he may have walked into the building with someone who knew and trusted him."

"I have a question," I said.

Steckworth's eyes swiveled to me. His expression was guarded. "Yes?"

"What were *we* going to use Intuit for?"

Steckworth blinked as if he couldn't understand why I would ask something so obvious. "To target and kill our deadliest enemies."

That's what I'd thought, but it still shocked me a little to hear it out loud. "Why aren't we trying to kill these people the old-fashioned way?" I asked next with just a *hint* of sarcasm. "You know, with a bunker buster or a gun or something less . . . well . . . toxic?"

"Against the enemies we're targeting, Ms. Cooper, the method of death is crucial," Steckworth said frankly. "Blowing our enemies into vapor only turns them into martyrs. They feel a sense of glory dying by bullet or a bomb. The dart we've developed is quite small with a very thin needle and is designed to drop off after impact. The target would experience only a sharp prick slightly more than a mosquito bite, and then within a minute or two they would become very, very sick indeed. As the toxins spread, the target would cry out in pain, vomit, lose control of their bowels, froth at the mouth, their faces and limbs would swell, and they'd convulse until they died. Their death would be as unromantic and inglorious a thing as can be imagined. Those around them would immediately suspect poison and treachery from within, which would further undermine the terrorist establishment. Using Intuit to pinpoint the target and kill them with a toxin serves our purposes on multiple levels."

"Unless someone spots the dart and puts two and two together," I pointed out.

Steckworth nodded. "Yes, but as I said, the dart is quite small, and in the desert, such things get lost in the dirt quite quickly."

I sighed. This whole topic was turning my stomach. The things we planned to do to our enemies and the things they planned to do to us just sickened me, and at that moment, I will admit, I wanted to back out.

Dutch seemed to read my mind and he reached out and grabbed my hand. Squeezing it gently, he said, "It's a dirty business, Abs. But someone's got to step up and do it."

I looked sharply at him. There was something in his eyes I didn't like. Leaning over, I whispered, "Do you mean to say that if I decide to opt out, you're still in?"

Those midnight blues looked deep into mine and held firm. "Yes."

Aw, shih tzu.

Steckworth finished lecturing us on Intuit and before the next round I was allowed a short break to visit the ladies', then returned to the conference room to find CIA director Tanner and FBI director Gaston there with Dutch and a folder.

"Do you feel up to looking at some photographs?" Agent Tanner asked.

I took my seat. "Sure," I said. "What am I looking for?"

The director laid the folder out in front of me and opened to the first picture, of an Asian man with a very flat face and a big blue mole on his nose. Immediately I got the sense that he was one seriously bad dude.

"These are photographs of known weapons dealers with the capability to pull off the drone heist. We'd like you to look through the file and flag any that seem suspicious to you."

I used my finger to flip quickly through the photos. "They *all* look suspicious," I said, smiling at the little joke until I saw Dutch's disapproving stare. "Sorry," I said before taking a deep breath, closing my eyes, and switching on my radar to point it at the file.

I studied each and every photo, being very specific when I searched the ether around them for anything that might indicate one of the men had taken the drone. In the end I separated out two photos: one of a short fat man with a beard and mean-looking eyes, and another of a tall dark-haired man with brown eyes and a square jaw. The second man looked very familiar to me in a way I couldn't quite pinpoint. I knew I'd never met him, but he reminded me of someone; I just wasn't sure whom. "I'd look more closely at these two," I said finally, pushing the photos forward toward Director Gaston.

He took them and turned them over to read the names on the back. "Viktor Kozahkov and Richard Des Vries," he said.

I nodded. "The short fat dude is the one that feels the most suspicious," I said pointing to the first photo I'd set in front of him. "But let me clarify that. I'm not sure he's actually responsible for stealing the drone. He feels like he might be coming into this from the side."

"From the side?" Director Tanner repeated.

"She means his relationship to the thief is tangential," Dutch said, eyeing me to see if he got that right, and I nodded. "In other words, he didn't steal the drone, but he probably knows who did and is in on the deal to sell it."

"Lookit that, cowboy," I told him, nodding in approval. "Three years together and you're finally speaking psychic."

"And Des Vries?" Gaston asked, holding up the other photo I'd flagged.

"Same thing but even more distant. I'd say at most he might have heard about the drone being stolen, but he didn't actually take it. Still, he feels connected to this in a singular and significant way, but his connection feels even more sideways, yet equally significant."

Gaston turned the photo back around and squinted at the picture thoughtfully. He then looked at Dutch and a sly smile played at his lips. "Agent Rivers," he said. "May I see you privately for a moment?"

"Yes, Director," Dutch said, getting up and following Gaston out.

Agent Tanner then gathered up her folder and photographs and thanked me for my input.

"There's just one more briefing to go before we'll turn you two loose for the night. They should be in shortly."

She left me then and I leaned back in the chair, closing my eyes and relishing the peace and quiet. After a while I went to the door and looked out into the hallway. Dutch was nowhere in sight. I wondered what Gaston had wanted with him, and why it was taking so long. About ten minutes after that, the door opened and two men in uniform with a whole lotta brass attached to the lapels came in, carrying several files with them. Along for the ride was a guy dressed completely in black, head to toe, with slicked-back black hair, brilliant green eyes, and a thin firm mouth set in a square but fairly handsome face. He moved with the stealth of a panther, and entered the room with an air of pernicious intensity. This is the part in the story where I also admit that he personally scared the crap out of me, which was just awesome, 'cause I don't think I'd been scared enough for one afternoon.

The men introduced themselves, starting with the brass.

The first man, who looked a whole lot like a walrus, said, "I'm Lieutenant Colonel David McAvery." I believe I forgot his name in the very next second.

His military buddy, who walked like a penguin, said, "I'm Colonel John Hughes."

The MIB (man in black) said, "Agent Frost. CIA."

Think I'd be skipping him on my holiday card mailing list.

"Agent Rivers stepped away with Director Gaston," I said.

"We're not waiting," Frosty the Snowman snapped, taking his seat and looking pointedly at the brass.

The two of them wasted no time getting down to business. "We believe the drone is somewhere in the Canadian province of Ontario,"

Walrus said. "Due to the highly sensitive nature of Project Intuit, the drone itself was equipped with several tracking devices. These were all removed once the drone reached Canadian soil, and separately mounted onto freight trucks, each heading in different directions all across the country. It took us several days to track down the devices and conclude they were not still attached to the drone."

"How do you know it's in Ontario province, then?" I asked. "I mean, it could be in another country by now."

Walrus looked at me like I'd spoken out of turn, and Agent Frostbite narrowed his eyes at me, which made me squirm.

"We're fairly certain it's still in Canada," Walrus said. "Professor Steckworth received a signature ping off the software somewhere in the lower Ontario province area, and we believe Intuit is now somewhere within the Greater Toronto metropolitan area."

I raised my eyebrows at Walrus. *"Signature ping?"* I asked. What was with these guys and their inability to speak plain English anyway?

"As a precautionary measure, Professor Steckworth equipped Intuit with its own locator beacon, so to speak. The device is designed to send out a small pulse every forty-eight hours, which can be detected by any passing satellite. By calculating the angle of the ping, we can approximate the area where Intuit is located."

"Okay," I said, understanding better. "Where in Toronto did the signal say Intuit was?"

Walrus nodded to Penguin, who opened up a folder, took out a piece of paper, and said, "The radius of the ping only narrows it to a twenty-square-mile area within the greater metropolitan area. It doesn't give its exact location."

Of course it didn't.

"At this point we're waiting on another ping, set to happen within the next two days, from the device, and if we're lucky, it will bounce off a different satellite, which could help to narrow the search area."

"Do you have any leads at all on where it might be stored, or who might want to buy it?" I asked.

Walrus and Penguin looked to Agent Frostbite. "Yes," he said, without any further elaboration.

Ah, charm. Watching it in action really warms the cockles.

"Could you be a little more specific?" I asked, silently patting myself on the back for having the guts to do so.

"No."

"Helpful," I said, with a big ol' smile.

"We are narrowing the list," he said crisply. "We will give you a full briefing before you leave on your assignment."

"We?" I repeated, hoping there was someone—*any*one—a little warmer than ol' Jack Frost here who could give us the final lowdown.

"Me," he said, looking me square in the eye like he'd really love to take me outside and personally show me the many, many ways to interrogate a terrorist. "I will be giving you a full briefing. And I will be your handler while you're in Canada."

Of course he would. If it weren't for bad luck, I'd have none at all.

Chapter Two

* * *

Dutch and I were finally turned loose around eight o'clock that evening. My eyes felt dry and gritty and my normal slightly sarcastic side was starting to take on a real edge. It's a tough thing when you know you're acting inappropriately and you're still unable to rein it in.

The truth was that I was flippin' scared. Not necessarily of going in undercover to find and recover a lethal weapon, but of failing in that mission. The consequences of either being discovered by the enemy or not returning with Intuit were far too big for me to deal with, and I felt like what I really needed was a phone call home.

So while Dutch was in the shower, I called my sister, Cat. "Hey," I said, feeling weary down to my DNA.

"Hi, honey!" she said, all perky. "Did you get my e-mail?"

"No," I said. "I haven't had a chance."

"Busy at the conference, huh?"

I'd told Cat that I was going to Washington for a weeklong conference on crime fighting. As lame as that story was, Cat bought it. "Yep. There's just *so* much information to take in."

"Oh, I know how those things go. The way to play it is to absorb only what's useful and toss out the rest. That's what I always do."

I nodded dully—like she could see me. "What was in the e-mail?"

"Wedding dresses. Well, more specifically, pictures of wedding dresses."

I pinched the bridge of my nose between two fingers. "Cat, Dutch and I haven't even set a date yet. I mean, I've been engaged for less than a week."

There was an excited squeak on the other end of the line. "Can you *believe* you're getting *married*?"

I smiled and eyed my beautiful ring. Four carats of soft emerald green reflected in the lamplight. "God, I love that man," I said, thinking dreamy thoughts about my soon-to-be husband.

"Anyway, I'm thinking mid-October might be good."

My attention returned promptly to the phone. "October? You mean *this* October?"

"Yes," my sister said as if I were slow on the uptake. "Why not?"

"Uh . . . 'cause that's in, like, six months!"

"So?"

"Cat," I said, using my best "I am going to be reasonable" voice. "I can't get married in six months."

"Why not?" Cat said.

"Why not?" Dutch echoed from the door of the bathroom.

I looked at him and winced. "What I mean is . . ."

"Yes?" said Cat.

"Yeah?" said Dutch.

"See, the thing of it is . . ."

"What?" said Cat.

"What?" said Dutch.

I stood up from the bed. "Will you two stop that?!"

"Stop what?" said Cat. "And who else are you talking to?"

Dutch was eyeing me moodily from the door.

"Cat, I gotta go," I said. I hung up the phone and flashed my fiancé a big ol' smile. It worked about as well as the last time I'd used it.

"Why can't you get married to me in October?"

My smile faded. "It isn't that I can't get married to *you* specifically," I said. "I can't get married to anyone in October."

Dutch crossed his arms. "Anyone? You mean you're fielding other offers?"

I shook my head. "No! I don't mean anyone-anyone. I meant . . . I mean . . . the thing is . . ."

"You don't want to get married to anyone, including me?" he said, and I could hear the hurt in his voice.

I lifted my chin and yelled, "Aaaaagh! Why are you taking me so literally?!"

"Why are you telling me *now* of all times that you want to back out?"

I glowered at Dutch, really glowered at him. And then I marched over, placed my palms on his shoulders, and said, "Cowboy, you just don't get it, do you?"

He didn't say anything, which was probably wise, so I continued. "I don't want to marry you in six months because it's only six months to plan the most amazing day of my life. The day I get to be Mrs.

Dutch Rivers, and sugar, I want that day to be so perfect that I just don't think I can rush it."

Dutch's granite expression cracked into the most amazing smile and he curled his arms around me, pulled me close, and said, "Well, why didn't you just say so, dollface?"

He kissed me long and deep then, and I went with it. Later, when we were curled up in bed, he said, "How about November?"

I laughed. "Push, push, push," I said. "Why the rush, anyway?"

"I like November," Dutch replied. "It's a great month to get married. Not too cold. Not too hot."

"It's too soon," I told him.

"Then when?"

I sighed and turned to spoon against him. "I don't know. . . . Maybe next summer?"

"Too long," he said.

I closed my eyes. I was so exhausted I could barely talk. "Later," I told him. "We'll set the date later."

I was fast asleep soon after, but I didn't stay that way for long. My dreams were moody and turbulent, filled with poisonous darts and the feeling of being chased. And then, I had the worst nightmare of all. I dreamed that I was free-falling from a very great height. There was no indication of what I'd fallen off . . . a bridge maybe? All I knew was that the landscape came rushing up to greet me and there was nothing to slow me down. The moment I struck was the same moment I sat straight up in bed with a loud gasp.

"Edgar?" Dutch asked, using his favorite pet name for me, after famed psychic Edgar Cayce.

"I'm okay," I told him, still breathing hard.

He mumbled something and took my hand, holding it to his chest. I could feel the beat from his heart against my palm. More than anything, that helped to calm me down, but it was a long time before I actually got back to sleep.

The next day Dutch and I were separated. This bothered me for a whole lotta reasons, but I didn't want to let it show. . . . That worked for all of two seconds and then I started shrieking at the poor guy who came to deliver that piece of news. "What do you mean, you're splitting us up?!"

"Abs," Dutch said cautiously.

"I don't want to be separated, Dutch! You're supposed to be my partner! These guys freak me out with their poison darts and their pings and their superspy stuff!"

"Ms. Cooper," said the agent who'd suggested the idea. "There are certain aspects to your preparation for this mission that will be redundant for Agent Rivers, and there are certain aspects to his briefings that it would not benefit you to know."

"Like what?" I challenged. I can be a real pistol when I want to be.

"Well," said the agent, "we understand that you have limited weapons training. Is that correct?"

I narrowed my eyes at him, irritated that he'd pulled that particular fact out of my file. "I've probably killed more people than you, Agent . . . uh . . . *you*." What was his name again?

"Agent Rosco," he reminded me with a smile. "We know about the shooting in Waco. Is there someone else you were forced to eliminate?"

I crossed my arms and thought. "You mean, as in someone else I personally shot?"

"Yes."

Crap on a cracker. I'd never been so ticked off that I hadn't actually killed more than one guy in my life. "Well, no."

Agent Rosco smiled, but it wasn't exactly what I'd call a friendly sort of grin. "I had seven kills last year alone in Afghanistan."

I scowled. "Don't tell me," I said to him. "You're my weapons trainer."

"Yes, ma'am."

I sighed and looked up at Dutch, who was actually grinning. "You're enjoying this, aren't you?" I asked him.

"Yep."

Dutch had been trying to get me to learn how to use a gun properly for weeks, and I'd barely managed to hold him off after the one time we actually visited a gun range together and he'd forced me to fire a few rounds. With a sigh I said, "What *specifically* does this specialized training I'm supposed to endure entail?"

"Extensive weapons training, self-defense, survival skills, interrogation techniques, and basic first aid along with syringe practice."

I looked at him in astonishment. Was he kidding?

"Why the syringe practice?" was all I thought to ask.

"You'll need to practice injecting yourself and a partner with the antidote should you or Agent Rivers get hit by one of the toxic darts."

Gulp.

Agent Rosco took advantage of the fact that for the moment he'd managed to shut me up, and handed me a blue folder embossed with the CIA's seal. He gave an identical one to Dutch. "Agent Rivers, someone will be along shortly to brief you on the next item on your schedule. Ms. Cooper, if you would follow me, please?"

I trucked along behind Rosco without a backward glance to Dutch, still a little miffed that he was enjoying this so much. We walked to the elevator and Rosco pressed the down button. Once we'd stepped off the elevator on the basement level, he led me to the women's locker room and said, "In locker number seven you will find a duffel bag. In that duffel bag will be a change of clothes, earplugs, noise cancellation earphones, and protective eyewear. Please change and meet me back here in ten minutes."

I barely resisted the urge to grumble a complaint and simply got on with it by marching into the locker room. Once I'd changed into the dark blue tracksuit with gold piping (which I was seriously hoping was a party gift, 'cause it was super cool), I met Rosco out in the hallway again and followed him to a set of double doors where he swiped his ID card and we went in.

Not surprisingly, we ended up at the indoor shooting range, where several agents in similar tracksuits were lined up in small cubicle-looking slots shooting off all manner of weapons. Well . . . no grenade launchers, but the day was young.

Inside the range it was loud. Like, surround-sound loud. Even with the earplugs and earphones on I still jumped at every pop, bang, boom.

Rosco led me to the last booth and unholstered his weapon. He offered it to me, muzzle down, and said, "Let's start you off with a Ruger SR9c nine-millimeter and see how you do."

I eyed the gun suspiciously, wondering if it could go off by itself. Rosco waited me out and I took the gun much like you'd pick up a dead smelly fish.

Attempting to remember the "training" Dutch had given me a few weeks back, I pulled back the clip, cupped the deceptively heavy weapon, and held it up level with my right eye. Working to ignore the hail of bullets being fired feet away from me, I took a breath . . . exhaled . . . held perfectly still . . . and squeezed the pad of my finger against the trigger.

The gun fired and kicked up, hurting my wrist a little, but it wasn't too bad. I then lowered the muzzle, held it between my two fingers (dead-smelly-fish style), and attempted to hand it back to Rosco.

He looked at me like I had to be joking.

"I don't like guns," I told him.

"You're kidding," he said woodenly, refusing to take the gun from me.

With a scowl I turned and laid it on the counter in front of me, then pointed to the target. "I got a hole in one," I said. My black target was showing a nice round hole in the chest area.

Rosco crossed his arms and eyed the target. "Yep. You probably punctured his lung. Too bad he's only wounded. Too bad he's just popped off six rounds into you. Too bad now you're dead."

"What do you want from me?"

"I want you to pick up the weapon and shoot the shit out of that target!" he shouted in a voice so icy I felt cold down to my toes. Apparently there was a darkish side to Agent Rosco.

And I don't cotton to darkish sides. "Or," I snapped, "since I'm dead and all, maybe my ghost will just move on outta here!"

With that, I edged past him and made like a bullet out of the shooting range.

Twenty minutes later, an older female agent in a smart business suit found me crying in the women's locker room. "Ms. Cooper?" she asked before sitting down next to me.

I wiped my eyes and sniffled. "Yeah?"

"I'm Dr. Sherrod. I'm the staff psychologist here at the agency. Would you like to come to my office and talk?"

Great. Now they were siccing the shrink on me. I sniffled again. "Sure, why not?"

"Come on," she said kindly, wrapping an arm around my shoulders and helping me up. "It's not far."

We went up to the third floor and down to the end. She held the door of the office for me and I headed in, plopping down on the cushy-looking leather couch. She took the suede wing chair opposite me and smiled again. "Tough morning?"

"I don't like guns. And I don't mean the dislike you say when you're talking about liver and onions—I'm talking about the dislike you say when you realize your house is sitting next to a nuclear silo."

"Who told you that you had to like guns?"

Just like a shrink to turn the question back on me, right? "No one, but I feel like everyone expects me to be okay with all this stuff, and I'm not okay with it! I hate guns. I hate darts. I hate poisonous toxins and allies who are really enemies and . . . and . . ." I took a breath here, trying to figure out exactly how I could sum up what I was feeling. "Dr. Sherrod, three years ago I was a peaceful, animal-loving, junk-food-eating, not-a-care-in-the-world psychic with a small but faithful list of clients, a few good friends, and a pretty mundane but totally predictable life. Since then, do you know who I've turned into?"

"Who?"

"Ange-friggin'-lina Jolie!"

Dr. Sherrod laughed, and her laugh was nice: soothing even, just like her voice. "Abigail," she said, shaking her head and grinning at me, "I know it must feel like you've fallen down a rabbit hole, hmm?"

My lower lip began to quiver again and tears pooled in my eyes. I had to swallow hard before I could reply. "How did I get here?" I whispered. "I am so over my head right now, ma'am, it's making me freak out."

Dr. Sherrod sighed and leaned back in her chair. "You came highly recommended," she said. "So highly recommended that all manner of exceptions were made to obtain you for this mission. And I understand that your intuitive input has already been very helpful. Still, Abigail, you should know that as a rule we never send in a civilian, but I understand that this particular operation is so vital to our national security that we simply *had* to have you."

I turned my face away and stared out the window as the tears leaked out and ran down my cheeks. "I don't know if I can *do* this, Dr. Sherrod."

"If you truly don't believe you're capable, then I will have no choice but to recommend that we not use you."

I bit my lip. "If I back out, would you still want Agent Rivers to go in on his own?"

"Yes. We have already acquired the perfect cover for him, which matches his credentials and closely resembles his appearance. He has actually become as vital to this mission as you, especially since he speaks fluent Dutch and Russian."

My heart was pounding in my chest. Suddenly, I wasn't such a huge fan of the kindly doctor anymore. "If he goes in alone, what are his chances?"

"Without you?"

"Yes."

"Probably fifty-fifty."

I swallowed hard again. "And with me?"

"Significantly better, in the sixty to sixty-five percent range. You have a very special gift in being able to read people and pinpoint their hidden agendas. That is exactly the type of person we need on this mission, and exactly the type of person we will need to aid Agent Rivers with his cover. But your participation in the mission depends solely on how the rest of your training proceeds. We only have a few days to prepare you, Abigail. And if you want in on this mission and to keep your partner safe, you're going to have to step it up."

I wiped my cheeks and took a calm, steadying breath. "Dr. Sherrod?"

"Yes?"

"Would you please call Agent Rosco for me, and tell him I'm very sorry for my earlier outburst. If it's all right with him, I would truly love to pick up where we left off and shoot the shit out of that target."

I arrived back at the hotel after eleven p.m. My wrist, shoulder, and back ached from the three and a half hours of target practice, and my brain was swimming with all the details I had to remember, but for the most part, I'd managed to get my head on straight.

Dutch was asleep when I crawled into the room. He was lying on his side with his back to me, and for the longest time I just sat in a chair by the bed and listened to the sound of his deep breaths.

I thought about what I'd said to Dr. Sherrod, how three years ago my life had been so relatively ordinary, and then this extraordinary guy had walked into my life and *everything* had changed. What I couldn't really admit to myself until I was sitting in her office was that all of it was worth it, if only because at the end of the day I got to come home and listen to the most beautiful man I'd ever met breathe in and out.

Snaking my way into bed, I curled up to him and whispered, "We can do it, cowboy. Together our odds are better than anyone gives us credit for."

The rhythm of Dutch's breath never changed cadence, but his hand flopped down off his hip and onto mine. He squeezed my fingers and for the next few hours, all was right with the world.

I barely saw Dutch for the next six days. By the time he made it back to the hotel every night, I was already asleep and my wake-up calls always came at five a.m.—his apparently came later. I made sure to dress in the dark and sneak out of the room so he wouldn't be disturbed, and when he came in, he did the same for me. On the last day of my training, I woke up to find that Dutch hadn't come back to the hotel at all.

I wasn't worried per se—I knew he'd likely pulled an all-nighter—but still, I realized I hadn't spoken to or seen Dutch in the daylight even once in nearly a week, and I missed that silky baritone and those midnight blues something fierce.

At that moment I was pretty sick of all this prep work and the intense training I'd been put through. And when I say intense, it doesn't really even come close to the level of concentrated effort being focused on yours truly.

In the mornings there'd been weapons training and target practice, followed by two hours of martial arts defensive maneuvers, followed by more lectures from Steckworth on Intuit's software and how to deprogram it if our lives were in imminent danger and we couldn't bring it back safely (oh yeah, they made it really clear that making sure the software didn't end up in enemy hands was *far* more important than us coming back alive).

Then, after all that marvelous activity, I'd be "treated" to lunch. Same thing every day: turkey on wheat with mayo, lettuce, and tomato, a bag of chips, and a soda. I will be happy if I never see another turkey sandwich as long as I live.

After lunch the program usually varied; one day I was trained for two hours on the proper way to administer the antidote to the toxins the drone carried. And it wasn't a happy experience, let me tell you. The syringe carrying the antidote needed to be plunged into the chest cavity so that it would reach a vein close to the heart. Two syringes were required, one on each side of the sternum. I practiced on a dummy for an hour, and then they actually forced me to try the technique on a real person by sending in a big beefy marine. Trust me, that was one soldier who would never "volunteer" for that duty *ever* again. . . .

Another day I was given a lesson on how to read a person's body language to detect if he or she was lying.

Now, you would've figured the CIA would believe me when I told them I was already an expert on that one—as I'm pretty sure my own body language could attest—but they didn't take me at my word and insisted I sit through it anyway. (Weren't they surprised, though, when I passed their test with one hundred percent accuracy?!)

Throughout all of it I made sure my attitude was superlative. It was "Yes, sir!" and "Yes, ma'am!" with no arguments, eye rolls, or frowny faces. I believe even Rosco was impressed. Especially when I unloaded his SIG Sauer into the heart of the target—all eight rounds with nary the blink of an eye.

On the last day of training, the very day I'd been missing my fiancé so much, I was led into a small conference room and told that the "others" would be joining me shortly. I sat down with a sigh and a small groan, as I was sore to the bone from all the target practice and judo moves. I rubbed my cheek while I eyed the clock, which read six p.m. Earlier in the day I'd caught a foot in the face during the self-defense class, and when I made a comment about it leaving a bruise, I was told that might not be a bad thing. The meaning of which I was still trying to figure out.

Leaning back in the comfy chairs, I laid my head against the back and closed my eyes. Man, I was tired.

My back pressed against something knobby, and I pulled out the small but highly effective stun gun I'd been practicing with that morning. I'd forgotten to put it back after the exercises were over. Eyeing it now with fondness, I decided to keep it, as it might come in handy on the mission. Discreetly I tucked it back into the waistband of my tracksuit, before leaning back again and closing my eyes.

I heard someone come in a moment later and I opened one eye. It was a man with no visible badge, dressed in a sharp black suit, a metallic maroon tie, and gold cuff links.

He had very dark brown hair and a somewhat lighter-colored goatee and mustache. His eyes were brown, his complexion was olive and tanned, and he was really striking in a way I should hardly be ogling, now that I'm all engaged and stuff.

I gave him a half smile, and he looked at me with a smoldering grin. I'm embarrassed to say I may have blushed a *weeeeeee* bit.

"Hello," I said.

"Good evening," he said, a beautiful Eastern-bloc accent lightly coloring the words. He had a deep seductive voice, not unlike Dutch's, and I squirmed slightly in my chair, reminding myself that I was *engaged* for crying out loud.

I cleared my throat and discreetly pivoted my chair away from him. "Have you been here long?" he asked.

"No," I said, focusing my attention on the door. Jesus, were my palms sweating? "I'm waiting for my fiancé. He's probably going to be joining this last briefing."

"Your fiancé?"

I nodded curtly. Could he please stop talking? I go weak in the knees when I hear a man with a sexy accent.

"He nice guy, this fiancé?"

I cleared my throat again. "He's the best," I said, and that warm gushy feeling flooded my heart. "In fact, he's the best person I know."

"Sounds like good guy."

Was it me, or was this guy being a little nosy? "I'm Abigail Cooper," I said, finally deciding I might be acting rudely, and turned to extend my hand.

"I am Richard Des Vries," he said with a bright white smile that could melt butter.

I pumped his hand just once and let go, feeling little beads of sweat form on my head and the small of my back grow moist. Okay, and maybe someplace else too, but that's personal.

His name sounded familiar, but I am notoriously terrible with names, so I figured somewhere along the line he'd been pointed out to me by someone and I'd been too preoccupied to remember who he was and what his job was here at the agency.

I laid my head back again and closed my eyes. Where was everybody?

Des Vries's cologne wafted under my nostrils. God, I love a great-smelling guy.

Wait. No, I don't! I love *my* guy.

My guy. Love. My. Guy.

My guy, who wasn't here yet. I was alone with a great-smelling dude in a gorgeous suit with a really sexy accent and hot smokin' smile. . . . "Maybe I'll just go see where everyone is," I said, getting up with a nervous laugh and preparing to bolt for the door.

Just as I was attempting to make my getaway, a team of agents and bigwigs came marching in, including the MIB aka Agent Frostbite . . . er . . . Frost, CIA director Tanner, Dr. Sherrod, FBI director Gaston, the air force team of Walrus and Penguin, and my weapons-training BFF, Agent Rosco.

"Did you need something?" Director Tanner asked me, obviously noticing my hedge toward the door. "No," I said quickly, and plastered a smile on my face. "Just thought I'd get a drink of water."

Tanner punched a button on the intercom in the center of the table. "Dawn, could you please bring in some refreshments before we get started?"

I smiled even brighter and took my seat. Of course, I didn't take the actual seat I'd been sitting in earlier. This time I moved a little farther away from Richard Des Sexpot.

When we were all seated and refreshments had been served, Director Tanner got down to business. "Welcome to your last briefing," she began.

I looked nervously at the door and raised my hand.

"Yes?" she asked me.

"Uh . . . ," I said, feeling a bit foolish, but I had to ask, "aren't we going to wait for Dutch—I mean Agent Rivers?"

Director Tanner's forehead creased. "Excuse me?"

Okay, so now I was *really* feeling foolish. "I thought he would want to be included in the final briefing."

"He is," she said to me.

I looked around at all the other faces save Sexpot's, but I could feel his eyes on me. I knew I was turning a big ol' shade of red, but there was nothing I could do about that. "Is he on the other end of the intercom?" I asked, looking at the small star-shaped object in the center of the table.

"Abigail," said Sexpot.

"Hold on," I told him, still trying to figure out where my fiancé was.

"Edgar," Sexpot said next, and just like that, I realized who Richard Des Vries actually was.

"Holy freakballs!" I squealed, whipping my head around to really look at him now.

"You didn't know it was me?" he asked, his voice losing any hint of the former accent.

"No!" I said, my eyes all big and goggly. "I mean, I thought your voice sounded familiar, honey, but I was trying to avoid really looking at you, and the whole accent and dark hair really threw me off." I squinted at him and studied the person that Dutch's voice was coming out of. He did indeed look totally different; the olive tone to his skin was much darker with the tan, his cobalt blues had been turned to dark brown, and his eyebrows were either thicker or just darker so they looked thicker. All that with the goatee had totally transformed him. "Did you bleach your teeth?" I asked him, squinting some more.

It was Dutch's turn to blush and I suddenly remembered who else was in the room. I coughed and quickly scooted my chair closer to the table. "Sorry 'bout that," I said. "I wasn't aware you guys had done such a good job turning Agent Rivers into someone else."

To my relief, Director Tanner appeared immensely pleased by my reaction, and she and Gaston exchanged a knowing look. "Yes," she said. "He does resemble Mr. Des Vries to a remarkable degree."

"You mean there's a *real* Richard Des Vries?" I asked. There was that name again. . . . Where had I heard it before? And I looked at Dutch again. . . . I swore I'd seen someone who looked exactly like him, but where and when?

In answer, Director Tanner clicked her remote control and on the screen behind me flashed a picture that brought it all back to me. "That's the guy in the lineup of photos I sorted through last week," I said aloud.

Tanner nodded. "It is."

"So, is the real Des Vries locked up?" I asked. I was already getting hits off his energy, which told me the man was currently behind bars.

Director Gaston smiled. "He is, although he's not being held by us. He's currently in an Israeli prison awaiting trial for illegal weapons dealing. We're trying to get him extradited to the U.S. for a round of interrogation with us, but that's highly unlikely. The Israelis have wanted him for years and they're not about to let him go."

"How'd they get him?" I asked.

Gaston said, "Des Vries was on a flight from Jordan to Bucharest when he began suffering an acute case of food poisoning. His commercial plane had to make an emergency medical landing in Israel. The minute the Mossad heard about who'd just landed at their Tel Aviv airport, they were all over him."

"Why did the Israelis want him so bad?" I asked him next.

"He's earned a reputation for selling arms to the Palestinians and

Iranians to use against the Israelis. He's also been known to work a deal or two with Hamas and the Taliban. He's unscrupulous and notorious, not to mention a murderer, smuggler, and thief, but in the world of weapons dealing, he's still fairly small-time. Word is that he's been looking for a big weapons deal to put himself on the map, and the Israelis have taken him out of the game before he had a chance to do that."

"Ah," I said, noting again the uncanny resemblance between the real Des Vries and Dutch, which was probably why Gaston had smiled like a crocodile when I'd told him to look at Des Vries for the missing drone. That reminded me of the mission and I asked, "Did you ask the Israelis if Des Vries stole the drone?"

Gaston nodded to Tanner, who answered me. "Yes, and as a favor to us during their interrogation of him, they got him to admit that he knew the drone existed, but he claims he had nothing to do with its disappearance. He pulled something similar with the British several years ago, when he managed to hack into a drone carrying facial recognition software and steal it away from them to resell it to the North Koreans, so you showed great skill in pulling his photo out of the pile. Still, we don't think he's responsible for the theft of our drone because Des Vries was captured a full five days before the drone went missing and the Israelis can be *particularly* persuasive during their interrogations, I'm inclined to believe him."

"But what if he was working with someone else who went ahead with the plan after his capture?" I pressed.

Tanner shook her head. "Every piece of intelligence we've obtained from both our sources and the Israelis suggests that Des Vries works alone, and nothing in his recent history points to him orchestrating the theft. Still, his capture by the Mossad, his uncanny facial resemblance to Agent Rivers, and his ties to Toronto have provided us with the perfect cover to go after the real thief."

Tanner then put up another slide, and I recognized the unattractive heavyset man as the second suspect I'd pulled out of their file. "We agree with you that Viktor Kozahkov is a very likely suspect. He lives in Toronto, does a fair amount of weapons dealing, and he's got some close ties and connections to the biggest guns in the Chechen mob."

I eyed the director. Her convincing argument didn't match the wave of doubtful energy coming off her. "What's bugging you, then, about making Viktor for the drone thief?" I asked.

She shrugged. "This heist seems way above his sophistication level," she said. "Viktor's smart, but we didn't think he was this smart, and he's never been more than a midlevel player in the weapons-dealing trade, buying caches of weapons in bulk and selling them in smaller bundles for more money. Stealing the drone just feels like it'd be out of his league."

"Maybe he had help," Dutch said.

Tanner nodded. "Maybe," she agreed, but her tone suggested she was still unconvinced.

She then clicked to another slide and up came the photo of one seriously mean-looking dude. A large, rotund man with beady little eyes that were cruel and cunning came onto the screen. I sat back in my chair and shuddered.

"This is Vasilii Boklovich," Tanner said. "If you're right, Ms. Cooper, and Viktor Kozahkov has either stolen the drone or come by it from another source, then he will no doubt attempt to auction it off through this man."

Gaston took over the conversation again. "Boklovich is *the* man to know if you have a weapon of either great quantity or great value to sell. He's tied in to all the major terrorist organizations around the globe and has been known to host special auctions where these things eventually go to the highest bidder. We've wanted him for years, but he's proved especially elusive.

"Several intelligence reports suggest that he's hiding somewhere in Ontario province at this time. The first two agents we sent into Toronto were tasked with discovering if Boklovich had the drone in his possession yet, because one way or another we're certain it will end up with him at auction."

I shuddered again when I remembered what had happened to those agents. One look at Boklovich's photo told me that if he'd discovered they were agents, he'd dealt with them swiftly and cruelly.

"In the final report they sent back before their deaths," Gaston continued, "they made it clear that Boklovich did not yet have the drone, and there's been no chatter yet about an auction or something as valuable as the drone and Intuit up for sale. So, either Viktor Kozahkov is dragging his feet, or whoever has the drone hasn't made contact with Boklovich yet."

I frowned, wondering how Dutch's cover was going to help get back the drone. Gaston answered that question next. "Two years ago, Richard Des Vries purchased an old vacant warehouse near the water in downtown Toronto. Since then he's been renovating the building, turning it into a high-end condo complex with eight luxury units, which we knew he was getting ready to sell, keeping the largest unit for himself of course.

"We believe his venture into real estate was a calculated one. Europe and the Middle East have been heating up for Des Vries—he's made some serious enemies in the recent past—and we know he badly wanted in with the Chechen crowd in Toronto. The Chechen Mafia dominates the weapons-trading market worldwide to a large degree.

"Des Vries, however, is an outsider. He was born in Holland and making alliances with the Chechens would prove difficult. The drone's disappearance actually gives us an angle to work."

Tanner took over again. "What we're proposing is to have Agent Rivers assume Des Vries's identity, move into the condo in Toronto, and make contact with Kozahkov. If Kozahkov reveals that he has the drone, then we'll set up surveillance on him until he attempts to move it. If Kozahkov doesn't have the drone, then we'll use him to get you two into the auction."

Dutch shifted in his chair. "I've been poring over the file on Des Vries, and his assets don't make him wealthy enough to bid on the drone."

"Oh, he won't be bidding on the drone," Tanner said. "He'll be providing something else even more valuable."

My interest was piqued when Tanner motioned to Gaston again to explain the plan. "We've set up a very carefully timed leak through very specific channels we know are being monitored by Boklovich," he began. "We're going to acknowledge that one of our drones has been stolen, and that it was carrying a prototype of a very sophisticated weapon, and while that is a cause for concern, we're not overly upset because the prototype had a fail-safe."

"A fail-safe?" I repeated.

Gaston nodded. "We're going to suggest that Intuit was designed to work only a handful of times before self-destructing, and as it typically takes hundreds of demonstrations for a competent computer programmer to reverse engineer a highly sophisticated device like Intuit, it would be useless to anyone who might want to buy it for mass production, or to use it beyond one or two missions."

"Is that true?" I asked, thinking that if it was, I'd be pretty ticked off that we'd been suckered into such a dangerous mission when all they had to do was wait for the stupid thing to mechanically fail on its own.

"No," said Tanner. "The rumor is not true. Intuit's software will continue to work normally and could most definitely be successfully reverse engineered, but we're counting on the rumor being taken seriously by Kozahkov, Boklovich, and the drone thief. If any of them buy into it, they'll all be anxious to get rid of the drone quickly before the rumor can spread to every potential buyer willing to pay big money for the technology."

"Ah," I said, understanding the ruse.

"Agent Rivers will pose as Des Vries," Tanner continued. "Once the two of you move into the condo, he'll set up a meeting with Kozahkov to determine if Viktor has the drone. If he does have it, then Agent Rivers will tell the Chechen that he's heard a rumor that Intuit will be useless past one or two demonstrations. If Kozahkov hasn't yet heard about it, he'll check, and after he verifies the rumor, he'll be highly motivated to set up an auction with Boklovich. The minute Kozahkov attempts to move the drone, we'll go in and nab it."

"And if Kozahkov didn't steal the drone and he doesn't have Intuit?" Dutch asked.

"Then you are to offer him yet another story," Tanner said. "You'll tell Viktor that you've been able to acquire a copy of the actual software for Intuit straight from Professor Steckworth's computer. Tell him that you've managed to get a clean copy on a disk that doesn't contain the fail-safe mechanism and can be duplicated without all the difficulties that come with reverse engineering. The software will be like the goose to the drone's golden egg, and Kozahkov will jump at the chance to help you sell it by promising an introduction to Boklovich in exchange for a percentage of the eventual sale. With Viktor's help, you're a shoo-in to get an invite to the auction where we *know* that Boklovich won't hesitate to offer both the drone and the software for sale. Knowing him, he'll offer them separately to help drive up the price for each."

"Will you actually provide me with a copy of Intuit's software?" Dutch wanted to know.

"Yes," said Tanner, a bit stiffly. "We will give you an encrypted copy of it. We'll also give you a password to allow you to get past the encryption should you be required to demonstrate that you do in fact possess the real software. But be forewarned, Agent Rivers: We're certain that Boklovich will require proof that you possess what you claim to have, but by no means should you give him your password or an unencrypted copy. He'll kill you the moment he thinks he doesn't need you anymore."

"Noted," Dutch said.

Tanner nodded like she was satisfied with his answer; then she said, "Your mission will be to determine if Kozahkov has the drone. If he does, your part is largely over. If he doesn't, then you'll need to get Kozahkov to set up a meeting with Boklovich, have him agree to offer your software at the same time he's offering to auction off the drone and Intuit, and at the auction either steal Intuit back or destroy the device."

I noticed she left out the part where she told us we'd also need to make it out alive. . . .

Tanner continued. "We've received two more pings from Intuit, and our best guess is that the device is still hidden somewhere near the Greater Toronto metropolitan area. By having Agent Rivers pose as Des Vries and live at the condo, we have access to a ready-made command center to run our operations out of without causing any unnecessary suspicion. It also helps us greatly that the condo building itself is currently unoccupied. Des Vries hadn't offered any of the units up for sale yet, so it's the perfect place to set up shop for us."

I thought of something that worried me. "Do you know if Kozahkov and Des Vries have ever met?"

Tanner's eyes swiveled to Gaston, and I didn't like the look they exchanged. "We don't know," she admitted. "If they have, it was likely only briefly. We know that Des Vries has spent considerable time in Toronto, but on many levels Kozahkov is his competition, so it's unlikely that the two would have spent much time mixing together in the same circles. It's far more likely that they would have attempted to avoid each other."

I glanced at Dutch, convinced that the uncertainty of her answer would set off alarm bells for him too, but he merely shrugged. "I know you're worried," he said, "but we'll just have to take our chances with it."

I didn't like that one bit, but didn't argue. Instead, I asked another question. "So what's my cover going to be?"

Tanner clicked the remote again and a photo of Rick Des Vries popped up with his arm around two beautiful women, scantily clad. "Des Vries likes the ladies," she said. "Especially blondes. We're going to send you in posing as Des Vries's newest girlfriend."

"Does he have an old girlfriend I need to worry about?"

Agent Tanner smiled. "I'm sure he has several," she said, flipping to another image of one particularly busty blonde dressed in a peekaboo halter top that was less peekaboo and more peekaboob. "This woman seems to be his most steady girlfriend. We did a thorough background check on her, and what we've found isn't impressive. Both her parents were drug addicts, so she spent most of her youth in foster care, and repeated the tenth grade twice before dropping out of high school. She tried modeling, acting, and was a makeup artist on the set of Canada's *Flashpoint*, but lately she's been flying the friendly skies for Air Canada working the Prague-to-Amman junket to be closer to Des Vries. We've arranged it so that her flight schedule is booked with back-to-back trips for the next week, so you're not likely to bump into her if she begins to worry about Des Vries's absence and comes looking for him."

"Does she know that Des Vries has been taken in by the Mossad?" Dutch asked. "I mean, she could have been working the flight he was on."

Tanner shook her head. "We checked, and she wasn't. Her work itinerary showed us that she was working her regular flight to Amman the day Rick was taken in by the Mossad."

"Does anyone else know?" he pressed, clearly worried that word would get out.

Again, Tanner shook her head. "No one knows," she stated. "Des Vries was taken off the plane in Israel by Mossad agents posing as paramedics, and at our request, the Mossad have been keeping his incarceration *very* quiet. As far as we can determine, no one should get wind that anything's amiss with Des Vries for at least another week or two."

I eyed the woman on the screen again moodily. Cup size aside, she was at least four inches taller than me and about ten pounds less. Clearly she needed a turkey sandwich, a soda, and a bag of chips.

"I look nothing like her," I said.

"Don't worry about it," Tanner said easily, which of course only made me worry about it even more. "You don't have to take on her identity, just portray the type of woman that Des Vries would be seen with: dumb, blond, and pretty. While Agent Rivers is working to locate Intuit, you can give your feedback on Kozahkov or any other suspects you identify directly to him. It's actually a terrific cover for you, as no one would ever suspect Des Vries's arm candy as being an undercover agent, which means that no one's likely to perform an extensive background check on you."

Great. Dutch got slick arms dealer, and I got flouncy bimbo. "Okay," I said with a sigh. "I'll do what I can."

Tanner beamed at me. "Excellent. After this briefing I'll have Dawn take you downstairs for your new wardrobe and a selection of blond wigs. Your identity has already been created, and we didn't want you to worry about slipping up when introducing yourself. Your new name will be Abigail Carter, Toronto native."

Tanner then tossed me a blue and gold passport and I opened it to a photo of me that had obviously been Photoshopped because in it, I had platinum blond hair and, shall we say, rather enhanced cleavage.

"What's my occupation?" I asked.

Tanner smiled tightly. "You don't have one," she said. "The less we have to fabricate, the easier it is to believe you are who you say you are, but we've managed to arrange for a cover story. An American named Robert Carter, now living in Canada and married to a very wealthy heiress, owes his country a favor, and we've called it in. He has grudgingly agreed to admit to an extramarital affair some thirty-odd years ago resulting in a love child named Abigail Carter. He's recently set up a monthly stipend and is interested in keeping the story very hush-hush."

"Ah," I said, because what else could I say? I mean, they were trying to pass me off as a love child? What idiot was going to buy that? Still, there wasn't much I could do about it, so I kept my mouth shut.

Tanner got back to the briefing. "To make the lure of the original software even more appealing and give legitimacy to Des Vries showing up in Toronto with it, we've made it look as if he knew all along that the drone was about to be stolen, and he let the real thief take the bait because he also knew about the device's software glitch. Hence, when the drone went missing, it would cause us to double-down our security on the *real* code to the software, revealing where it was being hidden. Last night, we snuck Agent Rivers into Canada. Once there, we had him book a flight to Las Vegas, posing as Rick Des Vries, and made sure he was seen in the neighborhood of Dr. Steckworth's home near Lake Mead."

I turned to look at Dutch. "That's where you were?"

He nodded.

Agent Tanner continued. "This morning we posted an internal alert to most of the federal securities agencies that there had been a major breach to a secure facility located in the area of Lake Mead."

"There was?" I asked.

Agent Tanner shook her head. "No," she said patiently. "There was no security breach. We just made that up because we knew it would be leaked. What we are attempting to orchestrate is a smoke screen. We want to create a bit of a paper trail to make it look as if Des Vries was able to steal a copy of Intuit's code should anyone like Boklovich question its sudden appearance."

"Ahh," I said. "I get it."

Tanner continued. "We'll get you two into Canada tomorrow morning, and from there Agent Rivers will make contact with Kozahkov and ask for a meeting."

The director then hit the remote control again, clicking to a gorgeous-looking building. "This is a photo of Des Vries's condo in downtown Toronto. We're working to change the security code to his alarm as we speak. You'll have no trouble getting in, but I want to warn you that even though Des Vries is fairly small-time, we know this building has been monitored by the CSIS ever since they learned that it belonged to Des Vries."

"CSIS?" I asked. I had no idea who or what that was.

Tanner explained. "The Canadian Security Intelligence Service. It's the Canadian equivalent to the CIA."

"Are they joining us in the effort to get the drone back?" I said.

There was a perceptive shift in posture from several members of the staff in the room. "No," Tanner said carefully. "We have not asked them to join in the mission because we cannot trust that someone within the CSIS won't compromise Agent Rivers's identity."

I stared at her in amazement. "If they're monitoring Des Vries, won't they *know* you guys are around?"

Gaston answered my question. "We've mentioned to them that Des Vries was recently recruited to assist the CIA in a global investigation, and we've gained their permission to monitor Des Vries for a few weeks until he leaves the country again."

"They agreed to that?" I was a little shocked the CSIS agents were willing to allow the CIA to tread on their territory.

"They have," he said simply. "But it's with the understanding that their surveillance will also remain in place. We already suspect the doorman at the condo may be a CSIS plant, and we also think Des

Vries's condo unit will be bugged, so use caution and stay completely in character until you've swept it for microphones and recording devices."

Tanner then looked keenly at me and issued a warning. "Ms. Cooper, there is also something you should know about Rick Des Vries."

Uh-oh.

"What?" I asked.

"He has a violent temper that extends to his women. We've obtained police reports from Amsterdam that suggest he put four former girlfriends in the hospital. One woman he dated for several years in the late nineties, Anna Wyngarden, went missing shortly after Des Vries scored his first big arms deal. She's never been seen since and is presumed dead. It was Anna's disappearance that finally forced Des Vries to flee his home in Holland when the police began closing in on him as the primary suspect in the case."

I felt my face drain of color. "Are you saying that you want Dutch to beat me up?"

Tanner licked her lips and appeared uncomfortable. "No," she said, "but it might not hurt for him to act angry and aggressive toward you and for you to appear frightened of him when you two are out in public."

Dutch's brow lowered dangerously, and I could tell he didn't like that idea one bit. "I'm not okay with that, Director."

"I didn't say you should hit her, Agent Rivers," Tanner replied coolly. "I'm merely suggesting that you—"

Dutch cut her off. "No," he said firmly, and the granite expression he wore brooked no argument.

Tanner eyed Gaston, whose expression seemed to say, "I told you so."

With another sigh she finally said, "Very well, Agent Rivers, but Ms. Cooper, I cannot stress enough that the real Richard Des Vries would not tolerate a woman who talked back to him and it would seem *quite* out of character for him if he did. Do you understand?"

"Fully," I said woodenly. I was to keep my trap shut and look scared. I knew I could manage the latter at least.

Tanner nodded. She then folded her hands together as if that was about all she had to brief us on. "Do you have any questions?"

I did. "How will we make contact with you to keep you in the loop about our progress?"

"Agent Frost will be close to you at all times," she assured me. "And of course we'll have a team of agents ready to mobilize quickly should the need arise or should your lives be in imminent jeopardy."

I tried to keep my facial expression neutral, but it was really, really hard. My personal assessment of Agent Frostbite was that he didn't much care if we made it through or not. In fact, when I glanced at him across the table, he seemed far more interested in his manicure than in the topic at hand.

And that meant that Dutch and I would have to look out for each other, which, I decided, wasn't anything new.

Chapter Three

• • •

That night back at the hotel my thoughtful fiancé drew me a delightfully warm bath and ordered me into it. Our room was actually a suite, and the tub was huge, so I wasn't surprised when Dutch climbed in with me.

"How's your shoulder?" he asked, sitting behind me and working his fabulous fingers into my sore muscles.

I replied with something witty like, "Oooh . . . ahhhh . . . yeah baby . . ."

Dutch chuckled. "So, did you really think I was someone else today?"

I sighed contentedly and leaned a little to the right so he could work my other shoulder. "Yep."

"Seriously?"

"Dude, you look totally different."

"Different how?"

"Different dangerous."

Dutch seemed to consider that.

"Different sexy," I added to keep those fingers moving.

"Sexy?"

"Yep. Like, Daniel Craig sexy."

"The double-oh-seven guy you keep telling me that if you two ever meet and the opportunity presents itself, you get to have sex with him and it doesn't count as cheating?"

I squeezed his knee. "Bingo."

Dutch's fingers moved to the middle of my back. I wasn't sure if he knew it yet, but he was definitely going to get lucky here in about three minutes.

"Who're you more attracted to?" he asked.

"Daniel Craig."

Dutch's soft laughter echoed off the wall. "Smart-ass."

"You walked right into that one, cowboy."

"Okay, okay," he conceded. "So, James Bond aside, between me and Des Vries, who're you more attracted to?"

My radar pinged with a little warning. I'd just been asked a seriously loaded question and I was in danger of totally ruining the mood—not to mention a good massage. I turned to look at him over my shoulder, so glad I could once again stare into those midnight blues now that he'd removed the colored contacts. "Dutch Rivers, you are the sexiest man I have ever—and I do mean *ever*—seen, met, or heard of. You are manly beyond all imagination and you clearly rock my world both day and night."

Dutch's eyes narrowed. "Des Vries," he snorted. "I knew it."

"Are we really going to have this argument?"

"Is it the goatee?"

I sighed and leaned my head on his chest. "Yes, Dutch, it's the goatee. Happy?"

"It itches a little," he admitted, scratching his chin.

"Wanna see if it tickles too?" I cocked my head to look at him playfully.

His eyebrows shot up. "What'd you have in mind?"

I smiled wickedly. "Why don't you and I have a little fun role-playing? You can be the secret service agent, and I can be the Russian spy."

Dutch grinned. "Why, Svetlana, it's so lovely to meet you. Have you been in D.C. for long?"

"Oh, *nyet*, Agent Beefcakes, I am here for conference on being good vooman for mail-order brides."

As for the rest of that bubble bath? Well, let's just say there wasn't a whole lotta water left in the tub once Svetlana was finally carried off to bed.

The next day we arrived in Toronto on a commercial jetliner, which taxied to the hangar in the pouring rain. Dutch was decked out in another of those charcoal suits with a dark gray shirt and a metallic silver tie.

I was dressed in my new "uniform": a low-cut cashmere cream sweater that fit like a second skin, black leggings, and thigh-high boots. Also, "the ladies" had been pushed up, pushed out, and crowded with foam to enhance their voluptuousness. They were now protesting mightily. I couldn't wait to get to the condo and take off my bra. I also couldn't wait to take off my blond wig, which kept getting in my eyes and itched something fierce.

My engagement ring had been stuffed into the bottom of my purse, and my left ring finger felt naked without it.

I stuck close to Dutch as we deplaned and went through customs. I flashed my new passport and a smile, but the agent was far more interested in my chest. He sent me through with barely a look at my face to confirm the photo in the passport.

I waited for Dutch, but he'd been pulled to the side. I knew he was using his fake Dutch passport, and I could see him talking calmly to the customs agents as they asked him a variety of questions. Finally, one of them made a phone call and without further delay he was allowed through.

When we were out of the customs agents' hearing range, I asked him, "What was that about?"

"The CIA warned me that Des Vries's name might cause some issues, but they also assured me that the Canadian government is cooperating with our investigation, as long as we keep a very low profile, that is."

"Hence the quick release once they made the phone call."

"Exactly."

After getting our luggage and finding our way via cab to Des Vries's condo, we had a little trouble with the key card the agency had provided Dutch to enter the building, but a helpful doorman came to our rescue. He took one look at Dutch and said, "Welcome home, Mr. Des Vries! I'm Daniel, your new doorman."

Dutch nodded curtly and handed him the faulty key card. "This doesn't work," he snapped.

"Oh, I'm so sorry, sir," said the doorman. He rushed behind his desk and rummaged through a drawer, coming up with two new white key cards, which he handed to Dutch. "Those will work in all entrances and exits, and will give you access to the penthouse, sir."

Dutch snatched the key cards out of the doorman's hand without so much as a thank-you.

I thought he was being a little rude, but then I remembered he was supposed to be an arms dealer who probably didn't have much of a warm fuzzy side. The doorman smiled brightly, however, and said, "Will you and the lady need assistance with your bags?"

"No," Dutch said, walking to the elevator without looking back.

I couldn't help it; I smiled apologetically to the doorman and hurried after Dutch, but as my six-inch heels clicked along the slippery floor, I lost my footing and nearly went down. Waving my arms like a pinwheel and making a little "whoop!" sound, I managed to keep myself erect, but was thoroughly flustered by the time I reached Dutch's side. I didn't look at him or the doorman; instead I busied myself trying to hike up the boots so the shoes would stay on my feet a little better. While I was bent over and tugging on the leather cuff of the boot, my wig fell off.

It plopped to the ground and lay there like a big blond rat. I gasped as the cool air hit the back of my scalp, and I looked up at Dutch, who eyed first me with large round eyes, then the doorman, who just happened to see the whole thing and was staring at me also with big Wile E. Coyote barooga eyes.

"Don't panic," Dutch whispered as the elevator doors opened. "Just pick up the wig, tuck yourself back in, and step into the elevator."

I could feel my cheeks heat with color and I snatched the hair off the marble floor and dove into the elevator. Mortified, I stood against the wall and stared meanly at Dutch, who inserted his key card, pressed the P for "penthouse," and did his level best not to laugh. . . . He failed.

"Ha-ha," I snapped, watching his shoulders shake as the laughter overtook him.

Dutch inhaled deeply and got control of himself. "Could have been worse," he said.

"How exactly?"

"Both ladies could have popped out."

It took me a second to understand what he was talking about, but then with a gasp I looked down and noticed that my left one had come out for air. "Oh, for Christ's sake!" I cried, tugging at the bra and the cashmere sweater. "Why didn't you *tell* me?"

"I did!" he swore. "I told you to tuck yourself back in, remember?"

I growled and turned away, absolutely mortified, and that's when I caught a glimpse of myself in the polished brass sides of the elevator. "Oh! This is no use. I look ridiculous!"

Dutch considered me carefully. "Let's get into the condo and discuss it, okay?"

I made a face at him, but then the doors opened and we entered a lovely entryway. The minute the doors shut, I opened my mouth to argue that this disguise would likely fool no one, but before I could get a word out, I saw Dutch raise a finger to his lips and cast me a warning look.

I held perfectly still and watched him walk around the condo holding out a small device he'd dug out of his inside pocket, and all the while he was saying things like, "That dumb-ass decorator! This was *not* the look I approved!" He walked slowly and carefully around the condo, holding up the gizmo, pausing every once in a while to comment on a picture or lamp. When he was done, he eyed me carefully, and pointed to a small nook by the door where hooks were set up to hold coats. He mouthed, "Stay still" when I was in place, and then he went on a rampage, smashing all the things he'd commented on one by one in the spacious living room, the utilitarian kitchen, and what I assumed was the master bedroom.

When he was done, he looked at me with satisfaction.

I looked at him like he done lost his mind.

He grinned. "Bugs," he said, and understanding blossomed in my mind.

"Whoa," I said, eyeing the mess. "That's a lot of surveillance."

I helped Dutch sweep up the mess and, sure enough, in between the broken shards of glass and porcelain were small silver disks and bits of wire.

When we had finished cleaning up the mess, I began pulling out the pins holding up my hair and eyed the wig sitting on the arm of the sofa with meaning. "Can we talk about this disguise thing?"

Dutch sighed. "I had my doubts when they mentioned the identity they had in mind for you. I've been studying Des Vries for six days, and I knew you'd have trouble pulling off the dumb-bimbo thing."

"Should I take that as a compliment?"

Dutch moved over to wrap me in his arms and kiss the bridge of my nose. "Definitely."

"So what do we do?"

He stepped away and moved to his attaché. Opening it, he pulled out a thick file and flipped through some of the pages. "Des Vries has had a string of personal assistants over the years. Always the same type. A pretty young brunette fresh out of college and naive about the monster they were about to go to work for. None of his assistants ever lasted longer than a few weeks. My feeling is he got handsy and they got out, but there is room in Des Vries's world for someone like that, and bringing you in as my assistant wouldn't be out of character for him."

I felt a bit of my temper flare. "Why the heck didn't the CIA give me that cover initially?"

Dutch grimaced. "They may have thought you were a little too mature for the role."

"That's a nice way of saying I'm too old," I snapped.

Dutch's mouth quirked again. "I thought 'mature' might be safer."

I sighed dramatically. "Okay, so can we call Agent Frostbite and get some clearance for this new identity?"

Lickety-split Dutch had his cell out and made the call.

It took some arguing on his part—the CIA definitely wasn't into changing covers for me so quickly—but Dutch never let up and eventually Frost relented.

Once he'd hung up, he smiled and said, "See? Piece of cake."

I rolled my eyes but couldn't help smiling. "Yeah, yeah." Then I looked down at my outfit and over to my luggage and a small wave of panic hit me. "All the CIA gave me for clothes was stuff like this."

Dutch reached into his back pocket and pulled out his wallet, extracting an American Express platinum card and the spare key card Daniel had given him. He handed both to me and said, "Take the elevator down to the parking garage. There'll be a car in slot one-A with the keys inside. I'll draw you a map to the shopping district. Get yourself some proper business attire and anything else you think you'll need to pull off being my personal assistant."

"What about my background?" I asked, worried that I'd need some sort of employment history.

"Leave that to me," he said. "I have a good friend who runs an employment agency here in Toronto. He owes me a favor. He'll be able to give you a job history."

I held the credit card between my fingertips and considered how much I was about to charge to it. "You gonna clear this with Frost too?"

"I am," Dutch assured me, adding, "Tomorrow. I'll clear it with him tomorrow. Now go shopping, dollface. And that's an order."

Later that night I completed the final touches of my new look by tying my long hair into a bun and throwing on a pair of fake prescription glasses. I twirled in front of the mirrored doors located in the spare bedroom on the opposite side of the condo, quite happy with myself, when I heard the elevator doors open. Thinking it was Dutch back early from his rummaging around at Des Vries's office in downtown Toronto (there'd been a note on the kitchen table telling me where he'd gone), I walked out to show him how assistanty I'd become.

I stopped dead in my tracks when I discovered a tall, leggy blonde standing in the hallway, wearing skinny jeans, a tight-fitting low-cut sweater, a huge Bottega Veneta purse, and toting two large suitcases. Protruding from her mouth was a familiar white key card. Upon seeing me, she let go of the suitcase handles and pulled out the key card. "Who're you?" she demanded, her hands finding her hips real fast.

I lifted my chin and tried to control my surprise. "Abigail Carter. I work for Mr. Des Vries," I told her, thinking I knew exactly who she might be. Still, I thought it wise to double-check and make sure. "The better question is, who're *you*?"

"Mandy Mortemeyer," she told me, taking those hands off her hips to fold across her bosomy chest. "Rick's girlfriend."

"Ah," I said. The stewardess who was supposed to be in Prague.

My mind whirled to figure out how to compute this new twist. "I'm his personal assistant."

The girlfriend narrowed her eyes at me. I could feel that she was about to grill me good and I was so ticked off at the CIA for not anticipating her arrival. "Rick doesn't have a personal assistant," she snapped.

I pointed to the new iPad lying on the table in the foyer, which I'd recently acquired. (So, yeah, the Apple Store had been right next to the clothing boutique and I figured the iPad would make me look like a real assistant, 'cause didn't they walk around with clipboards and checklists and wasn't the iPad just a fancy clipboard?) "Shall we send Mr. Des Vries an e-mail and ask him if I truly am his newest employee?"

Grillfriend glared at me. "Where's he at, anyway?" she demanded. "He hasn't returned any of my calls."

"He's at his office," I answered easily, moving to the iPad and touching the screen like I knew exactly how to use it. (Which I didn't, but she didn't know that!)

"Here in Toronto?" she asked, and I saw the surprise in her eyes.

"Yes," I answered coolly. "Didn't you know that?"

Mandy appeared flustered. She attempted to cover that by rummaging around in her purse and pulling out a plastic bag filled with what looked like wrinkled navy blue material. "Sometimes Rick gets all wrapped up in his business stuff and he's not so good about checking in with me. I got tired of waiting for him in that smelly condo in Prague, and I was homesick. So I figured I'd come back to Canada. I mean, I knew he'd come home sooner or later, but I didn't exactly know he was here now." She looked up from her purse again. "Didn't he tell you he had a girlfriend?"

"Uh . . . not in so many words," I said, still trying to figure out how I wanted to play this.

Grillfriend eyed me suddenly, her eyes suspicious. "*When* did he hire you, exactly?"

"Yesterday," I told her.

Again she appeared quite surprised. "And when did he get into town, again?"

"This morning. I picked him up from the airport myself, actually. You two probably just missed each other."

"If he hired you yesterday and you picked him up today, then how did he meet you to hire you?"

"We had a virtual interview last week, and he called me yesterday to offer me the position."

"A virtual what?"

"Interview."

"How does that work?" I could tell she was stalling, feeling me out, so I just went with it.

"Skype," I said. "He has a webcam and I have a webcam and we can speak to each other and see each other over the Internet."

"You mean like webcam sex?"

"A bit like that, yes," I said. "Only no sex. Just an interview." Oh, boy, Tanner hadn't been kidding. Des Vries did like 'em dumb and slutty.

"Well," she said, moving into the condo and over to the TV, "you can go home now. I'm gonna wait here till he gets back."

Crap. Now what? In desperation I sent a text to Dutch. "I'll just let Mr. Des Vries know that you're here and tell him that I'm leaving for the evening," I said merrily.

She didn't even look up from the couch. "Whatevs," she said, sifting through the plastic bag to pull out a blue blazer, matching skirt, red and white scarf, and what looked like an ID badge. She then got up to toss the whole bundle into the fireplace.

"Don't like your uniform?" I asked, curious about her actions.

"I got fired," she said testily. "And it was total bullshit. I mean, you spill one pot of coffee on an Arabian prince, and it's like you murdered someone or something." Mandy then moved over to the switch by the side of the fireplace and flicked it. Flames sprouted immediately and began to consume the clothes. She smiled at the sight of the flames consuming her clothes. "The condo in Prague didn't have a fireplace," she said.

"Are you going to get a new job?" I said, eyeing the screen of my phone anxiously. Where was Dutch?

Mandy made a *tsk*ing sound. "Rick told me that if I ever got sick of working for the airlines, that I should just quit, so this is practically the same thing. I only flew a couple of times a month anyway, and that was only so I could fly free when Rick had one of his business meetings out of the country and he wanted me along."

"Ah," I said again, just as my phone pinged with an incoming message.

When I read the text, I nearly laughed, but it would have been mean, so I held in the chuckle and took the phone over to show Grill-friend, holding it up for her so she could see the text. "He sent you a message," I said.

She leaned forward from her seat on the couch and squinted at the screen to read the text line by line . . . out loud. "'Tell Mandy to get her ass out of my condo. I've met someone else. It's over between us.'"

Grillfriend squinted at the message for about ten more seconds and then she burst into tears.

I spent the next hour trying to convince Mandy to leave the condo. She had a meltdown to end all meltdowns. There were a lot of waterworks and Kleenex, and I knew that until she left, Dutch couldn't come home. Short of zapping her with my stun gun and dragging her limp self into the elevator, I didn't know how to remove her from the premises.

"Mandy," I said evenly, after a fountain of tears and nonstop wailing. "You gotta go. I need to get home soon, and I can't leave Mr. Des Vries's condo with you still here."

"I love him!" she wailed. "He's my soul mate!"

The urge to roll my eyes was really strong, but I kept them staring straight ahead while I tried to think of something to say. Normally I would've dipped my toe into those intuitive waters and come up with a few insights for her, but two things stopped me: First, I didn't want to tip my hand that I had that kind of ability, because I didn't know if this girl knew any of the real Rick Des Vries's associates and would blab to them that he had a new psychic sidekick, and two, the girl was just a mess, and where the heck was I even going to start? I mean, she thought a misogynistic, abusive, cutthroat, murdering weapons dealer was her *soul mate*. The girl had issues . . . serious, *serious* issues.

"You know what I always do when a guy dumps me?" I said carefully.

"What?" she blubbered into her snotty Kleenex.

"I go shopping!"

Mandy began sobbing again in earnest. "Rick always gave me money to shop!" she wailed. "Now I don't have any money for clothes or my nails or to get my hair done! *And I just lost my job!*"

In desperation I snuck off to the bathroom and called Dutch. "I don't know what to do!" I told him. "She won't leave!"

"Sweetheart, you've got to *make* her go."

"And how do you propose I do that?" I snapped. "I can't call the police because we're not supposed to involve the authorities, and so far I haven't been able to get her to stop crying long enough to pick her face up out of the tissue and listen to me!"

Music erupted in the background on Dutch's end, and it was so loud I didn't hear what he said next. "Hello?" I said. "Are you there?"

The music subsided again. "Sorry," Dutch said. "I didn't realize it was going to be so loud in there."

"Where are you?"

"A bar."

I could feel my temper flare. Here I was dealing with a blubbering ex-girlfriend and Dutch was out getting a beer. "Nice," I said, in a voice that clearly suggested it wasn't.

"Easy there, Edgar," Dutch said. "I'm meeting Kozahkov here."

I inhaled deeply and let it out slowly. "Sorry," I said.

"Listen, Abs," Dutch said. "I gotta go meet Viktor; if you can't get Mandy to leave the condo, don't worry about it. I'll be back there in about two hours and I'll deal with her."

"She'll recognize you for an impostor," I told him.

"Then start feeding her some wine," he suggested. "Get her drinking and keep 'em coming until she's good and drunk. If she's still conscious when I get there, she'll be looking at me through beer goggles, and I doubt she'll notice I'm not Des Vries. It should be fairly easy to pour her into a cab and have one of Frost's guys drive her car back to her place. She'll wake up tomorrow and think it was all a bad dream."

"Is there any alcohol here?"

"There is," he said, and I could tell he was smiling. "I had a chance to bring in some groceries while you were out shopping. Check the wine rack. I'm pretty sure you'll find enough there to pickle her."

I felt better immediately. "Okay. And you be careful," I warned him.

"I will," he promised, and the blast of music told me he was once again entering the bar.

After hanging up with Dutch, I moved out to the kitchen, bypassing Mandy, who was still weeping dramatically on the sofa, sifting through pictures on her phone, presumably of her and Rick in happier times.

On the way I noticed that Dutch had left out on the counter some of his files on Des Vries, Kozahkov, and other members of the Chechen Mafia, and I discreetly moved all these to one of the kitchen drawers so that Mandy wouldn't see them and suspect our ruse. I then rummaged through the cabinets until I found the wine goblets, and set one on the counter before thinking better of it and reaching for a second glass. After uncorking a bottle of red, I poured us each a generous portion and went back to the sitting area.

"Here," I said, waggling the wineglass above her.

Mandy lifted one mascara-smudged eye out of her tissue. Without a word she took the glass, sat up, tilted it back, and guzzled it down.

Classy.

She then reached for the other glass I held, and with a shrug I gave it to her and took the empty back to the kitchen.

Just as I set that one in the sink and was getting another clean glass for myself, there was a buzzing sound from the intercom by the elevator. I left the kitchen and headed over to the control panel just as my phone gave a chirping noise. I focused on the intercom first, and it buzzed again, causing me to jump a little. Timidly I hit the TALK button and said, "Yes?"

There was a pause, and I realized I needed to release the button. Once I did, the voice of the doorman came through the speaker. "Yes, ma'am, this is Daniel, your doorman."

I frowned. What did he want? My phone chirped again, but I ignored it for the moment. "Yes, Daniel, what can I do for you?"

"Your guests have arrived," he said.

Huh? "My guests?" I asked.

"Yes m'am. Three gentlemen who would rather not give me their names, but they assure me they were invited to personally stop by and see Mr. Des Vries."

"Mr. Des Vries isn't here," I said to him.

There was a pause, then, "They would like to wait for him in the penthouse, ma'am."

I blinked at the intercom. "Uh . . . okay," I said, wondering what to do.

"Perfect," came Daniel's cheerful reply. "They're on their way to you." I realized belatedly that Daniel had mistaken my *Uh . . . okay* for *Go ahead and send them up!* I thought about buzzing him back to have them wait there, because without Dutch at my side, I didn't really know what I should do.

I had pulled my phone out of my blazer pocket to send Dutch a text when I saw that Frost had already sent one to me. It read: *Your flowers have arrived.*

The text was code. It meant the company in the lobby wasn't good company to have without a gun handy. As I lifted my hand to press the buzzer again and tell Daniel to hold on, the elevator pinged and the doors, which had remained open since Mandy arrived, began to close.

"Oh, sheep!" I hissed. Thinking quickly, I stuck out my arm, allowing the door to hit it and retract; then I pulled one of Mandy's suitcases halfway onto the elevator to prevent the doors from closing and hold the car at our floor. Once that was done, I considered my options. If I buzzed the doorman back and told him that I'd changed my mind and ordered him not to send up the "guests," wouldn't that look suspicious? Our cover was so tenuous that I hated to do anything that could be out of character for Rick's assistant, and I realized that if I really *was* Rick Des Vries's newest employee, I'd never insult his company by keeping them in the lobby to wait for him. I'd let them come up and serve them refreshments like any good personal assistant would.

The elevator pinged again and the doors attempted to close, bouncing off Mandy's luggage in an impatient manner. I scowled, then turned and ran back over to Mandy.

"What?" she said, looking up at me with her puffy eyes and runny mascara.

"You need to leave," I told her, nearly in a panic. *"Right now!"*

"But I want to talk to Rick!"

Fueled by fear, I reached down and clenched my hand on to Mandy's arm, pulling her to her feet and not caring that she spilled some of the wine onto the floor.

"Hey!" she protested, but I wasn't having it.

"Out!" I said firmly, pulling her forcefully down the hall toward the elevator doors. "And I mean it, Mandy. We've got company in the lobby, and if you know what's good for you, you'll make yourself scarce, *capisce*?"

"Is it another girl?" she demanded, standing stubbornly at the open elevator and mightily resisting my efforts to shove her inside.

I stepped back and tried a different tack. "Do you know what Mr. Des Vries does for a living?" I asked.

She blinked at me. "He does something with imports and exports."

I forced a smile. "Yes, that's correct. Mr. Des Vries is in the import/export business, and right now a few of his *very* important clients are on their way up here. I will have to entertain them until he gets home, and I don't have to tell you, Mandy, that if Mr. Des Vries arrives here later to find you in a state of emotional distress and embarrassing him in front of his associates, he will likely be *very* upset. Furious, even."

I emphasized that last part so that she would clearly understand what I meant, and the trickle of fear in her eyes let me know she did. "I should go," she said, stepping quickly to grab her luggage and wheel both suitcases into the elevator.

She then turned around and held her hand on the door to prevent it from closing. "Would you please tell him I miss him?"

"Absolutely," I promised. "I will tell him personally the moment he gets here how much you truly miss him."

Mandy opened her mouth to add something else, but I cut her off. "I will also tell him how gorgeous you looked and how impressed I was with you and that he is a fool to consider letting you go. Now *please* leave, Mandy, and exit out the garage—okay?"

She nodded and her eyes welled again, but she said nothing more, only offered me a small wave as the doors closed.

With a sigh I looked at my phone, which was chirping again.

Text from Frost: *Your flowers are beginning to wilt in the lobby.* I hurried into the living room and began to collect all the tissues and mop up the wine.

Another ping made me pause and eye the phone again. Text from Dutch: *I'm on my way back. Stay put and get rid of Mandy!*

I growled and rushed to the kitchen to throw out the Kleenex and dump the remaining wine in Mandy's glass down the drain. I was about to text Dutch back that Mandy had been dealt with when I got an incoming text from Frost: *Your flowers are in the elevator. You will need some water.* (This was code for "grab your gun and be prepared for anything.")

I grabbed my purse, which held both my pistol and stun gun, fished them both out, then tucked them into the waistband of my skirt against the small of my back, making sure my jacket covered them. Then I texted Frost, *Who sent me flowers?* I was hoping he could give me a clue as to who was in the lobby and on their way up.

He replied, *They're from your good friend Victor.*

Victor? Did he mean Viktor Kozahkov? The guy Dutch was meeting? If so, what the heck was he doing here instead of meeting Dutch at the bar?

My phone pinged again with an incoming text from Dutch: *A.C., please respond! Is she gone and have you gotten the flowers yet?*

I texted Dutch immediately: *GF gone. Flowers on their way up. Where r u?*

Before he could even respond, however, the elevator doors opened and a short guy with a pronounced gut and thick mop of salt-and-pepper hair stepped out to eye me with interest. He was flanked by two of the largest goons I had ever seen.

The short guy was like a midget next to these two, and both of them literally had to duck their heads to exit the elevator.

I gulped and typed quickly into my phone to both Dutch and Frost: *Flowers here. BIG bouquet!*

The short guy stepped up to me, flapping the white key card that Daniel seemed to hand out like candy. I gripped my phone tightly and steadied my nerves. "Hello," I said casually. "May I help you?"

"Who are you?" said Viktor.

"I'm Abigail, Mr. Des Vries's assistant. Did you have an appointment with him?"

"Ver is he?" Kozahkov asked, pivoting his head around as if looking for Rick.

My smile widened and I held up my cell. "He just texted me that he's on his way home. May I tell him who's stopping by?"

Viktor didn't appear to like me. Maybe it was the way his lip curled when I spoke, or the way his goons stepped closer together to completely block the exit. It was really hard to hold my ground, but somehow, I managed. "Tell him Viktor Kozahkov is here for za meeting," he said a bit impatiently.

I eyed him quizzically. "Mr. Kozahkov, I believe Mr. Des Vries intended to meet you at another location," I said carefully. "It was my understanding he was to meet you for drinks."

Kozahkov looked thoroughly irritated. "I receive message we meet here!"

I offered him a slight bow. "I sincerely apologize for the mix-up, sir. He's on his way back here and should be home shortly. May I invite you in to wait?"

I turned to lead the way into the living room when I felt a firm hand clamp down on my arm. Without warning, I was spun around to face the mean little man, whose eyes betrayed his intentions and sent all kinds of warning bells to sound in my head. "Maybe you should entertain me while your boss is avay, eh?"

My eyes flickered to the goons. They stood with their arms crossed and feet spread wide. If Kozahkov wanted to rape me, they weren't about to stop him; in fact, I had little doubt they'd help hold me down.

Tamping down my fear, I plastered a smile on my face and managed to wink at the beady-eyed beast. "Of course," I said easily. "After all, it's part of my job description to entertain Mr. Des Vries's guests."

Kozahkov appeared disappointed. I could see that he liked to brutalize and strike fear into women. I eyed his goons again, knowing much of the danger I was presently in was caused by their close proximity. Switching my phone to silent, I tucked it into my blazer pocket and said, "I've got some toys in the back bedroom. Why don't you and I head there and have a little fun?"

Kozahkov's expression was wary. I could tell he didn't completely trust me. Without letting him think about it for too long, I said to his goons, "If Mr. Des Vries arrives while we're partying, tell him we'll be out soon, okay, boys?"

They in turn looked to Kozahkov. With a sick smile he said something in Russian. The goons folded their arms over their massive chests and took up their post by the elevator doors.

Kozahkov then turned back to me and said, "After you."

I led him to the spare bedroom at the back of the condo, thinking furiously of a plan. I didn't believe for a second that Kozahkov would allow me to stop and send a text that I needed help with the flowers, so I kept my phone in my pocket.

I still had my gun tucked into my waistband, which was good, but if I shot Kozahkov, we'd lose the one contact we had to both the drone thief and Boklovich. Plus, the sound of a gun would definitely bring the goons running.

Still, I also had my stun gun tucked next to my pistol. Either way,

I'd have to be quick and I'd have to be clever if I intended not to get raped.

The moment we made it through the door, Viktor turned into an octopus. His hands began to grope me from behind, and it took everything I had not to fight him off. "Hold on a second, baby," I cooed, tasting the bile at the back of my throat as his fat hands felt me up.

"Take off your clothes," he ordered.

I ran my hands over his, removing them from my chest, and worked my way over to the dresser, where I turned so that it was at my back. I then shrugged out of my jacket and tossed it at him with a playful laugh. He caught it and growled, attempting to show me his ferocious side. It was so pathetic and awful that I had a hard time keeping my nerves in check. "Oh, you big tiger, you!" I said, moving to the buttons on my shirt.

Viktor shrugged out of his tweed blazer and flung it on the floor. "Strip for me, baby," he said, adding another growl.

Again I tasted bile at the back of my throat, but then I remembered something I'd read once about lion tamers and how they worked with big cats. The article suggested that it was all in the attitude. Wild animals would stand down to anyone they felt was dominant to them, so when tamers cracked their whips and yelled their commands, they were essentially saying, "I am the alpha and you will obey me!"

I thought I'd give that a try. I stopped fiddling with the buttons on my shirt and eyed Viktor sternly. "You first," I said. "Take off your damn clothes, Viktor. Now."

The ploy worked. He smiled hungrily and began to tear at his clothes, stripping away his dress shirt, exposing a dirty undershirt that didn't quite cover his extended belly. "Keep going," I demanded.

To my relief he did. He got all the way down to his tighty whities, when I held up my hand for him to stop. "Turn around," I ordered.

"Why?" he said, a bit of wariness creeping into his voice.

I stepped up to him with my hands firmly on my hips. "Because," I said, staring down my nose at him, "I think you've been a very naughty boy and you need a spanking."

The repugnant man giggled and turned around, wiggling his big wide butt at me.

Quick as a flash I reached to the small of my back, pulled out my stun gun, and zapped him with enough volts to topple a gorilla.

Kozahkov made a rather loud, squeaky, strangled sound and I covered that by shouting, "Oh, Viktor! You animal! Do it to me, baby!"

He hit the floor with a muffled thud and I just continued to hold down the trigger until the stun gun ran out of juice.

Viktor quivered and jerked on the floor and I stepped over him carefully, retrieved my jacket, and moved over to the window.

I'd seen the fire escape earlier when I'd had a chance to explore the condo. With effort I got the window open and stepped out onto the landing. I was about to text Dutch to warn him about the goons when a peek back into the room revealed Viktor flailing his arms and legs, struggling to get to his knees. I decided to get my butt to safety first and wasted no time moving to the ladder and working my way down it.

Climbing down a fire escape is much more difficult than you'd expect—after all, I was in a pencil skirt and heels, and it was forty degrees and windy outside. By the time I reached the bottom, I was out of breath, and shivering uncontrollably. I also didn't quite know where to go.

As I was pulling my phone out of my pocket, however, a black sedan with smoked windows pulled up next to me. Uh-oh.

The window rolled down and a voice inside said, "Nice thong."

I glared hard at the car's interior, even though I couldn't see the driver in the darkness. I then reached for the handle, which was locked. "Let me in," I said curtly.

The locks were released and I tucked inside. The window slid up and I nearly sighed with relief as the car's warmth wrapped cozily around me.

"Where's Dutch?" I asked Frost.

"He went in a minute ago."

"He *what*?" I shouted. "Dude! I just Tased Viktor!"

Frost's eyebrows rose appreciatively. "You did? Why?"

"The son of a toad wanted to rape me," I told him. "He suggested that I had to *entertain* him until Rick got there, so I coaxed him into the back bedroom away from his goons and zapped him."

Instead of being alarmed, Frost actually snickered before putting the car into drive and taking us around the block to a discreet corner location where we could watch the front of the condo without being detected.

Once he'd parked, he pulled out his phone and typed a message into it. He didn't tell me what the message said, and I could only hope he was sending Dutch a warning. "You have to go in there," I said when he made no further move to assist my fiancé. "Seriously, Frost, when that guy recovers, he's gonna be hoppin' mad."

"Probably," our handler agreed, eyeing the windows at the top of the building. "But Rivers is armed and he knows how to handle himself."

My cell vibrated again. With relief I read Dutch's text: *Where r u?*

I texted him back that I was safe and in the car with Frost. I also added a note that the bouquet held one small rose, which was so "stunning" that I'd placed it in the back bedroom, but I'd left the two daisies by the elevator because they were big daisies. Big, BIG daisies. I could only hope that Dutch picked up on all my subtext before he got to the penthouse.

I waited anxiously for him to reply, but he didn't. "Shouldn't you go in there?" I asked again after about ten minutes.

"And blow his cover? No. I think we should sit tight and see what happens."

I stared up at the third floor and could see the lights on, but all the shutters had been drawn and there was no way to see what was happening. "Why didn't Kozahkov meet Dutch at the bar?" I asked when it occurred to me again that the plan had changed without either Dutch or me knowing it.

Frost didn't look at me when he answered, but continued to stare right at the building. "Dunno. Kozahkov's appearance here caught everybody off guard. We expected him to show up at the strip club where Rivers was waiting for him."

"Strip club?" I asked, my eyebrows rising. "I thought it was a bar." My fiancé was going to have some explaining to do.

Frost snickered. "Kozahkov likes his strippers," he said. "I had Rivers suggest one of Viktor's favorite hangouts to get him to show up. I have no idea why he switched the meeting place on us." Frost then eyed me. "It might have had something to do with you, though."

"Me?" I said defensively. "Why would I have anything to do with it?"

Frost shrugged. "He might've heard that Des Vries got a new girl-friend and he wanted to check her out."

"I'm not the girlfriend anymore, remember?" I snapped, moody about being forced to sit with Agent Asshole.

Frost eyed me again. "Oh, right," he said. "You're the *assistant* now. And I saw that you added a few things to your wardrobe on the Company's dime."

I could feel my face flush. "The hooker clothes weren't working for me."

"Yeah, well, the iPad's going back," he said firmly.

I narrowed my eyes at him. I was really wishing I had that iPad with me. I'd use it to smack Frost over the head. "You must be a *blast* at parties," I told him.

"This ain't a party, Cooper."

"Duh," I told him. "What's your issue with me anyway?"

Frost lifted a Styrofoam cup of coffee from the cup holder on his console without answering me; his eyes remained trained on the building.

By now at least twenty minutes had passed since Frostbite had picked me up and I was really starting to get nervous about Dutch. Waiting and watching weren't getting us anywhere, so I used the only other tool at my disposal—my radar.

I closed my eyes and focused on my fiancé. I could feel him inside the building; his energy was tense and focused, but I didn't sense any pain. I let go of the little breath I'd been holding. "He's okay," I whispered.

"Who's okay?" Frost asked.

"Dutch."

"Did he send you a text?"

"No."

"Did you see him in one of the windows?"

"No."

"Then how do you know he's okay?" I couldn't help but detect the slightly mocking edge to Frost's tone when he finally turned away from the building to look at me.

"I can feel it," I told him bluntly. "My radar says he's unhurt and working his way through the situation."

"Right," Frost said, that mocking tone ratcheting up another notch.

"Don't take my word for it," I told him. "See for yourself."

With that, I motioned to the front doors, where Viktor and his goons were just now emerging, and my pal Daniel was holding open the door for them. Kozahkov looked mad enough to kill someone, and I'll give you three guesses as to whom he'd pick first for target practice.

His bodyguards were on either side of him, each one supporting him under the arms because he was definitely struggling to keep his legs under him.

My radar pinged suddenly and I sat forward, alert and focused. "Something's not right," I whispered.

Frost was watching Viktor and the goons. "You really did zap him, Cooper," he said, ignoring what I'd just said. "Text Rivers and see if you can get him to respond."

I put my arm on Frost's shoulder, my radar insisting that there was some unseen danger approaching. In my head a warning sounded so loud I winced. *Duck and cover!* it commanded. My attention whipped to a car parked well down the street. Its lights came on and it maneuvered out of its parking place with a jerk. "Frost!" I yelled. "Something's not right!"

"Shhhh!" he warned me. "Cooper, keep your voice dow—"

That was all he got out before we heard the squeal of tires. The car down the street had revved its engine and it was now roaring straight at us. I used my hand on Frost's shoulder to pull him toward me, to the side, and down low. In the next instant a hailstorm of bullets tore the quiet night apart.

Chapter Four

. . .

Before I could even cover my own head, I was pulled sideways and a heavy weight fell right on top of me, mashing my face into the leather upholstery. I heard sounds like golf balls pounding against the metal of the car. Over our heads, glass crackled and splintered, while outside there were shouts and one piercing scream, and all the while it continued to rain bullets. The assassin's car roared past, but it seemed to hit something, because there was a loud thud mixed into the cacophony of noise.

Even after the car had passed us, the assassin continued to shoot bullets, but when the car got to the end of the block, it squealed at the turn and was gone. For the next several seconds, all was quiet. Well, save for the sound of my panicked breathing and thundering heart.

I was still smunched against the leather seat, so I used my hands to try to get up from under the weight on my back. "Stay still!" Frost growled.

I stopped struggling. "Are you okay?"

"Yeah. You?"

"Freaked-out, but otherwise I'm okay."

"Good. Stay down and don't move until I tell you it's clear." The pressure on my head and back lifted as Frost moved off me.

Once he'd had a chance to survey the area, he said, "Okay, you can get up now."

I moved and heard the sound of tinkling glass. Sitting up slowly, I could see that our windshield had been struck by a hail of bullets, many of which were still stuck in the glass. Two bullets had made it all the way through, however, and one of them had lodged dead center into my headrest, and that hit me like a ton of bricks. If I hadn't ducked at the exact moment I had, I'd have been dead for sure.

My car door was suddenly yanked open and Dutch's panicked face filled my vision. "Thank Christ!" he said, reaching into the car to pull me out and hug me so tight I couldn't inhale.

"I'm fine!" I squeaked. "Dutch, sweetie, please let go. I can't breathe."

Dutch released me from the embrace only to hold me at arm's length and inspect me head to toe. "You've got a cut on your cheek," he said, wiping his fingers gently at the side of my face.

"It's nothing," I told him, really hoping it wasn't.

The other side of the car opened and Frost stepped out. "You okay?" Dutch asked him.

"Fine," he said, eyeing something lying in the middle of the street. I looked to what had caught his attention and my stomach lurched. "Ohmigod!" I said, pulling out of Dutch's grasp to hurry to the corner and lose my dinner.

After I'd stopped retching, I felt Dutch's hand on my back. "How you doin', Edgar?" he asked.

"I'm fine," I managed to say, before wiping my mouth with my sleeve. "Jesus," I whispered. "Who would *do* that to someone?"

Dutch looked over his shoulder at what remained of Viktor Kozahkov. From what I'd seen, he'd been shot up but good before being run over. It was an image I didn't think I'd ever get out of my mind.

"Someone who wanted him very dead," I heard Dutch say to Frost.

"Cooper could have just as easily been the target," our handler replied. "Did you catch the bullet holes on her side of the car? It looks like someone was aiming at her."

At that, I turned and looked more closely at Frost's car. Sure enough, most of the bullets that had landed on our car had favored the passenger side. It was a miracle I was still alive. "How is it that we weren't hit?" I asked.

Frost knocked the side of the car. "Bulletproof," he said.

I said, "Maybe the shooter fired at us using his left hand and most of those that favored my side of the car were just wild?" I was thinking there was no way I could have been the target, and it made sense to me that the driver was likely trying to steer the speeding car with his right hand and shoot out the window with his left. Dutch looked at me doubtfully, and I had a moment to consider that a professional hit man would probably be pretty skilled shooting either right- or left-handed while maneuvering a speeding car. "Yeah, scratch that," I said with a gulp.

Dutch appeared seriously stressed, especially when he went over to inspect my side of the car. "Let's get inside," he told me as we heard the first sirens approach.

"Keep away from the windows," Frost told us. "I'll be up later and we'll talk."

It turned out that there was one more victim besides Viktor and his two bodyguards. The doorman we'd suspected was a spy for CSIS was dead in the doorway with several shots to the chest and head. I felt terrible, because even though he'd been working undercover to keep an eye on us, and in spite of the fact that he'd given Mandy a key card, knowing full well Rick Des Vries had arrived with another woman, he was still technically one of the good guys.

It also took until Frost was through with the police—about three hours—for me to stop shaking. Dutch had made me some tea, which helped, and he held my hand and told me I was okay, which helped even more. He also received a text from Frost, who was meeting with a high-ranking member of the CSIS. Dutch showed me the message and I grimaced. So much for keeping under the Canadian radar.

Our CIA handler came up close to midnight, and by then I was slumped in my chair, heavy with fatigue.

"How'd it go with CSIS?" Dutch asked him before the guy even had a chance to sit down.

Frost tugged on his tie to loosen it and took his seat. "Not as bad as expected," he said. "They're not happy that we're working with Rick Des Vries, but they weren't sorry to see Kozahkov taken out. It was a little stickier because their agent got hit."

"I liked him," I said dully. "He seemed like a nice man underneath the subterfuge."

Frost nodded and rubbed his eyes tiredly. "Yeah, it sucks, but as bad as losing one of our allies is, I still have to point out that it works in our favor."

"How's that, exactly?" I asked, disgusted that he could find the agent's death beneficial.

"We offered to put one of our own guys into the building under-cover and take the risk. CSIS took the offer, no questions asked. We'll feed them a few tidbits about Des Vries's comings and goings, and that should keep the heat off of us for now at least.

"It's going to be even more important, though, Agent Rivers, for you to keep your identity a secret. We can't risk the CSIS finding out that you're an impostor working for us. They'd never trust the CIA again."

I wondered why anyone would trust the CIA in the first place, but I kept that thought to myself.

"When word gets out that Kozahkov was hit outside Des Vries's condo, it could attract a little too much of the wrong kind of atten-tion. You two are going to have to work to keep a low profile from here on out," Frost warned. "No paper trails or run-ins with the local authorities. Obey all traffic laws and local ordinances. If one of you gets sick or hurt, don't go to the doctor; we'll send one of our guys in to check you out."

"Wait," I said, putting up my hand. "You're including me in that mandate? You think the CSIS would be interested in *me*?"

Frost sent me a piercing stare. "They've already asked about you, Cooper. They had more intel on Des Vries's regular girlfriend than we did. Candy something . . ."

"Mandy Mortemeyer," I corrected, liking that, for once, I knew more than he did.

"Yeah, her." Frost yawned and scratched his chin. "We didn't anticipate that she'd lose her job and show up here. What a pain in the ass. And we didn't even know she'd entered the building until Rivers texted me."

"How is that possible?" I asked. Weren't they watching us like hawks?

Frost sighed heavily. "She came in through the garage, and our guy on watch by the entrance—who's been reassigned—thought she was you in the blond wig again. He didn't spot her until she came out driving one of Des Vries's cars."

"That must have been where she got the key card to the penthouse in the first place," I surmised, feeling bad that I'd blamed the doorman. "How many cars does Des Vries have?" I'd driven one on my shopping spree and Dutch had obviously driven another. From memory there'd been a few cars parked in the garage when I'd gone out to do my shopping.

"Three. She took the only one worth less than a hundred grand."

My eyebrows rose. "You guys gonna track her down so she doesn't come back?"

"We're working on it," he said irritably, which let me know Mandy had given some other errant agent the slip. I wondered if he'd been reassigned too.

"I broke up with Mandy by text," Dutch said. "She's got to think Rick's a tool for breaking up with her that way. I bet she moves on by tomorrow."

I turned and smiled at Dutch. "But you're her *soul mate*, Richard. Didn't you know that?"

Dutch rolled his eyes. "Do you think she'll be back?"

I shrugged. "Probably."

"We'll find her," Frost assured us. "And we'll make sure she gets the message. Anyway, the important thing here is that CSIS knows you're not Des Vries's regular girlfriend, Cooper—they've already run you through their facial-recognition software."

My eyes widened.

"You haven't come up in their system, which makes them extra curious about your identity. I've told them only that you work for us, but that's not going to satisfy them for long. I have a feeling they'll be trying to figure out who you are the whole time you're here. They'll be searching for any information they can find, and they'll dip their fingers into any medical records, driver's license, passport info, et cetera, if they can, so you *can't* end up at a doctor's office or the hospital, and you *can't* file any police reports or get a ticket, okay?"

"We get it, Frost," Dutch said. "Low profiles and no paper trails."

A short silence fell on us until I asked, "Did the CSIS have any theories about who might have killed Kozahkov?"

Frost eyed me. "No. And I didn't share with them that you'd gotten a good look at him either."

That got my attention. "But I didn't see him."

It was Frost's turn to look surprised. "Then what tipped you off before the shooting started?"

I sighed. My first day of actually being a spy and I was already tired of this. I tapped my temple. "My radar gave me a warning."

Frost seemed to take that in. "You seriously didn't see anyone? Maybe someone walking suspiciously up to their car before they got in and came at us?"

"Nope."

Frost drummed his fingers on the table, probably reevaluating his estimation of me.

Dutch took the opportunity to speak next. "Whoever it was, he was a pro. Any theories on who might've ordered the hit?"

Frost's fingers stopped drumming, but he continued to stare at me with scrutiny. I tried not to squirm. "Viktor Kozahkov had a list of enemies a mile long, including a few members of his own family. He was deep inside the Chechen Mafia and made enough waves to be forced to leave the homeland in a hurry. It was a foregone conclusion when we looked into his history that he was living on borrowed time. The important question is not who killed him, but did he know who stole the drone? Or even, did he have a hand in the operation and, by extension, was killed because of it?"

Dutch shook his head. "He didn't take it," he said firmly.

I frowned. "You're sure?"

"Yes," Dutch said. "Granted, he was still pretty out of it by the time I got here. . . ." Looking at me, Dutch asked, "By the way, Edgar, what'd you do to him? The guy could barely talk."

I gave him a sly smile and pulled my stun gun out of my blazer pocket. "I hit him with about a thousand volts of stop-groping-me-you-Russian-pig."

Dutch grinned. "Glad to know you can take care of yourself."

"Why do you think he didn't steal the drone?" Frost asked, his tone impatient.

"Kozahkov told me that he'd just scored a major deal. He said he'd made a connection to a newcomer who'd acquired some cutting-edge technology from the Americans and he stood to make a killing on it when he took the newcomer to Boklovich," Dutch said.

"The drone thief!" I whispered. "*That's* why I kept getting a sideways connection to Kozahkov. He really didn't steal the drone!" For the record, I seriously love it when I'm right.

"Did he tell you who this newcomer was?" Frost asked anxiously.

Dutch shook his head. "He wouldn't even give me a hint, and when I got pushy about it, I could tell he started to get suspicious, so I had to back off. He wanted to know why I was so curious, and I told him, point-blank, that I knew what the new guy was offering, and I also knew it was defective. I told him I had the real McCoy and just like the newcomer, I needed his help getting it to Boklovich's auction."

"What'd Viktor say to that?" I asked.

"He got real interested real fast. I told him that I'd acquired the original software code, which meant no one would have to bother with the reverse engineering. I also told him that the other guy didn't even know his product was defective, and that the device in question wouldn't work past a few demonstrations. If Viktor wanted to risk selling a defective product to someone, then he could have at it."

"His reaction to that?" Frost wanted to know.

"He had no problem with it," Dutch said, shaking his head ruefully.

"I'm beginning to see why someone would have wanted this guy dead," I said.

"Yeah," Dutch agreed. "Just like we hoped, Viktor wanted to use the new information to his advantage. He was willing to set me up with Boklovich and help arrange an auction. I knew he was thinking of pitting the copy of the software against Intuit to drive up the price."

"Which was exactly what we wanted to happen," Frost growled, his frustration written all over his face because now that Viktor was dead, so was our access to Boklovich. "Do you know if he'd already introduced the thief to Boklovich?"

Dutch shook his head. "I'm not sure, but I got the feeling that he hadn't had a chance to contact Vasilii yet. He seemed eager to leave the penthouse and I did see him starting a text message when he and his two bodyguards got into the elevator. Maybe the text was to Boklovich?"

Frost pulled out his cell phone and placed a call. After putting the phone to his ear, he said, "It's Frost. See if the Canadian authorities recovered Kozahkov's cell phone tonight, and if they did, steal it from their evidence room. We need to know the number to the last outgoing text on that phone." There was a long pause on Frost's side, then, "Shit, Jack. Just shit!" Frost then punched his thumb hard on the end button and pocketed the cell. "Kozahkov's phone was found in over a dozen pieces and the SIM card had a bullet hole through it.

"We'll try to tap into the Canadian phone logs to figure out the number," Frost continued bitterly, "but that's a process that'll take days. Maybe even weeks."

Something occurred to me then and I turned to Dutch. "Did Kozahkov explain to you why he switched meeting places from the strip club downtown to here?"

I was not at all unhappy when my fiancé blushed slightly. He knew I knew about the strip club. "Sorry, Abs," he said quietly. "I didn't want to upset you."

"Honey," I told him, "I don't care who you look at as long as it's me you come home to."

Frost cleared his throat loudly and looked pointedly at us. "Can we please focus here?"

I scowled, but Dutch got back to the point. "I asked him why he'd shown up here and he said that he'd gotten a text that I was changing the venue."

"Who sent him the message?" I wondered, and both of us turned to look at Frost, who merely muttered, "Shit!" again.

"It had to have been the assassin," I said into the silence that followed. My intuition was telling me I was on to something there.

Dutch looked at me again. "Kozahkov didn't give you any hint when he got here as to who told him the meeting place had changed?"

I shook my head. "Nope. He was way more interested in groping me than making small talk. I should have stuck around to recharge the stun gun and zapped him for another round."

"Yeah, well, he was ready to kill you if he ever laid eyes on you again, so I'm glad you weren't here when I got home."

"How'd he let you off the hook for Cooper using the stun gun on him?" Frost asked.

Dutch shrugged. "I played it cool. I told him if he cornered the new girl in the back bedroom against her will—he had it coming. A guy like Viktor could appreciate that he'd been outmaneuvered, although I'm positive he would've shot her on sight, which is why I'm not sorry he's dead. If he'd gotten me in with Boklovich, I could never have taken Abby with me to the auction. Without her sixth sense, there's no way to scope out who has the drone before the bidding begins."

"So, getting back to Kozahkov's murder," I said, feeling like my brain was a mixture of too much information competing with too many intuitive signals. "You really think it was the hit man who made the call and not the drone thief? I mean, if word is getting out that the drone is defective, maybe the drone thief called Viktor to change the venue and throw everyone off. Maybe he then killed Viktor after he saw he was talking to you."

Dutch considered that. "I don't think we can rule anything out. If it was an assassin from Chechnya finally catching up with Kozahkov, or if it was our drone thief suspicious of Viktor meeting with me, it almost doesn't matter because our access to both the thief and Boklovich are now cut off."

"So we're at a dead end?" I asked.

Dutch stroked my hand. "I might be able to find another angle by sifting through Des Vries's files. His computer is pretty clean, and I'm digging through his e-mail, but the guy was careful. He didn't exactly leave a Rolodex of possible contacts with access to Boklovich."

"What if we tried to call someone close to Kozahkov?" I asked. "Maybe someone in his camp knows Boklovich and can hook us up?"

Frost and Dutch shook their heads. "Viktor was killed outside Des Vries's condo, Cooper," Frost said. "They're likely to hold Des Vries responsible."

"Should we be worried about payback?" I asked.

"We should be worried about everything," he said grumpily. "We'll make sure, however, to send cash to one of our guys embedded in Chechnya posing as a hit man and leak that the payment was for the Kozahkov hit to make it look like one of the markers on Kozahkov's head has been paid in full. That'll buy us some time should Viktor's people think about pinning his murder on Des Vries."

And then a thought seemed to occur to him and he said, "Let me also talk to the Mossad and see if they'd be willing to share the contact list on Des Vries's cell phone. There might be a few local names there we can try."

My radar broke through the haze of exhaustion with a suggestion. "How's the investigation into the pilot coming?" I asked Frost.

At this he almost brightened. "We think we have our first solid lead," he said. "The pilot was seeing someone, and we think she was someone with a connection to Kozahkov."

Frost had my full attention. "Tell us," I encouraged.

"Phone records for the pilot indicate several calls a few weeks ago to a number registered to a Chechen national with ties to both Canada and the U.S."

"Whoa!" I said. "Bingo, right?"

Frost nodded. "Maybe," he said. "We're having a hard time locating the girl, though."

"What's her background?"

"Oksana Fedotova is a twenty-three-year-old girl from Chechnya who came to Canada as a mail-order bride. She never went through with the marriage, though, and about six weeks after she arrived, she ditched the poor guy who paid for her to come here. She then got involved with the son of one of the major Mafia players in Ottawa, where Kozahkov used to live before he came to Toronto. These Mafia guys all swim in the same pool, so we think there could be a connection."

"How'd Fedotova end up meeting the pilot?" Dutch asked.

"She got caught up in a drug sting when her boyfriend was nabbed by the Canadian authorities for selling massive quantities of meth. While Oksana was awaiting trial, she jumped bail and somehow managed to sneak into the States.

"We traced her to an escort service in Vegas, which is where we believe she met our pilot. He was stationed at the airbase nearby, and a credit card receipt shows he purchased some company back in March."

"And now you can't find the girl?" I asked, an uneasy feeling creeping over me.

Frost shook his head. "Nope. Her apartment's been abandoned and she hasn't paid May's rent. None of her neighbors have seen or heard from her in a while."

"Did you put a BOLO out for her car?" Dutch asked.

"Yep, and so far we've got a big fat nothing," Frost told him, clearly frustrated that the woman was proving so elusive.

I could understand his frustration. My radar was suggesting that the whole thing was suspicious and that the pilot's call girl definitely had something to do with the missing drone. "Have you thought about interrogating the old boyfriend?" I asked. "I mean, you said yourself these Chechen boys all stick together. Maybe he knows what she was up to or maybe he was the one who orchestrated it?"

"He's dead," Frost told me. "Died in a prison fight about a year ago."

"Crap," I said, out of both energy and ideas.

"Was Oksana smart enough to pull this off on her own?" Dutch asked.

Frost shook his head. "I doubt it. She's a twenty-three-year-old girl with an eighth-grade education. I can't imagine she would have the sophistication to pull off something this big."

Still, my intuition was insisting there was a thread there to follow. "Keep digging, Agent Frost. There's something there."

I stifled a yawn then and looked wearily at the clock. It was well after one. "Come on," Dutch said, helping me up out of the chair. "Let's get you to bed, hot stuff."

I nodded dully and followed after him without a backward glance at Frost. I'm pretty sure he didn't mind or even notice my failure to wish him a good night.

Dutch and I were out of the condo early the next morning. I could have gone for a few more hours of sleep, but duty called and I was the schmuck who answered. "Dutch, can we at least stop for coffee?" I asked grouchily, slumped in the passenger seat while he navigated the morning rush-hour traffic.

"There's a coffee place right next to the office building," he told me. "And you have to start calling me Rick, or, better yet, Mr. Des Vries."

I frowned moodily. "I'll call you anything you want for a damn cup of coffee."

Dutch slanted a look my way, no doubt irritated that I now owed a quarter to the swear jar. Still, he put on his turn signal and pulled into the parking lot of a Tim Hortons. After putting the car into park, Dutch looked at me expectantly.

"I'll take a large coffee with extra milk, two sugars, and a glazed doughnut," I told him happily.

He scratched his goatee. "Tell that to the guy inside, Abs. Remember, we're in character, and you work for me. So bring me back a tall black coffee and a blueberry muffin."

I took a deep breath, knowing he was right, then plastered a big ol' smile on my face, saluted, and said, "Yes, sir, Mr. Des Vries, sir!"

The line inside was long, but the smell of the coffee and doughnuts was soothing enough to make me wait patiently. After purchasing our breakfasts, I balanced the two coffees in one hand, and the bag of goodies in the other, and headed back out to the car.

Once I was in the parking lot, however, I stopped dead in my tracks. Dutch was out of the car with his back pressed against the door and he was surrounded by three tough-looking thugs. One of them must have felt me staring at him, because he turned his head toward me and glared.

If I had been just a pedestrian noticing something odd in the parking lot, I might have ducked my chin and proceeded straight to my car, but I wasn't and that was my fiancé they were threatening. So I stood there for a few beats, wondering what to do. The guy glaring at me got even angrier, and he pulled aside his coat to show me the metal butt of a nickel-plated gun tucked up next to him.

It was unnecessary. I knew he was dangerous, so I continued to stand there and stare. Dutch did not once look in my direction, although I'm sure he knew I was there. I could see the tense set of his shoulders and feel the ether between us crackle with warning.

I really wanted to try to help him, but I had no idea how, so I just stood there, bearing witness, waiting for an idea to come to me, and that's when the guy glaring at me crooked his finger and motioned for me to come close.

Hesitating only for a second to adjust the coffee and the bag of pastries, I moved in their direction. "Good morning," I said when I got near. "Mr. Des Vries, I've brought you your breakfast."

Dutch did not look at me. Instead, he snapped, "Go back inside and wait for me there."

"Who's this?" one of the men asked, eyeing me from head to toe.

"I'm Mr. Des Vries's assistant," I said, all nice and friendly-like. "And I am so sorry to interrupt, sir, but you have a very busy morning with several appointments lined up. Would you like me to call and reschedule them all?"

"Appointments?" said the guy in front of Dutch. He was a man of average height with greasy blond hair, a long scar from the corner of his mouth to his ear, and two different-colored eyes—one brown, one green. "Who're you meeting with, Des Vries?"

"Oh, several people," I said, setting the bag of doughnuts and Dutch's coffee on the top of the car and playing with the lid on my coffee. My fingers were shaking and I was trying to keep it together long enough to help him.

"Like who?"

"Ms. Carter!" Dutch snapped. "If you would like to keep your job, then I would suggest you return to the restaurant, and wait for me there."

Dutch had adopted the slight foreign accent again, I noticed. "Certainly, Mr. Des Vries," I told him. "But let me just give you your coffee first."

I set my coffee and the lid quickly on top of the car and got his down, flicking the top off with my thumb before moving to offer it to him. Just as I started to extend my hand, however, I changed directions and flung it into the face of the guy with the gun, who reeled backward, clutching his hands to his face.

The other two whirled to face me and I grabbed the other cup of hot liquid, throwing it at the guy closest to me. It hit him square in the chest and he stepped backward and made a hissing noise.

As that was happening, Dutch swung his hand up, clocking the guy in front of him in the throat, then elbowed the hisser in the ribs before bringing his knee up and smashing the guy's nose in.

He went down like a sack of potatoes, and the greasy guy was struggling to breathe, while Coffee Face was shrieking. "It burns!" he cried, and I thanked God for Tim Hortons' hot mug of joe!

"Get in the car!" Dutch yelled, grabbing the hisser by the shoulders before spinning him around and tossing him into the grass.

I ran around to the passenger side and ducked into the car as fast as I could, but Dutch was faster and already had the car in reverse before I'd even closed my door.

We backed out of the space like hell on wheels, and there was a slight bump on Dutch's side, followed by a high-pitched howl.

Dutch spun the wheel and threw the car into drive and we hauled butt outta there.

I checked the rearview mirror continually for several blocks, but no sign of the bad guys appeared. And then I noticed that I still held my empty coffee cup in my shaking hand.

"Who the hell *were* those guys?" I demanded.

Dutch's eyes flickered to the rearview mirror. "Some very bad dudes," he said. "It appears that Des Vries is a bit of a gambler and lately he's had a really bad losing streak."

I sucked in a breath. "He owes them money?" I asked, guessing where this was going.

"Yep."

"How much?"

"Half a million."

"Dollars?"

Dutch nodded. "Canadian dollars, that is."

I waved my hand around dramatically. "Oh, well, with the exchange rate, that's, still what? *Half a million dollars?!*"

"Abby," Dutch said, his voice impatient. "*I* didn't run up the tab, remember?"

I glared at him but didn't reply. *How* could the CIA have missed the fact that Des Vries owed so much money in gambling debt?

I said as much to Dutch and he said, "It's in the file that Des Vries likes to gamble, but he's a very skilled player and almost always comes out on top. This poker game was probably a high-stakes game played and lost right before Rick flew to Jordan. During his interrogation with the Mossad, I doubt Des Vries would have mentioned it."

I turned in my seat and looked behind us. "So, Des Vries owes those guys half a million dollars," I said again, more calmly this time.

"Yep."

"And they bought that *you* were Des Vries?"

"Those guys don't hold the mark, doll. They're the enforcers. They've likely only seen a security-camera picture of Des Vries, and I'll remind you that this is Rick's car we're driving."

"Great," I said moodily. "Do you know who sent them?"

"No," Dutch admitted, and I could tell that was the part that really bothered him. "I didn't get a chance to feel them out for a name before you came out with breakfast."

I sighed and set down the empty cardboard cup in the holder. "So, what're we gonna do?" I asked. "I mean, they'll come looking for you again, right?"

Dutch peered out the windshield intently. "We'll contact Frost when we get to the office and go from there."

Agent Frostbite was totally unsympathetic and, I noticed, not really surprised when Dutch told him he'd been accosted by three men in the parking lot of Tim Hortons looking for payment on a gambling debt. "Let me get a team on it," he said perfunctorily from the speakerphone in Des Vries's office, and hung up.

"What does *that* mean?" I asked Dutch when he disconnected the line.

"It means we hang tight until we hear from Frost," he said.

"What? Like just *sit* here?"

Dutch reached for my hand and kissed it. "Not exactly," he said. "I'm going to look through Des Vries's computer files again and see if

I can't come up with another possible contact that can introduce us to Boklovich. And I'll search his log history to see if I can't find out who he owes money to."

"What am I supposed to do?"

Dutch pulled out a thick file from the briefcase he'd carried in from the car, similar to the ones I'd shoved in the drawer back at the condo. "Here," he said, handing it to me. "These are known members of the Chechen Mafia in Toronto. Look through that and see if your radar dings on anyone who might either be responsible for the drone heist or can get us in with Boklovich."

"I thought Kozahkov said the thief was a new guy?"

"He did," Dutch said. "But there has to be a prior connection, maybe to that Oksana woman. Otherwise, how would the thief know to contact Kozahkov?"

"Good point," I said, opening the folder, which was full of photographs and notes on nearly two dozen men, all of them sending out waves of dangerous energy.

I pulled up one photo right away. "You don't have to worry about this guy," I said.

Dutch squinted at the heavyset Chechen with black hair and a thick mustache. "Why?"

"He's dead," I said, laying the photo on the desk and picking through the others. "Along with this guy," I added, pulling out another one from the pile.

Dutch took the photo and studied it. After a minute he asked, "Anyone else?"

"You mean, is anyone else dead?"

"Yeah."

"No, but this guy's friend now has a broken leg."

I pulled out a photo that showed a man with short-cropped hair, a high brow, and a broad square face. His individual features weren't especially attractive until you put them all together, and then they became sexy as hell . . . oh . . . dolly. Centered right above his top lip he had a slight divot, like Tom Brokaw in his younger days, that made him even more seductive. He exuded a sexual energy that, I hate to admit, affected me. Next to him stood the guy who'd tried to intimidate Dutch earlier—the very one whose leg we'd run over on our escape from Tim Hortons.

"Aw, shit," Dutch said, taking the photo and studying it.

"Do you know who he is?"

Dutch set the picture on the desk and ran a hand through his hair. "Maksim Grinkov," he said gravely.

"You know him?"

"Yeah, I read about all these guys last week." Dutch scratched thoughtfully at his goatee again. "The intel I read on Grinkov suggested that he used to be in deep with the Mafia here in Toronto, but in recent years he seemed to be toning down his criminal activity. It looks like he's still running some illegal gambling deals, though."

I moved around to sit in the chair opposite Dutch.

"And now Des Vries owes this guy half a million dollars?"

"Looks that way."

I thought about all the damage we'd done to Grikov's goon squad. "What'll they do if they catch you?"

Dutch barked out a hollow laugh. "They'll probably torture me for a while before they kill me."

"Unless you give them the half million, right?"

"Right."

"Maybe the CIA will come through, then," I said hopefully. "Maybe they'll pony up the cash and then, once everything's even Steven again, we can get back to business." My radar went off and I made another connection. "Hey, do you know if Grinkov knows Boklovich?"

"I'd be surprised if he didn't." Just then our eyes met and I knew he was thinking what I was thinking.

"Make a payment; get an introduction," I said easily.

Dutch phoned Frost immediately. He told him our idea and that we'd need to start the dialogue by making a payment on the half-million-dollar debt.

"These guys don't take installments," Frost snapped, like that was the dumbest idea he'd ever heard.

I glared at the speakerphone. "Do we really have a choice? I mean, if we don't pay these guys, they'll eventually find Rick, aka Dutch, and kill him. Do you really want your one shot at getting Boklovich to be a top FBI agent wearing cement shoes?" Okay, I was being a bit dramatic, but desperate times call for desperate measures.

Frost was silent for so long, I was beginning to think we'd lost him. "It'll take some time," he said at last.

"Time isn't something we're in large supply of, Agent Frost," I told him. My intuition was saying that it was important we move quickly.

There was another pause, then, "Let me see what I can do." And the line went dead.

Dutch clicked the off button on our end before leaning way back in his chair. Putting his feet on the desk, he looked like he was going to take a nice long nap.

By now, I was way too wound up and I began to pace the room.

After a while he said, "You're going to wear a tread in the carpet, Edgar."

I stopped. "I think I'm hungry."

Dutch opened one eye. "Okay," he said, digging into his pocket to pull out some cash. "I saw a bagel joint half a block down."

I didn't wait for him to change his mind and was quick to take the cash. "You want something?"

"Onion bagel with cream cheese."

I eyed him skeptically. "When you eat those things, I find it hard to kiss you, ya know."

Dutch smiled wickedly. "Fine," he said. "Make it a garlic bagel with cream cheese."

I rolled my eyes and trooped out the door.

It was starting to warm up a little and I enjoyed the feel of the sunshine on my face. I felt like I'd been cooped up in buildings for the past several weeks, mostly 'cause I had.

After getting Dutch a cinnamon-raisin bagel with cream cheese and an onion bagel for me (let's see how *he* liked it!), I headed back to the office. About halfway there, I felt my radar tug me back toward the bagel joint. I felt like it was suggesting that I'd left something behind.

Annoyed but knowing that I'd better pay attention to the heads-up, I twirled around and hurried back. "Did I leave something here?" I asked the clerk when I got through the door.

The clerk looked around the cluttered counter. "I don't think so," she said.

I frowned, and scanned the worn Formica myself. Nothing looked like it belonged to me. Checking in with my crew—that small band of spirit guides clustered around my energy—I couldn't figure out why they'd wanted me to come back, but I had the feeling it was some sort of warning to stay put.

I glanced up at the clock; it was already well past ten. "What?" I mumbled, completely confused when no additional information was forthcoming and nothing happened in the bagel shop to make me feel like the return trip had been worth it.

I got no reply from the crew and no further clarification for that matter. With a sigh and slightly frustrated, I began to march to the door again, but just as I reached it, I felt this tug on my mind. *Wait!* was the message.

"For what?" I whispered.

Just wait.

So I did. I stood near the door, waiting, while peering anxiously out the window—for what I had no idea, but I knew something would happen sooner or later.

And just when I was about to give up . . . something did.

Chapter Five

. . .

It was as I was reaching for the door in my second attempt to leave that I saw them. Two big thug types dragging Dutch toward a black town car. Even from half a block away I could tell they'd been beating on him.

He was slumped in between them, barely able to hold his head up. For a long moment I stood completely frozen; the shock of seeing two men abducting my fiancé caused all my synapses to fire at once—the overload left me temporarily immobile.

It wasn't until the thugs started to jam Dutch into the car that I dropped the bag of bagels and took off running. I closed in on them fast, mindless of the people scurrying out of the way along the sidewalk, focusing only on reaching Dutch.

One of the thugs saw me coming, because he paused in his effort to shove Dutch into the car and looked me dead in the eye.

I waved my fist at him and roared a kind of carnal, angry scream.

He countered with a big ol' gun aimed steadily in my direction.

Point to bad guy.

"Let him go!" I shouted, weaving slightly to the side at the sight of the gun but still pounding down the pavement toward the two men.

At that moment, Dutch shoved one of them aside and reached for the gun. It went off and glass broke right next to me. People screamed and crouched down. Someone yelled, "GUN!" and more people screamed and ducked.

I continued to race right for the town car, but as I got to within about ten feet of it, the two guys wrestled Dutch inside, slammed the door closed, and turned to me.

One pointed his gun at my heart; the other drew his and took careful aim. I knew that the next time they fired, they wouldn't miss. I stopped, my chest heaving and my blood boiling. Without a word the two men stepped to the front doors of the black sedan and got in. A moment later, they gunned the engine and the car roared to life, jumping forward—right at me. I dove to the side, straight into a couple of trash cans, sending one of them directly into the sedan's path.

There was a thunderous clash of metal, garbage flew up in the air along with the can, and I covered my head as much of it came raining down on me.

When the dust settled, I got to my feet and tried to catch the sedan's license plate. "Are you okay?" asked a middle-aged woman in a long camel coat.

I nodded, and took a step out into the street just as the sedan was turning the corner. "Miss!" she said. "You're bleeding, honey."

Sirens sounded in the distance and it seemed the whole street was looking anxiously at me. "The police will be here in just a minute," the kindly woman said.

I nodded because I couldn't really talk. I was still processing what'd happened. "Did you know that man?" she asked, her brow creased with concern.

I tore my eyes away from the corner where the sedan had turned and disappeared, staring at her for the first time. "What?" I whispered.

"The man they abducted," she said, pulling me gently over to a stoop. "Did you know him?"

I swallowed back the large lump forming in my throat. The sirens were getting closer now, the police were closing in, and I had nothing to tell them. Dutch and I were in deep cover, and I'd been warned not to leave a paper trail or call attention to myself under any circumstance.

"Where's my purse?" I asked, searching the ground desperately.

"It's right there," said the woman, pointing to my new purse, now covered in coffee grounds. I took a step toward it and winced. "You should see a doctor about that cut," she told me.

My knee was slashed up pretty good, but there was no way I was going to take the time to worry about it now. Wiping away some of the grime, I dug through my purse and lifted out my cell phone.

The helpful pedestrian was looking at me curiously, and I attempted a small smile. "I need to make a call."

She nodded, but continued to stare at me curiously. The sirens were much closer now. The police would be here in about ten more seconds. Looking back to the woman, I pointed to the bar we were right next to and said, "I'll just be in there for a minute to make my call, and then I'll be out to give the police my statement."

"I'll tell them," she assured me.

"Thanks," I said, before ducking quickly into the establishment.

There were no patrons inside, and most of the staff were ogling out the window. When I entered, one of them stared at me in shock and said, "Shit, lady! You almost got run down by that car! You okay?"

I nodded. "Is there a restroom I could use? I want to get some water on my knee."

"Sure," he said, and pointed to the back of the bar. "Head down that hallway. It's right next to the exit."

"Thanks," I said. "If the police come in here looking for me, would you tell them I'll be right out?"

"I will," he said, before handing me two clean, folded bar towels. "Use these to clean your knee," he instructed.

I took the towels and hurried away. The screech of tires outside let me know the police had arrived. Ducking into the back hallway, I cruised right past the ladies' room and snuck out the back exit, which put me in an alley.

Moving through the narrow street, I turned right the first chance I got, and continued to work my way west until I was about four blocks away from the scene.

Once I was safely out of police range, I flagged down a cab and gave the address for the condo. He gave me a once-over before putting the car into drive. Looking down at myself, I could hardly blame him.

As he drove, I pressed one of the bar towels to my knee, and finally selected Frost's number from the contacts list on my phone. I waited anxiously until he picked up. "What?" he asked, getting right to the point.

I was about to tell him everything that had happened before I remembered that I had an audience. "Meet me at the condo in ten minutes," I instructed and, not wanting to argue about it, I simply hung up.

Twenty minutes later I'd told Frost everything I knew about Dutch's abduction. My knee was still bleeding pretty bad, but I was so worried about Dutch I hardly cared. "I never should've left him!" I growled, so angry at myself for making a food run, for cripe's sake!

Frost had his phone up to his ear, waiting on hold for Director Tanner. "If you'd been there, Cooper, they'd have shot you first."

I considered that for a minute, and realized that was probably why my crew had made an effort to keep me away from the office until I'd seen Dutch being dragged out. Still, it didn't make me feel any better to know that I'd been unable to help him or prevent his abduction.

"Yeah," said Frost, his voice tense and edgy, "I'm still waiting for the director." He shook his head and rolled his eyes at the person on the other end of the line. "I don't care if she's in a meeting!" he practically yelled. "You get her a message from me to take my call right now, goddammit!"

I watched as Frost clenched his fist and turned away to pace the floor. It reminded me of what I'd done earlier that morning, and what had inspired the pacing, and I felt immediately that I knew what I had to do. "Hang up the phone, Frost," I commanded.

Frost pivoted and held up his index finger in a "hold on a minute" gesture.

"Hang up the phone, Frost!" I yelled so loud he jumped.

He looked at me in stunned surprise, then pulled the phone away from his ear and hit the speaker button. It was the best compromise he could offer me, I guess.

"You have to get me a phone number for Grinkov," I told him.

"Why?"

"Will you just do it?!" I yelled. "I think I know how to help Dutch, but we have to move on it right now, okay?"

Frost stared moodily at me, probably trying to decide if he should tell me to go sit down, shut up, and let him handle it.

I got up from the chair where I'd been sitting, and approached him. When I was well into his personal space, I said, "You have no reason to trust me, but you know I love Dutch more than anything in the world. I would *never* put him in jeopardy, Frost. And the only way I can help him now is to listen to my intuition, which is insisting that you get me that number so I can call Grinkov."

"There's no way we'll get approval for the half mil today," Frost told me bluntly.

I didn't even blink. "I know. I have something else in mind."

Again he wavered for a minute before sighing heavily; then he hit the end button to disconnect the line. Scrolling through his own contacts, he found the number he wanted and tapped it. A moment later he said, "Agent Dobbs, it's Frost. I need a number. . . ."

Fifteen minutes later I sat on the white leather sofa staring at my cell phone on the coffee table. The display showed a keypad and the number I'd just plugged in. Out of the phone's speaker came the tin sound of ringing, and finally the line was picked up. "Ya?" a male voice asked.

"I need to speak with Mr. Grinkov," I said crisply.

There was silence on the other end of the line, but I could hear some background noise, so I knew that whoever answered hadn't hung up on me.

"Who is this?"

The man on the other end had a smooth masculine voice and a very slight Slavic accent.

"My name is Abigail Carter. I am Richard Des Vries's business partner."

Across from me Frost's eyebrows rose and he looked at me skeptically.

On the other end of the line there was a long pause, and I waited with bated breath for the guy to react or speak or tell me "wrong number" and hang up.

"Richard has been very bad boy," said the voice, and I closed my eyes and used every ounce of control I had not to shriek or cry or beg the man to spare my fiancé's life.

Swallowing hard, I said, "I understand Richard is late on a payment or two for a loan taken out with Mr. Grinkov."

There was a chuckle on the other end of the line that sent a chill up my spine. "Is that what he told you?"

I ignored that. "*Is* this Mr. Grinkov?"

"Maybe yes, maybe no," he replied coyly.

"I see," I said, not really knowing where to go with that.

"Why are you calling?" he demanded.

"I would like to make payment on Mr. Des Vries's debts," I said. "And I would like Mr. Des Vries returned. Alive and in one piece."

Across from me, Frost looked at me sharply, but I ignored him, and waited for my answer. "The loan must be paid in full," said the caller.

I almost sagged with relief. He wouldn't have said that if Dutch had already been murdered. "It will take a bit of time to gather the money," I told him.

"How much time?"

"Two or three days," I said, squeezing my eyes closed and crossing my fingers that he'd give me that long to reach Dutch's best friend and business partner, Milo, and liquidate some assets.

The man on the other end sighed dramatically. "This is no good," he said. "I need some money now, Miss Carter."

My eyes shot open to meet Frost's. He shook his head. He couldn't promise that.

"Of course," I said easily, my heart thundering with anxiety. "I knew you'd want some sort of deposit in good faith. But I'd also like some assurances that Mr. Des Vries is unharmed."

"You would, eh?" he said, his voice mocking. "Well, unfortunately, Mr. Des Vries had a little accident on his way to meet with me, Miss Carter."

I gripped the arm of the sofa, hard. "But he's still alive, correct?"

"He is," he assured me. "For now."

"I will bring you the money tonight," I said. "I have fifty thousand dollars."

"That's not enough," the man said. "I will need one hundred thousand of the five hundred he owes me."

I was afraid of that. "Yes, all right," I said, glaring hard at Frost. "I will need the afternoon to gather the rest of the money together. Can you give me until this evening?"

"Yes, of course," said the man. "I'm not unreasonable, after all. You will come by and have dinner with me. We will discuss the terms of repayment."

Frost was shaking his head vehemently and mouthing the word, "No!"

"That sounds fine," I told him. "Tell me where to go and I'll be there."

"*Are you out of your fucking mind?*" Frost shouted the moment I'd hung up. Hmm, I doubted I'd be able get him to cough up a quarter for the swear jar. "Cooper, you can't go to Grinkov's house! We'll never see you again!"

I stood up and limped over to the sink, dousing one of the towels under the faucet and holding it to my knee. "If you guys want to fire me, Frost, then go right ahead, but I'm going there tonight and I am going to make sure Dutch is still alive. And then I'm going to negotiate the terms of his release."

Frost followed me over to the counter, where he stood angrily with his arms crossed over his chest. "I can't give you a hundred thousand dollars, Cooper! Do you know how many people would have to sign off on that?"

I glared hard at him. "One," I said, and limped back over to my phone. There were three people I personally knew that I could ask for a loan as large as one hundred thousand dollars, but only one of them wouldn't ask me too many questions.

I dialed the phone while Frost watched me as if I'd just gone mad.

"Abby!" Milo said. "Long time no see, girl. What's up?"

"Dutch is in trouble," I told him, getting right to the point.

I could practically see Milo snap to attention. "Where?"

"I can't tell you," I said, blinking back the moisture that was flooding my eyes. I couldn't involve Milo in our espionage, but that didn't mean I didn't long for him to fly in and help me rescue Dutch. "I need money to help him, Milo. A lot of money."

"How much?"

"Two hundred thousand."

"How soon?" He'd said that without even a pause, and the moisture leaking from my eyes got harder to hold back. God love Milo!

"As soon as humanly possible."

"Can you e-mail me some wiring instructions to the nearest bank?"

My eyes flickered to Frost. He nodded. "Yes, Milo, I can."

"You'll have it by five," he assured me. "And Abs?"

"Yeah?"

"If things get worse and you need me, you call back, you hear?"

I could barely speak, but I managed a throaty, "Thanks, buddy. I will."

It was nearly eight when I pulled into the long drive at the top of a very big hill overlooking a tony part of the Toronto suburbs called Yorkville. The house I rolled up to wasn't really a house—it was more like a compound . . . or maybe a castle. It didn't have a turret, but it seemed to have a tower. I wondered briefly, as I waited at the gate, if that's where they were keeping Dutch. My stomach clenched again. I had no idea what little "accident" had befallen him, and just prayed he was okay.

The guard approached the car and asked me to step out. I complied and he first searched my purse, then the small attaché I'd brought along; then he gave me a good pat down. He didn't take the opportunity to cop a feel, which I mentally gave him credit for, and finally he swept some sort of handheld gizmo over my body and told me to stretch out my arms and legs.

The gizmo made little crackling noises, but other than that, no loud squeaks or squeals went off, much to my relief.

Appearing satisfied, the guard stepped back from me and held out his hand. "Cell phone," he said.

My brow furrowed. "Why?"

"You want to go in there?"

"Yes."

"Then you give up your cell phone."

I hesitated. What if he went through all the numbers loaded onto my phone? What if he called people and asked them about me? What if he downloaded my pictures and saw the cute ones I'd taken of Dutch and me right after he'd proposed?

The guard squinted at me, and I knew I had little choice. "Fine," I said, reaching into the car and pulling it out. He went to grab it, but I held it away from him. "Just a second, buddy," I said tersely, pulling out the clip holding my hair up and using one of the prongs to depress the button that released the SIM card. "You may have my phone," I told him once I'd tucked the small piece of plastic into my pocket and locked the phone with a password. "But you can't have my personal information."

He scowled at me but made no further argument, taking my phone and motioning for me to get back into the car and go through the gate.

Once I was safely tucked back in my car, I used the rearview mirror to put the clip back into place, pulling a section of my hair back but leaving the sides long to cover my ears. Once I'd secured the clip, which hid a tiny camera and microphone and which Frost had insisted I wear, I clicked the teeny button on the side and felt it vibrate slightly. "How's the angle?" I whispered.

In my ear I heard Frost say, "It's fine. What took so long?"

I nodded to the guard as I passed by him through the gates. "I got the pat down," I said. "And he took my cell."

"Shit!" Frost said. "You let him have your cell? What numbers are on there, Cooper?"

I smiled. "None. I took the SIM card and locked the phone."

There was a pause, then, "Good thinking," which I thought might be the highest form of praise from Agent Frostbite.

I parked the car and took a small moment to collect myself. I knew the odds of coming out of here with Dutch were very, very low, and I had no idea if he was alive or dead, or even what condition he was in, but I knew that the most important thing for me to do was to remain calm, cool, and collected. I couldn't react to anything that I saw or heard, because that could tip our hand, which would ensure our swift and immediate demise.

Frost had also warned me (at length) not to mention the drone or the code we were trying to shop. "If he knows you've got something as valuable as Intuit's code, he'll keep Rivers hostage until you cough up the disk—then we'll be totally screwed."

So, I was left with nothing but my own wits and my sixth sense to see me through the night. I knew that in order to utilize both to the fullest, I needed to collect myself and gather my courage. While I took a quiet moment in the car, I did what I usually do before I see my clients. I tucked all my emotions, feelings, judgments, and ego into a secure place in my brain, before stepping fully into the character of Abigail Carter, badass business partner to Rick Des Vries.

I then got out of the car and approached the house, carrying my purse and the small attaché. I raised my hand to use the knocker, but the door opened before I even had a chance. "Good evening," said a man well into his sixties and sporting a British accent and a walking stick. "Ms. Carter?"

"Yes."

"Very good to meet you," he said, extending his hand. "I am William Eddington, Mr. Grinkov's butler."

"Pleased to meet you," I said, shaking his hand.

"If you'll follow me to the dining room?" he said with a slight bow before turning and moving through the large foyer, his walking stick clicking on the marble floor as we went.

The interior of the house wasn't that surprising. I'd expected expensive, and that's what I saw. Mostly brownish tones with olive green and gold accents and walls decorated with a great deal of expensive-looking art in gilded frames. By the looks of it, Grinkov favored the Impressionist era, but I found the overall effect of the house's color and decorating style to be heavy and too serious for me.

We entered a large dining room with a cherrywood table polished to a bright sheen. Chairs that looked like thrones were positioned just so around the table, and two place settings had been arranged—one at the head of the table and one just to the left.

William indicated the seat on the left and pulled my chair out for me. I sat and folded my hands in my lap. "Would you care for a cocktail?" William asked me.

"No, thank you, William. Will Mr. Grinkov be long?"

"Good evening," said a voice to my right. I swiveled slightly and into the room walked one of the sexiest men I'd ever seen. . . . (Uh . . . next to my fiancé of course . . . cough, cough.)

I stood as he approached, and switched my radar on to its highest setting. Maksim Grinkov was slightly shorter than Dutch, but I'd still put him close to six feet. He had a body that he took very good care of and he walked with the grace and power of an athlete. He had a broad chest, well-set shoulders, and a trim stomach. I had little doubt underneath his dress shirt he was sportin' a six-pack.

He strolled into the room confidently, wearing black silk slacks and a blue dress shirt with the sleeves rolled up to reveal tanned muscular arms.

His face was square and roguish, his lips full and inviting, and his hazel eyes locked with mine, causing my pulse to quicken even despite the knowledge of who this man was and what he'd done to my fiancé.

In that moment I could tell he also liked what he saw. I felt my stomach muscles clench, and I wondered if I'd just done something incredibly stupid, like entering the den of a lion while wearing eau de antelope.

"Ms. Carter," he said smoothly, stopping in front of me to take my hand and kiss it formally.

"Mr. Grinkov," I answered, quickly quelling the burble of nervous tension in the pit of my stomach.

"It is a pleasure to meet you," he said, standing tall again to pin me with those deadly, sexy eyes.

"Likewise. And thank you for inviting me to dine with you." I worked on making my words formal and clear, hoping my manner and tone showed that I was all business.

Grinkov motioned for me to take my seat again, and I did. William, who'd been standing beside us the whole time, assisted me with my chair before moving off again, the sound of his walking stick fading into the distance.

"My chef has prepared a wonderful meal for us tonight," Grinkov said, unfolding his napkin and placing it in his lap. "I hope that you stay long enough to enjoy it."

I nearly sucked in a breath at the implied threat, but managed to keep my mounting fear in check. Forcing myself to laugh lightly, I said, "As I do enjoy a nice meal, Mr. Grinkov, I hope so too."

Grinkov raised his eyes to meet mine again. "Please, call me Maks."

I nodded slightly and placed my hand over my heart. "Abigail."

William returned at that moment, pushing a cart loaded with a rocks glass loaded with ice and vodka for his boss, and I was given a tall glass of bubbling water with a wedge of lime on the rim.

"You will not be having a cocktail?" Grinkov asked me.

"No," I said, staring right at him. "I believe that business matters should be discussed with a clear head."

The corner of Grinkov's mouth quirked, but he made no further comment about my sobriety. Instead he raised his glass to me before taking a long sip. "So, tell me, Abigail, how did you and Richard become business partners?"

Grinkov's eyes roved my face and chest again, and it was very obvious this particular lion loved the scent of antelope. I wondered if I might use his obvious attraction to me to my advantage like I'd done with Kozahkov, and decided to go with it. "The usual way," I said coyly, lifting my own napkin to unfold it and place it in my lap.

"What usual way is that, exactly?"

"We had some great sex over a three-day holiday, and in the few times we came up for air, we discovered that we had similar . . . uh, *financial* interests."

Grinkov tilted his head back and laughed. I could tell that whatever he'd expected me to say, it hadn't been that. He sobered quickly, or shall I say, he smoldered quickly. The man was oozing virility, and in the very back of my head I was at least relieved he didn't physically repulse me like Viktor. "And do you still share his bed?" he asked.

"Des Vries?"

"Yes," he said, eyeing me intently, looking for any hint of dishonesty.

"No. I do not share my bed with Rick Des Vries. Our arrangement now is strictly business."

Grinkov sat back in his chair when William came back into the room, pushing his cart again, but this time it was loaded with a tray of toasted bread and three small dishes mounded with a black substance. Setting down the contents of the tray in front of us, he pointed to each individual dish and said, "Imperial Iranian osetra, Russian osetra, and Siberian osetra. Please alert me, sir, if you require more toast."

William then departed and I was left to consider the idea of eating caviar. *Fish eggs, blach!*

Grinkov motioned for me to go first. Luckily, I've been to enough of my sister's big Christmas shindigs to know the proper way to eat the slimy stuff.

I worked my way through a sample of each of the dishes and smiled and made little *mmm-mmm* sounds.

Grinkov continued to watch me closely, but he also continued to sip at his vodka, and it wasn't long before he was given a refill.

Once the caviar was removed and replaced with a potato-leek soup, which was heavenly, Grinkov said, "Tell me about your business dealings with Des Vries."

I wiped demurely at my mouth with my napkin before answering him. "No."

Grinkov's spoon stopped midway to his mouth. "You refuse me?" he asked, a dangerous undertone in his voice.

"Yes," I said, without flinching.

Grinkov set down his spoon and his hands rested beside his soup, clenching and unclenching. I knew he was waiting for me to elaborate, but I wasn't about to, especially given Frost's warning. I also knew that I couldn't make something else up because I knew that Grinkov would check it out and then Dutch and I would be toast.

My host inhaled deeply, then exhaled slowly and said, "You must give me a detail to confirm that you and Richard are partners."

"Fine," I said, reaching down to pick up my attaché. Being careful not to bump my soup, I opened it and took out ten packs of Canadian one-hundred-dollar bills. "There's the hundred grand I promised you as a down payment for Mr. Des Vries's debts," I said. "That should be proof enough."

Grinkov did not even look at the money; instead he continued to eye me in frustration. "Very well," he said at last, his tone a bit icy now. "But we must discuss the arrangement of the other four hundred and fifty thousand."

This time I couldn't help it—I let out a gasp. "He only owes you four hundred thousand more, Mr. Grinkov."

Grinkov smiled. He liked that he'd finally pushed one of my buttons. "Interest," he said by way of explanation. "And please, call me Maks."

Again I had to work hard to rein in my emotions, but I managed. "I would like to see Rick to make sure he's all right."

William appeared at my side to take my soup bowl, and Grinkov waited until his butler had replaced the dish with pan-braised trout and succulent-looking vegetables before he said, "We will eat a little first."

I had no choice; I had to sit there and pick at my food, waiting for Grinkov to give the okay to let me see Dutch. It wasn't until William came in again to refill his rocks glass that Maks finally made a small hand gesture to his butler, who nodded and left us alone.

As Grinkov was finishing his final bite of trout, the butler returned with a computer tablet. Grinkov took it from him and flipped the screen on, swiveling it around to show me. The image on the monitor revealed Dutch, sitting down and leaning heavily against the wall in a small room with no furniture. His shirt was torn and stained at the collar with blood, and I could see he'd been badly beaten.

I forced myself to take a slow steady breath, pushing down the fury the image inspired. "How do I know he's alive?" I asked.

Grinkov calmly removed his cell from his pocket and made a call. He spoke in Russian and while I watched, someone entered the room, causing Dutch to pick his head up slightly. The man looked up at the monitor with a sick smile and kicked Dutch, who reacted by lunging at the assailant and wrapping his arms around the thug's leg, trying to wrestle him to the ground. Another man ran in and shoved Dutch off his partner's leg, punching my fiancé in the head for good measure before both thugs departed.

It took everything I had, and I do mean *everything*, not to burst into tears and stab Grinkov with my fork. But none of those actions would help Dutch, so I dipped my chin and took a deep breath once. Twice. Three times, waiting for the panic, fear, rage, and gut-wrenching heartache to pass. It didn't, but I managed to get beyond it—at least temporarily.

"Motherfuckers," I heard in my ear. Frost had seen the image on the monitor and it was the first time I'd heard from him since I'd entered the home. His voice in my ear reminded me that I wasn't completely alone in all this. That, more than anything, helped me focus and come up with a plan.

"You've beaten him," I said, my voice hollow and cold.

Grinkov was again watching me intently. "Richard knew there would be consequences for nonpayment."

"Easy, Cooper," Frost whispered.

"He requires medical attention," I said.

"You may take him to the hospital the moment I receive all that is owed to me," Grinkov said in a tone that didn't allow for argument. "Besides," he added, his mouth turned down in disgust, "Richard has given far worse beatings to his women—or hadn't you heard about that?"

I swallowed hard again. "I've heard."

Grinkov eyed me with steely eyes. "And yet you and he are friends."

The statement was more a question and I knew I had to offer up some sort of explanation, so I said, "Richard is not my friend; he is my business partner. Even though we connected under intimate circumstances, we no longer have that kind of relationship, and Richard knows that if he ever laid a hand on me, I'd kill him dead."

Grinkov appeared to take that in. "Well, at least you have some sense," he said to me. "But you will forgive me if I do not pity Richard's little accident today. I saw a girl he'd gotten cross with once, and I can assure you, her physical condition was *much* worse."

I tried to remember that Grinkov fully believed Dutch was Richard Des Vries, and that it was obvious the former mobster didn't especially advocate violence against women, and he'd maybe ordered his boys to be a little rougher with Dutch because of it, but now I knew what was in store for my fiancé if I didn't get him out of there tonight, and it chilled me to the bone. My ankle tapped against the attaché at my feet, where I'd replaced the money before we'd been served our final courses. "Let me ask you something, Mr. Grinkov—"

"Maks," he corrected.

I forced a smile and leaned in to look him in the eye. "Maks, I wonder if you and I might find a way to settle Rick's debt tonight?"

Grinkov laughed and reached out to stroke my wrist seductively. "I have had many high-priced whores in my day, Abigail, but never one that cost four hundred and fifty thousand dollars."

I lifted my hand away from Grinkov, only slightly insulted. "You misunderstand," I said to him. "I'm not offering you my body. I'm offering you an opportunity to double your money."

Grinkov cocked one eyebrow at me. "What did you have in mind?"

"Poker."

Eddington came to the table again and lifted away my plate, loading it onto his cart. I tried not to imagine how much Dutch might be suffering while I dined on a gourmet meal and offered to play cards with his captor.

"So, you enjoy gambling as much as your business partner, then, eh?" Grinkov asked. To my relief, I could tell he was intrigued.

"I do. That's how he and I cemented our partnership, actually. I kicked his ass in a high-stakes poker game about a year ago. He'd put up half the ownership of his import/export business in the match, and he lost."

Grinkov pursed his lips. "You believe yourself to be a skillful player, then?"

I gave him a sideways smile. "Oh, I know I'm good. The question in front of me is, are *you*?"

"Nice," Frost whispered.

Grinkov circled his finger around the rim of his rocks glass and considered me with those smokin' hazel eyes. "Oh, Abigail, I am good," he assured me, and I knew he wasn't just talking about his gambling abilities, but I also knew I had a chance. "What are the terms you're proposing?"

I reached again for my attaché and pulled out the first hundred thousand plus another ten bundles of cash, which was all the money Milo had wired me. "Texas hold 'em. Ten grand minimum. We play until either Rick's debt is clear, or I've run out of money."

Grinkov tapped his finger thoughtfully on the table. Frost whispered, "Come on, you son of a bitch, take the bait."

Finally, Grinkov sighed and leaned back in his chair. "I don't think that is all you can offer me," he said.

Uh-oh. I lifted the attaché and showed him the empty interior. "As I said, this is all the money I was able to liquidate on such short notice. I won't be able to bring more until Monday, when the banks open again."

"Yes," he said smoothly, his eyes again boring into mine. "And yet, you have come here with another currency, Abigail. One I find I quite desire."

Gulp. I had to resist the urge to look away, and stare steadily into those eyes. "You want me to sleep with you?"

"Yes."

My breath quickened and my pulse raced and something inside of me unexpectedly stirred . . . and I hated myself for it. Still, I did nothing to hide my reaction because, again, I knew I could use it to my advantage. "All right. If I lose, then you may keep all my money; Rick will still owe you the four fifty, and tonight, I will rock your world."

"Not just tonight," he corrected, leaning in to hold my hand, lifting it to kiss the inside of my wrist. "You will stay with me until Monday morning when I will escort you to the bank."

I swallowed hard, forced a smile, and reached out to stroke the side of his face. "Assuming you'll have the strength come Monday, right, Maks?"

Maks's pupils dilated so far his eyes were all but black. "Yes," he whispered, leaning in to kiss me.

I pulled away and shook my head. "Business first," I cautioned. "Pleasure second."

Grinkov laughed long and low. "Very well," he said. "I will have William bring the cards and the chips."

Before Grinkov could call for his butler, however, I put my hand on his arm. "I'd like you to speak to the two men guarding Rick, first. I'd like you to tell them not to lay another finger on him until our game is finished."

Grinkov's brow rose. "Oh?" he said, and he clearly didn't look pleased that I'd made such a request.

I was quick to explain, lest he change his mind about our terms. "I need to make sure Rick lives long enough for me to collect him. He's no good to me dead, Maks."

"I see," he said, but he still seemed suspicious. "I don't give up something for nothing, Abigail."

"I wouldn't expect you to," I said, praying that Dutch could forgive me someday, and I leaned forward, grabbed Grinkov by the back of the head, and kissed him passionately.

I wanted to feel nothing but disgust and distaste, but the truth was, there was an intense chemistry between us that sparked when our lips touched, and the kiss sealed it. After a long, lingering moment I pulled my lips away, but our foreheads remained touching. My breath was coming quickly and those home fires were burning. Jesus! What was wrong with me?

Grinkov lifted his phone to his ear and gave the order for his men to lay off their prisoner. Then he cupped my face and kissed me again, and I knew I was going to hell.

Chapter Six

• • •

"Cooper!" Frost barked into my ear. My eyes flew open and just like that, the spell was broken. I backed away from Grinkov and straightened out my blouse. "Are you ready to play?" I asked him.

He chuckled and called to his butler. William appeared and cleared away all our remaining dishes. A minute or two later, he and his cart returned loaded with a snifter of brandy for Grinkov and some coffee for me. Once he'd set those down, he limped off again, only to return with an attaché, which he opened facing Grinkov.

Maks reached over and took all the money I'd laid on the table, exchanging my two hundred thousand for one hundred thousand in chips.

William then proceeded to deal out five cards facedown on the table between Grinkov and me, then two each to us. I peeked at my first two cards, praying for something good. I had a pair of tens. "Thank you, God," I heard Frost whisper.

I threw a stack of thousand-dollar chips into the middle of the space between us. "Ten thousand," I said.

"Call," said Grinkov. Cool, he was matching my bet.

William then turned over three of the five cards in the center of the table. One of those was a ten. I threw in another stack of thousands. "Ten more," I said.

Grinkov eyed the cards in the center and I could detect the slightest smile on his face, but I could also sense something else. It wasn't exactly the *liar, liar, pants on fire* message I normally got when someone wasn't telling me the truth, but I could see the bluff forming in his energy. "Raise," he said. "Your ten plus twenty more."

I threw in another twenty without hesitation.

Eddington then turned over the fourth card. It was a jack.

Before placing my next bet, I scanned Grinkov's energy. His luck hadn't improved. "Ten more," I said, tossing in one of my last stacks.

"Call," said Grinkov.

William turned over the final card. It was a ten. "Cooper," Frost whispered. "Turn your head. I can't see the last card."

I turned my chin a little and heard him whistle appreciatively. "You are one lucky woman," he said.

William cleared his throat. "It's your bet, miss."

I eyed my remaining stacks of cash. Should I toss it all in? What if I was wrong and Grinkov pulled out the winning hand? I'd need as much of what I had left to finish the rounds of betting. I decided to play a little conservatively, and tossed in one thousand-dollar chip, hoping Grinkov wouldn't try to raise the bet.

He tapped his finger on the table, noticing the change in confidence, but he didn't pounce, probably because he had a crappy hand. "Call," he said.

We both laid our hands down at the same time. He had a pair of twos, and there was one more in the middle of the table, which was no match for my four of a kind. I reached out and collected my winnings and Frost said, "Good job, Cooper. A few more hands like that and we'll be home free."

The night of gambling was not as smooth as I'd hoped. My sixth sense definitely gave me an advantage over Grinkov, but he was one heck of a good poker player and at one point he had me down to my last twenty thousand. Still, I managed to rally, and by three a.m. I had completely cleared Des Vries's debt and had an extra one hundred and fifty grand to spare. That worked out okay for me, as I figured Dutch could bill the CIA and probably get back the fifty grand I'd had to leave with Grinkov.

"I told you I was good," I said to Maks after the final hand and he called for his men to bring out Des Vries and load him in my car.

I was a bit anxious when Maks shut off the monitor, and he must have noticed the change in my expression because he said, "My men will not injure him further. The debt is paid and we are in good standing again."

I had to admit, his consideration puzzled me. I wanted to believe he was a real SOB, but he'd actually proved that he was something of a gentleman by honoring our agreement, and further, when it became clear that I could hold my own at the poker table, he'd called for a break in the game, and told William to administer some attention to Des Vries. William had bowed to us and left the room, and Maks had turned the monitor around to allow me to watch as William went into Dutch's room, offered him water, some pain pills, a wet cloth, and a pack of ice for his face.

Grinkov had even left the monitor on, so that I could periodically look up from my cards to see how Dutch was doing, and I was encouraged that although Dutch looked far worse for wear, at least he was conscious enough to keep the ice pack on his face. Around one a.m. I saw that he even nodded off.

"I would like to see you again," Grinkov said, catching my wrist, as Dutch was being carried out to my car. "I would like to take you out for dinner, Abigail."

"Negative!" Frost barked.

I watched as Grinkov's two thugs eased my fiancé into the backseat of my car. There was no way I was breaking out of character this close to our escape. "Perhaps," I said to Grinkov. "I had a better time with you than I expected, Maks."

Grinkov wrapped his arms around my middle and pulled me close to him, giving me that long smoldering look again. "Stay the night," he whispered.

"Cooper! Get out of there!"

I inhaled deeply and let it out slowly. "I'm tired, Maks," I said. "And I've still got to get Rick home and make sure he's okay."

Maks eyed Dutch contemptuously. "You know that Richard is a violent man, Abigail. What I don't understand is, why would you associate with such a man?"

His question surprised me, and I had to think fast. "Since we established our partnership, Rick has always been completely professional with me. What he does in his personal life is none of my concern."

"Unless there are gambling debts to pay," Maks said.

I smiled coyly. "Yes," I agreed. "But I hardly minded helping my partner out tonight, especially when the evening proved so entertaining."

"Then stay with me," Maks said again, squeezing his arms around me.

I cupped his face and stroked his temples. He had smooth skin and his cologne smelled amazing. "Some other time," I promised, then kissed him lightly and pulled out of his grasp. I was stunned when the gentle but firm ploy worked and he let me go.

I wasted no more time and got into the car, started it up, and drove away with only a small wave. As I approached the gates at the end of the drive, I had to will myself not to punch the gas. I wanted out of there so bad I was shaking.

The guard inside didn't open the gates, though; instead he came out of the little guard booth and held his hand up for me to stop. "Why's he stopping you?" Frost asked.

"I don't know," I whispered anxiously.

Again I considered gunning it, but the gates looked very strong and I wasn't sure I could crash through them and hold it together long enough to get us out of there, so I braked and waited for the guard to approach my window. "I'd like to leave," I told him a bit snappishly.

He scowled at me. "You want this back?" he asked, holding up my cell.

I felt a flood of relief and held my hand out for the phone. "Yes, thank you. Sorry I snapped, it's just been a very long evening and I need to get my associate home."

The guard was still glaring at me, but gave me the phone and said nothing more. Instead he turned and went back into the guard-house and a moment later the gates began to open. I tapped the steering wheel with my thumb, mumbling, "Come on, come on, come on!"

When at last they were open enough to let me through, I pressed on the gas and sped out of there, and I didn't even care if the guard thought that suspicious.

I drove very fast for several miles, but I was soon shaking and crying so hard that I had to pull over. "Cooper?" Frost asked into my ear when I'd put the car into park and bent over the steering wheel to sob.

At the sound of his voice I ripped the earpiece out of my ear and yelled, "Shut up!" I also reached up and unhooked the hair clip with the tiny camera and microphone attached. Holding it close to my lips, I shouted, "Just give me a friggin' minute, would you?!"

And then I dissolved into even more tears. All night I'd battled to keep my emotions in check, and now here they were, tumbling out of me like ants from an anthill. "Edgar?" I heard Dutch call weakly from the backseat.

I sucked in a blubbery breath and held very still. Jesus, I'd even forgotten that my battered and bruised fiancé was in the car! "I'm okay," I whispered, wiping my eyes quickly and trying to get my shaking hands to grip the steering wheel again.

I heard the squeaky sound of the leather seat behind me as Dutch pushed himself to sit up. Looking in the rearview, I caught sight of his swollen and puffy face again, and I couldn't help it—I began balling in earnest again. "I'm so sorry!" I told him, feeling so incredibly ashamed of myself I could hardly even stand it. How could I have kissed the man who had done *that* to Dutch?

He reached over the seat and squeezed my shoulder. "It's okay," he said. "Honey, I'm a little beat up, but I'll be okay."

He was misunderstanding what I was really sorry about, and the guilt was crushing. And I couldn't explain it to him. Ever. So I simply nodded, sucked it up, and put the car back into drive.

Still, the tears continued to roll down my cheeks the entire way back to the condo.

Frost met me at the elevator with a physician in tow. I didn't know where he managed to find a doctor willing to make house calls at four in the morning, and I wasn't about to ask. I was just grateful that the kindly physician with the receding hairline was treating Dutch with great care and concern.

I watched from the doorway of the bedroom with my arms wrapped tightly around me, afraid the doctor would say that Dutch's injuries were even worse than they looked.

After stitching a cut on his forehead, the doctor managed to pry open Dutch's swollen eyes enough to remove his brown contacts; then he dabbed some ointment around his face, wrapped his ribs, and felt all along his abdomen and limbs for any signs of internal bleeding or broken bones. Finally, the doctor got up from the bed and motioned for me to follow him.

Frost was in the kitchen on the phone, but he quickly hung up when he saw us. "How is he?" the agent asked.

"Banged up pretty good," the doctor said. "I wish I could get an X-ray of his ribs and a CT scan of his head, but I understand you need to be discreet about this."

"Very discreet," Frost agreed.

"Well then, we'll skip the X-ray and the CT. His lungs are free of fluid, which is a good sign, but those ribs are definitely bruised and one or two may have a hairline fracture. He'll be quite sore on his left side for the next few weeks.

"He also has a slight concussion, but he answered all of my questions well, and his cognitive and reasoning skills are intact."

I let go of the breath I'd been holding and wiped at my eyes. I couldn't seem to stop crying tonight. "Thank God," I whispered.

"He should stay in bed for at least a few days," the doctor cautioned. "And if he suddenly becomes dizzy, nauseous, or has issues with his vision or balance, I will insist that he go in for a head scan."

"Absolutely," I promised, not even looking at Frost. If Dutch showed any sign that he was getting worse, I'd personally fight off the CIA all the way to the hospital if I had to.

The doctor departed shortly after that, leaving me with several prescriptions to fill. I grabbed my purse and started for the exit.

"Where're you going?" Frost asked.

I waved the three pieces of paper at him. "I saw a twenty-four-hour Shoppers Drug Mart about three blocks from here. Dutch is going to be in some pain when he wakes up, and I want to make sure he's got his prescriptions filled. I'll be back soon."

Frost stepped in front of me as I moved toward the elevator. "I'll go," he said.

That caught me off guard. "You will?"

He took the slips out of my hand and turned away. As he was leaving, he said, "You did good tonight, Cooper. You kept your head and you stayed in character, which was the only way you got out of there alive. I might have underestimated you."

Before I could even fully absorb what he'd said, Frost had slipped into the elevator and closed the doors. I stood there stunned by my handler's compliment for a few beats, but I was weary down to the bone and I turned away from the doors and drifted back into the bedroom. Once there I peeled off my clothes and slipped into some comfy pj's, then got into bed next to Dutch and moved very carefully under the covers to snuggle next to him.

He murmured softly when I laid my head next to his on the pillow. "You okay?" I whispered, thinking maybe he was trying to tell me something hurt.

One puffy eye opened and that midnight blue iris looked right into mine. "Love you," he said.

I felt my lower lip tremble, and I tried to bite back the urge to confess my sins, but the guilt was too heavy. "Dutch," I began, my voice wobbly and emotional. "In order to get Grinkov to agree to the poker game, I had to pretend that I was attracted to him, and I—"

"Edgar," he interrupted, lifting one hand to lay it on my cheek. "It's okay. You got me out. It's okay."

For a long, long time, I could do nothing more than weep and listen to the sound of his breathing. But eventually, I found the courage to forgive myself and finally drifted off to an exhausted slumber.

The next morning I woke with a start. Someone was brewing coffee. Dutch was still asleep next to me, and I noted the prescription bottles on the side table next to him. One of them already had the cap off, and the half-empty glass of water next to the lamp suggested that Frost had made sure that Dutch had gotten his medication.

Quietly I wrapped a robe around myself and shuffled out to the kitchen. Frost was reading the paper with a steaming cup of black brew right next to him. "Morning," I said, my voice all croaky.

"Cooper," he said tonelessly without looking up from his paper. Was he just a bucket of sunshine or what?

"Mind if I join you?" I asked.

He looked up in surprise. "Sure. The mugs are in the cabinet next to the fridge."

I yawned while I poured myself some coffee, then shuffled back to the table. "Thanks for making it," I said, lifting the cup in a little toast.

"Sure," he said, back to his paper.

We sat silently for a little while, Frost intent on the paper, me wondering how to start a conversation with this snowflake.

Out of sheer boredom I flipped my radar on and began to scan his energy. A few things there surprised me. "You're a widower?" I asked before I could stop myself.

Frost's head snapped up. "How'd you know that?"

I pointed to his left hand. "My symbol for widowhood is a white ring."

Frost looked down at his hand. "I'm not wearing a white ring," he said.

I smiled. "I know. It's not a hallucination; it's sort of a vision I get in my mind's eye when I look at your hand."

He cocked his head. "You see me wearing a white ring?"

I nodded.

"Why is it white?"

"It symbolizes death," I said.

Frost looked back to his hand, and circled his ring finger. "Huh," he said.

"You're pretty young for a widower," I said, really curious now. I mean, the guy couldn't be a day over forty if he was even that old. "What happened?"

Frost sipped his coffee and eyed me suspiciously. "You tell me."

I sighed. Why were these law-and-order types always such pricks? "She was murdered," I said, seeing a dagger in my mind's eye, which didn't mean she'd been stabbed; it was just my symbol for murder.

Frost's brow rose, but he didn't comment.

"And she was murdered by someone she knew," I added. How ya like me now, Mr. CIA boy?

"Yes."

I sat back and folded my arms, satisfied that I finally had his attention, and then I focused further on the jumble of symbols twirling about in my mind. "I can't figure it out," I said after a bit. Maybe I was still too groggy, but the murder of Mrs. Frost was more than it appeared. "Someone close to her murdered her, and it almost feels like she knew it was going to happen. In fact, I'd swear that she accepted some of the responsibility for her own death."

Frost was studying me intently, but otherwise his expression was unreadable. He didn't look upset to be reminded about his wife's death; in fact, he almost appeared detached. "What happened?" I asked into the long stretch of silence that followed.

Frost folded his paper and set it aside. "It's classified," he told me.

I laughed. I thought he was joking, but when his expression didn't change, I knew he wasn't. "Uh . . . okay," I said, preparing to get up and leave this awkward conversation.

Frost stopped me, however, when he asked, "What else do you pick up about me?"

Huh. Even I didn't see that one coming. "I'm sensing you're a decent cook," I told him after focusing on him again.

For the first time since I'd met him, Frost actually gave in to a tiny smile. "I am," he admitted.

My stomach rumbled. "How are you with breakfast?"

"I'm a rock star with breakfast."

"Awesome. I like omelets. You make me one of those, and I'll give you a reading."

Frost was a much easier read than I would have guessed. Only very rarely do I sit with a client who has amazingly loud energy. These people are a welcome rarity because when I read them, it's as if they're projecting their futures onto a big screen with the volume turned way up loud.

Most people I read for project at medium to low volumes, which is why tuning in for someone is such exhausting work. You have to really, really listen and pay attention to so many subtle nuances to give a good reading to someone.

But Frost was one of those few exceptions whose energy held vivid details and plenty of stuff to select from. "I'm seeing Hawaii," I told him after he'd served me a piping hot pepper, cheese, and mushroom omelet.

That slight smile returned. "I was born there."

"You're going back," I said.

"Yes. Next month."

"You should stay longer," I advised after taking a bite of the eggs. Frost was right about one thing—he could knock an omelet out of the park. "You could really use a nice long vacation, Frost. Thaw out a bit." I tried to hide a smile but he was on to me and my pun.

"Yeah, yeah, Cooper," he said, his tone softening and a smile forming at the edges of his mouth. "What else can you tell me?"

We went on like that for half an hour. The reading was loaded with details about Frost's career, which had seen a bit of a lag since his wife's death, but which was about to move forward in a new and interesting way. "You'll be traveling quite a bit again," I assured him. "Mostly to Europe, but specifically to France."

"I'm fluent in French," he said.

"Good. You'll need it. There's a little bit of activity in the Middle East, but I'm thinking that won't occupy too much of your time. You should also consider holding on to your town house in D.C."

Frost opened his mouth to say something, but I interrupted him. "You'll lose money if you sell now. The market's still too soft. Give it two years, and rent it out while you're away so that it won't hurt you financially any more than it has to."

And on went the reading. By the end, I felt like I knew Frost far better than if we'd had a six-hour conversation together. Even if I didn't know the details of his wife's murder, I knew pretty much everything else.

The one thing that didn't come up in the reading, however, was romance. He seemed to notice, because when I asked if he had any questions, he said, "You didn't bring up dating. Do you see a woman in my life?"

I wadded up my paper napkin and tossed it onto my plate. "Nope."

Frost's features didn't reveal how he felt about that, but I could see it in his energy and I decided to elaborate. "Maybe what I need to explain to you is my personal understanding of the future. I don't foresee only those things that will happen; I see those things that could happen too. And that means that the future isn't a set and definite thing. I believe it's malleable, and if I had a recipe for what the future was made of, I'd take one part destiny and add two parts free will. In other words, if you continue to do nothing to extend yourself romantically, then your life will continue to be very solitary, and at times even lonely. But if you take a chance and come out of your shell and *try*, well then, that's a game changer."

He seemed to think on that for a bit, because he took his time replying. "So, what you're telling me is that if I want someone in my life, I have to do something about it; it's not just going to happen on its own."

"That's exactly what I'm saying. In other words, if you do nothing to alter your solitary status, no love will come into your life. At least not in the foreseeable future, which is about the next five years. And now that I know you a little better, Agent Frost, I can tell you that that would be a real shame."

His eyes came up briefly to meet mine. "Thanks, Cooper," he said. What he said next surprised me. "Have you ever considered a career with the CIA?"

"Ha!" I laughed. "You're kidding, right?"

"No. I'm dead serious. You're a very talented person, and I think you could be a real asset to your country."

I sat back in my chair and considered him. "Are you trying to play the patriot card with me?"

He grinned. "Yeah."

I shook my head. "Sorry, buddy. That only works for the long term on someone like Dutch. I pay my taxes, keep my nose clean, use my radar for the good guys, and after this mission is over, that's all the asset I'm willing to be."

Frost made a circle on the tabletop with his finger. I had the feeling he was thinking up another angle to try on me, so I decided it might be time to take my leave of him. I looked at the clock, noting that it was well past eleven and that gave me a good out. Getting up, I stretched and carried my plate to the sink. "I'm gonna hit the shower and check on Dutch. Then we can chat about how to approach Grinkov and get an intro to Boklovich."

Chapter Seven

· · ·

Dutch was able to shuffle out to the table to sit with us while we talked through our options. Looking at him hurt my heart. His eyes were both still badly swollen and there were some ugly bruises forming, especially on the left side of his face. But the voice that came out of that body was strong and sure. "It looks worse than it feels," he told me when he caught me staring at him.

"I'm so sorry," I said again. "I wish I could have been there sooner, but I had to wait for the money."

"Where'd it come from?" he asked.

I fiddled with some lint on my sweater. "Milo."

"You gave Grinkov half a million dollars of Milo's money?" Dutch said, clearly displeased by that idea.

I was quick to shake my head and then I got up and brought over the attaché with one hundred and fifty thousand dollars in it, which I gave to Dutch to inspect. "Milo wired me two hundred thousand, which got me in the door and was enough to start a poker game. I won enough to cover Des Vries's debts and only lose out on fifty grand."

Dutch's face swiveled to Frost. "I'll reimburse my friend the full two hundred grand, and you guys will reimburse me the missing fifty. You got that?"

"Got it, Agent Rivers," Frost said tersely. "I've already put in for a check. It'll take a few days, but we'll make sure you're reimbursed."

I got up from the table and retrieved from the freezer one of the ice packs the doctor had left us. Moving over to Dutch, I handed it to him and he laid it gingerly on the side of his face. "Thanks, dollface," he said.

"They worked you over pretty good," I said, taking my seat again.

"Most of the damage was done at the office," Dutch said. "They used a Tazer, then beat the crap outta me. When we got to Grinkov's, he actually stopped them from killing me, and had me thrown into a locked room until he could decide what to do with me."

"So he bought the disguise?" Frost asked. "He really thought you were Des Vries?"

"Hook, line, and sinker," Dutch said. "Of course, I was a bloody, bruised mess by the time he saw me, and now that I think about it, getting roughed up by him may really work to our advantage."

"How do you figure?" I asked.

"Grinkov's going to spread the word that he worked me over—it's the only way to ensure that everyone else pays up on time—and meanwhile, anyone I come into contact with who might personally know Des Vries is going to expect to see a few differences, if only from the bruises."

"Rivers is right," Frost said. "We can use this to our advantage. If he meets anyone Des Vries has previously met at the auction—assuming we get in with Boklovich—they're not going to scrutinize too much why his speech is a little off or why he might not look exactly like the Des Vries they remember. We should move forward and work on connecting with Grinkov again, convince him to get us an introduction to Boklovich."

"The tricky part is going to be finding a reason why Des Vries would want to bury the hatchet so quickly," Dutch said. "I mean, if I call him up right away and ask him for the introduction, he'll probably get suspicious."

"I could do it," I offered. "I mean, he had no problem taking my call yesterday."

Dutch's jaw bunched and he winced. "No," he said firmly. "I want you out of it."

"Maybe she should make the call, Rivers," Frost said. "She and Grinkov seemed to have some real chemistry there."

My eyes shot daggers at Frost. "It was an act!" I nearly shouted. (Think I doth protest too much?)

"Well, you're a great actress," Frost replied blandly, and my hands curled into fists.

"Hey," Dutch growled. "She did great last night, Frost. Leave her alone."

"I *know* she did great last night, Rivers. That's what I'm saying. She can handle herself, and I think that we should let her make the call. She's quick on her feet, and she might be able to get us that meeting."

"No," Dutch said again, and this time, his tone was deadly serious. "If I know Grinkov's type, which I do, he'll want to meet with her again . . . alone. I'm not going to let her go off on her own. She's too green and she's been in enough danger already."

Waves of barely restrained jealousy were pouring off my fiancé, and I knew better than to argue with him. "Okay, Dutch," I said. "You make the call and set up a meeting. But not today. Today, you need to rest."

"I'm fine," he said grouchily.

I squinted at him. There was a line of sweat on his forehead and I moved my hand to his brow. "You've got a fever," I said.

"I'm fine," he repeated.

I stared at Frost with a look that said, "Dude! Help me out here!"

"We can wait a day or two," he said to Dutch. "I've got people monitoring the airwaves, and so far, we haven't heard any chatter about an auction. The minute we do, however, we'll need to move on it fast."

Frost left us after that for a meeting with his team and his superiors to brief them on our game plan. He had let us know that CSIS was going to be in charge of watching the building, but they'd agreed to let him know if any nefarious-looking types approached. He'd added that they would call us with an alert and he and the team wouldn't be far away. He also promised to be back in a few hours to give us the lowdown on what Dutch should say to Grinkov. In the meantime, I helped my sweetheart get back to bed, and made him comfortable.

He was far more bruised on the left side than he was on the right. "Both of Grinkov's thugs were right-handed," he explained when I ran my hand very gently over his swollen cheek.

I leaned in and gave him a soft kiss. "Do you want another pain pill?"

He shook his head. "I'll brick it out."

I frowned and thought of an idea. "How about a smoothie?"

Dutch brightened. "We have stuff for a smoothie?"

I'd spotted both frozen blueberries and strawberries in the freezer when I'd gotten Dutch his ice pack. "We do," I told him, scooting off the bed and discreetly tucking the bottle of pain pills into my sleeve. "You sit tight and I'll be back in five minutes with one."

I rummaged around in Des Vries's pantry and came up with some protein powder, and his fridge revealed a pint of vanilla yogurt. Mixing all the ingredients into the blender, along with one of the pain pills, I pressed the blend button and smiled when the contents turned a pinkish purple.

I carried the glass back into the bedroom, quite proud of myself, and Dutch took a good gulp of it, pronouncing it delicious. "Your cooking's improving," he said.

I laughed. For the record, my cooking is so bad the local firemen know me by name.

"Yeah, yeah," I said, waving my hand at him. "Just drink that down, okay?"

Dutch did, and within minutes after he'd finished, his eyes closed and he was fast asleep.

I had moved into the kitchen with the empty glass when I heard the elevator doors open. "Frost?" I called, looking at the clock. He'd been gone only an hour.

No one answered and I felt the hairs on my arms stand up on end.

"Hello?" I said loudly, grabbing a breadboard and holding it high like a baseball bat.

Footsteps sounded in the hallway. I waited for the person to identify himself, shaking slightly and hoping it wasn't Kozahkov's assassin coming back to finish off the witnesses.

Around the corner came someone familiar and completely unexpected, holding flowers and offering me a shy sad smile. "Hi," she said, before spotting the breadboard in my hands. "You gonna hit me with that?"

"What the freak are you doing here?!" I yelled. My heart was pounding in my chest from the implied threat of someone unknown entering the condo.

Rick's girlfriend held up the flowers. "I heard he'd been roughed up by Grinkov!" she explained, and tears filled her eyes with moisture.

I lowered the breadboard. "How did you get past the doorman?" I demanded. Stupid CIA, couldn't even keep out a simple dumb blonde!

Mandy held up a set of keys and her key card. "I came up from the garage and used my card," she said.

I wanted to yell at someone right then—preferably Frost for trusting the CSIS to guard the building while he and his team were out. Send us an alert my aunt Martha. "Mandy," I said firmly. "You have to leave."

"But—"

"Now."

Mandy's hand went to her mouth and she choked on a sob. "But he needs me!"

"Abs?" I heard Dutch call groggily from the bedroom.

Mandy's face whipped around at the sound of Dutch's voice. "Rick!" she cried, and before I could catch her, she darted around the corner and ran down the hallway into the master bedroom.

I tore after her and caught her by the wrist just as she pulled up short in front of the bed, staring in horror at Dutch while he lay propped up on pillows.

His one good eye opened a little more in surprise. "I'm sorry!" I told him. "She had a key card to the elevator and she used it to get in."

"Who the hell are you?" Mandy yelled, pointing at Dutch accusingly.

"Mandy," I snapped, gripping her arm tightly and trying to pull her out of the bedroom. "You need to come with me."

"Where's Rick?" she demanded, trying to pull out of my grasp. "You tell me where he is right now or so help me God, I will start screaming bloody murder!"

"Oh, yeah?" I replied. "And who do you think is going to hear you, huh? Des Vries owns this whole building and there's no one in it but us!"

"Who are you and *where* is my boyfriend?!" she shouted again, slapping me hard on the cheek before launching herself at me, scratching and clawing with her long nails.

I pulled my head back after the slap and tried to duck away from those nails, but she was like a rabid cat. After getting raked on the side of my neck, I shoved her hard to create a little room, then stepped forward and swung for all I was worth.

My fist connected with the side of her cheek, and she went down like a lead balloon.

"Son of a beast!" I hissed, shaking my hand and dancing above her. "Sweet Jesus, that hurt!"

Dutch was attempting to get out of bed and struggling to do so. "You okay?"

I held up my hand. It was already swelling. "No!"

Mandy moaned.

"I think you knocked her out," Dutch said, looking down at the crumpled form of our houseguest.

"I didn't have much of a choice," I told him, feeling zero sympathy for the wretched woman.

"Help me up, would you?" he asked me.

I went to his side and gently lifted while he pushed. I heard him suck in a breath as he clutched his side, but he managed. He then shuffled over to squat down and inspect Mandy. "Hey," he said, shaking her shoulder a little.

She moaned, but otherwise didn't respond.

"We need to call Frost," Dutch said, standing tall again, clearly troubled. "She knew I wasn't Des Vries right away, even with all the bruises."

I stared at him in surprise. I hadn't even thought of that. "You're right!"

I looked from him to Mandy. "But how could she tell?" I said. "Honey, you barely look human. You could pass for anyone with dark hair and a goatee."

"Gee, thanks."

"Sorry," I told him. "But it's true, cowboy. There must have been something that tipped her off, and we need to know what it is before we set up another meeting with Grinkov. What if he has a chance to get a close look at you and starts noticing some differences?"

Dutch nodded. "Okay. Let's get her to wake up and interrogate her. Then we'll call Frost and have him take care of her."

It took a faceful of ice water to wake Mandy up. And it took a bucket of ice to make the swelling on my hand go down. "You hit me," she said sullenly, using the towel I'd handed her to mop her face.

"You started it," I told her meanly, tapping the gun I'd borrowed from Dutch's holster on the table just to let her know we meant business. I didn't like Mandy so much after getting raked by her claws and slapped.

"Fuck you," she said, glaring hard at me.

I guess the feeling was mutual.

"Mandy," Dutch said from the chair I'd pulled over for him. "Why did you come here today?"

"I heard Rick'd been roughed up by Grinkov," she told him. "And I wanted to see if he was okay."

"How'd you hear that?" I asked her. After all, I'd brought Dutch home only the night before.

"Rick's bookie called me. He said he'd heard that Rick got the shit kicked out of him by Grinkov after being picked up off the street. He wanted to know if Rick was still gonna be able to cover his bets. Where is Rick anyway?"

"He's safe," Dutch told her.

She scowled at him doubtfully.

"He is," I assured her, and she cut me a look too.

"Why should I believe anything you say? You could've killed him for all I know!"

"Yeah," I agreed. "We could have. And we could've killed you too, toots, but we haven't." Tapping the gun again, I added, "Yet."

Mandy held the towel to her chest protectively and her lower lip trembled. "Are you going to?" she asked hoarsely.

"No," Dutch told her.

I frowned. In my opinion he'd given in too easily. "We won't," I said quickly, "as long as you agree to tell us what we want to know."

Mandy swallowed hard and looked absolutely petrified. "Is this about Rick's gambling, or about his weapons dealing?"

My brow rose in surprise. "You know a little something about Rick's business?"

Mandy nodded. "He talks on the phone a lot. I pretend not to listen."

"What types of things have you heard him say?" Dutch asked curiously.

"Well, he talks a lot about guns and bombs and explosives and stuff. I figured out after the first two weeks we were together that he was selling weapons and shit."

"To whom?" I asked carefully.

Mandy shrugged. "Anyone willing to pay. A lot of them have names I couldn't even pronounce if I tried."

"Have you ever met any of Rick's associates?" Dutch asked her.

Mandy nodded. "Yeah."

"Would you know if any of them would recognize you if they saw you?"

She shrugged. "Sure, I guess. I mean, he likes to take me to meetings sometimes and he shows me off at parties. Hey," she added, as if the thought had suddenly occurred to her, "if you've been posing as Rick, does that mean that he hasn't really broken up with me?"

I turned my head away so only Dutch could see and rolled my eyes. He ignored me and said, "We appreciate your willingness to cooperate, Mandy. And yes, you're right, as far as we know, Des Vries hasn't broken up with you."

"Who are you guys, anyway?" she wanted to know.

"The good guys," he told her.

Mandy's eyes moved back to the gun in my hand, and she rubbed her swollen cheek. "Sure, you are."

"One last question, Mandy," I said. "How'd you know it wasn't Rick Des Vries in the bed when you came in here?"

Rick's girlfriend frowned distastefully. "It was the pajamas," she said, pointing to the royal blue silk pj's Dutch was wearing. The very ones I'd gotten him for Christmas. "Rick wouldn't be caught dead in those. In fact, no *real* man would."

I growled low in my throat. "Shih tzu," I grumbled, glaring hard at Mandy.

Dutch glanced sideways at me. "What?"

"I wish my hand didn't hurt so much so I could smack her again."

Mandy flinched. "You asked!"

Dutch sighed. "Let's call Frost. And Abs?"

"Yeah?"

"Better let me hold the gun."

Frost wasn't at all happy to hear about Mandy. In fact, he was down-right furious when he found her with both hands cuffed to the chair in the kitchen and my iPod playing tunes in her ears. "She's a Cana-dian citizen!" he hissed as we all huddled in the living room, just in case she could hear us over the music. "Do you know how much trouble this could cause?"

"She knew Dutch wasn't Des Vries the moment she laid eyes on him!" I countered. "What were we supposed to do, Frost? Just turn her loose so that she could go out there and tell every one of Des Vries's as-sociates that Dutch is an impostor? She's already admitted that she knows his bookie! She could make *one* phone call and get us both killed!"

"She knows too much for us to cut her loose," Dutch added. "She's fully aware of what Des Vries buys and sells and she claims that he takes her along to some of his arms deals."

Frost had his hands on his hips and was looking completely exas-perated. But when Dutch told him that, his posture changed in an instant. "She said that?"

I nodded. "Yep. We showed her some faces of known weapons dealers and she pegged three guys right off the bat. And if I were Rick Des Vries's girlfriend, and I cared about him as much as she appar-ently does, I would stop at nothing to try to find out where he was and try to help him. And I'd start by calling his bookie. She tells that guy and it's all over for us. Word'll get back to Grinkov, who will no doubt tell everyone else—including Boklovich. She could blow our cover right out of the water with one phone call, and we wouldn't know it until it was way too late."

I wanted Frost to take Mandy away to some nice quiet cell for a while where she couldn't cause any more trouble until all this was over. But I also knew that her being a Canadian citizen really complicated things for the CIA. "We can't hold her," he said, confirming my fears. "And we can't hand her over to CSIS. They'll interrogate her, and she'll spill the beans that the guy they've thought was Des Vries is an impostor, and then they'll start asking us too many questions. But, if we let her go, we'll have to call off the mission."

"So . . . where does that leave us?" I asked.

Frost sighed, took out his cell and began to punch the display. "We have no choice. It's over."

I slapped my hand on his wrist. "What if there was another option?"

Frost frowned, switched the phone to his other hand, and placed it to his ear. "There is no other op—"

I squeezed my hand on his arm, urging him to listen to me. "What if we *recruited* her?"

Through the earpiece of Frost's phone I could hear someone answer the ring. I stared right into Frost's eyes, willing him to at least hear me out.

Our handler hesitated. The person on the other end repeated the greeting. I nodded, knowing Frost was close to agreeing to listen to my idea. "Director," he said at last. "I'm sorry to have disturbed you. I'll have to call you back."

I breathed a sigh of relief and let go of his arm.

"All right, Cooper," he said once he'd disconnected. "You have sixty seconds."

I pitched my idea to both Dutch and Frost, hoping they'd go for it. "Think about it, guys. Mandy said it herself: Rick brought her to meetings to show her off. And you used her image when you set up my original cover, right?"

Frost's brow furrowed and he stole a glance at Mandy, who was now singing—off-key—to Beyoncé.

Turning back to me, he said, "What's your point?"

"My point is that she's obviously memorable, and she could further cement Dutch's identity as Des Vries. We can totally use her to our advantage! If we make it to the auction, Mandy and Rick can look like the happy couple everyone remembers, while I mingle in with the crowd to figure out who has the drone. With those boobs and that hair, she's the perfect distraction. No one's gonna look at me or Dutch twice with that eye candy around."

"Don't sell yourself short, hot stuff," Dutch said.

I grinned broadly at him. Such a good fiancé!

"How the hell do you plan to convince her to go along with it?" Frost argued.

"By promising to reunite her with Des Vries."

Frost's eyes widened. "*Are you insane?* Cooper, I can't promise her that! Des Vries is in a secure location being held by the Israelis!"

"We don't have to bring Des Vries here," I snapped, eyeing Mandy over my shoulder to make sure she hadn't overheard. She was still singing along to Beyoncé.

"Then what're you suggesting?" Frost asked.

"We just have to get the Mossad to agree to let the two of them meet," I said. "I mean, it shouldn't be hard to sell them on a visit of, like, ten minutes or so, whatever it takes to get them to agree to let the two see each other, and we can be vague on the particulars when we offer that as an incentive to Mandy. In return, we get her to agree to help us and not tell the Canadian authorities about holding her here against her will for the past two hours or so."

Frost glanced at my knuckles. "Or about assaulting her, huh?"

"Hey, that was self-defense," I told him.

"It was," Dutch agreed. "I'm the witness."

Frost's hands went back to his hips and he hung his head while he thought the idea through. "Fine," he said at last. "See if you can recruit her and I'll try to sell the idea to the director. Assuming she goes for it, I'll have the paperwork drawn up and Mandy can sign it this afternoon."

"Perfect!" I said, feeling really confident.

An hour later I was feeling notably less confident. "Let me get this straight," I said through gritted teeth as Dutch and I sat with Mandy and worked through the terms. "You want one hundred thousand dollars *and* a guaranteed spot in the *Canada's Got Talent* semifinals?"

Mandy nodded. "I'm an awesome singer," she said. "I know you'll have to rig the judging for the first round, but if I make it into the semis, I'm pretty sure I can go all the way."

I turned to Dutch. "I'm so sorry."

I couldn't be sure, given the swelling, but I thought he was smiling a little. "For what?"

"Obviously, I hit her too hard. She's delusional."

"I am not!" she yelled at me. "I *do* have a good voice!"

I rolled my eyes and texted Frost the terms. A minute later, after receiving his reply, I said, "There is no way we can guarantee that. The best we can do is fifty grand, and a spot in line for *CGT*."

"And I want to see Rick."

"He's in custody and we're trying to clear that," Dutch told her.

"Well, then, when this is over, I want a conjungle visit with him."

I blinked at her. "A con*jungle* visit with him?"

She had the nerve to look at me like *I* was stupid. "Yeah. You know, where you get to have hot monkey sex with a prisoner? Conjungle visitation is what they call it."

I handed Dutch the phone. "You get to text Frost that one," I said, moving away while I could still resist the urge to slap her.

Frost brought over the paperwork later that night. It'd taken much longer than we'd thought to get the CIA, the State Department, and the Mossad to iron out a "conjungle" visit between Rick Des Vries and Mandy, which she flat-out insisted was put into the agreement. The issue was that the Mossad admitted that they'd used some rather inventive ways to extract information from Des Vries, and they weren't sure that he'd be able to . . . uh . . . *perform* any act of lovemaking— "conjungle" or otherwise. They didn't want to agree to something that might not be physically possible. Can you believe *that* was the sticking point?

Anyway, we got around it by putting the wording in that it would be completely up to Mandy to arouse Des Vries once the two were put together sometime after the auction was over and we'd recovered the drone. It didn't surprise me that she didn't actually read the agreement before signing it in big swirly letters. She just assumed we had met all her demands and would keep our word.

We then sat up with her late into the evening, picking her brain about all of Des Vries's business dealings. The more we knew, the better prepared we'd be when we got to the auction—assuming we got to the auction, that is.

Mandy knew far more than she'd originally let on, which didn't really surprise me. My radar had suggested she'd been holding something back and she was. She knew a great deal about Rick's weapons deals, and the information was pure gold.

By the time we'd finished at two a.m., Dutch was completely wiped out and Mandy was yawning and whining that she was tired. I motioned to Frost that it was time to quit, and helped get Dutch to bed while he showed Mandy to the spare bedroom, locking her inside. "You'll want to post someone at the bottom of the fire escape," I whispered to Frost as he shuffled tiredly out from the hall. "Those windows open right onto it."

Frost nodded, then texted to someone and a moment later said, "It's done."

I stretched and yawned, getting down a glass to pour Dutch some water so that he could take his medication before he drifted off to sleep. "That was a good call," Frost said to me.

I eyed him over my shoulder. "What was?"

"Recruiting Mandy."

I gave him a sideways smile. "Thanks."

"Dutch can reach out to Grinkov in the morning."

"You should send Mandy along for the meeting," I said. "It'll look like Des Vries's girlfriend is nursing him back to health, and Grinkov won't eye him too closely."

"Exactly. We just have to make sure she keeps her mouth shut and doesn't say something that'll blow his cover."

"Dutch can handle her," I assured him. When Frost eyed me skeptically, I added, "Hey, he handles me pretty well, doesn't he?"

For the first time since I'd met him, Frost actually laughed. It was a lovely sound and I felt sad that he didn't make it more often. "You've got a point there, Cooper."

And then the moment passed and Frost was back to his serious self. "Okay, I'm gonna crash out on the couch. Why don't you give Rivers his pain pill and get some rest yourself. Tomorrow's going to be a long day."

"Got it," I said, and headed off to bed. I hoped the next day wouldn't be too bad. Okay, so, what I really hoped? That when Dutch called Grinkov, Maks wouldn't mention that whole part about kissing me.

Needless to say, sleep was a long time coming that night. No surprises why.

The next morning I was up by eight along with Frost, but Dutch was still fast asleep and so was Mandy. "I want to let Dutch rest," I told Frost before he'd even taken a sip of the coffee I'd poured him. "We pushed him too far yesterday."

Frost sighed and looked at his watch. "Yeah, okay. We'll give him another hour or two."

I took a seat at the kitchen table opposite Frost. "No," I said firmly. "We'll give him the day."

Frost opened his mouth to protest, but I cut him off. "Listen," I said. "He's in no shape to do this today. He's been beaten to a pulp, and he's still running that low-grade fever, plus he's exhausted. The doctor told us we needed to give him a few days of rest, and so far we haven't given him any time at all. It's Sunday, and Grinkov's probably taking the day off anyway. Let's give everybody until tomorrow morning."

"Cooper," Frost said stubbornly, "I don't think we should wait. For all we know, whoever stole the drone could be working on moving it out of the country right now."

"They're not," I told him.

"How do you know?"

I tapped my temple. "My radar says they're not."

Okay, so that was a total fib. I had no idea if Intuit was still in Canada, but if it was currently on its way out of the country, there'd be little we could do about it anyway.

Frost scratched his head and considered my request. "Fine," he said. "I guess if there's going to be a slow day, it's probably today."

"Thank you," I told him, feeling a flood of relief. "I really appreciate it."

"Yeah, well, you can thank me properly by cooking breakfast this morning."

"Are you sure?" I asked. "I'm not very domesticated, you know."

"You're kidding," he deadpanned.

"It's that obvious?"

"Yep."

"I could run out and get us something?" I suggested.

Frost seemed up for that and after a quick shower, and another check on Dutch, I was ready to forage for food.

I left the condo wrapped in a beautiful oversized beige cashmere sweater, chocolate leggings, and brown suede platform boots with a killer heel. The clothes had been purchased on my shopping spree, and I wasn't feeling even a little guilty about spending the CIA's money on something cool and comfy after being shoved into tight and trampy when we'd left D.C.

I stepped off the elevator to the parking garage, digging through my purse for my keys, when a black limo pulled up in front of me. Before I could even think through what was happening, the car came to a stop and the back window rolled down. "Good morning, Ms. Carter," said the passenger.

My heart skipped about six beats, but somehow I managed to keep my composure. "Mr. Grinkov," I said. "What're you doing here?"

Maks moved closer to the window and eyed me up and down. "You look lovely this morning. Although . . . you are far away from your apartment across town."

I had an apartment across town? "I stayed here last night," I told him. "Rick is still recovering from his playdate with you."

Maks inhaled and let it out slowly. "An unfortunate necessity of my business," he said, not looking the least bit sorry for pummeling my business partner. "If I did not set an example now and then, no one would ever think to repay me."

"Maybe you need a new line of work?"

Maks smiled charmingly, and damn him, that handsome face and pleasing smile stirred that little fire in me again. "May I join you wherever it is you are off to?" he asked.

I returned his smile. "Oh, I doubt it," I told him. "I'm headed to church, and I'd worry the place might be struck by lightning if I let you come along."

Maks laughed heartily. "Touché."

I eyed my car and wondered if the heels I was wearing would allow me to sprint for it. I could also turn back and make a run for the elevator, but I'd have to wait for the doors to open. The stairs were also on the other side of the garage. "I'm wondering why you're here, Maks,"

I said, still trying to come up with a plan. I had the feeling I was in trouble, but how to get out of it without getting hurt was going to be tricky. "Rick's debt to you is paid in full, after all."

"It isn't Des Vries I came to see," Maks said, his hazel eyes focused and intent on me.

Aw, shih tzu. "Ah," I said, only then remembering the stun gun was in the bottom of my purse. Could I get to it in time?

"I came to see you, Abigail."

I made a show of looking at my watch. "Well, Maks, I'm sorry you came all this way when I had other plans. Maybe next time you could call?" I began to walk purposefully away, aiming right for my car and hoping he'd give up.

He didn't.

The limo driver threw the car into reverse and backed up right beside me. "Perhaps I can convince you to join me for breakfast?" Maks said.

I shook my head. "Like I told you, I'm on my way to church."

"Which church?"

Uh . . . "The church of . . . of . . . St. Mary's . . . the Virgin Mother . . . of His Holiness Our Father." (As you can probably tell, it's been a *long* time since I visited a church.)

Maks was amused. "I'm not familiar with that congregation. Where is it located?"

"On the corner of Queen and University." The intersection just popped into my mind for some reason, so I went with it.

Maks looked at his driver. Even through the glass I could see the chauffeur shake his head. "There's a Laundromat, bank, and a Coney Island Hot Dog on that corner," he said to Maks.

Ahhh, Coney Island Hot Dog. *That's* why I'd remembered it.

I stopped walking, knowing the jig was up and there was no way Maks was going to let me out of that garage. "Fine," I said, moving to his door. "I'll have breakfast with you. But I want to let Rick know where I am and who I'm with, okay?"

Maks smiled wickedly. "You don't trust me?"

"Not by a long shot."

Chapter Eight

...

"Do *not* get in that car, Abby!" Dutch growled, his voice low and threatening.

Maks's chauffeur had already gotten out of the car and had come around to open the back door for me. His presence behind me let me know I was boxed in.

"All right, Rick, as long as you're feeling better. I promise not to be long."

"Abby!" Dutch called angrily. I tried not to wince as I had the phone pressed very tightly against my ear so that Maks couldn't overhear the conversation.

He was looking at me intently, however, and I knew he was getting close to forcing me to both end the call and get in the car. I couldn't stall any longer, so I said a cheery good-bye and clicked off the line before bending low and ducking into the limo.

Our driver closed the door behind me the moment I was seated, and I tried to resist the urge to open it up again and make a run for it, but my radar kept telling me that I'd be okay as long as I remained calm. We were too close to our goal now to blow our cover by acting nervous and arousing suspicion. Plus, maybe I'd get the opportunity to mention to Maks that Rick and I would appreciate an introduction to Vasilii Boklovich. After all, what could it hurt?

"Where are we going?" I asked once I'd tucked my cell back into my purse.

"Are you hungry?" Grinkov asked.

"No," I told him just as my stomach gurgled. "Well, maybe a little."

"You will eat with me again," Grinkov said. "And we can tell everyone that we had dinner and breakfast together."

The limo turned in a circle, preparing to head out of the garage, when I saw the elevator doors start to open. I knew Frost would be inside, and I could only hope that he'd get to his car in time to follow us.

We didn't drive far, thank God, and I didn't want to risk craning my neck to see if Frost was behind us. The driver turned onto Queen Street of all places, and there wasn't a church in sight, but there was a charming little bistro named Joy's that looked open for brunch.

I took heart in the fact that although Grinkov had all but kidnapped me, at least he'd taken me to a public place where I'd get a good meal out of the deal.

It was turning into a lovely morning, and Maks suggested we sit outside. I readily agreed, as this would put me in the most public place and allow me to scan the street for any sign of Frost's car.

From the menu I ordered the eggs Joy—a version of eggs Benedict—and Grinkov ordered the same. I also told the waitress that I'd need three more orders to go after our meal.

"Three orders?" Grinkov said. "Who else are you bringing food to?"

"Uh, you mean besides the two orders I'm sure Rick will eat on his own now that he can move his jaw again?" I said, thinking fast. I knew I'd need to explain three separate meals to Maks.

"Yes."

"I thought I'd bring an order back for his girlfriend, Mandy, too." In truth Mandy, who was painfully thin, didn't strike me as the type to eat breakfast. Or lunch. Or much of anything really, but maybe we could coax a few calories into her.

Grinkov's brow rose. "Rick is still with Mandy Mortemeyer?" he asked.

"You've met?" I asked, pleased to think that our plan to recruit Mandy might actually pay off.

Grinkov scowled distastefully. "Yes, we've met."

I couldn't help but smile, but then I remembered that I was supposed to be working on keeping our cover intact. "She's been helping to nurse Rick back to health while I look after our business investments."

The expression on Grinkov's face surprised me. For the first time I thought I saw a hint of guilt, but he didn't comment further. Instead, he turned the conversation back on me. "I'm still intrigued by this business relationship between you and Richard. You do not seem the type of woman to partner with someone like him."

I smirked before taking a sip of coffee. "He's a bit on the brutish side, right?"

Maks nodded. "Yes. He's not well liked, you know."

"Oh," I told him, "I can only imagine what his reputation must be. I mean, believe me, I *know* what he can be like. But right now Rick has hold of a golden egg, and I'm not letting go until I get my fair share."

"A golden egg?" he asked. I could tell that I'd piqued his interest.

"Yep."

Maks stirred cream into his coffee and studied me. He seemed to do that a lot actually. "You won't tell me what this *egg* is?"

I tilted my chin to the sun, enjoying the warmth of midmorning. "Maks, do you know a man named Vasilii Boklovich?"

My question seemed to surprise him, and not in a good way. "I might," he said cautiously. "What is it you want with Vasilii?"

"A meeting," I said, cutting right to the chase. "Rick has acquired some very valuable technology and we'd like Boklovich's help auctioning it off."

I could see in Maks's expression that he really wished he'd known that the other night, but he didn't comment on it because our server arrived with our food. I took the opportunity to sneak a look at the street. To my immense relief I was able to spot Frost's car parked half a block away. Once our server left us again, I waited for Maks to comment on what I'd said.

But he didn't. Instead he continued to consider me as if he was deciding something . . . like whether he should let me live past my eggs Joy.

Taking the hint, I tried a different track. "Maks, you obviously didn't ask me here to discuss Rick's business dealings, so what am I doing here?"

Grinkov casually cut into his eggs. "I have been thinking about our poker game," he began. "And there are things that I find very curious."

I nearly laughed. "Like the fact that I beat you?"

"Yes," he said honestly. "I am very good poker player."

"You are," I agreed. "Do you think I cheated or something? Because I can assure you, I didn't." Well, at least not *technically*.

"I know you didn't cheat, Abigail. You would not have left my home if you had." I felt a small chill down my spine. "What I'm wondering is how you knew I was bluffing."

I blinked. "Excuse me?"

"Every hand you won was a hand where I was bluffing. Every hand you lost was due to your inexperience and lack of skill. It's how I knew you weren't a professional. I would like you to tell me what I did to alert you to the bluffs. I know it wasn't my mannerisms or my expression, so what was it that tipped you off?"

This time I did laugh. "You're serious?"

Maks was not laughing. Heck, he wasn't even smiling. "I am."

"Why is it so important to you that I tell you?"

"Oh, you must tell me," he insisted.

And I guessed at the reason why. "You're worried that if I was able to pick up on your bluffs, other people will too?"

"Yes."

"You take this game really seriously, don't you, Maks?"

"I do."

I sat back in my chair, knowing I had a bargaining chip and wondering if I had the cojones to use it. "Do you think you could find a way to help Rick and me in return?"

Maks set down his silverware, but he didn't look up at me.

Uh-oh.

"Perhaps," he said, and I exhaled. "It depends on your answer."

I took a long sip of water to steady my nerves. I'd just jumped into the big-girl pool and it was a little late to wonder if I should have brought along the floaties. "You have nothing to worry about," I told him. "There is nothing you physically did that alerted me to your bluff."

"Then how did you know?"

I tapped my temple. "Because I'm psychic," I said, making sure not to smile or appear coy in any way.

Still, he thought I was kidding. "Abigail," he said, his voice low and even. "You must stop playing with me. Tell me how you knew."

I leaned in really close to him. "I'm not playing, Maks. I am an honest-to-goodness psychic."

He squinted at me as if trying to peer through a lie.

I smiled winningly at him, then shrugged and got back to my breakfast, even though I was now so nervous I could barely taste the food.

"All right," Grinkov said carefully. "If you are psychic, what am I thinking right now?"

I couldn't help it—all the tension that had built up in the moments after our food arrived was suddenly released by that silly statement. I laughed heartily. "I have no idea! That's not how it works."

"Then how does it work?"

I set my silverware down. "Well, when I focus, I can pick things up about people. I can sense their personalities, and events coming into their futures, and I can also almost always tell when they're lying. That's how I knew you were bluffing the other night. Your energy didn't out-and-out suggest a lie, so to speak, but at times there was a hint of mistruth there coupled with concealment. I knew that every time your energy combined those two things, I needed to bet high and keep my fingers crossed, and when I felt no concealment in your energy, I needed to bet low and keep my fingers crossed."

Grinkov's head tilted slightly. "This is really how you won the match?"

I nodded. "Well, I did have a streak of good luck there too."

Grinkov considered me for a moment. "I have two brothers and one sister. Is this true or a lie?"

I rolled my eyes. His lie was really obvious, but I knew he wouldn't be satisfied by my telling him just that. So I peered into his energy and said, "You're an only child, Maks, but you're the father of two boys. The boys are also very close in age—I'm thinking that they're twins even, but their energies are unique enough to make them fraternal rather than identical."

Grinkov's brow lifted in surprise. "How do you know this?" he whispered, and just by his reaction I could see what I revealed was a closely guarded secret.

"Don't test me if you don't want me to pull stuff out of the ether."

Grinkov wiped his mouth with his napkin and nodded to the bus-boy who'd seen his empty plate and silently asked if he could take it. "I see now why Rick finds you so valuable."

"We make a good team," I agreed.

"Perhaps the three of us could make an arrangement," Maks said.

That got my attention. "You'll help us get a meeting with Boklov-ich?"

"I have heard some rumors. . . ."

"What rumors?"

"I have heard that something very valuable to the Americans was taken right out from under their noses. A small drone was piloted away from a military base carrying something that would be highly prized."

I kept my face as neutral as possible. "Then you're abreast of current events," I told him. "But that is not the item we've been able to acquire. What we have is even more valuable."

"Oh?"

I wondered if it was a good idea to be putting all our cards on the table, and wished that Dutch could be sitting here with me to take over the conversation. He was much better at this stuff than I was. Still, at this point, what did we have to lose? "We've got the code," I said simply. When Maks's expression revealed his confusion, I elaborated as subtly as I could. "The item taken over the border has a faulty component. If it's used more than a few times, it'll malfunction and render the device unusable and impossible to reverse engineer. We have the original code to the item in question. No reverse engineering required. Production on a large scale could begin immediately."

Maks leaned back in his chair, the surprise and interest clearly evident in his features. "Vasilii would be most interested in this," he said smoothly. And then he grinned. "I will arrange a meeting," he said, "for a cut of the deal and a few terms."

My radar pinged. Uh-oh. "What did you have in mind, Maks?"

"Forty percent," he said, "and your services for an evening."

I sucked in a breath. "I don't know which is more offensive, the fact that you want more than a third of the money or the fact that you think I'm a whore."

Grinkov looked taken aback. "Forgive me. I did not mean to imply that you were for sale sexually. I meant to request that you assist me with some business tonight."

I hesitated. I was officially *way* in over my head here, and I didn't know if it would be prudent to accept Grinkov's terms outright, or to try to stall and figure it out with Dutch and Frost later. In the end, I decided I needed to demonstrate a little negotiation power and not appear too eager. "I'm willing to go to Rick on your behalf for thirty-three percent, Maks, but not a penny more."

"Forty."

"How can you justify more than a third?" I demanded.

"Vasilii is a highly suspicious man," he told me. "He does not meet with just anyone, and every person recommended to him must be trustworthy or all parties will face the consequences. Richard has already proven to me that he is less than trustworthy, so the percentage is based on my own risk in arranging for him to meet Vasilii."

"And you really think that risk is worth an extra seven percent?"

"I do. Do not forget that I can also help to legitimize your admittance into the meeting," he added. "Vasilii would normally never think to negotiate with a woman of questionable credentials."

"Questionable credentials?" I repeated. "What's questionable about my credentials?"

"You have none to speak of," he said, looking directly into my eyes. Ahh, so he'd done his homework. "Other than receiving a monthly allowance from your father, who would like to keep your connection to him a secret, and working for a temporary agency, your existence and connection to Richard Des Vries is a bit of a mystery, Abigail. You come with nothing to substantiate your legitimacy in a world where personal history is everything."

Another ding from my radar told me to quit while I was ahead. "Fine," I said with a sigh. "Rick's not going to like it, but I'll recommend the forty percent."

"It will come out of your share," Grinkov said.

I knew that were I dealing with the real Rick Des Vries, it would in fact come out of my share. "Probably," I agreed.

Grinkov shrugged. "It will still be quite profitable for you."

"Let's hope so."

The waitress came by and dropped off our checks along with my to-go order. As I was reaching into my purse for money, Maks slid the check out of my hand and handed it to our server with his credit card. I started to protest, but one look told me I'd lose that argument too. "Thank you."

"You're quite welcome," he said, his eyes studying me intently again.

While his credit card was being run, Grinkov asked, "You did not agree yet to the second part of my terms."

Aw, crap, he'd noticed. "I don't know that I'm really comfortable with loaning myself out like that."

"Why not?" he pressed.

I couldn't think of an answer that might satisfy him, so I went with telling him that I'd have to clear it with Rick.

That seemed to frustrate Grinkov, but he didn't comment further. Instead, he signed the tab and we were on our way.

The moment I walked through the door of the condo, I took one look at Dutch's worried, swollen face and felt like a dog. He got up from the couch, grunted in pain, and walked stiffly over to me. Before I could even say anything, he'd wrapped me in his arms and pulled me to him gently. "Jesus Christ, Edgar!" he whispered in my ear.

"Honey, I'm *fine*," I assured him.

The elevator doors opened again and a voice demanded, "Is she okay?"

I turned awkwardly in Dutch's embrace and waved my to-go bag at Frost. "I brought everybody breakfast."

"I don't eat breakfast," Mandy said sullenly, filing her nails in front of the TV. "Breakfast is for fat chicks." She made a point then to give me the up-down with her eyes before adding, "And I wouldn't eat anything *you* brought me even if I were a fat chick." She then went back to filing her nails.

I stepped back from Dutch and reached into the to-go bag, pulled out a plastic utensil, and held it aloft. "Hey, Mandy," I said, waiting for her to look up. "Fork you."

She offered me a well-manicured middle finger. Such a charmer, that one.

"What happened?" Dutch and Frost asked together, pulling my attention back to the subject at hand. I glared one last time at Mandy, who was still practicing her sign language, and coaxed them both into the kitchen. "First, Dutch, you need to eat," I told him firmly. "And I'll tell you all about it over brunch."

I spent the next hour giving them the details, and the moment I mentioned the second part of Maks's terms, Dutch slapped his hand onto the table and growled, "Not on your life!"

One glance at Frost, however, said he wasn't opposed to the idea. "It might help us win Grinkov's trust, Rivers."

"She already has his trust," Dutch countered.

"I doubt it," Frost said. "From what I've been able to gather, Grinkov doesn't even trust his own mother. The guy has one of the lowest profiles in organized crime. He keeps everything about himself a safely guarded secret and we're still unable to identify much about his background. He's something of a ghost to us."

Now it made sense why Maks had looked so surprised when I'd mentioned his children.

"Exactly why we need to keep our distance from him," Dutch

pressed. "We don't know enough about him to trust that he won't hurt her."

"He won't hurt me," I said, and both Frost and Dutch looked at me.

"How do you know?" Dutch asked.

I shrugged. "He likes me." Dutch's expression was unreadable, but there was a tint of the green-eyed monster in his energy. "I don't mean like *that*," I told him quickly. "I mean, he thinks I'm amusing. And he thinks I'm useful. He's not about to do anything that'll jeopardize my potential usefulness to him."

"She's got a good point," Frost said. "And if Grinkov can get us a meeting with Boklovich, then we've got to take the risk."

Dutch was still shaking his head, however. "I don't like it."

I reached out and took his hand. "I'll be very careful. And Frost is going to have my back, just like he did when I went in to get you out of Maks's house, right, Agent Frost?"

"Absolutely."

"See?" I said to my fiancé. "The sooner we recruit Grinkov, the sooner we can arrange the meeting with Boklovich and get an invite to the auction so that we can flush out the thief. Honey, it's win-win, and the only thing we have to do is wait for me to get through tonight."

Dutch lifted my hand and kissed it. "I don't like it," he repeated. "But I guess we don't have a choice."

I sighed with relief. My radar said that meeting with Maks was the right way to go.

"Hey, are you guys talking about Maks Grinkov?" Mandy asked from her place on the couch.

"Yeah," Frost said. "You know him?"

Mandy got up and walked over to us, her high heels clicking on the wood floor. "A little," she said with a shudder. "I went to a party at his house once, right before I met Rick. I was dating this other guy, Zuri, who supposedly did a lot of business with Grinkov, and he introduced us and I told Zuri I thought Maks was hot, 'cause I was trying to make Zuri a little jealous so he'd take me on a cruise.

"Anyway, Zuri told me that I shouldn't even think about getting mixed up with Maks, because he knew for a fact that Grinkov had been married once, like, ten years ago when he was still living in Russia or something, and one night, Maks walks in and catches his wife in bed with another guy and he gets so mad that he kills them both. But he didn't kill 'em right away, nuh-uh. I heard that he took his time, you know, torturing them to death over a couple of days. First he tied 'em up; then he shot each of them in the foot; then he left 'em there for a while to bleed and stuff; then he came back and shot 'em in the other foot; then he left 'em alone; then he came back and shot them in the shin, then the other shin, then the knee, then the other knee, then the thigh, then the—"

"Mandy!" I snapped.

"What?" she snapped back.

"We get the picture, and you're not helping."

Mandy offered me her middle finger again, then turned on her heel and stalked away.

I looked at Dutch and Frost as if to say, "Can you believe her?" But I noticed that both of them were looking at me as if to say, "Aw, shih tzu."

Grinkov's driver came to pick me up at seven. I had dressed up a little more from that morning, wearing a charcoal gray wool-blend suit with a dusky-rose-colored shell and patent leather pumps. The suit was beautiful, and as the limo came to a stop right next to me, I had the distinct and somewhat morbid thought that I hoped I didn't get blood on it.

I'd worn my hair loose, and at the last moment I'd told Frost privately that I wouldn't be wearing the hair clip with the camera or the earpiece again. He'd protested. I'd insisted. He'd threatened to tell Dutch, who would make me wear them, and I'd threatened to walk out on the deal if he did. My radar had absolutely *insisted* that I not wear any kind of a wire, and experience has taught me not to ignore such warnings.

I waited for the limo driver to come around and open the door for me, but both of the front doors to the car opened and out stepped a big guy in a navy suit holding the same electric gizmo the guard at the gate to Maks's house had used to sweep me for bugs.

This time I was treated to a pat down before I could even get in the car, and the gizmo was swept over the entire length of my body, from the top of my hair, all the way down to my toes. I was asked to remove my jewelry, my shoes, and the contents of my purse, and the wand was swept over all of it.

Thank God I'd listened to my own internal warnings—I'd have been made for sure as a spy.

The big man then confiscated my phone—which was fine. I'd backed it up to Dutch's computer inside the condo and I'd restored the phone to its factory settings. No one could get anything personal off it.

I was then allowed into the backseat of the limo and we drove in silence until we reached Grinkov's front gate, which opened smoothly and allowed us to enter without stopping.

Grinkov's British butler greeted me at the door and led me deep into the house through a winding series of corridors. By the time we reached Grinkov's study, I was a little disoriented, but I had a feeling we were probably somewhere at the back of the house, because there were large windows flanking the far wall that overlooked a beautiful and well-tended garden. "Abigail," Grinkov said warmly when I was shown into his study.

"Maks," I replied, just as warmly. Maybe tonight wouldn't be so bad after all?

Grinkov was dressed casually in a lightweight black sweater with matching dress slacks and wine-colored loafers—no socks. His wrist was adorned with a beautiful gold watch studded with sapphires, and I had no doubt it was a Rolex. He looked relaxed and sexy and tempting as heck. I tried to remind myself about the mission and to whom I was engaged.

"Would you like some wine?" he asked.

Now, I wanted that wine like you cannot believe, but I knew that if I had a glass, my defenses would start to peel away, and that was just too risky for obvious reasons. So I offered him a polite excuse that I hoped he'd accept. "Thank you, Maks, but I find that alcohol interferes with my sixth sense, and as you've asked me here in a professional capacity, I think it's wise to remain completely sober."

The corner of Grinkov's mouth twitched. "Pity," he said.

When he didn't offer another topic for conversation, I made a show of looking around the room and noticed several photos of Maks engaging in various extreme sports. Curious, I walked over to a row of framed photos and examined them. One showed him midjump from a helicopter, wearing a set of skis and facing a very steep slope. In another he was mountain climbing, in a third he was skydiving, and a fourth showed him leaning against the hood of a race car in full racing attire. "I see you're an adrenaline junkie."

Maks came to stand next to me, allowing me a whiff of his cologne, which was, like the rest of him, sexy and dangerous. "I like to combine speed and risk, if that's what you mean."

I turned to him and flipped on my radar. "Is that how you hurt your hip?"

Maks's eyes widened a bit. "Yes," he admitted. "I injured it last year right after this picture was taken." He pointed to the one of him jumping out of the helicopter to ski down the side of a very steep mountain. "It's been bothering me quite a lot lately."

I waved a hand in a circular motion around his right hip. "I can sense the pain." Maks opened his mouth to say something, but I cut him off. "Frankly I don't know why you're putting off the surgery. Your hip is shot, Maks. It's time to replace it."

Maks's eyes got even bigger before he seemed to rein in his reaction and he considered me seriously. "You are a most remarkable woman."

I smiled. "Thanks. Now, what was it you needed my help with?"

Maks waved me over to his desk and I followed behind, curious to see what he'd have me tune in on. On the desk was a rolled-up blueprint, and right away I started getting stuff off it. Maks began to unroll the paper and I said, "You're building an ice rink?"

His hands froze. He stared down at the half-unrolled blueprint and said, "If I did not know better, Abigail, I would think you were a spy."

Immediately sweat formed on my palms and at the small of my back and I barely managed to keep my wits about me. I forced myself to laugh lightly and turn it into a joke. "Ha! Oh, Maks, that's rich. Yes, I've been sent here by CSIS to interrogate you about your ice rink. Give it up for the Crown, buddy."

To my immense relief, Maks laughed too and continued to unfurl the blueprint. "What else are you picking up?"

"Well," I said, thinking about it for a minute and attempting to sort through the mix of visual images entering my mind. "I can sense lots of sports-type things—hockey and figure skating—but also other stuff like classrooms and computers. There's going to be a lot of kid energy focused here, right?"

Maks set two paperweights on each side of the blueprint and stood back to gaze at it with pride. "It will be a youth center," he declared. "And I want to place it in one of the poorest neighborhoods in Toronto."

I looked at Grinkov with a new perspective. Either he was very good at hiding some sort of ulterior motive, or he really did have a charitable good side. "You want to help disadvantaged youth?" I asked, my voice betraying my disbelief.

Grinkov looked sharply at me. "Yes. Is that so hard to believe?"

I remembered what I'd read about this man from the file Frost had provided earlier in the day, how he'd been orphaned at a young age and raised on the streets in Chechnya, surviving by his own wits and cunning. He'd left his homeland abruptly ten years ago, and I wondered if it'd been because he was running from the murder of his wife and her lover.

Still, I imagined much of who he was had been formed on those rough streets when he was a boy, and it wasn't hard to see why he'd want to help other young boys and girls avoid the same hardships. "No," I told him honestly. "It's not hard to believe when I think about it."

"What do you mean, when you think about it?"

I shrugged. "It fits your energy. There's a side of you that's very conscious of how difficult life can be for those from more humble beginnings. I can sense that much of your own youth was spent in hardship."

Grinkov's stance relaxed, and I could tell he accepted my explanation. "Yes, this is true," he confessed. "I would like to save even one
child from a similar experience."

I turned my attention back to the blueprint, waiting for Grinkov to
tell me what he wanted to know about the project, but I was already
picking up lots of political and quarrelsome energy around it, so I just
dove right in. "There are some big issues to overcome before you can
break ground—am I right?"

"Yes."

I closed my eyes and felt my way through the ether. "You've got
some major opposition, Maks, both political and social. People have
heard of you in those circles where individuals with your connections
are whispered about, and I know you've been working to establish
some legitimate contacts, but the rumors persist and let's face it—
they're true anyway."

I opened one eye to check his reaction; to my relief he appeared
only curious, so I closed my eye again and continued. "You want
people to trust that this youth center will be good for Toronto, and
while the people who could allow you to build this thing know that,
what they're afraid of is being linked to you during their next run for
office. It's a huge obstacle you'll have to personally overcome and it
isn't one that will be resolved quickly if you go it alone. I see it taking
many years to win these people over, in fact."

"What would you recommend I do?" Grinkov asked me.

I opened my eyes again and shrugged. "You mean if I were you and
I had all this facing me?"

"Yes."

"I'd get a partner."

"A partner?" he repeated.

"Yes. Someone with impeccable credentials, someone who could be the face of this youth center and help buffer the fallout for the politicians. You need a champion, Maks. Someone to help you gain access to the building permits currently eluding you, along with the extra funding you'll need to finish the project and keep the youth center going for the long term. This can't be the Maks Grinkov youth center. It has to appear to be someone else's."

The hard set to Maks's mouth told me that he didn't like that idea at all. "But it's my idea," he insisted, as if he could argue with me to change the outcome.

"It is your idea," I agreed. "And it's likely to stay just that—an idea—if you don't consider bringing in someone else and making them the face of the youth center. So, Maks, the choice is yours: You can have a great idea that you'll continue to try to get off the ground for years and years until you're out of time, energy, and patience, or within the next two years you can have a fully functioning youth center where hundreds, perhaps thousands, of underprivileged youths will benefit and one day be hugely grateful for it, even if they don't know the *real* person to thank."

Maks adopted a pensive pose. I considered that although he was willing to finance this incredibly generous act, he was having a hard time letting go of the fantasy of being seen as a great man by so many adoring youngsters. With a sigh he lifted off the paperweights and began to roll up the blueprint again. "Your advice is very good," he told me. "I will look for someone to partner with tomorrow."

"Make it a sports hero," I told him, already seeing a hockey jersey in my head. "And if you can find anyone who made it all the way to the NHL from that particular neighborhood, you'll have a partnership made in heaven."

A sly smile spread across Maks's face. "I am beginning to envy Rick more and more," he told me, and when he looked up at me, his eyes were smoldering with desire.

I felt a blush hit my cheeks. "Can I have some water?"

Maks pushed a button on his desk and within seconds Eddington the butler appeared. He was sent to get me some water, and Maks led me over to a group of chairs, where we sat and were soon served my water and a plate of cheeses and fruit. I nibbled at the cheese while Grinkov and I made small talk. He was very curious about my radar and asked all the usual questions: When did I first realize I was psychic? And what goes on in my head when I get an intuitive feeling?

Conscious of how anxious Dutch and Frost likely were about my absence, I kept many of my answers short and sweet and it wasn't long before I was able to steer the conversation back to why I'd been brought here. "So, is the youth center the only thing you wanted to ask me about?"

Before Grinkov had the opportunity to answer, Eddington came into the room. Bowing slightly for the interruption, he said, "Would you care for more cheese and fruit, sir?"

"No, William, but I would like to ask Ms. Carter something in your presence, if you don't mind?"

My radar *bing*ed the moment Grinkov began speaking, and the shift in energy was so abrupt that it caught me a bit off guard. Maks's tone had not changed in pitch or pleasantness, yet I detected some subtle and immediate danger. "Of course, sir," said Eddington with another bow.

Grinkov turned to me and I could feel my heart beating like a wild bird in my chest. Something bad was on the verge of happening and I couldn't identify quite what it was. "Abigail," Grinkov began. "With regard to my butler, William, do you suspect, as I do, that he might be stealing from me?"

The breath caught in my throat much the way I'm sure it caught in Eddington's. I chanced a very quick glance at the butler and saw the immediate fear in his eyes and how the color faded from his cheeks. I forced myself to swallow and remain calm. "Why do you suspect your butler?" I asked, stalling so I could think on how best to answer.

Grinkov's manner was still completely relaxed, but I knew that he was much like a coiled snake, ready to pounce on his servant the moment I said go. I also knew that I likely held Eddington's very life in my hands.

"I would rather not reveal what has caused me to be suspicious," he said curtly. "Please, observe his energy and tell me what you can glean from it."

I hesitated. Grinkov was a masterful poker player with his own terrifically honed intuitive sense, and I wondered if he suspected his butler just because Eddington appeared to have something to hide. I focused my radar at Grinkov and found that same signature wave of energy I'd hit on a few nights before when he had a bad hand and was trying to bluff his way through it.

"Now, please!" he snapped, which pulled me immediately away from focusing on him.

I flinched but swiveled in my seat and lifted my eyes to meet Eddington's. The elder gentleman stood rigid, with his chin held high, but there was a slight tremble to his lower lip, and he was gripping his walking stick so tightly that his knuckles had turned white. He was radiating fear through the ether and I felt awful for him. "Fine," I said to Grinkov. I closed my eyes to shut out the haunted look from the butler, attempting to work my way first along Eddington's energy and then along very carefully chosen words.

"I can see why you're suspicious," I told Grinkov as in my mind I could see a tangle of images that were somewhat complex given their context. I saw my symbol for jail, and for justice and also a crown. I could feel Eddington's past might be coming back to haunt him, and I thought I knew a way out for him.

"Tell me what you see," Grinkov insisted.

"Your butler has a past," I told him. "One that he's not exactly proud of. As you know, he comes from Britain, but what he hasn't revealed to you is that he once spent time in prison."

I opened my eyes to look at Eddington again. His expression practically begged me to keep quiet, and I wished I could somehow convey to him that he could trust me.

"What was he in prison for?" Grinkov asked.

I tapped my finger on the sofa, trying to figure that part out. I'm usually really good at stuff like that, but I was a bit nervous and feeling pressured. I focused on Eddington, who was doing his level best to try to conceal his energy, and subconsciously he was fairly adept at hiding himself from my radar now that he knew what I could do. In desperation my eye roved to the far wall and lit upon one of Grinkov's many oil paintings. There had been a hint of an artistic element in Eddington's energy, so, as I was running out of time, I decided to improvise and make something up. "I believe it was forgery. Art forgery, isn't that right, William?"

The poor butler opened and closed his mouth, words failing him.

"He has the energy of an artist," I told Grinkov. "I believe he was quite a talented painter in his youth, and if I had to guess, I'd say that he was copying some of the masters and passing them off as the real thing."

Eddington's gaze never left mine. He looked absolutely terrified at where I was headed with this.

"Your butler's time in prison was many years ago, however," I added. "And I believe he served his time, then left England for Canada to make a fresh start and leave all that behind."

"Is my art collection in any danger from him?" Grinkov asked me.

At this I actually laughed, because it was ludicrous to think that this frail-looking butler would ever consider pinching more than a grain of salt from someone as dangerous as Grinkov . . . and yet . . . at the edge of all this energy, something tugged at me. Something I couldn't quite place but had to ignore. "Your art collection is perfectly safe," I assured him. "Mr. Eddington learned his lesson long ago, and today he is very much your faithful servant." I swiveled back to Eddington and looked for anything I could use that would help assure Maks that his butler wasn't capable of the crime I'd invented. I noticed a considerable amount of pain emanating from his left knee, which was likely why he used the walking stick; but he also had some degree of discomfort coming from the knobby knuckles of his right hand, and I pointed to it. "Your poor butler has a terrible case of arthritis," I said, as if to prove that Eddington couldn't possibly pull off another forgery. "I doubt he can wield a paintbrush with the skill he exhibited in his earlier years. Am I right, Mr. Eddington?"

The butler managed one shaky nod.

Still, there was something off about his energy, and I had little doubt that the butler had stolen from his boss at some point or another, but there was *no way* I was going to call Eddington out in front of Grinkov and watch as Maks either murdered him or had one of his thugs do it. No, tonight I was going to save this man's life if it killed me . . . which, frankly, it could.

To my immense relief Grinkov seemed to accept my take on it, because he regarded his butler with a shrewd look before nodding. "Yes," he said after a moment. "All right. You weren't wise to keep your past from me, William. The man I used to investigate your employment history before I hired you was dismissed long ago for incompetence, so it doesn't surprise me that you escaped scrutiny. Still, you have served me well these past ten years. But you should remember that I always know when people are keeping secrets."

Eddington bowed very low and there was a slight tremble to his frame. "My apologies, sir," he said. "But it is exactly as your guest described. I was reckless in my youth, I was caught, and I served my time. Since then, I have been a loyal and honest servant."

I looked at Grinkov and with some relief I could see that his servant's bald-faced lie was evident only to me.

I stood up abruptly and walked over to the butler. I didn't want Grinkov focusing overlong on his servant, and decided it might be time for the both of us to make a hasty exit. "Maks," I said in my most businesslike tone. "It's late, and I would like to be on my way."

Grinkov appeared surprised. "You won't stay for dinner?"

I shook my head. "No, thank you. I've overworked my sixth sense tonight, and I now have a splitting headache. What I need is some rest. But please call me or Rick when you've arranged for us to meet with your friend." I didn't want to mention Boklovich's name in front of the butler, because I didn't know if that might upset Maks.

He smiled slyly. "I will want to meet with Richard and finalize the terms first," he said. "And as I said, my friend is a difficult man to arrange such things with. I imagine it will take some time to convince him that a meeting is in order."

Crap. Time was something we didn't have a lot of. Still, there was no sense pushing it, especially when I knew it was more prudent to get my butt out of there before Maks insisted I stay.

I turned back to Eddington. I didn't want to leave him alone with Grinkov, who might grill him more on his shady past. "Mr. Eddington, would you please escort me to the front door?"

The butler offered me his right arm, his expression quite relieved. "Of course, ma'am," he said.

He and I then walked purposefully from the room, neither one of us daring to look back. As soon as I was out of hearing range, I said very softly, "You've been a naughty boy, William."

The servant beside me didn't say a word, but he did stiffen and I added, "I saw a hint of your dishonesty in the ether, and I'm not talking about your stint in jail back in England. If you don't want Maks to know what you've been up to, then you'll need to make reparations and do it quickly. Understand?" I wasn't sure what Eddington had stolen, but whatever it was, I wanted him to put it back, posthaste.

"I understand perfectly," he said tersely.

We arrived at the door and he opened it for me without meeting my eyes. "Good evening, ma'am," he said.

"Good night, Mr. Eddington," I replied, holding back from sprinting to my car. "Sleep tight, and remember what I said."

With that, I left Maks's house without a backward glance.

Chapter Nine

• • •

Dutch's phone rang early the next morning. It was Grinkov. He wanted to meet with Dutch. Alone.

I knew why and it really bothered me. "You can't go alone," I told both him and Frost over breakfast. "Seriously, honey, you can't."

Dutch sighed and held the ice pack up to his jaw again. It'd been bothering him more than anything else save his ribs. "I'll be fine," he assured me.

"Oh, I know you'll be fine. Grinkov has no intention of hurting you again, at least until you double-cross him. That's not why he wants to get you alone."

"Then why does he want to get him alone?" Frost asked.

"Because he wants to negotiate the terms of the partnership without me there to call his bluff."

Dutch eyed me sideways. "*Do* you need to be there to call his bluff? I mean, Abs, this is a fake agreement. We're not really going into business with Grinkov—we're just using him to get the ball rolling."

I sighed and took a bite of my bagel, chewing while mulling that over. "I suppose not," I admitted. "I mean, as far as the negotiations go, I'm positive you can handle them, but sweetie, you don't really know this guy like I do. He can smell a bluff a mile away. He's got great radar in his own right, and he'll use it to feel you out. If you sit down with him, he may probe you because he'll sense something's a little off. You'll have to be very, very careful with him, and when you go in there, you'll have to do more than act like Des Vries; you'll have to *believe* you're Des Vries."

Frost looked unsure. "Maybe she's right," he said. "Maybe you should insist on taking Cooper with you. At least then she can help divert Grinkov's attention away from any inconsistencies."

Dutch shook his head. "Des Vries would never insist on bringing along a woman, even if it was his business partner. He's got way too much machismo for that. Trust me, if asked, he'd go in alone and with an attitude."

That alarmed me. "Grinkov isn't going to tolerate you going all alpha male on him, cowboy."

My fiancé moved the ice pack from his jaw and took my hand. His fingers were cold. "I know," he assured me. "It'll be a little dicey, but I can handle him."

I looked to Frost, thinking he'd back me up, but his expression told me that he was now leaning Dutch's way. "Okay, Rivers," he said. "But if you go in alone, we can't risk the wire or the camera. You'll be on your own."

I scowled at both of them, but I knew I'd just been outvoted. "Fine," I said. "But remember he'll look to take you by surprise, Dutch. And he'll definitely try to test you, so please, be on the alert."

Dutch leaned in and kissed me lightly on the lips.

"Blech," we heard from across the room. "You two should get a room."

I backed away from my sweetheart and glared hard at Mandy. That woman was getting on my last nerve.

"Easy, killer," Dutch whispered with a chuckle. "Remember, it's all for the cause."

"Easy for you to say," I growled, and left the kitchen to stew over Mandy and worry about Dutch.

As it happened, I was decidedly less worried when Dutch left for his meeting with Grinkov, because he wasn't able to drive a car. The pummeling he'd taken to his ribs had made it difficult for him to raise his arms and steer the wheel, especially since he was now refusing all pain meds beyond two Tylenol every few hours. So Frost donned a chauffeur's uniform and drove Dutch to Grinkov's offices, which were located only a few miles away from Des Vries's office, which allowed me to get away from Mandy for a few hours to go along with them as far as that and get dropped off downtown. The plan was to meet back at Des Vries's office after the meeting and brief me and Frost about how it had gone.

Mandy was left back at the condo, locked inside and with a guard posted at the door, lest she get any ideas about venturing out on her own.

After the boys had dropped me, I paced the floor again until I had an idea, and I sat down at the desk and closed my eyes, focusing on Dutch's energy to make sure he was okay.

To my immense relief I could clearly feel him in the ether—our link was so strong it was nearly telepathic. I smiled because I had the clear sense that Dutch was thinking of me too. I don't believe he knew I was tuning in on him, but I could feel him reciprocate that strong connection to me, which helped me all the more to figure out what was happening around him.

Inspired, I picked up the phone and called Frost. "You okay?" he asked me.

"I'm fine," I told him. "I just wanted you to know that I'm tuning in on Dutch."

There was a pause, then, "I'm not sure what that means."

"It means that we're no longer totally blind to what's happening in this meeting between Dutch and Grinkov."

"Really?" Frost said, his tone interested. "What're you seeing?"

I took a deep breath and felt out the ether. "Dutch's energy is calm, but guarded, which is to be expected. He's being careful, but he's confident, which means that Grinkov hasn't tried to test him yet. I can sense Grinkov there, and his energy feels guarded but engaged. And there's another person in the room. . . ." My voice trailed off as I focused on the newest member to the group.

"You there?" Frost asked me.

"Yeah," I told him. "I was just trying to get a bead on the other guy."

"Who is it?"

I shrugged, then realized Frost couldn't see me. "I don't know. I'd guess him to be a bit older than Dutch and Grinkov, maybe by ten years or so. He's also an extremely powerful man. I'm thinking he's the head of something big, and he's loaded. We're talking *big* money here."

"Do you think it's Boklovich?"

I frowned. "It could be."

"What're the initials you get for him?"

I realized Frost was trying to help by pointing me this way and that, but my radar didn't work in the way he thought it did, and his constant questions were only serving to distract me. "I don't know," I said tersely. "I don't get names or initials."

"Okay, so can you describe him physically?"

I sighed. For the record, linking in quasi-telepathically to a meeting between three people miles away is really, *really* hard. "The most I can tell you is that he feels big."

"Huh?" Frost said. "You mean like fat?"

"No . . . well . . . maybe . . . but more like he has a big presence. He might be a large man, it's really hard to tell."

"How about complexion or hair color?"

I rolled my eyes. It's not like I had a video camera in my head, peering into the room. "You'll have to wait for Dutch to give you that. I can only describe his energy."

Frost paused, probably taking that in before asking me his next question. "Is there anything else you can tell me that might be relevant?"

"Yeah. It feels like the guy with the power is directing the meeting. Grinkov feels like he wants to defer to him. If I had to guess, I'd say that he's either brought along Boklovich or one of Boklovich's henchmen."

"That could be a good thing," Frost said.

"Or it could be bad."

Frost blew out his own sigh. "Okay. Keep your ESP pointed at the meeting and call me if you get anything else."

"Got it."

I hung up and refocused all my attention to the meeting. I kept my radar trained on Dutch, because I was worried about him and would be able to tell in a moment if things turned ugly. His energy remained calm but alert, and there was also a feeling there of being pleased with how the flow of the meeting was going. I took this as a very positive sign.

An hour later I called Frost. "They're wrapping it up."

"That was quick," he said. "I was prepared to wait another couple of hours."

"It was a good meeting, and they accomplished what they wanted to. We'll have Dutch fill us in."

"He's coming out of the building now," he told me. I felt a wave of relief. "We're on our way back to you. Sit tight and we'll see you in a bit."

I leaned back in the chair and put my feet up with an exhausted sigh. Focusing my radar on Dutch for so long had really taken it out of me, and in about three deep breaths I'd drifted off to sleep.

I couldn't have been asleep for long, because the next thing I knew, I was awake and in a full state of panic. I couldn't breathe and my windpipe was being squeezed closed while something wrapped itself painfully around my neck.

Flailing my arms and legs instinctively did nothing to ease the terrible constriction. My hands then flew to my throat, pulling at the piece of cord digging into my skin. My mouth opened and I tried to gasp for any amount of air, but none came.

I dug my nails into the crevice between the cord and my skin, pulling and tearing at it in desperation. Excruciating pain vibrated straight down my index finger as the nail caught and was ripped away from the finger. Darkness started to cloud the edges of my vision, and my ears filled with the sound of my pounding heart.

I kicked again at the desk, my heel making a thunderous noise on the wood top, and then, in one last moment of clarity, I thought to bend my knees and hook my heels on the edge of the desk. Using all my reserve strength, I shoved away from the desk, pushing the chair into the person standing behind me pulling hard on the cord.

My assailant stumbled backward, pulling me and the chair too. As if in slow motion I felt myself tip all the way back, and the chair's two front wheels left the ground. In an instant, the tension on the cord around my neck eased and I took a ragged, desperate breath before my head hit the corner of the cabinet. A lightning bolt of pain erupted in my head, and then the darkness took me.

I woke up to an argument. "Call them!" I heard Dutch shout from right above me.

"I'm calling the doctor who treated you."

"Goddammit, Frost!" my fiancé roared. "You call the fucking ambulance now, or you'll need to call another one for yourself!"

"Stop yelling!" I croaked, my hand going straight to my head, which was sticky and wet.

"Jesus!" Dutch whispered, and he moved my hand back down to the floor. "Don't move, Abs. We're getting you some help." And then in a much more terse whisper he said, "I mean it, Frost. You call for an ambulance *now*!"

I managed to open one eye. Frost was holding the phone to his ear, looking very unsure and a little pale. "We'll blow the mission," he said softly.

"Fuck the mission!" Dutch snarled.

"No," I said, moving my hand to Dutch's. "I'm okay."

Dutch's attention came back to me, and in his eyes I saw panic and worry and anger. "You're definitely not okay, Edgar," he said frankly. His fingers then brushed my neck, which was competing with my head for what could hurt the most. And then the pain from my lost fingernail kicked in again and it was a three-way tie.

"The doc can be here in five minutes," Frost told Dutch. "She's alert, talking, and coherent, so why don't we let him examine her, and if he wants her to go to the hospital, then I won't hesitate to call an ambulance or take her myself."

I closed my eyes again. The world was starting to spin and I thought I could be sick, which would be *seriously* bad news given the state of my throat. "She's bleeding pretty bad," Dutch insisted.

I felt Frost step close to me, and gentle fingers probed around my temple. "She might need a few stitches."

"Oh, great," I muttered. "I just got the staples out of my head a month ago, and now I have to go through ten days of bedhead again?"

"See?" Frost said lightly. "She's even making jokes! She'll be fine, Rivers."

"Fuck you, Frost."

"Please shut up," I told them. "You're giving me a headache worse than the one I already have."

The doctor arrived about five minutes later. He told me to lie very still and inspected my limbs and the back of my neck. After determining that I had no serious injury to my spine from the fall out of the chair, he instructed Frost to carry me to the couch. I groaned when he set me down. So much hurt that it was hard to focus.

The doctor tended first to my noggin, which I gathered was much less seriously injured than it looked. "Head wounds always bleed a lot," he said.

"Are you going to give me stitches?"

"Yes, but not the kind you're thinking of. I've got a liquid-based medical adhesive that we can use, which will minimize the scar and allow you to take a shower."

I gave his arm a pat to say thank you, because frankly it hurt to talk.

Next he examined my throat. "You're very lucky, Ms. Cooper. If the cord used to strangle you had been an inch lower, it would have likely broken your hyoid and there'd be nothing I could do for you."

"It hurts to swallow," I told him.

"Yes," he agreed. "I'm sure it does. The muscles around your larynx and esophagus have been bruised. You'll be sore for a few days, but otherwise you should be fine."

"How bad is my finger?"

The doctor lifted my hand to inspect it. "The nail will grow back, but that will likely cause you the most discomfort over the next few days. I will put the same liquid bandage over the raw skin to act as a temporary buffer against the elements, and recommend that you take one of Agent Rivers's pain pills now, and then again before you go to sleep tonight."

"You're sure she doesn't need a CT scan or something?" asked my oh-so-protective fiancé.

The doctor smiled kindly at him. "Her pupils are normal and she seems quite coherent. Also, the bruising around the gash in her head is minimal. I think that her temple only grazed the corner of the cabinet, and it was the sudden rush of blood flow to her head when her assailant let go that caused her to black out. With some rest I'm sure she'll be fine."

Frost gave Dutch a look that said, "See? I was right to call the doctor instead of the ambulance!"

Dutch gave Frost a look that said, "Yeah? Well, fuck you anyway."

Frost helped me into the limo and the three of us drove back to the condo in silence. No one had yet asked me what had happened in the office, for which I was grateful, because that would mean I'd have to talk, and that hurt. Still, Frost had given me a black shoelace that he and Dutch had found still wrapped around my neck when they'd come into the suite and found me on the floor.

I could read Frost's expression when he'd handed it to me. He was hoping I could tune in on it to identify my attacker. The guy'd been watching too many lame movies about psychics or something if he thought I could get anything off a shoelace.

When we got to the condo, the agent guarding Mandy checked in with Frost, then made a very quick exit. I had no doubt that he found her company as enjoyable as we did.

Frost carried me to the bedroom with Dutch right behind. Dutch handed me one of his pain pills, and Frost hurried to get me a glass of water. After considering the enormous pill, and the hard time I had swallowing even a tiny sip of water, Dutch kindly took the pill into the kitchen, and returned with a small cup of very smooth ice cream. "I mashed up the pill and blended it into a smoothie, just like you did for me the other day."

I smiled. He'd been on to me from the start. I managed to get most of the sweet dessert down and then I laid back on the pillows and shut my eyes. I was asleep within seconds.

W hen I woke up, the room had the dusky feeling of late afternoon. I blinked tiredly, still feeling very groggy, and pushed up from the pillows, wincing as I felt the soreness in my upper shoulders and back from the struggle that morning.

"Hey," said a familiar baritone.

I looked to the corner of the room. Dutch was sitting in one of the chairs, his face hidden in shadow. "Hey," I said, my voice hoarse.

"You feeling better?"

I nodded.

"Are you up for telling me what happened?"

I nodded again. "Frost?"

Dutch sighed. "Yeah. He should probably hear it from you."

He got up and left the room, returning a minute later with the CIA agent in tow. "How're you feeling?" Frost asked.

"She's better," Dutch said crisply.

Ah, so these two hadn't made up while I'd been napping. "Play nice," I begged them.

Dutch looked chagrined. "Sorry."

When they were both seated, I took a notepad off the side table and began to write out what had happened at the office, peeling off the pages as I wrote in large block letters and handing them to Dutch, who read them and then handed them off to Frost.

"Did you see who attacked you?" Dutch asked me when I'd finished.

I shook my head.

"Did he say anything to you while he was strangling you?"

Again I shook my head.

Frost asked, "How do you know it was a he?"

"Strong," I whispered.

"And you didn't hear anything or see anything that might give you a clue as to who they were?" Dutch asked.

I shook my head.

Frost tapped his finger on the arm of the chair. "What about your radar? Did you pick up anything off the shoelace?"

I sighed, reined in my impatience at his ignorance, tapped my temple, and shook my head.

"What does that mean?" Frost asked, looking at Dutch to see if he understood.

"She can't pick up anything off a shoelace, for Christ's sake, Frost," my fiancé growled. "Jesus, what movies have you been watching?"

If my throat weren't killing me, I would have laughed out loud, especially at the way Frost's face flushed bright red. Of course, my fiancé forgot that only three years ago he'd been just as ignorant.

Frost cleared his throat and leaned forward to put his hands into a steeple and rest his chin on them. "That's the second attack on your life in the past few days, Cooper," he finally said.

Dutch looked sharply at me. "What's he mean, *second* attack?"

I knew Dutch had forgotten Kozahkov's assassin's hail of bullets, which had fallen heavily on my side of the car, so I held my arms like I was shooting a rifle to remind him.

"Send her home," he said quietly after a pause.

"What? Why?" I demanded, too loudly for my throat to handle. My hand flew to my neck and I winced.

"You want me to take Cooper off the case?"

"Yes."

I shook my head vehemently, which was not a comfortable thing, let me assure you. "No!" I whispered, glaring hard at Frost. "Do not!"

Frost's gaze was pivoting back and forth between me and Dutch like he was watching a tennis match.

"Do not!" I said at the top of my voice—which wasn't very loud. I added a determined finger point at him too, just to let him know I meant business.

"I can go it alone from here," Dutch argued.

I was so mad, I threw the pad of paper at him. It hit his knee and bounced harmlessly to the floor. "Need me!" I whispered desperately.

But Dutch wouldn't look at me. His mind was made up and I was furious because every ounce of my intuition told me the deadly outcome if Dutch attempted to go it alone.

Frost eyed me like he might be considering sending me home and I moved off the bed and over to him. Kneeling down, I literally begged him. "Please!" I cried, then pointed at Dutch. "Won't come back!"

Frost held my gaze and I took his hand, squeezing it hard, willing him to keep me on the mission. "Someone's trying to kill you, Cooper," he said softly. "You're definitely a target, and so far, Rivers is pulling off Des Vries's identity. Maybe he should go it alone."

I glared hard at him and shook my head vigorously again, mindless of the pain to my sore muscles. *"No!"* I cried and pointed to my temple, shaking my head.

"I'll be fine," Dutch told him. "Really, Frost. I can handle it."

My eyes filled with tears. I wanted to scream, and had I been able to, I know I would have. But in that moment something in Frost's expression changed, and he seemed to read my sense of urgency and understand what I was trying to say to him. "Your radar is telling you that if he goes in alone, he won't come back out?"

I nodded.

"And if I keep you on this mission, what will happen to you?"

I paused. Holy crap! I'd never even considered that. I let go of Frost's hand and sat back on my heels, really taking a moment to think about it. I could follow the energy of my going forward with Dutch on the mission like a current moving along a river. There were rocks, rapids, and twists and turns to come, but I could feel the strength of our combined force and knew we had a chance. "Make it out," I whispered, and pointing back and forth between me and Dutch, I added, "But only together."

Frost pursed his lips and gazed sideways at Dutch. "I think I'm with Cooper on this one, Rivers."

Dutch clenched his fists, gave Frost a murderous look, then got up and stormed right out of the room without another word. It hurt to watch him leave, but I had to accept that I'd won, and gotten my way, which was all I truly cared about.

"You know," said Frost into the silence that followed, "if this thing goes south, Cooper, it'll be my butt on the line for not pulling you off the mission when I had the chance."

I offered Frost a small smile, then reached out to squeeze his hand. I mouthed, "Thank you" to him before turning around to crawl back to bed. The pain pill I'd taken was adding to the exhaustion I felt. Once I'd lain down, Frost got up and came over to cover me with an afghan. "You rest. We'll talk more in the morning."

*   *   *

The next day I woke up early and tiptoed to the bathroom to take a long hot steamy shower and get the dried blood from my head wound out of my hair. All things considered, I felt pretty good and the only thing that still really hurt was my blasted missing fingernail.

When I came out, Dutch was awake and watching TV. "How're you?" he asked.

"Better. You?"

"Better."

I caught our reflection in the mirror over the dresser. "We look like Mr. and Mrs. Smith after they've tried to kill each other and their house has been destroyed."

Dutch grinned. "Match made in heaven."

I went over to sit next to him on the bed. "You still mad at me?"

He looked at me quizzically. "I'm not mad at you."

"Oh, really?" I said, not believing him for a second. " 'Cause the way you stomped out of here last night, I could've sworn you were miffed."

Dutch reached out and squeezed my knee. "I was ticked off at Frost, not you."

"Don't be mad at him, Dutch. He's only doing his job."

"By letting you get killed?" The playful tone he'd started the conversation with had vanished and there was now a flinty edge to his voice.

"I'm not going to get killed," I told him, *really* hoping I was right.

"Someone wants you out of the way."

I sighed. "Wouldn't be the first time."

"Abs," he said curtly. "This isn't a game. We have no idea who's trying to kill you. It could be that Grinkov's working to set us up, and thinks that your intuition's going to figure that out sooner or later, so he had us separated yesterday, and quietly sent someone to take you out of the picture."

"He didn't even know where I was yesterday," I replied, going quickly to Maks's defense.

Dutch's lips pressed together as if he was regretting something. "What?" I asked him.

"When I first got to the meeting, before Boklovich arrived, he asked about you. I told him you were back at my office waiting to hear about our meeting."

"Did he make a phone call or something to let someone else know that?" Maks had two perfect opportunities to take me out when I visited with him at his house. It didn't make sense that he'd wait for some innocuous tidbit about my whereabouts to send someone to kill me with a shoelace.

"No," Dutch admitted. "But he could have ordered the hit the minute the meeting was over."

"Honey," I said gently, stroking his arm. "My attacker tried to strangle me with a *shoelace*. Would you hire a hit man who resorted to something as unreliable as that?"

"He's a dangerous guy, Abs," Dutch countered defensively. "Don't underestimate Grinkov, okay?"

"Which is all the more reason why you shouldn't go it alone, cowboy."

Dutch shook his head and stared hard at the TV. Baloney, he wasn't mad at me.

I gave him a minute before I asked, "Do you *really* think Grinkov tried to kill me?"

"Who else could it have been?"

I thought about that for a minute. My intuition just didn't accept it. "Maybe it's simply another one of Des Vries's enemies," I suggested. "Lord knows the man must have plenty of them."

"No one's made an attempt on my life yet . . . except Grinkov."

I scowled at him, feeling like I wanted to defend Maks and move him out of the way as a suspect so that Dutch wouldn't fight me so hard on staying with him for the auction. "He didn't try to kill you, Dutch. He just beat you up a little, and he only did that because he wanted to make an example out of Des Vries."

"A little?"

I sighed. "Fine. He's a murderous son of a one-eyed snaggle-toothed she-beast and we're both likely to have shorter life spans the longer we hang out with him."

Dutch snorted. "That's all I'm sayin'."

I rolled my eyes and thought it best to steer the conversation in a different direction. "So, what happened at the meeting yesterday?"

Dutch put the TV on mute but continued to watch the screen while he talked to me. (Which reminds me, why *are* men only capable of carrying on a conversation while the TV is playing? Do they think talking to us sideways is *enjoyable* for us?)

"Frost told me that you'd hooked into my energy during the meeting and picked up some of what happened."

"Oh, I come with skills," I told him with a stroke to his sideburn.

Dutch grinned again. "Babe, I know all about those skills, and the minute these ribs heal and you feel one hundred percent, we're putting those skills to good use again."

"Hallelujah."

Dutch kissed my hand and got back to telling me about the meeting. "As you already know, Grinkov pulled in Boklovich."

"I didn't really know, but I had a pretty good guess when I tuned into the meeting and found you with Grinkov and another powerful man. I didn't expect him to show up so soon."

"That makes two of us."

"I'm assuming the meeting went well?"

"It did," Dutch said. "He agreed to host an auction, and he let it slip that he'd come across another seller with something similar to offer his clientele."

"The drone," I said knowingly.

"Yep."

"So, does Boklovich have it in his possession?"

"No," Dutch said. "But he knows who does."

My eyebrows rose. "Did he give you a name?"

"Nope," he said with a sigh. "He's keeping that pretty tight-lipped. But he is willing to put both of our items up for sale at his private home in B.C., and open it up to anyone interested. And by anyone, I mean every terrorist and corrupt government in the world will be able to bid on it."

"Yeah, but the main head honchos won't actually *be* there, right? I mean, he's not going to host all these well-known terrorists in his house, for God's sake."

Dutch's left eyebrow rose. "Of course they'll be there, Abs. What did you think all this time the auction would look like?"

I blinked. "I thought it would be a room full of representatives, you know, connected to phone lines and stuff, like the auctions at Sotheby's."

Dutch snorted. "It won't be anything like Sotheby's, toots. These guys are gonna be the heavy hitters and they'll show up to make sure they can take immediate possession of either Intuit or the code once they pay for it, and maybe even take out an enemy or two while they're at it."

My breath caught in my throat. "Holy shish kebab!" I gasped as the full weight of what he was saying sank in. "Dutch! What if one of these bigwigs recognizes that you're not Des Vries! I mean, he probably did business with a lot of these guys, and with enough of them together, they could start comparing notes about you and put two and two together! They'll kill you on the spot!"

"It's a risk I'm going to have to take," he said simply. "Which is why I don't want you along."

I grabbed the remote and turned the TV off; then I very carefully moved over to straddle him, making sure I put no weight on his rib cage. Taking his bruised and swollen face in my hands, I said, "You can't do this. Honey, it's way too dangerous!"

His one good eye stared out at me, and there was such sadness there. "I don't have a choice, Abs," he said.

"Yes, you do!" I insisted, my heart racing with the panic I felt. "You can quit!"

"Abby," he said seriously, reaching up to hold my wrists. "I took an oath to protect and serve my country to the very best of my ability. That oath didn't include the words 'or until it gets too dicey.'"

My eyes began to water and I felt a lump form in my throat. "You'd give up your life?"

"Yes."

"You'd give up *me*?"

Dutch didn't answer me for a long, long minute. Finally, he said, "You have to know that you're the most important thing in the world to me. But if I walked away from this, and someone important died because of it, I could never live with myself. It would change who I am inside. And I could never marry you and take you down that road, babe. In the end, it wouldn't be fair to you."

I was so choked up I couldn't speak. We'd been playing with fire this whole time, but this wasn't fire—this was a nuclear bomb.

Dutch gently wiped at my tears. "So now you see why you can't come with me," he said earnestly.

I shook my head and swallowed hard. "Like hell I can't!"

"Abs," Dutch said, his voice pleading with me. "If I go down at this auction, you'll have no chance, and I can't live with that."

"And you think *I* can?"

"One of us should make it home, and it should be you."

I was breathing hard now. I was so furious with Dutch, and so afraid for him, and so angry at having accepted this stupid suicide mission, that I wanted to scream.

Instead I leaned in, kissed him tenderly on the lips, and said, "If you do anything, and I do mean *anything*, to keep me from going with you, Dutch Rivers, I will not only *never* forgive you, but if you make it back to me, I will end our relationship there and then. I will never marry you, and I will go to work full-time for the CIA. I'm sure they could use my help on some of their most dangerous missions . . . don't you?"

Dutch sucked in air. "You wouldn't."

I sat back on his thighs and crossed my arms, my gaze unwavering. "Frost and I have already talked about it," I told him. "As far as he's concerned, I've proven myself in the field and he thinks I could be a real asset. He's actually already offered me the job."

"Abby . . . ," Dutch warned.

I moved off his legs and headed for the door. Without looking back, I said, "You take me with you this time, Dutch, or you'll lose me forever. Even if you don't come back, I'll still join the CIA, because what the hell will I have to live for anyway?"

The silence from the bed cut straight through me, but it was the only way to get Dutch to listen, and the only way I wouldn't go completely insane if he somehow managed to keep me from going with him to the auction.

I left him with those final words and even managed to make it all the way down the hallway before I had to lean on the wall to steady myself and wonder how the hell we were ever going to get out of this mess.

Chapter Ten

. . .

It took a few days to pull together the auction, which allowed both Dutch and me some good recovery time and afforded us an opportunity to do our homework. An unexpected hitch in the plan came up when Grinkov told us that Boklovich was still waiting to hear from the drone thief about whether he would attend. My radar insisted the thief would be there, but Frost and Dutch were still sweating it.

We'd tried to get a list of the attendees, but Boklovich seemed to be guarding that information tightly. The most we could do was to have the CIA monitor their channels and present us with a list of the most likely attendees. We knew the margin of error was going to be big, and we'd have to cross our fingers that of those people identified as having previous dealings with Des Vries, most either were not big enough to attend or wouldn't especially notice the subtle differences between Dutch and Des Vries.

The list the CIA gave us was pretty impressive in a holy-cow-these-guys-are-super-dangerous kind of way. Lots of names on the list sounded Middle Eastern. Several others were Asian, and the rest were mostly Eastern bloc and Ukrainian. "It's the United Nations of weapons dealing," I muttered, looking over Frost's shoulder at the list. In the background I could hear Dutch's smooth baritone singing Sinatra in the shower, and I would have laughed if what I was looking at weren't so sobering.

"Let's just say you wouldn't want to meet any of these guys in a dark alley," Frost agreed.

Frost clicked on the link next to the name of one Arab sheikh, opening up his profile.

"He looks like someone I'd like to avoid meeting in a dark alley," I said, pointing to the Saudi.

"Oh, you would—trust me," Frost said. "He's also stinking rich. His name is Sheikh Omar bin Muhammad. We've long suspected he's been supplying various anti-Western terrorist groups with money and arms."

"Is he Saudi?"

"His father was. His mother is from Yemen, where he's been spending a lot of time lately."

"We've got trouble all over the globe, don't we, Frost?"

"Cooper, we've even got it in our own front yard."

"Do you think he'll be at the auction?"

Frost sighed as if he was troubled. "I really hope not, but it's possible."

My radar pinged with a little warning. "Why do you hope not?" I asked.

Instead of answering me, Frost clicked over to another window

and pulled up a video. He pressed play and I realized I was looking at surveillance video of the sheikh and Des Vries sitting down
over coffee, talking business. "He knows Des Vries," I whispered
nervously.

"He does," Frost said. "And not in a good way."

"What does that mean?"

"Shortly after this video surveillance was taken, our operative in
Dubai reported that Des Vries backed out on an arms deal he had with
the sheikh. He left him high and dry and the Arab was furious. Not a
smart move on Des Vries's part, because this guy has a long memory,
and he will find a way to get even."

I felt a cold chill along my spine and I worried anew for Dutch's
safety. "What if he comes to the auction?"

"We'll have to hope that Sheikh Omar thinks Dutch is Des Vries
and doesn't scrutinize him too closely, and then we'll have to hope
that Boklovich maintains the peace and prevents the sheikh from killing Rivers long enough for you guys to steal back the drone and get
the hell out of there."

I watched the video in silence for a while. The audio was both terrible in quality and in a foreign language, so I couldn't follow what
the men were saying, but it was obvious they were negotiating something and not just trading small talk. The cameraman shifted the angle slightly near the end, and I noticed someone sitting behind Des
Vries.

Moving my finger over the mouse pad, I said, "Hold on a second . . . ," and rewound the section.

"What's up?" Frost asked me.

I squinted at the screen, then stood up straight and swiveled toward
the living room. Mandy was sitting on the couch, twirling her hair

and watching Nickelodeon . . . which I seriously considered might be over her head. "Mandy," I said.

"What?" she replied, never taking her eyes off *SpongeBob Square-Pants*.

"Come here a second."

"I'm busy."

I could feel my jaw clench. "I wasn't asking," I said through gritted teeth.

Mandy sighed dramatically, took her time getting up, smoothed out her hoochie skirt, and clomped her skinny butt over to us. "What?" she asked again.

I pointed to the screen, which I'd paused so that I could show it to her. "Is that you?"

Mandy made a face at me and bent over to squint at the screen. Frost was watching her with renewed interest. "Oh, yeah!" she said. "I remember that. Rick took me to Dubai three years ago for my birthday; only we didn't do much celebratin' 'cause he had some business or something. It was really hot there."

Frost pointed to the Arab man on-screen. "Do you remember him?"

Mandy snickered. "Yeah. He offered Rick five thousand bucks for me. He wanted to add me to his harem or something. Rick almost took it, but I talked him out of it. I'm worth *way* more than five thousand."

I opened my mouth to tell her exactly how much *I* thought she was worth, but Frost placed a hand on my wrist, silently warning me not to. Reluctantly I let the moment pass.

"Do you know if Rick and this man met again after this time in Dubai?" Frost asked next.

Mandy shook her head. "No. It was a onetime thing. Rick didn't like him so much 'cause he said he was cheap. I guess he tried to low-ball Rick or something, you know, like he did when he made an offer on me, and Rick didn't want to close a deal with him 'cause he didn't trust him."

Frost let go of my wrist and closed his laptop to consider Mandy before asking his next question. "I need you to give me your honest answer on this next question," he said.

"I've been honest!" Mandy replied defensively.

"I know, Mandy, and I appreciate it," Frost told her carefully. "But we're worried about your safety—as well as Cooper and Rivers. If we send the three of you to B.C. and someone there recognizes that Rivers isn't Des Vries, it could go bad for everybody, including you."

"I know," Mandy said; again she sounded defensive.

"So, what I need to know is, do you think that the Arab sheikh Rick met with in Dubai would recognize Rivers as an impostor?"

To add to my irritation with her, Mandy shrugged like she didn't know and didn't care. "Maybe," she said. "I mean, *I* can totally tell it's not Rick, but Rivers's face is all beat up. I guess he could pass for him."

Frost didn't seem to like her answer either, but he let it go. "Thanks, Mandy. You can go back to your TV show."

Mandy shuffled her way to the couch and did just that. I turned back to Frost and said, "Can I watch that video again?"

"Sure," Frost said, opening the laptop and hitting the PLAY button.

Something else about the video had caught my attention. I noticed that it was well after dusk, but everyone, save Mandy, was wearing sunglasses. Even Des Vries had on a pair. I remembered something my father once told me—he'd worked for one of the big three automakers in the international arena for most of his career, and he'd done a lot of traveling abroad and made a lot of deals in his day. He'd told me a story about meeting with a large group of Arab sheikhs in his London office on a rainy day, and all the men seated there had worn sunglasses, never taking them off, through the meeting. He'd told me it was a common practice, because the sheikhs believed you could actually give away a lot at the negotiation table by allowing the other person to see your eyes.

It was also the same reason why many poker players wore mirrored shades when they gambled, and it gave me an idea. "I gotta go out," I said.

Frost's attention snapped to me. "Why?"

"I need to run an errand."

"Where?"

"The nearest department store." Frost eyed me skeptically. "I won't be gone long," I told him impatiently.

"Fine," he said, "but check in with me every half hour—and that's a direct order."

"Okay, okay," I said, grabbing my coat, purse, and keys.

"Can I come?" Mandy asked, jumping off the couch and following me into the front hall.

"No," I told her firmly.

"Oh, come on!" she yelled. "I've been cooped up here for days!"

"Not my problem," I said, hitting the button for the elevator.

"Fine," she snapped. "But don't count on me to back up your boyfriend when he needs it."

I paused. Frost and Dutch were both insisting that Mandy come with us to the auction, as it would help back up the story that Dutch was Des Vries. Mandy had been with Des Vries for three years, and had met a lot of the nefarious folk that Des Vries hung out with. Frost and Dutch argued that she could be a valuable tool to help Dutch avoid direct contact with someone who might recognize him for an impostor.

Still, she was a total pain in my butt and I disliked the woman intensely. There was no way I wanted to spend even one more second with her than I had to. "Whatever, Mandy. The answer's still no," I repeated, and pressed the button for the elevator again.

"Hey, Cooper?" Frost said, and my shoulders sagged.

"What?" I already knew what he was going to say.

"If it's a quick errand, would you mind taking her, just to keep her happy?"

I sighed and let my head knock against the steel doors. Stupid men. "Fine. But I'll need the company credit card."

Frost had taken away the credit card we'd been given when he saw my tab from the shopping spree. I heard him push back the chair and walk up behind me. "Here," he said, handing it to me over my shoulder. "And please, try to keep it reasonable this time, okay?"

I took the card without promising him shih tzu. "Mandy!" I snapped.

"Yeah?"

"Get your coat. We're going shopping."

She was next to me in a hot second. "You'll need to find me a nail place," she told me like I was her servant or something. "I gotta get a manicure and a pedicure."

I turned my head and glared at Frost, who did his best to look guilty. He failed. "Every half hour," he reminded me when the doors opened. "And if she doesn't behave, call for backup, or use your stun gun."

Mandy's sharp intake of breath was audible, and I smiled evilly at her while directing my comment back to Frost. "Yes, sir," I said, stepping inside the elevator. I patted the wall next to me and added, "Come on in, Mandy. There's plenty of room for you, me, and my stun gun."

Even with the threat of electrocution, Mandy still spent most of her time with me in the car picking a fight. She was looking forward to a long day of shopping, getting her nails done, more shopping, and doing her best to annoy me.

I was looking to make one quick stop at a department store, find an opportunity to stun her, then get back to the condo, so as you can already tell, our agendas didn't match.

"You are such a bitch," she told me when I parked the car but refused to let her out of it until she promised to stick close to me and do as I say.

"Sticks and stones, honey," I told her mildly. "Sticks and stones."

"Look at my nails!" she screeched, shoving both hands right under my nose.

I swatted them away. "They look fine."

"No they don't! The cuticles are all screwed up and this one has a chip in it!" Mandy held up her middle finger to show me just how messed up it was.

I leveled my eyes at her. "That one-finger salute is really getting old."

"It'll only take an hour," she begged. "Come on, Cooper!"

I sighed and wished my best friend, Candice, were with me. She'd know exactly how to deal with someone like Mandy. *"Fine!"* I said, giving in and hating myself for it. "But if you do *anything* to jeopardize our mission, I'll make sure they take away your conjungle visit with Des Vries."

She clapped her hands and stuck her tongue out at me all at the same time. God help me, I wanted to zap her but good. Instead I got out of the car just as my cell went off. Digging it out of my purse, I noticed the caller ID said it was Rick Des Vries. "Hey there, cowboy. Did you enjoy your shower?"

"Where are you?" Dutch said, his voice tense.

"I had to run an errand at the Eaton Centre."

"Why?"

My brow furrowed. I didn't much care for his tone. "I had to pick up something. Is there a problem?"

Intuitively I could tell that Dutch was working to pull in his horns. "I don't like you going off alone," he said to me. "Not after what happened at the office the other day."

I looked sideways at Mandy, who was eagerly clomping along next to me like a kid on her way to meet Santa. "I'm not alone. I've got Mandy."

"I'm gonna kill Frost," Dutch muttered. "Can I convince you to come back to the condo right now?"

I pulled on the door of the department store entrance and motioned for Mandy to go first. "Honey," I said soberly, "I'm in a public place with tons of people around, and we're only going to pick up one small item and get Mandy a manicure. We'll be back in an hour and a half at most."

I could tell Dutch wasn't at all happy with the idea that I was insisting on running my errand, but he didn't push it any further with me, which was a relief. "Okay," he said. "But send me a text every half hour, okay?"

"Yes, Mom," I told him.

"Abs," he warned.

"I got it, I got it. Listen, I'm gonna let you go. Love you and see you soon."

With that, I clicked off and hurried after Mandy, who was moving down the aisles much faster than I'd ever be able to manage in heels that high. I grabbed her by the arm near the entrance to stop her from getting away from me. "Hold on there, sister," I said. "I have to go over there." I pointed to a row of cases lined with sunglasses.

"But the nail salon is right there!" Mandy protested, and I followed her finger to the salon, which was the first shop visible at the shopping center entrance, right next to the department store. I considered just letting her go on her own, but my intuition warned me to keep her in my sights.

"We'll head there right after I get what I came here for," I told her.

Mandy did the unexpected. She started throwing a fit. A very *loud* fit. She began shrieking at me, and I could tell that the several days we'd had her cooped up and under our thumb had frayed her nerves to the breaking point. Midway through her tirade, aimed mostly at me and how unfair I was being, a store manager approached and asked if there was a problem.

Mandy's face was by now bright red, and there were tears dribbling down her cheeks. "She won't let me get my nails done!" she shrieked. "She's a mean, mean lady!"

The situation was so ridiculous I hardly knew how to react. My hand had gone immediately for the inside of my purse and the stun gun, just in case she tried to make a run for it, but with so many wit-nesses now openly staring at us, I thought twice about using it.

"Ma'am!" said the store manager. "Please lower your voice!"

Mandy dissolved into a puddle of tears and I could tell from the faces of everyone staring at us that most of the crowd thought I was the bad guy. "Mandy," I said through clenched teeth. She continued to wail. *"Mandy!"*

"Stop . . . yelling . . . at . . . me!" she blubbered.

I sighed and looked to the store manager as if to say, "See what I have to put up with?"

He, however, was looking at me reproachfully. "Perhaps you should take her to get her nails done?" he said.

I gave him a tight smile and grabbed Mandy again by the elbow. "Come on," I growled. "Let's get you a manicure."

The tears and drama vanished immediately, replaced once again by an eager smile. I could feel my free hand clench into a fist. God, I hated this woman and her theatrics!

We got to the salon and Mandy approached the counter nearly dancing with happiness. How Rick Des Vries could have put up with her for three full years was beyond me. "I'd like a mani and pedi," she told the woman behind the counter. "The deluxe package on both."

"I know you," said the woman suspiciously, squinting at Mandy like she'd just picked someone out of a lineup. "The last time you were here, your credit card didn't go through and you said you didn't have any cash. You still owe us for last time. If you want service today, you'll have to pay us for last time and this time up front."

Mandy turned to me expectantly.

"What?" I asked her.

"Well, *I* don't have any cash!"

I inhaled a very deep breath and let it out slowly. Grumbling, I dug into my bag and produced the CIA's company credit card. If Frost wanted to insist that I personally babysit Mandy, then the CIA could pay for her nails.

I handed it over to the clerk, who took it and asked if I wanted my nails done too. "No, thank you," I said, noticing that Mandy had already moved to one of the pedicure baths and was dipping her feet into the water. She looked absolutely relaxed and happy, especially when her nail tech offered her a magazine and a soft drink. "Listen," I said, leaning over to the woman behind the counter. "Can you just keep the card and put whatever services she wants on it? I have a quick errand to run and I'll be right back to sign for it."

"Yeah, okay," said the clerk.

I hustled back to the department store and over to the sunglasses counter. The moment I got there, my cell rang again and it was a number I didn't recognize. "Hello?"

"Ms. Carter," said a silky male voice.

"Mr. Grinkov," I replied, a tiny smile forming automatically on my lips. I wasn't sure what it was that made me hold a small soft spot for this dangerous Russian mobster, but something about him caused me to like him, even against all my better judgment.

"I would like to share a meal with you again. Are you free for lunch?"

I looked at my watch. It was eleven thirty. "Actually, Maks, I'm a little busy right now."

"Where are you?" he asked, probably hearing the background music from the department store.

"I'm at Eaton Centre making a purchase."

"Lingerie?" he asked playfully.

I couldn't help it—I smiled. "Not this time," I told him. "I'm just picking up a few new things for the auction."

"Very well," he said. "A rain check for later?"

"Sure," I said easily. I mean, what were the odds that he'd get to collect on it?

"Excellent," he said. "Enjoy yourself." And with that, he hung up.

I stared at my phone for a moment. "That was weird."

"May I help you?" asked a woman's voice. Startled, I looked up to see a salesclerk looking expectantly at me.

"Yes," I told her, sneaking a peek over to the entrance of the salon. I couldn't see Mandy, but I could see the tech filing her toenails, so I relaxed and got down to the business of finding the right sunglasses for Dutch. I went through several pairs of shades until I felt I'd found the right ones. While I was purchasing them with my own card, I sent a quick text message to both my fiancé and Frost that we'd be on our way back the minute Mandy's nails were dry; then I took my small package and threaded my way through the crowd to the nail salon, which was now quite crowded. There was a line at the counter and I decided to just wait out in front of the entrance for Mandy to come out.

After forty-five minutes I was growing impatient. I'd done all the people watching I'd cared to do for the day and swung around into the salon to coax Mandy along. I searched the crowd of faces lining the walls and didn't see her anywhere. My heart began to pound in my chest and I hustled over to the woman I thought had been her nail tech. "Where did my friend go?" I asked her. She looked at me like she had no idea what I was talking about. "The skinny chick with the long blond hair and big boobs?" I asked. "With the short denim skirt and high heels?"

The tech shook her head at me. "She left like an hour ago."

My jaw dropped. "No," I insisted. "No, she didn't. I left her here an hour ago and she was getting a manicure and a pedicure. The deluxe package." I was willing this woman to remember Mandy and where she was. "Maybe she's in the restroom?"

The woman shook her head again. "Nuh-uh," she told me again. "I started to give her the deluxe, and she said she'd changed her mind and left almost as soon as she'd sat down."

Which had been right after I'd turned my back on her and gotten the call from Grinkov. My heart *really* started to pound then, and I had an awful feeling. Angry as all get-out, I marched up to the clerk at the front and demanded she give me the credit card back. "I don't have it," she said, thoroughly confused. "Your friend took it with her when she left."

Breaking my no-swearing rule with a colorful string of expletives, I dashed out of the salon and ran back through the department store while I tried to hold my phone steady so I could call Dutch. His phone went straight to voice mail. "Call me!" I told him, winding and ducking my way through the crowd while my eyes scanned the area, in hopes of finding any sign of Mandy.

When I got to the parking garage, I dashed down the concrete runway in the direction of the car, now in almost a complete state of panic. I held my phone up as I went, looking to make sure Dutch hadn't called. At one point I paused long enough to call his cell again, but being underground cut off the reception and the call wouldn't go through. "Son of a beast!" I swore, changing directions, and nearly getting hit by a sleek luxury car as I headed back up to the corner of the garage where I thought I could get the call to go through.

I found a corner where two bars lit up on the cell phone display, and I tried Dutch impatiently. It went straight to voice mail again. "What the freak!" I nearly shouted, before bringing up Frost's info and calling him.

"Frost," he said abruptly.

"It's Abby," I told him. "Mandy's miss—"

That's as far as I got before I felt the most god-awful pain on the back of my head, and out went the lights.

Chapter Eleven

. . .

"Owwwwwwwww!" I heard myself say as I climbed out of the dizzying dark depths of unconsciousness.

"Lie still," said a silky voice I recognized.

"What the freak hit me?" I squawked, paying no attention to the command and trying to sit up. My head was ringing like the Liberty Bell.

"We've sent for the paramedics," said the voice. "You'll want to go to the hospital."

I opened my eyes to squint at Maks Grinkov, who was crouched down and holding me in his arms. Behind him stood his butler, talking rapidly on the phone. "No ambulance!" I told him sharply, then quickly regretted it.

Grinkov appeared surprised. "But you fainted," he said.

I felt the back of my head where a good-sized lump was forming. "I didn't faint," I told him. "Someone hit me."

Grinkov's expression turned grim and he looked up at his butler, who was talking urgently into the phone. Seeing that his boss wanted him, Eddington asked the person to hold the line and said, "Yes, sir?"

"Did you see anyone strike Ms. Carter before you reached her?"

Eddington appeared shocked. "No, sir! She was lying on the ground and I assumed she'd fainted."

"Nope," I said, really wishing the world would stop spinning and the sharp pain in my head would abate. "Someone hit me in the back of the head."

"Who?"

I closed my eyes again. "I've no idea."

"The paramedics will be here shortly," I heard Eddington say.

Gripping Maks's arm tightly, I begged him, "Please, don't let them take me."

"Why not?" he asked.

And for a moment I was at a loss to explain to him why I wouldn't want to go to the hospital. "Hospitals freak me out," I said, making up something quick. "I mean, people *die* in there, you know?"

Grinkov laughed lightly. "I hardly think you will die from your injuries," he told me.

I swallowed hard and pulled my feet up; using him as a brace, I got unsteadily to my feet. Eddington looked at me warily and said, "I really think you should lie still, ma'am."

I nodded. I thought that too, but now that he'd called for an ambulance, I needed to get the heck out of there before any records were created or the police were called in, but I knew I was too shaky to drive. "Would you take me back to Rick's place?" I asked Maks.

Again he looked surprised. "You don't want to go back to your apartment?"

I made a show of glancing down at my watch and even though I couldn't quite get my eyes to focus on the dial, I said, "He's expecting me, and you know how Rick's temper is. I don't want to be late."

Grinkov frowned, and in his eyes I knew he didn't care one lick for Rick's tempestuous nature. "We'll take you," he said, and helped me to his car, which I realized was the very one that had nearly hit me when I'd spun on my heel and hurried back up the ramp.

After we were inside and the driver was told where to go, I asked Maks, "What are you doing here, anyway?"

He smiled. "Looking for you."

It was my turn to look surprised. "Why?"

"I wanted to see you," he admitted, his eyes smoldering with interest. "And I wanted to perhaps help you pick out something appropriate for the auction."

Uh-oh.

"Ah," I said.

An awkward silence followed until Grinkov pointed to my purse and said, "Perhaps you should check to see if your attacker took anything."

I looked down and blinked. I hadn't even thought of that. Digging through my purse, I saw that my wallet and my stun gun were both missing. "Great," I grumbled. "I've been mugged."

The moment we cleared the parking garage, my phone, which was still clutched in my hand, blew up with incoming calls from both Dutch and Frost. I tried to answer Dutch's first but got Frost instead. "What's happening?" he demanded.

"Hey, Rick," I said, trying to make my voice sound easy and relaxed. "I'm on my way to your condo. I had a little misstep when I was out shopping, but I should be there in about, what, Maks, ten minutes or so?"

"Yes," he told me. "About that long."

"Are you okay?"

"Oh, yeah, no problem. And hey, if you see your girlfriend, tell her I saw those shoes she likes at Neiman's. They were on sale, and she *really* has to go there *now* to grab them before they *run off* with someone else."

"Mandy took off?" Frost hissed, putting the coded message together.

"Yep."

"Shit!" he said, and hung up.

Subtly I switched the phone to silent, even though I could see that Dutch was still trying to reach me. I couldn't risk answering another call in the car with Grinkov.

My head was still pounding really hard by the time we got to Des Vries's condo. I so wanted to get out of the car and make it through the garage and over to the elevator on my own, but the sides of my vision kept clouding in and I couldn't seem to focus or keep my balance.

Maks helped me from the car, making repeated requests to take me to the hospital, and I kept insisting that all I needed to do was lie down and have a little rest. I didn't know what to make of the fact that he was so genuinely concerned for me, and my head hurt way too much to think it through.

So I allowed him to help me over to the elevator, and he stood there, waiting patiently while I buzzed the intercom, because the doors would open only if you had a key card, and mine had been safely tucked inside my now-missing wallet. After a moment I heard Dutch's voice say, "Yeah?"

"Hey, Rick. It's me, Abigail. I lost my key card, so could you send down the elevator? Oh, and Maks is here. He'd like to come up to say hi."

There was a lengthy pause before the light at the top of the elevator pinged, and a few moments later the doors opened. Once we got inside, I noticed that in the slot was Dutch's key card. I pressed the button for the penthouse while Maks held me up the whole ride, which was good because I would have most definitely keeled over if he hadn't.

When the elevator doors parted again, Dutch stood in the foyer, looking tall and imposing, wearing his brown contacts and an angry look. "Where you been, Carter?" he demanded, in full Rick Des Vries–impersonation mode.

I smiled tightly. "Sorry. Maks was kind enough to escort me here. I got mugged."

"Mugged?"

"Yes. Someone hit me on the back of the head while I was in the parking garage at Eaton Centre, and the mugger stole my wallet, which had the key card in it."

A small vein near Dutch's left temple began to throb, a sure sign that he was upset, but otherwise, nothing about his expression or manner indicated he was at all alarmed. "Did you call the police?"

"Not yet. I was worried about making our meeting."

Grinkov stepped forward, getting into Dutch's personal space, and I could tell he didn't care for the way Dutch was interrogating me. "Abigail sustained a serious injury to the back of her head," he told Dutch icily. "I think she needs some ice and a chance to lie down."

Dutch's brown eyes swiveled from Maks to me and back again, the vein at his temple pulsing intensely now. I knew he was having a hard time staying in character, and so I did my level best to stay on my feet and not give in to the waves of dizziness washing over me. I was certain that if he showed any uncharacteristic concern for me, it would tip Grinkov off. "Yeah, okay," he said as if he didn't really care, and he stepped to the side and allowed us to come in.

I nearly groaned when I realized Grinkov was going to stick close behind me. I wobbled once as I moved past Dutch and I saw his hand jerk toward me. Reflexively and with supreme effort I tilted away from him and back toward Grinkov, who caught me under the arm and helped to steady me as we made our way into the living room. Once I was on the couch, I sat down and inhaled several deep breaths.

Dutch got me some ice wrapped in a dish towel and handed that to Grinkov, who sat next to me and placed it behind my head. The cool compress was so welcome I could have wept. "Thank you," I whispered.

"Does it hurt much?" Grinkov asked me.

I gave a tiny nod. "It's a killer."

"Rick," Grinkov said, his tone once again testy. "You must have some pain medicine. Get her something to help with the headache."

I heard Dutch shuffling around in the kitchen and then down the hallway to our bedroom. He came back out shortly and I opened my eyes to see him hand me a glass of water and the pill. "Who mugged you?" he asked.

"I don't know. I got knocked on the head, and when I came to, my wallet was missing."

Throb, throb, throb went Dutch's temple. "Huh," he grunted.

"Are you sure you don't want me to take you home?" Grinkov asked me, and I could tell he clearly didn't want to leave me in the dispassionate company of Rick Des Vries.

"I can take her," Dutch said quickly. "After all, she and I still need to go over some of the details for the auction."

Grinkov sighed like he didn't like that idea, but he let it go, thank

God. Getting to his feet, he looked down at me. "Please call me later to let me know you're feeling better," he said.

I forced a small smile. "Absolutely. And thank you again for the ride."

Grinkov then turned to the elevator and we all heard his phone give a beep. He pulled it out of his pocket and read the display before turning back to us. "It's a text from Boklovich. He has heard from his contact in possession of the drone. They will be attending the auction."

I resisted the urge to look at Dutch, afraid my emotions would give us away. "Great," I said. "I look forward to seeing who will get the highest price."

Grinkov smiled devilishly. "Yes," he said. "It should be a very successful event."

The moment the doors closed behind Grinkov, Dutch was at my side. "Jesus!" he said, pulling away the ice pack and parting my hair to look at the lump on the back of my head.

I hissed as he fussed around back there. "Easy, cowboy," I whispered.

He kissed my cheek and eased my head back against the cushion, looking critically at me again. "I think you have a concussion."

"Yep," I said, closing my eyes again and just praying that eventually the world would stop spinning.

"I'm calling Frost and having him send the doctor over."

"Good idea."

Dutch moved off the couch, and while he was dialing the phone, I asked, "Where is Frost anyway?"

"Out looking for Mandy." Frost must have come on the line then because Dutch began speaking fast and furious to him. In short order I learned that Frost had located Mandy and was bringing her back to the condo, and by the sound of it, the trip home wasn't going smoothly. Frost also assured Dutch that he would send the doctor right over.

The kindly man appeared at our door not ten minutes later, and when he sat down in front of me, he said, "You two seem to attract more than your fair share of trouble."

"Tell me about it," I said to him.

He told me to follow his penlight, which I had a heck of a time doing, and asked me several random questions like, "What is today's date?"

"Aww, man," I said honestly, "I don't remember. Since I've been on this mission, I haven't really looked at a calendar. I know it's sometime in May, right?"

The doctor smirked. "What's your birthday?"

"December twenty-ninth." I eyed Dutch humorously. "See? Even with a concussion I can remember it. How come you can't?"

"I forgot it *one* time," he replied with a laugh.

"Who is the prime minister of Canada?"

"Beats the heck out of me," I said.

At this point Frost came in handcuffed to Mandy, who was pulling and tugging and beating on him like crazy. "I *hate* you!" she screeched.

In spite of the awful pain in my head I couldn't help but smirk at him in an "I told you so" way.

The doctor had turned his attention away from me and he seemed somewhat alarmed by the commotion. "Doc," Frost asked him in exasperation. "Can you *do* something with her?"

The good doctor blinked. "Like what, Agent Frost?"

"I don't know, sedate her or something?"

"No!" Mandy shouted, tugging and pulling and hitting poor Frost for all she was worth.

Dutch stood abruptly and moved menacingly over to her. He didn't put up with crap like that. Mandy took one look at him and cowered, shielding her face as she cried, "Wait! I'm so sorry! Please, *please* don't hit me!"

Every single person in the room stopped to suck in a breath. "Oh, man," I whispered as Mandy crouched low and held up both her arms, trying to cover her face and her head, while she shivered pathetically from head to toe like a frightened puppy.

Dutch immediately backed off, and the look on his face told me flat out that he was disgusted by the character he was being forced to portray. Frost dug into his pocket and extracted the key to the handcuffs. In short order he had Mandy out of them and gently guided her over to the opposite side of the room, where he placed a blanket over her legs and switched on the television. She continued to shiver and cower for long after that, but at least she'd settled down.

The doctor went back to examining me, concluding that my concussion was likely mild but severe enough that he wanted me to consider getting a CT scan, which I refused. He then prescribed bed rest and a pain pill every eight hours as needed, and told both Dutch and Frost to call him if I began showing signs of confusion, disorientation, or if I began vomiting; much the same as he told them about me only a few days before, and Dutch a few days before that.

Dutch moved my legs onto the ottoman and brought a blanket from the bedroom, then replaced the ice pack behind my head with a fresh compress. During all this he also brought Frost up to speed on what had happened to me at Eaton Centre, and about Grinkov escorting me home.

"How did Grinkov find you at Eaton Centre of all places?" Frost asked.

"He called me right after I dropped Mandy at the nail salon. He wanted to have lunch and I told him I was there shopping. I don't know why he decided to come find me, but he did."

Dutch eyed me coolly for a minute but didn't say anything, and I sure as heck didn't add anything more to the explanation, as I could clearly see the vein in his temple throbbing again. Instead I decided to change the subject. "Where'd you find Mandy?"

"Same place you left her," Frost said, looking over his shoulder at her as she watched a *Friends* rerun. "She was still running around Eaton Centre like a wild child."

That surprised me. "When she took off, I had no idea where she'd gone. I assumed she'd hightail it out of the shopping area as fast as she could."

"When you called us to tell us that Mandy was missing, I didn't know exactly where you'd gone shopping, so I put a trace on the credit card I gave you. There was a charge at a nail salon located at Eaton Centre, and a few minutes later one at Coach, then another at Michael Kors and on and on. Basically we just followed the bread crumbs."

"Wow," I said. "What'd she buy?"

"What *didn't* she buy? In an hour she'd rung up fifteen thousand in purchases." Frost glared at Mandy, who was totally oblivious to anything but the TV.

I barely managed to stifle a laugh. "Where is all the stuff?"

"Being returned," Frost said. "And how'd you lose sight of her, anyway?"

It was my turn to look guilty. "I dropped her at the nail salon while I went to get Dutch some sunglasses."

"Why do I need sunglasses?" he asked.

I pointed him to my purse, because I remembered the glasses I'd purchased were thankfully still in my bag. "I wanted to get you the same kind Des Vries wore in the video that Frost showed me this morning. I figured your excuse could be that you're trying to hide the bruises around your eyes, and if that Arab guy shows up and sees you in the same sunglasses, he might not wonder so much why you look a little different than the man he remembers meeting with three years ago."

Dutch poked through my purse and lifted out the small bag from Neiman's. As he held them up, he took note of the tag and whistled. "These were expensive, Edgar."

"Des Vries wouldn't be seen in anything cheap," I assured him.

"No," he said. "What I mean is, the person who mugged you took your wallet and your stun gun while leaving behind a pair of three-hundred-dollar sunglasses?"

"Someone's definitely after you, Cooper," Frost said in a way that sent a chill down my spine.

"Maybe it was just a mugger who didn't have time to grab the sunglasses before Maks and his butler showed up," I argued, wanting that to be the case but knowing in my bones that Dutch and Frost were right. Someone had my number and wanted me out of the way.

"I don't think so," Dutch said, and I could tell he was weighing the argument to get me bumped off the case. "I think this might be the same guy who tried to strangle you, and possibly even the same person that took out Viktor."

"But we don't know for sure," I insisted. There was no way I was going to let Dutch use this as an excuse to go in by himself. I'd never see him again; of that I was certain. "I mean, the pattern is a little off, don't you think?"

"No," said Frost. "What're you getting at?"

"Well, to Dutch's point, if this is the same guy who first tried to include me in the murder of Kozahkov and his bodyguards, then tried to strangle me, why only bump me on the head? Why not kill me with the same gun he used to kill Viktor?"

I could tell that stumped both of them, and I used that momentum to further my argument. "It's almost as if the violence against me is being subdued on purpose. Don't get me wrong, guys—my head is killing me, but it wasn't a lethal blow by any measure. If the goal had been to kill me, then that's what should have happened. Instead, someone merely conked me on the head, then sifted through my purse and took my wallet. No assassin is going to knock someone out and sort through their personals in a crowded parking garage for cripe's sake! Trust me, this isn't an assassin. It's simply a thief who took advantage of me when I was alone, distracted, and vulnerable, and maybe he already had a pair of expensive sunglasses, or maybe he just didn't have time to grab them too."

Dutch and Frost exchanged a long look, and I could tell I'd managed to put a little bit of doubt into their theory. Finally, Frost said, "Fine. You can stay on the mission, but you're done going anywhere alone. And I don't care if Grinkov really wants to have you over for dinner again—the answer to him will be, 'After the auction,' you got that?"

I nodded obediently, even though the action hurt. "Got it."

Dutch's lips pressed together in a tight seal and he said nothing more. Instead, he turned on his heel and headed to the bedroom.

A while later Dutch joined us again and began cooking dinner. I was feeling less woozy and Mandy was peacefully watching TV, while Frost checked in with HQ. When he got off the phone, he didn't look happy. "There's been a development," he said, coming over to sit in the chair opposite me.

"What?" Dutch asked from his place at the stove.

"We've found Oksana Fedotova."

Dutch turned around, his brow raised. "The one we think was involved with the drone pilot and had a possible connection to Kozahkov?"

Frost nodded.

"Is she talking?" Dutch asked.

Frost shook his head. "She's dead. Her body was found in her car parked at long-term parking near the airport. She had a ticket to Toronto in her purse and two big suitcases full of clothes in the trunk."

I swallowed hard. "How long had she been dead?"

"At least a week," Frost said. "Maybe longer."

"How was she killed?" I pressed.

"Strangled," Frost told me.

"With a shoelace?" Dutch asked, and I knew why he was asking.

Frost shrugged. "Hard to say," he said. "Decomp barely allowed the ligature marks to appear, but her hyoid's been broken and no other obvious signs of trauma were found, so someone used something like that to take her out."

Dutch turned back to stir his sauce, but even from the couch I could hear him sigh heavily.

"So we've come to another dead end," I said, belatedly regretting the pun.

"We have," said Frost.

At that moment, Dutch's cell chimed and he pulled it out of his pocket to check the text. We all waited for him to tell us what it said, and finally he picked his head up and addressed us. "That's Grinkov. The auction is set. We leave for B.C. on his private jet tomorrow at noon."

That night I sat in the bedroom feeling much better physically, although I still had to suffer through the coming-to-Jesus meeting that Dutch and Frost were having with Mandy out in the kitchen. And trust me when I tell you that it was a very LOUD coming-to-Jesus meeting.

From what I could overhear, Mandy was still really miffed at the fact that Frost had taken away all her purchases, and Frost and Dutch were attempting to remind her of her arrangement with the United States government.

"What you fail to understand, Mandy," Frost was saying, "is that if you screw this up for us, it's not just Agent Rivers and Ms. Cooper whose lives will be at risk, but your own too."

"*I'm* not a spy!" she spat at him.

"Oh, but you are," Dutch countered smoothly. "At least, that's what Grinkov and Boklovich will assume if our identities are compromised. You won't live to file another nail, sweetheart."

"Then I won't go," Mandy told them.

"Which means your deal with us is off and you'll never see your boyfriend again," Frost warned her.

"Oh, screw him!" she shouted. "I could do way better than Rick!"

Swallowing hard, I eased myself out of the bed and shuffled into the kitchen, where the three were arguing. "Mandy!" I said to get her attention.

Everyone looked up at me. "What?" she snapped.

"If you don't come with us, then I'll personally tell Grinkov that my intuition is suggesting that *you* are working with the CIA as a spy. You know how well connected Grinkov is, and because he likes me and trusts me, he'll do a little research and find out about your arrangement with us. He'll put a hit out on you like that," I said, snapping my fingers to show her I was serious. "So you either come along and cooperate, playing the role of Rick's doting girlfriend, or you die. It's as simple as that."

Mandy visibly paled and I didn't even wait for her to reply. Instead, I turned on my heel and headed back to bed.

Later, Dutch came in and snuggled up close to me, spooning himself against my back. "You awake?" he whispered.

"Yeah. How're you doing?"

He kissed my shoulder. "Honestly?"

"Of course."

"I'm worried."

I sighed and squeezed his arms, which wrapped a little more tightly around me. This would be the last night we'd get to spend together until after the auction. "Do you think Mandy's going to blow it for us?"

"I don't know," he admitted. "What's your radar say?"

"My head's still throbbing, honey. There's no way I can tune in tonight."

"Which is yet another reason why I'd prefer you stay behind on this one."

I half turned in his arms to face him over my shoulder. "Nice try," I said sarcastically.

Even in the dark I could just make out Dutch's frown. "You just don't get it, do you?"

"What am I slow on the uptake about this time?"

"I couldn't handle it if anything happened to you."

I twisted all the way around then to face him and cupped his face with my hands. "And you expect me to handle it okay if something happens to *you*?"

"Yes," he said frankly. "You're beautiful and you're talented and you'd find someone else in no time."

I shook my head. "My God, Dutch, I think you're probably the dumbest man on earth, and it's clear you don't understand women at all. You're right. Maybe you *should* go first."

I could feel his smile under my palms. "That's what I keep trying to tell you, Edgar."

I kissed him tenderly. "I love you every bit as much as you love me, cowboy, and you're not shaking me loose on this one. We go in together or not at all. Period."

"Okay," he said, a bit reluctantly.

"Really?"

Dutch sighed heavily. "Yeah. I guess we don't have a choice. But we're coming out of this alive, you hear me?"

I kissed him again. "Oh, I hear you. After all, we've got a wedding to plan, remember?"

"Just not in six months," he said, his expression playful.

"No way," I laughed. "I want *lots* of time to plan. Maybe next June or July."

"April," he teased.

I laughed again and kissed him. "Okay, April," I said, giving in.

"November," he said next.

My eyes widened. "You're pushing your luck, buddy."

"What?" he said, all innocence and boyish charm. "You gave in on April pretty easily."

"Yeah, but you're going all the way back to November now and taking off even more time to plan."

"I like November," Dutch told me. "It feels right."

I giggled. "Oh, so now *you're* the psychic?"

"Yeah," he said. "Maybe you're rubbing off on me. My parents got married in November and they've had a really great forty-six-year marriage. My brother and his wife got married in November too, and they seem pretty rock solid. It's a good omen, Abs. November is a great month for a wedding."

"What happened to my argument about not planning the wedding in six months because I don't want to rush it?"

"November is *seven* months away," Dutch insisted. "That's six months *plus* another whole month. Plenty of time."

I rolled my eyes and kissed him again. "There's no winning with you, is there?"

Dutch's face became serious again. "I don't want to wait," he whispered. "I want to marry you, Abigail Cooper, and putting it off feels wrong. We don't need a big fancy wedding. Just you, me, and the preacher."

I sighed. "I can't promise that I can do November, Dutch. I mean, I know you're thinking it doesn't matter what our wedding day is like, but it matters to me. I want it to be special, not rushed and last-minute, okay?"

"Okay," he said, squeezing my hand. "Just promise me that you'll meet me at the end of that aisle, okay?"

I looked him dead in the eyes and whispered, "I pinkie swear, cowboy."

That night I had that dream again. I was free-falling from a very high place with no explanation of where I'd fallen from, just the air rushing past my face and the ground approaching with frightening speed. I woke with a jolt and sat bolt upright, my back and neck coated in sweat. Beside me Dutch slept on, and I wanted to wake him to tell him about it, but knew he'd need his sleep to keep his wits about him for the auction.

I wondered what the heck my subconscious was trying to tell me, and tried to avoid the obvious: that the free fall was my panicked response to discussions of weddings and becoming Dutch's wife. But I couldn't avoid looking at it from that perspective.

The weird thing was that consciously I really *did* want to marry him and I really *did* want to take my time planning the wedding because I wanted it to be perfect and a day I would always remember.

But the dream was certainly telling. I had it only when he brought up the wedding and our discussion turned to rushing me down that aisle.

With a sigh I lay down again and decided that the moment this mission was over, I was going to look at a calendar and set a date that I was comfortable with and not give in to anyone else who wanted to pressure me into doing it sooner.

Still, when I closed my eyes to go back to sleep, I had the most unsettling feeling that I'd missed the point entirely.

Early the next morning we met with Frost and Mandy in the kitchen. Frost seemed agitated, and he told us he'd need to speak with us privately after he briefed us on the game plan for the auction. During the briefing, Dutch and I took diligent notes, while Mandy looked bored, but every once in a while I caught her subtly paying attention. "Boklovich has an estate just north of Victoria, B.C., on Salt Spring Island. The island is really only accessible by plane or boat, and Boklovich has got his own personal landing strip near his estate.

"The estate is heavily guarded, and there's nothing around it for miles but wilderness. In other words, once you guys are there, there's no way we can get to you quickly. You'll be completely cut off."

I tried not to gulp too loudly as I considered the satellite map of Boklovich's estate. The compound itself was massive, given the scale of it compared with the surrounding trees, and I could see the small brown strip nearby that must have been Boklovich's landing strip. Extending out in all directions from the main house was nothing but wilderness for miles and miles. If things went south, Dutch and I would be on our own all right.

"When you get in there, you'll need to identify the drone thief and gain access to Intuit. You'll be looking for a small black box six inches by six inches. If it's still mounted to the drone, it'll be right under the belly, cradled between the wings. If you can't steal it back, then you'll need to insert this into the USB port located on the top left-hand side of the device."

Frost held up a small silver flash drive and handed it to Dutch. "Once inserted, a virus will load which will render Intuit completely useless within twenty-four hours."

"Twenty-four hours is still plenty of time to do some damage," Dutch said, pocketing the flash drive.

Frost nodded. "Which is why you'll need to assess the situation early and load the program if you're unable to take Intuit with you when you make your escape. We would have instructed you to load the flash drive and devised it to kill Intuit immediately, but we considered that Boklovich will likely require you and the thief to hold a demonstration of Intuit's capabilities to legitimize the sale and also drive up the price. We're hoping that both devices will go to one individual, which will also help us identify who is most anxious to cause the U.S. and its allies harm."

"Will the software you gave us actually work?" I asked, noticing the small CD on the table.

"Yes," Frost told me. "But the CD has been loaded with two passwords to bypass the encryption code. One password will let you in and allow you to copy the software to any computer. The other password will let you in and appear to copy the software, but not before releasing a Trojan virus which will send a code back to our mainframes and lead us right to you. If we cannot locate the computer the software is loaded to within twenty-four hours, it will self-destruct, taking down any system it's connected to in the process."

"It's a time-release kill switch," I said, summing it up.

"Exactly. In the meantime you all know what your respective roles are. Mandy, you have to sell the attendees on the fact that Agent Rivers is the real Rick Des Vries. We can't know how many of these people have actually met Rick face-to-face, so you're there to sell them on the idea and help navigate him away from those people who may know Rick too well for Rivers to be able to pull off the disguise."

"I know," Mandy said moodily. My head was feeling better, so I used my radar to follow the thread of Mandy going along with the story that Dutch was Rick, and I was more than a little relieved to sense that she'd fully cooperate; however, there was also another thread that told me I couldn't fully trust her and I'd better keep my eye on her.

"Cooper," Frost said next, and I snapped my attention to him. "You and Rivers need to cool it."

My brow furrowed. "Cool what?"

"Your attraction to each other is palpable, and we're trying to sell your presence at this thing as Des Vries's business associate, not his lover. Mandy's filling that role, so you *have* to distance yourself from him emotionally. When you look at him, in your mind you've got to be looking at Rick Des Vries. Got it?"

I could feel my cheeks flush with anger. I thought I'd been doing a great job of portraying Abigail Carter so far, but as I chanced a look at Dutch, I could see that Frost's warning was sinking in with him too. More than anything, his expression told me there was something to the warning and I'd better listen. "I hear you," I told him. "He's Rick Des Vries, weapons dealer and a real son of a beast."

Frost's shoulders seemed to relax, and that tempered my attitude even more. I could clearly see he'd been worried about how I'd take the advice. "It would be a good idea for you to continue to play coy with Grinkov too," he added, looking at the tabletop. "He seems to like you, and that may work to our advantage."

Dutch's hand clenched once, but then he relaxed it. I knew he hated the idea, but he'd be good and play along. "Understood," I said, hoping our handler would move on.

Frost nodded like he'd gotten the hard stuff out of the way, then reached under the table and pulled out a small briefcase. Opening it, he began to extract items one at a time. "Here," he said, handing me a silver subcompact pistol no bigger than my hand. "It's small," he admitted, "but it'll do the job."

I took the gun, which was far heavier than it looked, and set it aside, nearly smiling when I realized that just a month ago I would have shaken my head and refused to accept the weapon.

Frost handed Dutch a much bigger gun. "This is Des Vries's actual weapon," he said. "It's a Beretta Px4 Special Duty with a custom grip and you'll note that it doesn't handle like your Glock, but I'm sure you can manage."

Dutch took the gun from Frost and inspected it moodily. I could tell he didn't like the Beretta, which I knew from my week of gun training was quite a different gun from the Glock, but Dutch nodded and said, "I'll make it work."

"Remember, the biggest difference between it and your Glock is that the Beretta's got a safety," Frost told him. "Pull the trigger with that safety on, and nothing's gonna happen."

"Got it," Dutch said, tucking the pistol away.

Next Frost handed Dutch and me two retractable ballpoint pens, one with a green cap and one with a red cap. He handed Mandy a pen too; her cap was also red. Mandy snatched hers, clicked the top, and immediately began to try to doodle on the newspaper. "Mine's broken," she announced when no ink appeared. She then threw the pen into the middle of the table and pouted like a five-year-old.

Frost gave her a look that was, well . . . frosty. "It's not a pen," he growled.

"Looks like a pen."

Frost inhaled a deep breath, then reached for the instrument and twisted the red cap. A tiny beep came from the top and five seconds later Frost's phone began ringing. He answered the line with a snappy, "Location and signal strength, please." After a pause he added, "Good. Please log this as a test, Agent Brewster. Thank you for the prompt alert."

I looked at my pens more closely. "Are these homing devices?"

"Yes," Frost said, handing the pen back to Mandy with a steely glare. "If you twist the cap on the one with the red cap, it will send out an alert signal and we'll know you've been compromised. We'll then dispatch a team to attempt your recovery. I want to make it clear that you should activate the pens only as a last resort, because the odds that we'll make it to you before you're hunted down and killed are running in the ten-to-twenty percentiles."

Ah, Frost. Ever the optimist.

"The pen with the green cap is an electronic scrambler. If you're in a position to make an escape, twist the cap and hide it anywhere within five feet of Boklovich's digital command center. It will turn all his video surveillance monitors to snow and give you guys the opportunity to get out of there without being tracked by camera."

"How will we even know where his command center is?" I asked.

"It will likely be somewhere in the center of his compound, inside the main building. You and Dutch will have to do some surveillance on your own to find it."

I looked uneasily at Dutch. He mouthed, "It's okay" to me, but I hardly felt better. This mission was proving to be far more complicated than I'd ever imagined.

"Carry the pens on your person at all times," Frost said to us.

I put the pen in my pocket and hoped I'd never have to use it.

Next, Frost pulled out what looked like two small manicure cases. Unzipping them, he revealed the usual toenail clippers, cuticle scissors, and nail file. Mandy leaned in, looking especially interested. "Where's mine?" she demanded.

Frost ignored her and focused on me and Dutch. "Pull out the clippers and the back panel will open," he said, demonstrating by removing the clippers and revealing a small tab that allowed the lining of the case to be removed. Behind the panel were several small syringes, lined up neatly and held in place by thin elastic bands. My stomach flipped over. I knew exactly what those were. "How many shots would we need?" I asked.

"Two," he said. "And they must be delivered in quick succession within a minute or two of getting hit."

"Are those drugs?" Mandy asked, her eyes large and immediately interested.

Frost turned to her, completely out of patience, and said, "You may be excused, Mandy."

Mandy stuck her tongue out at him and clomped off loudly to her bedroom, leaving her pen behind. Frost eyed it with such irritation that I picked it up and said, "I'll make sure she holds on to it."

Frost looked like he was working to rein in his temper, and after a minute he said, "I wish we didn't need her. But she's the only one who can help cover Rivers here as Des Vries."

"It'll be okay," I told him, only half sure it would be.

"Is there anything else?" Dutch asked, trying to get the briefing back on track.

"Yes, two things," Frost said. "First, I got a call this morning from the agent leading the investigation into whomever hacked into the drone's flight path to fly it over the border. We believe it was someone named Diedrich Wyngarden. He's a rather infamous hacker based in Holland, but we think he may have been on the move recently, and we think we've discovered an alias he uses here in Canada."

"Wyngarden," I said. Why did that name sound so familiar?

"Is he Anna's brother?" Dutch asked.

"Cousin," Frost told him.

"Wait, who?" I asked, still having trouble recalling the name.

"Anna Wyngarden was the girl Des Vries is thought to have murdered, and the reason he fled Holland," Frost reminded me.

My jaw fell open. "That cannot be a coincidence!"

"Exactly what we were thinking, and that explains why you thought there was some connection between the drone theft and Des Vries. We think Diedrich set up the heist to make it appear Des Vries took the drone, so that we'd go after him. The fact that Des Vries got nabbed by the Israelis was an unforeseen coincidence, and we doubt that Diedrich even knows about it."

I looked at Dutch. "Which means that Dutch's life is in serious danger if Diedrich shows up at the auction, because either he'll expose Dutch as an impostor or he'll buy the disguise and try to kill Dutch to avenge his cousin."

"Yes," Frost said simply.

"You guys have a handle on where Diedrich might be?" Dutch asked.

"No, and that's what's so troubling. Our guys have been able to trace his signature hacking tags right up until ten days ago; then nothing. It's like he's gone completely radio silent, which is highly unusual for this guy. He hacks compulsively, but now we can't find his signature anywhere."

"What's his connection to Kozahkov and the Chechen Mafia?" I asked.

Frost sighed. "So far, we can't find a connection," he admitted.

"Viktor did say he was contacted by a newcomer," Dutch reminded us.

I had an unsettling feeling about all of this. Something didn't fit, but I couldn't put my finger on it.

"In any case," Frost continued, pulling up a picture and showing it to us, "you'll need to be on the lookout for this guy."

I stared at the image. "No, we won't."

"Yes, you will," Frost insisted. "This is Diedrich Wyngarden."

"No," I told him. "*That* is a dead man who *used* to be Diedrich Wyngarden."

Frost turned the picture around to look at it. "How do you know he's dead?" he asked me.

I tapped my temple. "It's one of the many perks of my particular talent," I told him. "If you show me a photograph, I always know when someone's dead, and that guy has definitely expired."

"Shit," said Frost. "Then we've got another player in this and no idea who it is."

"Which is right where we were before we knew about Diedrich," Dutch pointed out. "I say we move forward with the plan, Frost."

Our handler nodded and got on with the briefing by handing us each a small compass and a map with a grid. "We know that Boklovich has an electronic scrambler of his own over most of his compound, so using your cell phones will be impossible. If you use the homing pens, you've got to get outside of the compound's perimeter. Their signal strength is good enough to get through the scrambler from about fifty yards outside the walls, but you won't be able to get a clear signal on your cells for several miles beyond that. If you activate the pens, try to follow the coastline on the east side of the island to this location." Frost pointed to a small section of the aerial map that had almost nothing but green around it. Faintly, however, when I looked closer, I could detect another patch of light green, as if the area was a large clearing near the water. "This is another unused airstrip," Frost said. "We should be able to drop in a helicopter or small plane to retrieve you if the worst happens."

My radar pinged when Frost said those words, but I didn't say what was circling around in my brain, which essentially was, *Expect the worst.*

Later, as I was packing, Frost found me and came into the bedroom to have a private chat. "You up for this, Cooper?"

My hands were shaking a little, and I had the most foreboding feeling about going on this mission, but what could I do? If I backed out, I knew Dutch would carry on, and sending him in alone was sending him to his death; of that I was positive. "I'm up for it," I told him hoarsely.

He was silent for a time, watching me pack, and I had to admit that his company actually helped to calm me. "You're attracted to Grinkov," he said suddenly, and the calm I'd been feeling left in a flash.

I even dropped the sweater I'd been holding. *"What?"*

Frost had a slight smile at the corners of his mouth; he knew he'd hit a nerve. "I've heard the two of you together," he said. "It's obvious that you're attracted to him, and that you like him in spite of who he is."

I didn't know what to say, so I just reached down and grabbed the sweater, turning away to refold it for my suitcase. "You can use that to your advantage," he added, and it felt like he was trying to goad me.

I rounded on him, angry and defensive. "What do you want me to say, Frost? I mean, how can I even respond to something like that? You saw what he did to Dutch! You know he's a ruthless criminal! How could you accuse me of being attracted to someone like *that*?"

Frost's eyes clouded with something unexpected. If I had to guess, I'd say it was regret. "You were right about my wife," he said softly.

I blinked. "Wait. . . . What?"

"My wife, who was murdered," he explained. "She was killed by the man who'd recruited her for the FSB."

"What's the FSB?" I said, still blinking and trying to catch up.

"Its former name was the KGB."

I sat down on the bed, clutching the sweater. "Your wife was a double agent?"

Frost nodded. "Yes."

"And you found out about it?"

"Yes."

Neither one of us spoke for several seconds. Finally, I told him what I thought. "Your energy is suggesting that you betrayed her in some way."

Frost looked steadily at me, but I didn't think he was actually seeing me as much as he was seeing what unfolded with his wife so many years ago. "I was going to turn her in," he admitted. "And I made the fatal mistake of hinting that I was going to do that. She told her superiors, who decided that she was too much of a risk to keep alive. She was run down outside of our home early the next morning. We never found the car and we never officially learned who ordered the hit, but I know that I caused her death, and it kills me just a little bit every single day."

In that moment I felt terribly sorry for Frost, especially now that I'd gotten to know him and found him to be a really decent man. "Why are you telling me this now?"

His eyes came back to focus on me again. "Because, Cooper, I wanted you to understand that it's possible to be attracted to your enemy. Hell, you can even love them, and still find a way to do the right thing. It's hard, but it's not impossible."

I smiled sadly at him. "Okay, Frost. I get it."

He stood and came over to me. "A lot of this hinges on you, you know."

"No pressure, though, right?"

He squeezed my shoulder and left.

Chapter Twelve

. . .

Dutch, Mandy, and I met Grinkov at the small Bishop Airport, where his private jet was docked. Eddington was there to help us load our baggage and see us onto the plane. I'd dressed casually in a pair of camel pants and an ivory sweater coat with faux rabbit-fur collar, and I was relieved to see Grinkov dressed in jeans and a navy blue blazer with a crisp white shirt. Dutch . . . I mean *Rick* was similarly attired in jeans and a brown tweed sport coat, while Mandy was in her usual hoochie skirt, six-inch stilettos, and tight pink sweater.

Her skinny knees were bright red from the cold—it was unseasonably chilly—and her teeth chattered as she boarded the plane. Still, I had to give her some credit; she was hanging all over my fiancé as if he were her one and only true love. Dutch was doing a great job of masking his distaste, which I picked up on my radar, but wasn't otherwise visually apparent.

Remembering Frost's words to me, I chose to sit near the front, where I guessed Grinkov would be, and I was happy that he did in fact choose the seat right next to mine.

"Are you comfortable?" Maks asked when he'd settled in.

I felt my pulse quicken. Sweet Jesus, he was sexy. To distract my-self, I looked around the luxurious interior filled with roomy creamy leather seats and polished wood. "Very much so, thank you."

The captain came on board then and nodded to Grinkov, who nodded back. "We'll be departing shortly, sir," the captain told him.

"Excellent, Bruce," Grinkov replied.

Eddington also appeared in the doorway, setting aside his walking stick to pull up the ladder and close the door before taking his seat in the back of the plane. I was a little surprised that Grinkov would bring his butler, but reasoned that Maks probably wanted to keep an eye on Eddington now that I'd pegged him for an art thief.

I still felt bad about that, but, at least I'd saved his life.

We were airborne shortly after that, and the moment we reached cruising altitude, Eddington began passing out flutes of champagne and serving us toast and caviar. I looked at the little black granules with barely hidden disgust and didn't notice that Grinkov was eyeing me curiously. "You don't like caviar?" he asked me.

I forced myself to smile. "It's not really my favorite."

Grinkov chuckled and removed the plate we were sharing from the table in front of us. "You should have mentioned it the other night," he told me. "I would have prepared you something else."

"Don't worry about it," I told him hastily. "I'm not very hungry."

Grinkov snapped his fingers, however, and Eddington appeared at his side. "Yes, sir?"

"Take this away and bring us something else, William."

The tray was removed and I felt instantly better.

"Are you looking forward to the auction?" Grinkov asked me next.

I took a sip of champagne and resisted the urge to look over at

Dutch. I had to keep mentally checking myself from glancing over at him to see how he was faring with Mandy. "I am."

"Vasilii will want a demonstration," he said, leaning in so that we couldn't be overheard. "Is the software encoded?"

"It is. But Rick and I both have the password." I offered him that tidbit so that he'd know Rick and I were truly partners in the deal, and not try to cut me out of the auction.

Grinkov's eyes squinted and I swore there was a hint of alarm there. "Tell no one that you both have the password," he whispered.

Eddington appeared at our side and Maks sat back to allow the butler to serve us a plate of assorted cheeses and fruit. Once he'd left us alone again, I leaned in toward Grinkov and asked, "Why shouldn't we reveal that we both have the password?"

"It's too dangerous," Maks said. "The people joining us at Boklovich's estate are some of the most ruthless, treacherous, and cutthroat men in the world. They will not hesitate to use any means possible to gain what they want, and believe me, Abigail, they are all most anxious to have this technology."

"You think one of them would try to kidnap me to get Rick to give up the software?"

"No," Grinkov said, and his answer surprised me. "I think they would kill Rick, steal the software, and torture you to get the password."

I gasped. I couldn't help it; the idea of that shocked me to my toes.

Grinkov squeezed my hand. "Don't look so worried," he said. "Boklovich has many armed men with orders to keep the peace and everyone safe, and I will be especially concerned with your well-being, but you'll still be wise to take some precautions. And one of those should be to keep your role as Rick's partner very subdued. We'll say that you are his accountant to take the mystery out of things."

I nodded dully. "Okay."

"After this is over," he said, his eyes lingering seductively on mine, "I would like you to consider another partnership altogether."

I cocked an eyebrow. "Oh, really?"

He grinned, and lifted my hand to brush his lips against my fingers. Heat seeped up into my cheeks and I tried in vain to keep my quickening pulse in check. "Rick is a bad choice in business partners," he said softly, and I was relieved he didn't look behind him to where I could feel Dutch's gaze boring a hole into my back.

"He seems to have been a good choice so far," I told Maks.

My companion's lips lingered delicately over my fingers again. His breath was warm against the skin of my knuckles. "Yes," he agreed. "But I'm convinced he is someone with an expiration date, and he may not live long beyond the auction."

I narrowed my eyes at him. "What do you know?"

Maks laid my hand down gently on the armrest and shrugged his shoulders. "There are rumors," was all he would say. "And if I were you, Abigail, I would consider, where there is smoke, there's fire."

"Someone's got a hit out on Rick?"

Maks shrugged again, as if we were talking about a sports game he wasn't especially interested in.

This time I did glance behind me. Dutch was looking pointedly out the window while Mandy snuggled close to him, and although he wasn't resisting her, his posture was stiff and distant.

I turned back to Grinkov, who was selecting from the assorted cheeses to put on a slice of apple. "Thank you for the warning," I said. "I'd be happy to discuss this with you further."

Grinkov must have thought I meant the partnership, because he said, "Excellent. I believe we will be a very good team, Abigail."

We landed several hours later at the small landing strip on a good-sized island not far from the city of Victoria, B.C. Looking down with rapt attention at the scenery as we approached our destination, I was struck by the beauty of the place. I'd never been to the Pacific Northwest and even from the air it was spectacular. Huge evergreens carpeted steep mountainous terrain, and breathtaking gorges opened to wide beautiful valleys, while snaking rivers twisted their way through the landscape. But gazing at all this beauty was also tempered by the realization that it was incredibly remote. For miles and miles and *miles* around there wasn't anything but wilderness, and it further clarified how precarious our situation was if things got dicey.

We landed a bit on the bumpy side, which earned our poor pilot a glare from his boss, but otherwise our flight was without incident. Eddington did his duty with the door and the short ladder, standing at the bottom to help me and Mandy climb down in our heels.

Once I was on the grass, I became aware of the chill this close to dusk. I hadn't brought a coat and was already regretting it. A limousine appeared and stopped in front of our plane. A chauffeur bounded out and hurried to help Eddington with our luggage. While we waited for them to load our gear, another vehicle appeared—an army green Hummer with several men in fatigues and assorted assault weapons.

At the sight of them, Grinkov swore under his breath, and every hair on the back of my neck stood on end. This was about to get ugly; I was sure of it.

Instinctively I edged a little closer to Dutch until I caught myself and moved in the other direction, closer to Maks. "What gives?" I whispered to him, lifting my chin in the direction of the armed guards.

"My friend Vasilii has chosen not to trust me," Grinkov snarled. He then wrapped a protective arm around me and whispered a warning. "Call no unnecessary attention to yourself and if asked, tell them you're with me."

I had a terrible feeling about this, but there wasn't much I could do, and sure enough, the clear leader of the soldiers approached Dutch and stuck a handgun right in his face. He barked something in a foreign language, which I guessed was Russian, and Dutch glowered at him before putting his hands in the air. The soldier never wavered as he held Dutch at gunpoint and another soldier stepped up and began to pat down my fiancé, while Mandy backed away and hid behind Eddington. Another order was barked and Dutch grudgingly spread his legs while growling something at the man with a gun in his face.

"A slight inconvenience, Richard," Grinkov told Dutch loudly, and I could hear the tone in his voice meant, "Simmer down, dude."

The soldier patting Dutch removed Des Vries's gun and held it out for his leader, who looked at it thoughtfully before tucking it into his belt. The soldier then discovered the CD with the Intuit program's software on it. This he also handed to his leader, who smiled like he knew exactly what he held in his hands before motioning to a man still in the truck.

The guy in the Hummer got out and carried with him a laptop computer. Opening the laptop, the soldier took the CD and inserted it into the disk drive. We all waited tensely while the computer booted up and the program loaded. More words I couldn't understand were exchanged and Dutch shook his head no.

The soldier with the gun in Dutch's face moved the muzzle slightly to the right and fired right next to Dutch's ear. I yelped—I truly couldn't help it—and Grinkov squeezed my waist and hissed, *"Shhh!"*

Next to me, still hiding behind Eddington, Mandy stood completely frozen in terror, but she found her voice the moment the soldier pointed the gun back in Dutch's face to bark his command again. "Give him the damn password, Rick!" she pleaded.

Several tense seconds passed while Dutch glared hard at the soldier, and then he said something too softly for me to catch. Again another tense moment seemed to pass until Grinkov stepped in. "Allow him to enter the code, Yurik. It's a reasonable request, after all."

I held my breath as Yurik glared hard into the eyes of the man I loved. I could tell a lot about this soldier—his energy was especially loud, and I knew he was cold-blooded and ruthless, capable of killing someone and not thinking twice about it.

Finally the soldier lowered the weapon to Dutch's chest and waved it at the laptop. Dutch cautiously stepped over to the computer and bent down to turn the screen away from prying eyes while quickly typing in the password. He then turned the screen around to show the soldiers. They all leaned in and eyed the screen almost greedily and then Dutch did something completely unexpected. He snatched the laptop and lifted it high before bringing it down with all his might on the ground, smashing it into a dozen pieces. In the seconds that followed and without even looking up at the soldiers, Dutch fished around the parts until he found the CD, and tucked it back into his pocket. He then got to his feet again, his arms back above his head, staring defiantly at Yurik like he was double-dog-daring him to shoot.

The stunned silence that followed was palpable in a god-awful way.

I'd stopped breathing and such a terrible foreboding crept over me while I watched the lead soldier raise his gun at Dutch's head again, his finger already moving to squeeze the trigger.

Maks let go of me and stepped forward very quickly. "Yurik!" he said in a commanding voice. "If you shoot him, Vasilii will not be able to auction off the program. His patrons will demand a demonstration after all, and without Rick, we lose the password."

I was trembling now as I knew that all Maks had to do was point to me and say, "She knows the password," and Dutch's life would be over. But he didn't, and Yurik's cold eyes suggested that he was thinking that over very carefully. Finally, he lowered his gun and began to turn away. I sucked in a ragged breath, completely relieved that the moment had passed, when all of a sudden, Yurik whirled back around and swung the gun viciously at Dutch's face, striking him an awful blow across the cheek.

Dutch's head snapped sideways and he lost his balance, falling hard on the ground amid the shattered pieces of the laptop.

It took every single fiber of resistance I had in me not to leap to Dutch's side when he fell, and I can't even fully describe the awful feeling of watching another woman go to his aid when Mandy dropped down next to him and attempted to stanch the flow of blood now gushing from his cheek.

"You son of a bitch!" I snarled, and Yurik turned to consider me, as if he was noticing me for the first time.

"Who is dis?" he asked Grinkov.

Maks's eyes shot to me, his look demanding that I say nothing more. "She's with me, Yurik."

The soldier sniffed the air, as if smelling my anger and fear. "Tell her to shut her mouth," he snapped. "Or I'll do it for her."

With effort I lowered my eyes. "My apologies," I said through tight lips. "Maks, I didn't mean to cause any trouble."

Maks came back to my side and took me firmly by the hand. "We'll discuss this later," he said coldly.

I nodded and did my best to avoid looking at Dutch. It hurt too much to see him on the ground, bleeding and beyond my help. Yurik barked a few more orders to his men, and when I looked up again, I saw that he was handing Maks Des Vries's gun while the other soldiers moved back to the Hummer. Yurik then got into the vehicle with the other men and took off without a backward glance.

The moment their SUV was in motion, I pulled out of Maks's grip and raced over to the back of the limo where the chauffeur was standing next to the open trunk. "Do you have a towel or something I can give him to stanch the blood?" I asked desperately.

"Let me look in the front of the car, miss," he said, and hurried to the front. I then began to dig through the bags to get to my own luggage for something suitable, but I had a hard time of it because several other bags were on top. Mandy's suitcase was huge and still had the old tags on it. I pulled and tugged it out of the way—it was just like her to pack too many clothes—and then yanked aside another smaller suitcase that was right on top of mine. Pushing it to the side, I saw something that shocked me down to my toes. Sticking out of a side pocket of the other luggage was the top of my wallet. I pulled it free just to make sure, and there on the side was the small tear I'd put in it a year ago. "You son of a beast," I whispered, eyeing Grinkov angrily while his attention was still on the departing SUV. The remaining bag had to be his, and I thought about what a fool I'd been to believe his story about finding me in the garage already unconscious. He'd been the one that'd struck me and taken my wallet, and I thought I knew why.

"I've found a towel," the driver said, and I jumped with a little squeal. Ramming my wallet back into the pocket where it came from, I turned and forced a smile, then took the towel and raced over to Dutch, who was being helped to his feet by Maks and Mandy. "Here, Rick," I said, handing over the towel. Dutch placed it on the side of his cheek and winced.

We all waited for him to stop the bleeding, and I ached to reach out and comfort him, but I didn't dare. Finally he nodded that he was ready to get out of the cold and we moved over to the limo, where the driver had all the doors open.

Inside, Dutch and Mandy took up the seats facing the back of the car while me, Maks, and Eddington took up the seats facing the front. Once the driver had shut all the doors and got in, Maks placed an arm around my shoulders and handed Des Vries's gun to Dutch.

Dutch stared at it for a moment, his eyes moving angrily from Maks, to the gun, to me . . . and then he lifted it out of Maks's palm and aimed it right at his face.

I held my breath, but Mandy squeaked and backed away from Dutch to plug her ears and close her eyes. "What the fuck, Maks?" Dutch growled.

Grinkov stiffened slightly next to me, and I looked sideways at him to gauge his reaction. His face revealed nothing but calm, cool, and collected, but next to him I did notice that Eddington had shifted his arm across his middle, and I had no doubt the butler was packing and reaching for his own gun.

"My apologies, Rick," the Chechen said blithely. "I believe your reputation precedes you."

"My *reputation*?" Dutch snapped, and the gun in his hand inched closer to Maks's face.

"Vasilii doesn't trust you," Maks said. "And after that stunt you pulled in Palestine, can you blame him?"

I had no idea what Maks was talking about. Dutch was far more familiar with Des Vries's background than I was, but something caught me off guard and I focused quickly on Maks's energy. He was bluffing. I wiggled the index finger of my left hand out of Maks's view to gain Dutch's attention and his eyes darted to it, then back to Maks. "*What* stunt in Palestine?" he snapped, and I could have sagged with relief that he'd read the warning signal correctly.

Maks smiled slyly. "Forgive me," he said. "I meant the stunt you pulled in Dubai."

I thought he might be referring to the arms deal that went south with the Arab sheikh, and Dutch must have assumed so too because he dropped the gun slightly and asked, "Is Sheikh Omar attending the auction?"

"He is."

Dutch put his gun back in his holster. "That's going to make things tricky," he said. "Omar and I have issues."

"Yes," Maks agreed. "And Vasilii will be forced to keep the peace until the auction is concluded, but he's already demonstrated where his loyalties run, Rick, and they seem to be leaning toward the man with the money."

Dutch wiped the rest of the blood off his cheek with the towel. "You'll run defense?" he asked Maks directly.

"I'll do what I can," Maks said, leaning in and lowering his voice so that the driver could not overhear. "Which is why I told Yurik that Ms. Carter is with me. If Boklovich suspects that she is your business partner, he will assume she knows how to access the disk. And I have little doubt that Vasilii will use any advantage he has to get what he wants."

I remembered how Grinkov had insisted I stay away from the meeting between him, Dutch, and Boklovich. "So you knew he'd react this way," I said accusingly. "You knew that Boklovich would pull something like that even before we came here."

"I knew it could go either way," he admitted, and his energy suggested he wasn't lying. "Which was why I arranged for Rick to meet with Boklovich last week without you. I had hoped that as well as that meeting had gone, that Vasilii would extend us a level of trust, but Boklovich is nothing if not unpredictable, which is why you would do well to keep on your toes, Rick, and pretend that you have only just been introduced to my companion, Ms. Abigail Carter."

Dutch's face was unreadable, but I knew he detested the idea of the new ruse being forced upon us. I wanted to try to make it easier on him, so I said, "It's fine, Maks. And I appreciate you doing your best to protect our interests and our lives. We'll play along just to get through the auction."

Mandy, ever the self-preservationist, asked, "Mr. Grinkov? Can I be your girlfriend too?"

Dutch rounded on her furiously and she did a great job of cowering in her seat, shivering and muttering apologies. Once she'd settled down again, Maks asked Dutch, "I'm assuming she doesn't know how to access the software?"

"You think I'd share that with *her*?" he snapped, as if that were the dumbest idea he'd ever heard.

Maks smiled. "No," he said. "Of course not."

Dutch moved his jaw in a way that suggested he was testing its soreness. When he lifted the towel away from his cheek, I could see the awful gash and bruise already forming under his right eye. The only saving grace was that now his face would be even more battered, which would make it harder to distinguish him from the real Rick Des Vries. "You might want to wear your sunglasses," I told him, while Mandy looked on with those big scared eyes again. "It'll help cover up that gash."

The limo made a sharp turn at that point and I had a chance to stare out the window. We approached a short drive and a set of large iron gates guarded by two men dressed in fatigues and carrying assault rifles. The limo was stopped and the soldiers opened our doors to have a look inside. After checking our names against those on a clipboard, they waved us ahead.

The gates opened slowly and I waited tensely in the limo, knowing that beyond the gates was a prisonlike fortress that we'd be hell-bent escaping from. I took in as much as I could about the security, just in case.

The gates themselves were attached to a ten-foot-high masonry wall with nothing in the way of foliage nearby to gain purchase and give one a boost up. All the trees were centered closer to the drive leading up to the main house, while along the wall armed soldiers patrolled.

As the limo moved ahead, I could see that mounted to every other tree lining the drive were cameras with high-tech video surveillance. I assumed that around the entire perimeter of the house the security was the same, and that no one got in or out without one of Boklovich's men knowing about it.

The house itself was a bit of a surprise; massive in scale and shaped in the neoclassical style, it had at its center a large rectangle topped with an equally large dome, flanked by twin wings three stories high. The exterior matched the gray of the walls with white shutters and Greek columns lining the front entrance.

Beautiful well-tended gardens decorated the front of the estate, where multicolored tulips and lilies bloomed beautifully. Given what I knew about the dangerous days to come, the setting was somewhat off-putting, a beautiful facade thrown over a ticking time bomb.

The limo stopped and the driver jumped out to open our doors. We climbed out and I looked about with sharp eyes, my adrenaline still pumping from all that had happened since we'd gotten off the plane. Immediately I noticed that a large, rotund man in a tan-colored suit stepped out of the front door and observed us with a pleased keenness I could associate only with a crocodile's smile. At his side stood Yurik, his posture stiff and predatory.

The rotund man lifted his hands in welcome and spoke in Russian to us. Maks moved to my side and firmly took my hand, while Dutch put his arm around Mandy and held her close.

Maks returned the greeting to the man I assumed must be Boklovich, and we inched closer to the several steps leading up to the front terrace. I noticed in passing that Eddington and the limo driver were busy unloading our bags, which only reminded me again that Grinkov had been the one to attack me in the parking garage and steal my wallet while pretending to have his butler find me after I'd been "mugged."

I stiffened a little next to him, thinking that I needed to get Dutch alone to tell him, but Maks must have detected the shift in my demeanor because he only gripped my hand more tightly to keep me firmly at my side.

Boklovich waited for us to come up the steps to him, and he greeted Maks warmly with a kiss on each cheek, then moved his fat ugly face to me and gripped my shoulders to have a better look at me. "Hello," I said without a hint of warmth.

Boklovich turned to Maks and asked him a question in Russian. Maks nodded and said something back, which made the two men laugh. I had a feeling I wouldn't like the translation. "Velcome!" Boklovich said to me, the volume blasting my ears. "So, you are Maks's new gurlfriend, eh?"

Boklovich's accent was thick and heavy, just like the rest of him. "It's nice to meet you," I replied. "Thank you for having us."

Boklovich laughed like I'd said something funny before he pulled me to him and kissed first my right cheek and then the left. He then let me go so suddenly that I had to catch myself from falling. Next, he turned his attention to Dutch and Mandy.

Mandy was clinging to Dutch like a scared kitten, but Dutch stood straight and tall without a hint of fear. "Richard," Boklovich said, shaking his head as if Dutch were an errant schoolboy. "Yurik tells me you give him leetle bit of trouble earlier, eh?"

"Vasilii," Dutch replied coolly, running his finger along his injured cheek. "You should have told me to bring my boxing gloves."

Boklovich laughed heartily and curled his hand into a fist before chucking Dutch under the chin playfully, then grabbing him by both arms to pull him into the same kiss-on-the-cheek routine. Dutch didn't flinch in the slightest, which made me so dang proud.

"You will come in and have drink!" Boklovich announced. "We will make truce and talk terms. If you want ice for your face, we get that too."

Dutch nodded and then he reached into his pocket and pulled out his sunglasses, putting them on in front of both Boklovich and Maks, which I thought was very smart. They wouldn't suspect anything if he wore them around inside, and the glasses were large enough that they hid much of his face quite well.

Once we were inside, Mandy and I were subtly shepherded away from our partners and guided by two members of Boklovich's staff, who helped Eddington with our luggage up to the second floor. Here I was shown into a suite of rooms including a nice-sized parlor and one large master bedroom. Eddington was told that the servants' quarters were at the other end of the house, and the two attendants told us that they would take Mandy to the room she would share with Dutch, then be back to collect the butler and show him to his quarters.

The moment they left, Eddington got right to work unpacking Maks's things. "Would you like me to unpack for you, Ms. Carter?" he asked politely.

"No," I said, thinking there was no way I wanted him to rummage around in my things and discover the syringes or the pens. "I'll take care of it, Mr. Eddington, thank you."

He gave me a curt bow and continued to hang up Maks's clothes in the closet, while I moved out into the sitting room and sat down. There was no television in here, which I found a bit odd. No radio either. Just a small library of books all written in Russian.

Swell.

I sat on the couch and waited for Eddington to finish. I couldn't wait for him to leave so I could search out Maks's things and find my wallet. I fully intended to take it back, if only to send him the subtle message that I was totally on to him. I also needed to talk to Dutch and tell him what I'd learned. I figured Maks had stolen my wallet because he wanted to run a background check on me, and I could only hope that if he actually did, the fake Canadian driver's license the CIA had set up for me would hold up under closer scrutiny.

Finally Eddington was done and about two minutes later there was a knock on the door, which he answered. The two attendants were there to pick him up and take him to his quarters, and he left with a polite, "Have a lovely afternoon, Ms. Carter."

The moment he was gone, I ran into the bedroom and pulled open the closet. Grinkov's luggage was stored there in the corner and I moved over to squat down next to it and rummage through the pockets. My wallet had been removed, but in one of the bottom pockets I found my stun gun and I pulled it out with a little, "Aha!"

At that moment I heard the door to the room open, and I had a moment of panic as I shoved the stun gun back into the pocket of the luggage, pushing the bag into the corner again before getting quickly to my feet.

Maks was already standing in the doorframe when I turned around. "Hello," I said casually. "I was just about to unpack my things."

Maks's expression was unreadable, but I thought I detected something like suspicion there. "Please," he said with a casual wave of his hand. "Don't let me keep you from your task."

I flashed him what I hoped was a relaxed smile and moved to the edge of the bed where my own luggage was resting. As I unzipped the top, I asked, "How did drinks go with Vasilii and Rick?"

Maks continued to watch me from the doorway and I had to force myself to keep my movements slow and calm. "Vasilii does not trust your business partner," he said, getting right to the point.

I eyed him over my shoulder. "That was pretty obvious at the landing strip."

Maks nodded. "Yes. But it seems his mistrust is based on something else altogether."

My radar gave a small ping of warning. "Like what?"

"There is a rumor," Maks said, stepping into the room. "One that he shared with me after Rick had been taken to his quarters."

I inhaled and exhaled purposefully. I knew that Maks was scrutinizing my every move, watching to gauge my reaction to this supposed rumor. "Does this rumor involve me or Rick?" I asked, refolding a sweater just to keep my hands busy.

"Rick."

I looked up at Maks and sighed. "Might as well tell me what this rumor is, Maks."

"One of Boklovich's sources suggested that Rick Des Vries had been captured by the Mossad three weeks ago."

My jaw dropped while my brain fired off all sorts of synapses and warnings. I decided to let my natural reaction speak for itself. "That's hilarious!" I said, and was actually able to give a credible laugh. When Maks still appeared uncertain, I knew I had an opportunity and I ran with it. "I mean, Jesus, Maks! You think Rick's being held by the Mossad? He's right here in front of you, for God's sake!"

Maks's face registered some confusion. "I know he's here," he said defensively, as if I'd just called him out for being silly. "What I wonder is, if the rumor is true, has he been recruited by the Israelis?"

I sat on the edge of the bed, my shoulders sagging with relief. Holy cow! These guys didn't suspect Dutch was anyone other than Rick Des Vries! We'd actually pulled it off . . . well, at least for now. And I let all that relief flood me with a gale of laughter. I'd been so tense and anxious and scared and threatened that it all came out in a gush of laughter, and it was several moments before I could collect myself to speak.

To add to my immense relief, Maks was looking like he felt foolish for even suggesting it. "Oh, Maks!" I said to him. "I really think that is the funniest thing I've ever heard! I mean, I realize I've known Rick a lot longer than you, but you have got to believe me when I tell you that Rick Des Vries would *never*, as in *ever*, consent to work for the Mossad!"

Maks didn't have to study me to see the veracity plastered all over my face. What I was saying was absolutely true—if only for the fact that the Mossad would never ever offer Rick Des Vries, the weapons dealer, a job working for them. The idea bordered on ludicrous, actually.

Maks seemed to relax and he came over to sit on the bed next to me. "You're right, of course," he said, laughing now himself. But then he seemed to think of something else, and he turned to me and said, "And you, Abigail Carter? You're not working for them either?"

I flashed another toothy grin, still riding the humor train. "No, Maks. I'm not working for them either." I even held up my little finger and added, "I pinkie swear."

Maks squeezed my knee and got up from the bed. "When you've unpacked, come downstairs and join us. We'll be dining early this evening."

He turned to go and I called him back. "Do you know what room Rick and Mandy are in?"

Maks frowned. "Yes," he said, offering me no further information.

"I'd like to talk to my business partner alone," I told him. "Just to make sure he's okay."

Maks shook his head and came back into the room to stand in front of me. Using two fingers, he lifted my chin and stared soberly into my eyes. "Richard is no longer your business partner, Abigail. As I said on the plane, I worry that there is a good chance he will not leave here alive, and it's best if you accept that and keep well away from him for the duration of your stay here. In fact, I'm afraid I must insist on it."

"And if I refuse?"

Maks let go of my chin and stepped back with a sad-sounding sigh. "I will have no choice but to reveal to Boklovich that you know the password to the software program Rick carries. It will mean certain death for Rick, but I may still be able to bargain for your life."

I could feel all the good humor of three minutes before wash right out of me. "*Why* would you do that, Maks?"

"Because I believe you could be a valuable asset, Abigail, and you and I could make a great deal of money together. Your business ventures with Rick will only get you killed, and I won't stand by and allow such a talented young woman with so much potential to be brought down by a lowlife like Richard Des Vries."

I couldn't think of a word to say in response, and Maks didn't seem to want to hear one anyway, because he turned on his heel and walked quietly out the door, leaving me alone, separated from Dutch and certainly doomed to watch him die.

Chapter Thirteen

. . .

I spent my time at dinner moodily pushing the food around on my plate while Dutch, Maks, and Boklovich talked in Russian. Mandy sat shivering in the chair next to Dutch, hardly touching any of her dinner—as per her normal skimpy caloric intake—and obviously feeling the cold of the chilly interior.

Boklovich must have noticed her discomfort because he switched to English and said, "Tomorrow the weather be better, you see."

Her brow crinkled. "Huh?" she said.

"A vwarm front coming in," he said, shoving a big spongy roll into his gap.

"Oh," she said timidly. "That's nice."

Boklovich nodded like he agreed. "Good for guests," he added, after swallowing down his roll. "Most of them from vwarm climate."

I tried to catch Dutch's eye, but he was wearing his sunglasses and I couldn't see behind the dark lenses. My great idea to help disguise him was proving to be a hindrance to our unspoken communication.

I'd thought earlier about sneaking him a note, but in the whole of the room I couldn't find a single pen, and the only pen I carried wasn't actually a functioning pen. Also, Grinkov was keeping a very close eye on me, and my stomach turned when I considered that at the end of the evening he and I would be faced with the night ahead in the same room together . . . and one bed.

I didn't quite know how I was going to get out of actually going to bed with him, and I was feeling incredibly boxed in and close to panic.

I remembered what Mandy had told me about Grinkov finding his wife in a compromising position with another man, and how Maks had gone about killing both of them. The thought made me sick. I also remembered his brutality against Dutch, and I really didn't care that he truly believed Dutch was Des Vries. The man was a thug, and I had little doubt, based on all of that and the fact that he'd hit me hard enough over the head to knock me out, that if he wanted his way with me, he'd darn well have it.

I shuddered involuntarily in my chair. "Are you cold?" Maks asked, leaning in to consider me with those smoldering hazel eyes. "I'm fine," I said curtly.

Boklovich's gaze shifted to me, as if he detected the small change in the atmosphere at the end of the table. "Tell me, Miss Carter," he boomed. "Where you and Maksy meet?"

I took a sip of water before answering. "At a poker game, Mr. Boklovich."

This seemed to surprise our host and he looked at Maks with great humor. "Who won game?" he asked, his attempt at English making him sound more and more like a caveman.

"She did," Maks said, smiling too.

Boklovich laughed and thumped the table hard enough to rattle the china. "Tomorrow we all play poker!" he announced. "And we dance too. Must have dancing!"

I eyed the fat Russian at the end of the table, and considered that he might be very drunk.

At that moment there was some noise from the front hall and Boklovich excused himself. I gathered that some of the invited guests had arrived. I also wondered if the drone and its thief were here yet.

I closed my eyes for a moment to focus on that, and sure enough I felt positive that both were here at the estate, but my concentration on the thief was interrupted when Maks leaned over and said, "Tomorrow afternoon Vasilii will be hosting a party for all his guests before the auction. I hope you brought a party dress?"

I opened my eyes and blinked. "Uh . . . no," I told him.

Maks smiled. "No worries. I will send Eddington by plane to Victoria to select something for you."

I saw an opening there to make contact with Frost and tell him what was happening here and I jumped at it. "Can't I just go to Victoria and find something suitable?" Maks seemed to study my reaction carefully. "I mean," I added quickly, "sometimes I'm a four and sometimes I'm a six. It just depends on the designer, so I'd like to try on a few things to find the perfect dress."

"I will arrange a selection," he said easily, which let me know that I wasn't about to be allowed off the estate until after the auction.

"Oh," I said. "Okay."

Boklovich joined us again and he seemed even more jovial. I had a sneaking suspicion that the thief had just arrived, and hoped he'd be shown in for dinner so I could scope him out. "Forgive interruption," Vasilii said to us, taking his seat again and going right for his wineglass. "Guests coming all day and night."

"Will they be joining us?" Dutch asked.

But Boklovich shook his head. "Long trip," he said. "Dey vill rest and join us tomorrow."

When everyone was distracted, I stared hard at Dutch and thought I'd caught his eye. I made sure to look meaningfully at him and scooted my chair back. "I think I'd like to get some air!" I said, standing and giving a slight bow to Boklovich. "Is it all right, sir, if I take a stroll through your garden?"

Boklovich was slightly taken aback, but he quickly recovered. *"Da, da,"* he said, waving his hand at me to go ahead. "But stay where guards can see you."

Smiling tightly at Maks, who leveled his eyes in warning, I hurried out of the room, praying that Dutch would get the hint and find a way to follow me.

I reached the French doors that led to the backyard and hurried outside. The temperature startled me. It was noticeably warmer than when we'd landed that afternoon. Well, Boklovich had mentioned that a warm front was moving through. Too bad his house was taking its sweet time to heat up.

I moved over to one of the terraces overlooking a series of small ponds that each fed into another, and waited . . . and waited . . . and waited. Dutch did not appear.

"Crap on a cracker," I muttered. I'd come out here for nothing. Finally I decided to get a grip and focus on the mission. I had to find the drone. I closed my eyes again and concentrated, and when I opened them, I began making my way down the steps to the garden and over to a section where several guards were focused on putting something together.

I approached cautiously and to my amazement I realized that they were putting together the drone itself!

It was much smaller than I'd considered, about three and a half feet long and in several parts that needed to be fitted together, but all the pieces seemed to be there, including a small black box, which I was sure contained Intuit.

One of the men looked up then and saw me standing there staring. He barked something in Russian and I knew I needed to move away.

"Sorry!" I said, holding up my hands and making a hasty retreat.

I found my way over to a quiet corner of the garden and looked around for Dutch again, but if he'd come out, he was nowhere to be seen.

I thought about going back inside, but I knew I was pretty anxious from the discovery of the drone and what Maks had told me about Dutch not being allowed to leave alive after the auction, so he and I would need to somehow recover Intuit and then get the heck outta there. I considered that if there was some big shindig that would take place the following night, that might be the best time to make our exit, and I knew that going out the front wasn't an option for us.

I moved out of the corner and began taking surreptitious looks around. Switching on my radar, I spoke directly to my own spirit guides, known collectively as "the crew." "Okay, crew, I need you right now more than ever. Find a weak spot in this defense system that Dutch and I can exploit to get our butts out of here."

Immediately I felt a tug on my solar plexus that pulled me over to the left.

Moving to the central garden, which was to the left of where the guards were still fiddling with the drone, I walked as casually as possible, trying to give off the appearance that I was simply out for an after-dinner stroll.

The tug on my middle continued, even though I knew I was getting closer and closer to the back wall. I passed another guard and his dog, and I smiled at him and said that it was a lovely evening.

He gave me a gruff smile and continued on without commenting. Obviously he didn't consider me a flight risk or a threat. Good.

Moving a little more cautiously now, I hedged my way nearer a section of the wall almost completely covered in ivy, and next to that was a small garden shack with the door slightly ajar and several gardeners' tools poking out. I moved to pass the ivy, but that visceral tug yanked me back, and I paused to consider the thick tangle of vines.

As I squinted at it, I realized that poking through the greenery were rusty iron bars. My crew sent a little note of warning to my head, and I quickly retreated from the rusted gate over to a low bench, sat down, and waited. Not a moment after I'd taken my seat, one of the guards walked by and took note of me as I sat casually and stared up, pretending to take in the lovely pink and purple early-evening sky.

The minute the guard was on his way again, I hedged back to the gate and pulled at the vines to get a better look. The bars were quite old, and the black paint coating them was peeling off in thin layers all around. The latch was secured by an old iron padlock, also coated in rust but still formidable. Through the bars on the other side of the wall I could see dense vegetation. I squinted in the dim light, and wondered if we'd be able to make our way through it to escape.

My radar gave another warning and I backed quickly away from the gate. Rubbing my hands together furiously to clear them of the dirt and rust debris, I moved at a trot until I found one of the pathways, then slowed my pace and walked calmly along as if I didn't have a care in the world. Someone was approaching me, but the light was fading and I didn't see who it was until he was quite close and I could see the slight limp and the walking stick that accompanied it. "Hello, Mr. Eddington," I said.

"Ms. Carter," he replied, stopping in front of me. "Mr. Grinkov is wondering if you're all right?"

"I'm fine. I was just out for a stroll."

Eddington seemed uncomfortable. He was a bit twitchy and jumpy, and I could only imagine that being in the den of so many lions was making us all a bit nervous. "He would like to see you," the butler said.

"Is he inside?"

"Yes, ma'am. He is waiting for you in your room."

Gulp.

I smiled tightly at him and said, "Thank you for telling me, Mr. Eddington. I'll be right up."

The butler returned my smile and seemed about to say something else to me, but a guard came close to us and he seemed to think better of it. Eddington then swiveled round to leave me when I thought of something and called him back. "Mr. Eddington?"

The butler stiffened. "Yes?"

"Do you know which room Mr. Des Vries and Miss Mortemeyer are staying in?"

Eddington looked over his shoulder, his face curious. "Yes, ma'am."

I hurried up to him and took his free arm as if he was my new best friend. "Would you please show it to me?" The butler seemed to hesitate, likely suspecting that his boss might not approve, so I held up my purse and said, "Mandy had mentioned needing an extra tampon, and I've got a supply in my purse."

Maks's butler turned such a bright shade of red he was nearly purple, and I could have laughed. He cleared his throat and said, "Yes, of course, ma'am. Right this way."

Eddington led me right up to the third floor and down all the way to the end. He left me quickly and I smiled as he retreated, still finding some humor in an old proper British man's reaction to our lady things. I raised my hand and knocked and after a moment Mandy opened the door. "Is Rick here?" I asked her softly, afraid to use Dutch's name even in a whisper.

"No."

I looked anxiously over her shoulder to see if she was lying, but I couldn't spot Dutch anywhere in the room. "Do you know when he'll be coming up?"

"No."

"Do you know if he's still with Boklovich?"

"No."

"Gee, Mandy, you're just a fountain of information, aren't you?"

"He's not here, okay?" she snapped.

I bit the inside of my cheek to keep from saying something rude back and instead said, "Fine. When he does come up, I need you to tell him to meet me in the garden by the tent tomorrow morning at six thirty a.m."

"Whatever," she said, looking incredibly bored.

"It's important," I insisted.

Mandy stared at me with half-closed lids.

I could feel my frustration mounting, so I turned away, knowing that I was very close to losing it with her. "Just give him the message," I said tersely, and hurried away.

When I made it back to my room, I took a moment to smooth out my clothes and take a deep breath. In the light of the hallway I saw how dirty my palms were from fussing with the gate, but there wasn't anything I could do other than try to hide them until I had a chance to visit the restroom.

With a feeling of dread I turned the handle, preparing myself to face the music. On the other side of the door, I came up short and stared in surprise as I took in Maks, reclining on the couch with a book, a pillow from the bedroom, and a thick blanket folded at his feet.

"Abigail," he said warmly. "I was beginning to worry about you."

I blinked and tried to collect my thoughts. "I'm fine," I assured him. "But if you'll excuse me for one minute, I really must visit the ladies' room."

With that, I trotted into the bathroom and scrubbed my hands clean. On the way in, I'd passed the bed and noticed that only one side of it had been turned down. I looked in the mirror after I was done scrubbing my palms, asking my reflection if Grinkov really could be something of a gentleman.

Leaving my purse on the nightstand, I moved back out to the sitting room again and found Maks in the same position, looking relaxed and quite content with his book. "You're sleeping out here?" I asked, getting right to the point.

Maks laid the book on his chest, a crooked smile on his lips. "Unless you'd prefer I join you in the bedroom?"

I felt relief flood through me right down to my toes. "That would be moving a little fast, wouldn't it, Maks?"

He sat up and considered me quite seriously. "Abigail Carter," he said. "You are a riddle wrapped in a mystery, you know?"

I sat down on a nearby chair. "You can't quite figure me out, is that right?"

He laughed. "That's right. But I find myself wanting to. I'm very attracted to you."

I didn't know what to say to that, so I stayed quiet.

"I realize," he said next, "that I forced you into staying with me here in my room, but you must understand that I did this for your own protection."

I had opened up my radar the moment I sat down, and I was studying his energy quite intensely. I could see many of the same things I already knew about him there, but I could also see something I'd missed before. "What happened to your wife, Maks?"

The question had an immediate reaction. His face went quite pale and he stared at me with haunted eyes for a long uneasy moment.

Still, even sensing the danger, I pushed a little more. "I can see that you're a widower," I told him, my mind's eye focusing on the white band that appeared around his left ring finger. "And I've heard the rumors, so I just want to make sure I know exactly who I'm getting involved with here before things go any further with us."

Maks's lips pressed themselves into a thin line and he tossed his book on the table. "Don't tell me," he said. "The story you heard was that I murdered my wife and her lover?"

"It was more that you tortured them to death over the period of several days."

Maks nodded and there was a sardonic smile at the corner of his lips. "Ah," he said. "The 'I shot them in each of their extremities before finally putting them out of their misery' story?"

"That's the one. Is it true?"

"No."

I could have sagged with relief. He wasn't lying. And that allowed me to thread my way along the energy of his wife's death. What I

found there was like a puzzle with odd-shaped pieces. "She was murdered, though," I said, and it wasn't a question. "And it was by someone you both knew and were quite fond of. What's odd is that I keep
sensing heartbreak around her. Like in her final moment there was
this shattering feeling around her heart because someone she knew
and loved murdered her."

"She was *not* murdered," Maks said, his voice bitter and hard.

I ignored him and continued to follow the thread. "It feels like
murder," I said to him. "And I don't think it was a suicide."

"Abigail, stop," he said.

But I was in too deep, and when I could finally find the end of the
thread, I gasped. "Oh, my God!"

My eyes grew wide and traveled up to his, which were haunted and
pained. "You know?"

I nodded. "Your son," I whispered, feeling the terrible heartache
coming off the man on the couch.

Maks got up and walked over to a credenza across the room. He
opened it and pulled out a tall bottle of vodka. Without another word
he poured himself a generous portion and swallowed it down in one
gulp.

After another moment he began to speak, his voice choked with
emotion. "Both of my sons are very clever," he said. "Too clever. One
day when they were six and while I was away, they discovered how to
open my gun safe. They figured out the code somehow and retrieved
my gun. My wife walked in on them while they were playing with it.
The gun went off. My wife died within seconds, shot through the
heart."

I now understood why I'd picked up the heartbreak around his
wife and the distance between Maks and his sons, which had formed

in the years after their mother's death. They were both physical and emotional clues. "You don't know which of your sons pulled the trigger," I said, still snooping around the energy.

"No," he said. "And if you know, please do not tell me!"

My radar offered the word *younger*, and I knew that it had been the second twin that had shot his mother. "Do they remember it?"

Maks nodded. "I believe so, yes."

"You haven't talked about it?"

Maks poured himself another drink. "No. They're living far away from me now, and we don't talk much."

"So, why the rumors?"

Maks came back and sat down heavily on the couch. "I would rather the world believe that I murdered my wife than have everyone know that one of my sons killed his own mother."

I got up and moved over to the couch to sit next to him. His energy and his posture were so sad that my heart went out to him and I reached over to take his hand and hold it.

We sat like that for a long time and all the while my radar kept making a suggestion that I was really fighting against, but finally my crew's insistence couldn't be ignored. "Do you have a pen, Maks?"

Numbly he reached into his shirt pocket and handed me a gold Cross pen. I reached for his book and opened it to the last page, which was blank. Ripping it carefully out, I tore the page in half and scribbled a name and a phone number on it, which I then handed to him. "Here," I said, and while he was distracted by the paper, I tucked his pen into my pocket.

"What's this?"

"It's the phone number to a really good friend of mine. She's a psychic medium out in L.A., someone who specializes in talking to the dead, and she's one of the best in the world. Call the number and her assistant will schedule you an appointment. Don't mention my name, though, because when Theresa reads for you, I want you to believe that I had nothing to do with the information that comes through."

Maks studied the paper like it held a secret code and I got up, discreetly taking the other half of the paper with me and moving to the bedroom. Turning back to him, I said, "You need to hear from your wife, Maks. You need to know that she doesn't blame you, and that it's not your fault. It was an accident, and you need to move forward and begin to forgive both yourself and your sons."

I left him still staring down at the paper and hurried into the bathroom, where I immediately turned on the shower. As the bathroom filled up with steam, I scribbled Dutch a note about what Grinkov had told me: that there was a hit out on Des Vries's life and that he wouldn't be allowed to leave the premises, and that I'd seen the drone and Intuit out in the garden, which meant the thief was actually here, and I thought I knew of a way out if Dutch could figure out how to steal back Intuit. On the other side of the paper I drew a map of the gate at the back of the garden, and told him that we needed to hightail it out of there during the party when all the other guests were busy, which might be the best time to steal Intuit.

Satisfied, I folded the note, tucked it into the pocket of my dress slacks, hurried into the shower simply to get wet, then got out and wore a towel around myself just in case Maks was still awake and watching for me from the sitting room.

When I came out of the bathroom, he appeared to be sleeping, and I noticed that the piece of paper I'd scribbled my friend Theresa's name on was neatly tucked next to his date book. On tiptoes I walked out and placed his pen beside them on the table before going to bed myself.

The next morning I crept out of the room at five thirty. I didn't know what time Maks would be up, and I didn't want to get stuck in the room with him, so I made sure to be up and out well before he woke.

I found a quiet corner near the patio doors to sit, huddled in my sweater because Boklovich's house was still cold; then around six I slipped out of the house and onto the back terrace.

I was surprised to find several workers out back, up early and preparing for the afternoon's festivities. So much hustle-bustle would provide good cover and I moved over to the tent to make it look like I was only checking things out. The drone was fully put together now, displayed on a pedestal with two armed guards beside it. One focused his beady eyes at me and I moved off quickly.

It was cozier out here than it had been in the house—the warm front had definitely moved into the area, for which I was immensely grateful. If Dutch and I were going to make our escape that evening, it would be nice not to freeze to death while we did it.

I glanced at my watch every few minutes and eyed the French doors, waiting for my fiancé, but as six twenty-nine became six thirty, no sign of him appeared.

My heart sank. Dutch was nothing if not prompt.

I waited another fifteen minutes before deciding that I needed to risk sneaking up to his room to deliver the note. I moved quickly back up the stone stairs leading to the garden doors, but immediately had to duck out of sight again because Maks was inside, his back to me, accepting a cup of coffee from one of the servants.

Grumbling to myself, I edged down the wall nearly to the end of the house and tried a door. It was locked.

I glanced back the way I'd come, looking for any sign of Dutch. He was nowhere around. There was also no other easy way to access the house.

Out of options, I moved back to the French doors and took a deep breath, peeking through the panes before going in. Maks was sitting in a chair reading the paper. I opened the door and moved inside, offering him a warm greeting. "Good morning!"

Maks turned and glanced over his shoulder. "Abigail," he said, setting down the paper. "You were up very early this morning."

I felt my heart beat a little faster. "Did I wake you?"

"I'm a light sleeper," he said.

"Ah. Sorry about that. I couldn't sleep, so I got up to check out the preparations."

Maks's knowing gaze traveled to the large tent outside. "You saw the drone," he said, and it wasn't a question.

I smiled, knowing that if I tried to deny it, he'd see right through me. "Yes."

Maks nodded and he seemed to relax into his chair again. He was about to say something else when a maid came into the room and curtsied. She asked me something in Russian and I shrugged my shoulders to show her that I didn't understand her. "She's asking if you would like coffee," Grinkov said.

"Oh, yes, please," I told her, pumping my head up and down, and the servant trotted away, only to return a moment later with a steaming cup of the good stuff. I took a seat and attempted some small talk.

I had little doubt that Maks was suspicious of my comings and goings, and I didn't want to give the appearance of being anxious to be off again. "Have all the guests arrived?"

Maks folded the paper and turned his wrist to check the time. "Some have already trickled in," he said. "But most will be arriving shortly."

I took another sip of coffee. "And have you met the other dealer? The one offering the drone for sale." Maks looked sharply at me, so I added, "I know that Rick is anxious to meet his competition."

"Why would he be anxious to do that?"

Again I detected the hint of suspicion in Grinkov's voice and I knew I was treading on thin ice here, but I also knew it could work to our benefit to stir the pot a little. "Because Rick has the better product," I told him. "Remember the rumors that the device on the drone is defective? It will work only a few times and needs to be reverse engineered, at that. Rick's disk is ready to roll with no bugs or system flaws."

"You've heard a lot of rumors," Grinkov said with more than a bit of mirth.

I tapped my temple. "My radar says I'm not wrong on this one, Maks."

He considered me thoughtfully. "I see."

"So have you met them?" I asked again.

"No," Maks said, and his energy insisted he wasn't lying, which I found truly frustrating. If he had been introduced to the thief, I could have searched the ether around him for clues. As it stood, I still had no idea what our thief looked like.

At that moment there was a lot of activity at the front of the house, and Maks and I both stood up to see what was happening. A whole troop of people poured into the front hallway and in the thick of them stood Boklovich, greeting his guests while a flurry of servants bustled about, taking coats and luggage.

At first glance it looked like a gathering of the United Nations. There were all manner of ethnic groups represented, with one individual standing out from the crowd. He was a very tall man dressed in flowing robes and the traditional Arab headdress. I noticed that the man's beady brown eyes took in everything around him, including me.

"Is that Sheikh Omar?" I whispered as Maks came to stand close to me and take my hand possessively.

"It is," he said, and I could hear the distaste in his voice.

The man in reference did something unexpected then; he pointed to me and said something that he was clearly directing to Boklovich. Boklovich turned to look at me too and he laughed as if the Arab had just said something quite funny. Then he gave the sheikh a slight bow and began walking over to us. Maks's hand gripped mine even tighter.

"Maksim Grinkov," Boklovich said formally, before speaking to him in rapid Russian. I could tell that I'd attracted the sheikh's attention, but I didn't know why, and all the while Boklovich and Maks were talking, the sheikh's eyes never left mine.

I finally looked away because he was making me uncomfortable, and I waited for Maks to translate what was happening.

Boklovich finally ended the conversation by shrugging and shaking his head, then walking back to the sheikh with a shrug and his palms turned up in an "I tried" gesture.

"What was that about?" I asked when Maks began pulling me out of the room and over to the stairs.

"The sheikh has taken an interest," he said. "He wants to purchase you."

I was offended. "Does he really think I'm a hooker?"

Maks shook his head and hurried me along up the stairs. "No," he said. "He does not want to purchase you for an evening, Abigail. He wants to buy you and place you in his harem."

At the top of the stairs I stopped and pulled hard on Maks's hand. "He *what*?"

Maks came close to me again and warned, "Lower your voice!" I piped down quick. "Come with me," he added less forcefully. "Please."

I followed him back to our room and Maks pulled me inside and shut the door. I rounded on him the moment we were alone and demanded he tell me what was going on.

"Sheikh Omar is a *very* wealthy man," Maks explained. "And as such he is quite used to getting what he wants. I was afraid he might take notice of you, but, as you insisted on coming, there was little I could do. He has set a price of one hundred thousand dollars for you."

"One hundred thousand dollars?" I was incredulous, and I didn't know if I should feel insulted, flattered, or a little of both. "What did you tell him?"

"No," Maks said. "Obviously. But the price will climb."

I could feel my stomach turn. "At what price will you accept his offer, Maks?"

He didn't answer me, which I found quite troubling. "I'm going to ask you to stay here for the duration of the day, Abigail. It's for your own good. I'm hopeful that the other women Boklovich has ordered to attend the party will take the interest of Sheikh Omar off you, but until they arrive, it's best for you to keep out of sight. I will have a guard placed outside the door to keep you safe while I attend to business."

My jaw dropped. "Is that really necessary?"

Maks's beautiful hazel eyes bored into mine. "Do not underestimate the predatory nature of Sheikh Omar," he warned. "He will not stop until he's gotten what he wants by whatever means necessary."

With that, Maks turned and walked out the door.

Chapter Fourteen

• • •

The moment Maks left me, I counted to fifty, then crept out the door quickly and quietly. Moving to the staircase, I tiptoed up the steps, profoundly grateful that everyone still seemed to be milling about downstairs in the main hall. Once I gained the third floor, I ran down to the end and began knocking on the door urgently.

Mandy opened it, looking groggy and out of it. "What?" she groaned.

"Where's Rick?" I whispered.

Mandy blinked. I could tell I'd just woken her up and she looked behind her in the room. "He's not here," she said, her attitude changing instantly to annoyed.

"Where is he?" I demanded.

"How the hell should I know?" she complained. "God! It's not like we're tied at the hip, you know!"

This time I was so frustrated that I didn't hold back. I reached up and grabbed her by the shoulders; shaking her slightly, I got right up in her face and hissed, "This is serious, Mandy, and I need you to shut up and focus!" Mandy's eyes bulged. She gave me an obedient nod and I let her go. "Did you give him my message?"

Mandy rolled her eyes dramatically, which I took for a yes.

"Do you know what time he left the room?"

"What am I, his warden?" she snapped.

I could feel the anxious feeling in the pit of my stomach intensify. Out of desperation I reached into my pocket, pulled out the note, and shoved it into her hand. "You've got to give this to Rick when he comes back to the room, do you hear me?"

Mandy nodded, her eyes still big and frightened. My radar pinged a warning and I knew I had to get back to my room. "Stay here until he comes back, okay?"

Again she nodded and I left her to bolt back down the hallway and race quietly to my room. No sooner had I reached it than I saw the black cap of one of the soldiers cresting the top of the stairs. I dashed into the room and closed the door behind me, exhaling slowly and leaning back against the door.

A few seconds later there was a knock on my door. I gathered my composure and opened it. A man in fatigues tipped his cap and said in a very thick accent, "I to guard you."

"Sure," I told him, and closed the door again.

I was left to pace the floor and worry about Dutch.

Around eleven a.m. there was another knock on my door and I opened it to reveal Maks's butler holding several garment bags and packages. "Hello, Ms. Carter," he said cordially, while the guard eyed him suspiciously. "Might I come in?"

I'd completely forgotten about Maks insisting that Eddington go into town and find me a dress suitable for that evening. "Of course,

Mr. Eddington," I said, giving a small wave to the guard to let him know it was okay.

Eddington came in and began to shut the door, but the guard put his foot out and said, "If she have company, I vwatch to make sure no hanky-panky."

I rolled my eyes and sighed heavily, taking a few of the bags from the butler's overloaded arms. "I've brought you an array to chose from," Eddington said. I could tell he was nervous to have the guard staring at us through the doorway. "Mr. Grinkov suggested you were between a size four and a size six?"

"Yes," I said, watching him hang the garment bags along the door to the bedroom and more than a little curious.

"I also guessed that you wear a size nine shoe?"

"I do," I said, surprised that he'd guessed correctly.

Eddington smiled and tilted his head. "I shall leave you to select the outfit which most pleases you for the party," he told me, and moved to the door. Pausing on his way out, he said, "Mr. Grinkov will be along at three thirty to collect you. Might I send up some lunch for you in the meantime?"

Given the state of anxiousness I was in, I wasn't very hungry, but then I realized I'd probably need my strength if Dutch and I were going to escape that night. Who knew how long we'd be stuck tramping through the wilderness before we could reach the other landing strip and signal for help? "Some lunch would be wonderful, Mr. Eddington, thank you."

"Very good, ma'am," Eddington said, and took his leave of me, closing the door and shutting out the probing eyes of the guard.

As soon as the doors were closed, I moved over to the array of garment bags. There were eight in all, and upon closer inspection I discovered that there were actually only four styles to choose from, but one of each in a size four and size six.

The instant I pulled back the cover of the second dress, I knew it was for me. I swept it immediately off the door where Eddington had hung it, and turned it around to admire it fully.

The cocktail dress was a black sequined Dolce & Gabbana number that looked almost liquid on the hanger, like a shimmering black river as the ebony sequins caught the light. The cut was short, to my upper thigh, and tight, but when I had it on, it was incredibly flattering. Also, the fact that the four fit me without being uncomfortable gave me a temporary ego boost.

I sifted through the other shopping bags to find a pair of black patent leather pumps and a matching sequined clutch. I moved into the closet to dig through my luggage and see what I had in the way of jewelry. My engagement ring was there, tucked safely among an assortment of jewelry, and seeing it brought me up short. I sat down on the floor of the closet, staring at my ring, and felt all the tension of this mission and the fear for Dutch catch up with me and I had myself a little pity party right there on the closet floor.

After about ten minutes I wiped my eyes, placed my engagement ring onto my right ring finger, vowing not to leave it or Dutch behind, and rummaged through my luggage again. Finally, I located the small handgun Frost had given me, and tucked that into my clutch along with the stun gun from Maks's luggage. The clutch was heavy, but I vowed to manage.

My lunch arrived just after I'd washed my face and collected myself again, and I ate every bite.

I then paced the floor until two, jumped in the shower, and stayed in the bathroom for the next hour and a half. When I was satisfied with my reflection, I emerged. Maks was standing in the bedroom as if he'd been waiting for me, and I sucked in a breath as much for the fact that he was there as for how the man looked.

Which . . . in a word . . . was breathtaking.

He wore black silk dress slacks that fit him beautifully, with a matching velvet dinner jacket. A crisp white dress shirt had several buttons open to reveal a bit of chest hair, and the outfit was completed by a beautiful purple pocket square with flecks of gold, and diamond and amethyst cuff links. "You look stunning," he said, catching sight of me.

I felt heat hit my cheeks again and inwardly I cursed my own attraction to this man. "Thank you," I said. "And might I say the same about you?"

He grinned sideways at me. "You may."

That made me laugh, which helped ease the terrible knot of tension that had been building inside me all day. There was a knock at the door and Maks moved over to answer it. I followed him out into the sitting room and peeked over his shoulder when he opened the door. I noticed two things immediately: The guard at the door was gone, and Mandy was there, looking nervous and fidgety. She was also dressed in a black cocktail dress, but her dress hugged her a little tighter than mine and showed off her long legs, small waist, and size DD boobs. In an instant I went from feeling confident to chopped liver as I saw how a tasteful and flattering dress on Mandy was all it took to transform her into something amazing. "Hey," she said, spying Maks immediately and doing a terrible job of tucking the note I'd given her earlier behind her back to hide it from him.

I stepped immediately to the door, alarm bells going off in my head. "Hi, Mandy!" I said with false warmth. "You look incredible, girlfriend! Did you need me?"

Mandy was a little slow on the uptake—no shocker there—and she replied, "Uh . . ."

"You needed to borrow some more lady things, am I right?"

"Uh . . ."

Maks was looking from Mandy to me, and he seemed to know something was up. "I have some in my bathroom, honey, so don't be embarrassed. Just come with me and we'll get you taken care of."

I then grabbed her by the hand, said, "We'll just be a minute" to Maks, and half pulled, half yanked her in the direction of the bedroom. "Right in here," I sang, moving her inside, where I shut the door and mouthed, "Where's Dutch?"

Mandy shook her head and held out the note to me. "He didn't come back to the room!" she whispered.

I eyed the door to the bathroom. I had little doubt that Maks was trying to eavesdrop on our conversation, so I said loudly, "These should do the trick, honey. And they're nice and small to fit into your purse!" I then motioned to the note and her purse and she caught on, thank God.

After she'd tucked it away, I leaned in close to her ear and said, "Go back to the room and wait for him there. I'll try to get away from Maks to find Dutch and send him to you. He's got to read that note far away from prying eyes, do you understand?"

Mandy nodded, but she didn't look happy. "I'll miss the party!" she whispered back.

I glared at her so hard she shrank away from me. "Okay," she said when I didn't ease off the glare.

I moved back to the door and opened it, smiling brightly at Maks, who was quite close to the door. "Is everything all right?"

"Of course!" I said, putting my arm around Mandy.

"Have you seen Rick?" she asked suddenly, and for the first time since I'd known her, I thought she'd asked an intelligent question.

Maks nodded. "He's downstairs with the others."

Mandy then turned to me and said, "I'm going back to my room for a bit; I've got cramps. Would you send Rick up to me?"

In that moment I could have hugged her. "Of course, Mandy."

We exited the room and Maks locked the door, pocketing the key in his jacket pocket. He offered me his arm and we left Mandy to go back upstairs while we headed down.

As we descended the stairs, I could feel the tension radiating off Maks. He knew Mandy and I were up to something, but as of yet, he hadn't asked me about it. I pretended I didn't notice that he'd noticed.

We got to the bottom of the stairs and I could see that most of the guests were already there. The large sitting room just off the back terrace was filled with people, and for every man I saw, there were at least three drop-dead beautiful women. "You weren't kidding when you said that Boklovich would be bringing in the ladies," I said to Maks, hoping to distract him from Mandy and me.

He grunted, his mind clearly still occupied by other things. When we reached the terrace, we could both see that Sheikh Omar was surrounded by no less than ten of the most gorgeous women at the party. I would have felt intimidated by their beauty too if I weren't so relieved that his attention had seemingly been completely diverted away from me.

And then I spotted Dutch off in a corner with Boklovich, who was waving to the crowd to gather round.

Maks had me around the waist and we edged closer. I wanted to break free and hurry over to Dutch, but the crowd and Maks's firm hold on me prevented that.

When everyone was circled around Boklovich, he began speaking in Russian. Several other men gathered around also began speaking, but softly and in a variety of languages.

I realized that they were translating the fat Russian's speech. I glanced over at Maks and without looking at me he said, "Vasilii will now give a demonstration of the drone and its technology."

On the wall of the tent a projection appeared, showing short clips of each guest arriving at Boklovich's compound. Around each guest were vivid bubbles of color. I saw a clip flash by showing our arrival, and got an unsettled feeling. Once that footage had played, another image appeared—an aerial view of the crowd emerged, a cluster of pulsing blobs of color distinct from the surrounding dull green terrain. Immediately I looked to the sky, trying to spot the drone, but there were thick dark clouds overhead and finding the small drone in the mass of gray was next to impossible.

I lowered my chin as the crowd began to murmur, and looked again at the projection on the tent. The aerial view was closing in on the crowd and a small circle appeared on one of the patches of color. I realized in an instant that the circle was a bull's-eye, and I also knew exactly whom Intuit was targeting—I'd recognize that signature aura anywhere.

"Dutch!" I squeaked, completely forgetting to use his alias.

Luckily, my reaction was lost in the increasing murmurs of the crowd, but Maks had heard me. I could feel his steely glare on the side of my face. I attempted to pull out of his grasp as the image on the tent drew closer and closer to its target.

Intuit was going to kill Dutch, and I had to get to him. "Let me go!" I whispered threateningly, pulling at Maks's hand around my waist.

"Stay still!" Maks ordered, and he wrapped his other arm around me.

I looked frantically over at Dutch, and in that moment his head swiveled to me and behind those dark shades I knew he was looking right at me. "DUCK!" I mouthed at him, and in the last second before the drone dive-bombed him, Dutch hit the deck.

To my immense relief the drone zoomed harmlessly over Dutch's head and came to land right next to the tent.

The crowd erupted, roaring its approval and clapping and laughing at Dutch, who got to his feet as quickly and gracefully as possible. I did not applaud, but stared hard at the drone, looking for the gun with the darts in it, wondering if it had shot my fiancé and he wasn't even aware of it, but the gun didn't seem to be mounted onto the airplane, just the small black box with the camera and Intuit.

I let out a long breath. Dutch appeared okay. "What are you two hiding?" Maks asked under his breath, and I knew we'd been made.

I turned in his arms and smiled at him, but it was only an act and I knew he could tell. "Hiding?" I asked. "Nothing, Maks. I would just prefer if my business partner weren't murdered right in front of me, if that's all right with you?"

Grinkov glared hard at me. "You play a dangerous game, Abigail," he warned.

"So do you," I told him tartly. By now I'd seriously had enough of the friendly pretense.

Maks let go of me abruptly. "I have forgotten something in our room. I will be back in a moment."

He left me then and I made my way through the crowd, working hard to catch Dutch's eye again. He was receiving a rough pat on the back and a glass of champagne from our host, who couldn't stop laughing and mimicking Dutch's rather inelegant fall to the ground. Dutch was wearing his cop face through all of it, but I knew he badly wanted to wipe that smile off Boklovich's face . . . permanently.

I waved frantically to my fiancé behind Boklovich's back, and I watched as he downed the contents of his glass in one swallow, motioned to it like he was going to get another one, and took his leave of Boklovich.

The vile man followed my fiancé with his eyes, and I knew it was too risky to have Boklovich see me talking to Dutch, so I subtly motioned to the bar and met him there.

"Boklovich is trying to kill you," I whispered.

"Tell me something I don't know," he murmured.

I remembered the note I'd given to Mandy. "You have to go see Mandy. She's not feeling well and she's asked to see you." I said this loud enough to be overheard.

"Where is she?" he asked, moving in front of me to place his drink order.

"Upstairs in your room."

Dutch looked around as if he was simply taking in the crowd while the bartender poured his drink. "I'll try to slip away," he said softly. "Boklovich's keeping a tight rein on me until after the auction."

"Mandy said it was urgent," I told him, hoping he could read the subtext.

Dutch thanked the bartender and turned away from the bar, allowing me to move ahead of him. "Got it," he whispered, his hand subtly brushing my arm as he left.

I could have wept there and then. I'd had my radar wide open all afternoon, and there was terrible danger threaded all throughout Dutch's energy, and it hadn't passed when he'd managed to duck under the drone attack. What if that soft caress was the last time he ever touched me? What if those were the last words he ever said to me?

I stepped forward to the bartender with these heavy thoughts tangling my mind but somehow managed to order my drink and, while I was at it, one for Maks, because I knew he'd be back soon.

I think that's why I didn't immediately realize it when another man stepped close to me and took me by the elbow. "Come with me," he said, his voice hard as steel.

"Excuse me?" I replied, trying to break out of his grasp while not spilling the drinks.

"Your presence is requested," the stranger said, his fingers tightening on my arm.

I looked up at him and saw that he dressed in the typical Arab fashion, except that he carried a sidearm tucked into a sash around his waist. I could see that he was trying to steer me over to the cluster of women gathered around Sheikh Omar and I dug in my heels and refused to move. "I'm here with someone," I told him firmly. "And I'll thank you to let me go!"

I'd said that last part a bit loudly, hoping someone in the crowd would notice and come to my aid, but no one paid us any attention and I was simply dragged along beside the unruly jerk until I was standing right in front of the sheikh himself.

He smiled wide when he saw I'd been brought in front of him, and I took the opportunity to pull out of his bodyguard's grasp. "I don't appreciate being manhandled!" I snapped.

"Apologies," said the sheikh, and he waved his hand to his guard like he was shooing away a pesky fly.

"Sheikh Omar," said a voice from behind me, and I wanted to sag in relief. "I would like to introduce my woman, Ms. Abigail Carter."

I took a step back to stand next to Maks and handed him his drink . . . or what was left of it. "Here you go, honey," I said to him. When he took it from my hand, I wrapped my arm around his waist and he wrapped his around my shoulder.

The sheikh spoke in Arabic and I was surprised when Maks replied to him in the same language. Turning to me, he said, "Sheikh Omar thinks you are very beautiful."

I smiled and waved my drink in the direction of all the girls nearby. "Not nearly as pretty as these women, though."

Maks didn't repeat what I'd said, and I suspected the sheikh understood every word, because he pointed to me and said, "Most beautiful woman here."

This won me lots of catty looks from the surrounding women, and I could only laugh like I thought he was very silly to think such a thing while I tried to wave it off. "Thank you, but I really doubt it."

The sheikh then spoke again to Maks and whatever he said made Grinkov redden slightly. Turning to me, he said, "Sheikh Omar would like to know if you are satisfied with me?"

I blinked. "Satisfied?"

Maks's lips thinned and I understood the subtext in an instant. "Oh! Um, of course I am!" When Sheikh Omar continued to scrutinize me, I added, "Maks is a wonderful man, and he is very good to me . . . in *every* way."

The sheikh swatted at his neck like he was slapping a mosquito just as a rumble of thunder echoed across the sky. The weather had been threatening rain all afternoon, and I couldn't have asked for more perfect timing. "Maks!" I said. "Don't you think we'd better move into the tent before we get wet?"

Maks nodded and bowed to the sheikh before moving off with me toward the tent. Another rumble of thunder reverberated overhead and I looked around to gauge its direction, spotting Dutch sneaking off into the house in the process.

I felt a flood of relief and almost didn't see it when Maks swatted at his own neck. "Mosquitoes must be out early," I said to him. He nodded and rubbed the side of his neck, and that's when I noticed something small and red drop to the ground.

I stopped walking, which forced Maks to stop as well. "What is it?" he asked.

Stooping down, I bent to retrieve the tiny dart from the ground and looked up at him in horror. *"Oh my God!"* I whispered.

Maks lifted the object out of my palm. It was no bigger than a thumbtack, with a tiny needle at the end pricked with blood. Automatically his hand went to his neck and he seemed to be putting two and two together.

I grabbed him by the hand. "Come with me now!"

"What was in the dart?" he asked, moving with me as fast as the crowd would let us.

"Don't talk," I warned, my stomach turning at the thought of what was about to happen to Maks. "Just move as fast as you can without calling a lot of attention to us."

Maks stuck to my side like glue and my heart hammered hard in my chest. How much time did I have to get him the antidote? A minute or two? Maybe less? I couldn't remember.

Maks stumbled suddenly as we were making our way up the steps. "I'm dizzy," he said to me.

I tightened my grip on his hand. "Keep moving!"

Behind us I heard a woman cry out. "What's wrong with him?"

I thought she was talking about us, so I chanced a look back and it was then that I noticed that the sheikh was being held up by two of his men, looking pale and sweating profusely. I remembered him swatting at a mysterious bug about two minutes before Grinkov. The sheikh was now beyond my help, not that I really would have helped a misogynist pig like that even if I could.

"Come on!" I urged as Maks and I got inside and were moving to the inside stairwell. Sweat had broken out all across his forehead and his breathing was labored. "Listen to me!" I snapped when he paused to grab the railing and wouldn't move. "If you don't make it up those stairs, *you'll die*! Do you understand me?"

Maks nodded dully. I lifted his arm over my shoulders and pulled him along with me up the stairs. By the time we reached the top, we were both breathing hard.

Our door was only a little down from the landing, thank God, as I was now supporting most of Maks's weight. "Please!" I coaxed. "Just a little farther!"

Somehow Maks was able to get his feet to cooperate and we made it to the door . . . which was locked.

"Where's the key?" I said frantically. Maks mumbled something and his now trembling hand came up to rub against his jacket pocket. I set him on the ground because I couldn't maneuver with him draped over me, and fished through his pocket, removing all the contents, including a folded piece of paper and the key. I inserted the key into the lock and got the door open, then pulled him limply into the room, because he was no longer able to stand.

His eyes were quickly rolling up into the back of his head, and foam began to form at the corners of his mouth. "Jesus!" I cried, dropping the key and the rest of the contents of his pockets next to him as I dashed into the bedroom, over to my luggage, and began rummaging through the contents.

I found the small manicure set right away and unzipped it with trembling fingers. Pulling out the toenail clippers, I extracted two of the syringes and ran back to Maks's side.

He was curled onto his side now, convulsing and frothing at the mouth. "Ohmigod!" I cried, shoving him onto his back and yanking so hard on the front of his shirt that buttons flew off in every direction. Straddling his torso, I lifted the syringe just like I'd been taught in my training and plunged it straight into the right side of Maks's chest.

He convulsed so hard he actually sat up and threw me off-balance. I fell sideways but managed to recover, then raised the other syringe and plunged it into the other side of his chest.

Maks gave one loud heaving breath and lay still.

I was panting so hard I was seeing stars, but I backed up off him and waited to see if he'd sit up and tell me that he was perfectly fine now, thank you very much.

He didn't.

My radar pulled my attention back to the syringes still in the cuticle case. I had an overwhelming urge to give him a second round of the antidote, but I hesitated for several seconds debating about whether that was a good idea. No one at the CIA had told me what giving an extra dose of the antidote would do, and I wondered if I'd kill Maks by injecting him with another round.

My intuition insisted that I needed to act quickly, and I needed to give him an extra dose. Steeling myself, I removed two more syringes and administered another dose, hoping they would do the trick.

But as I watched, Maks's color didn't return and his breathing remained very, very shallow and it seemed to me that he might be getting worse. I started to tremble and knew I needed to find Dutch. He'd know what to do. As I was getting to my feet, I reached for the key, and that's when I noticed the folded piece of paper lying next to Maks on the floor.

With a small gasp I realized it was the note and the map I'd written to Dutch and given to Mandy. *"Oh, no!"*

I grabbed the map, my purse, and the key and ran out of the room, barely managing to still my hands long enough to lock the door behind me. I then made a mad dash up the stairs to the third floor, and was only vaguely aware of the shouting and angry voices coming from outside.

Reaching the landing, I ran headlong down the hallway, panic fueling my every step, and to this day I don't quite know how I made it so far, so fast, in four-inch heels.

When I reached Dutch's door, I twisted the knob, not even bothering to knock, and thrust it open. Dutch was standing in the middle of the room looking at something hanging from the door to the bathroom. It took me a minute to realize that the blue-faced figure hanging grotesquely on the door by a black leather belt looped around her neck was Mandy.

I opened my mouth to scream—it was all a little too much for me—when I felt a hand clamp firmly over my mouth. I stared up at Dutch, my eyes watering, while he shook his head vigorously. "Shhhh," he said softly; then he let go of my mouth and curled me into his arms.

I sagged against him, suddenly so exhausted I could barely move. He set me down on the floor because my legs refused to hold me up, and I leaned next to Mandy's suitcase, which was parked next to the bed. "Jesus!" I cried. "Oh, poor Mandy!"

"It took me a while to get into the room," Dutch said, bending low to talk to me. "Whoever killed her locked the door after they left."

Numbly I lifted the key I'd taken from Maks, and pushed it into his hand. "Try that in the door, will you?"

Dutch took the key and moved away, and my eyes went back to her prone figure for a moment. She was so blue and still, and I felt like I was going to throw up.

I turned my head in the other direction, and the tags from Mandy's suitcase tickled my face. I pushed them away, but something about them caught my attention.

"The key works in the lock," Dutch said from across the room.

"Dutch!" I whispered, motioning him back over to me.

He came right over and I showed him the tags. "Las Vegas," he said, eyeing them, then Mandy.

"She flew in from the same airport where Oksana was killed!" I said.

Dutch looked back to me again. "Someone was using her and Oksana," Dutch said.

I nodded. "And when they were done using them, they killed them."

"Grinkov?" Dutch asked, holding his palm open to show me the key.

I shook my head. "I thought so," I said, "but now I'm not so sure. I think there's someone else responsible."

"How do you know there's someone else?"

"Because Maks has been shot by a dart!"

Dutch stood up quickly and pulled me up too. "Is he dead?"

"No," I said. "At least, maybe not yet. I gave him a double dose of the antidote, but I don't think I gave it to him in time."

"Where is he now?"

I was dizzy with all the recent events happening around me, and closed my eyes trying to get the world to stop spinning. I opened my eyes again and saw the urgency on Dutch's face. The window to the room was open and a strong wind gusted in, billowing the curtains and allowing me to see directly out into the garden, where it appeared the sheikh either had just died or was in the final throes before death, because the commotion around him seemed to be escalating. "He's in our room," I said. "It didn't look like he was going to recover, so I came to get you."

Dutch moved over to the window and peered outside. More thunder rippled across the atmosphere and the shouting below grew volatile. "Something's happened to the sheikh," he said.

I nodded dully. "He was also shot with a dart."

"You saw it?"

"I think so."

Gunfire erupted from down below, followed by screams and angry shouts. Dutch moved swiftly to my side and swept up my hand. "Time to go," he said, pointing out the obvious.

We paused long enough for him to grab Mandy's homing device, which she'd left on the nightstand, and as we dashed out of the room, he gave it to me with a stern, "Keep this with you."

I tucked the pen down my dress, clipping it to the inside of my bra, while we rushed down the hall and over to the stairs. We made it to the second floor, and just as we reached the landing, I saw Grinkov's butler knocking on Maks's door. "Sir!" he called urgently.

Eddington's face lifted and our eyes locked. "Go!" I told Dutch as the butler's mouth fell open, and we hurried as fast as we could down the rest of the stairs.

Gunfire continued to sound all around the premises along with screams and the shattering of china and glass. Dutch and I ducked low as we moved down the stairs to the ground floor, where chaos reigned. "Do you have your gun?" he asked, reaching into his blazer to pull out Des Vries's weapon.

I held up my purse. "Yes!"

"Good," Dutch said, and we ran out from the stairwell. Dutch began moving us toward the front, where everyone who was fleeing was naturally gravitating, but I stopped him and said, "No! We need to get to the back! There's a gate in the wall of the garden and I think we can get through it if we hurry!"

Dutch's lips pressed together like he didn't like the idea, but he trusted me enough to turn direction and pull me down a side hallway that ran along the back of the house. He seemed to know exactly where he was going, and my radar was telling me we were headed in the right direction, so I kept close to him and tried to keep my heels from clicking too loudly on the floor.

Of course, I shouldn't have worried; the chaos all over the grounds was enough to mask even Mandy's horse clomp.

At one point in our stealthy course through the house, Dutch paused outside a closed door where I could hear several voices yelling inside. There was also a loud static noise in the background, but I couldn't make out a single thing anyone was saying. Dutch pulled his scrambler pen from his dinner jacket, twisted the cap, and placed it on the ledge above the door.

The effect was immediate. From inside the panicked yelling increased dramatically. Dutch and I hurried away as fast as possible and barely managed to round a corner down a smaller hallway before we heard the door burst open and someone shout angrily in alarm.

"Keep moving!" Dutch said when I stopped to try to remove my shoes.

"I can't run in these!" I told him, mentally berating myself for not changing into different shoes before I'd left Maks to find Dutch.

"Keep them on!" he warned, and reached back for my hand again. "You'll cut your feet to shreds if you don't."

We made it to the end of the hall and Dutch stopped in front of another closed door. He tried the handle, found it locked, and stepped back from it, pulling me with him. "Stand clear," he said, right before he brought his foot up and karate kicked the door just above the handle.

It burst open and we darted inside, coming into a small library of sorts. Dutch moved to a single glass-paned door with a sheer curtain, the very one I'd attempted to open earlier that morning, in fact. As we moved to it, the glass suddenly shattered and a hail of bullets rained into the room.

Dutch threw himself over me and we went crashing to the floor. I heard him grunt in pain as he tried to shield me from the gunfire, and for one awful moment I was convinced he'd been hit.

The gunfire aimed at us diminished the moment another round of bullets sounded from across the lawn. I concluded that whoever was shooting at us had just gotten shot. "Dutch!" I said when the rain of bullets stopped threatening our lives. *"Dutch!"*

"I'm okay," he said with a groan, rolling off me but holding on to his left side where his bruised ribs were still healing. "Come on," he said, after taking a breath and getting to his knees. "We've gotta move."

Squatting down low, I followed him over to the ruined door, immensely grateful that he'd insisted I keep my shoes on when my feet crunched on the broken glass. Dutch kept me behind him as he chanced a look out onto the lawn. "Why is everyone shooting at each other?" I whispered.

"It's the death of Sheikh Omar," Dutch said softly. "I'm sure his bodyguards thought he'd been poisoned by Boklovich or one of the others who wanted to take him out of the bidding, and they started the gunfight. Since everyone here is armed to the hilt, it's likely everyone's shooting at everyone."

"Great," I said, wondering if our situation could possibly get any worse.

"Get your gun out," Dutch told me.

I dug into my purse and pulled out the small pistol, which brought me little comfort when I thought about the assault weapons being carried by every single one of Boklovich's guards.

I clicked the safety and held it in the manner that I'd been taught, waiting anxiously behind Dutch. My radar pinged and I nudged him. "Honey! We've got to go *now*!"

He looked over his shoulder to stare meaningfully at me, mouthed, "Love you," then took me firmly by the left hand and we dashed out to the terrace.

Chapter Fifteen

. . .

The first thing Dutch and I had to navigate when we came out onto the lawn was a dead body. To this day, I'm not sure if it was a man or a woman; I just knew the person was dead by the blood . . . lots and *lots* of blood.

My stomach clenched and I felt myself gag and double over. Dutch pulled me close and swept me up in his arms, not even pausing while he hurried over to the wall and began to run with me down the side.

Overhead small droplets of rain hit my face and a cool wind came with it. I swallowed hard and pushed on his shoulder. "I'm okay!" I told him, just as the sky really opened up and the rain came pelting down.

Dutch paused by a tree, where he set me down and we hid for a moment to catch our breath and assess the lawn. I peeked out through the rain and saw it littered with bodies. I tried not to look too close, but even that random observation told me that Boklovich appeared to be one of the casualties.

"Oh my God!" I gasped when I saw just how many people were down. Dutch was right—everyone *was* shooting at one another!

"Come on," Dutch said, reaching for my hand again. "We can't stay here."

"The gate is at the far end of the wall," I told him when we began to move again. I kept praying that we wouldn't encounter a guard, and judging by the stream of gunfire still echoing above the thunder, lightning, and rain, most of the fighting had moved to the front of the house. I was immensely grateful to my crew that they'd pushed us to the back, because as we continued to dart along the wall, I thought we might yet have a chance.

And with a small flutter of my heart I saw the ivy covering the gate just ahead. "There!" I said, pointing it out to Dutch.

In ten more strides we got to the gate and both of us began to tear the ivy away. It was slick and wet and clung to me, tangling around my ankles, but I was hardly worried about that. I just wanted out of that stupid yard and I didn't yet know how we were going to get beyond the padlocked gate.

I paused to look up. The top of the wall didn't seem to be ten feet tall anymore—it seemed to be twenty. "We can climb the ivy," I told Dutch as he stood back to survey the gate and the lock too.

He looked from the gate to me, and I swear he almost smiled. "In that dress, Edgar, that's something I'd like to see, but not today."

He then aimed his gun right at the padlock and fired three times in rapid succession.

The lock took all three bullets and held together. "Son of a bitch!" he swore, stepping forward, about to yank on it.

All of a sudden the brick next to me exploded and I screamed, dropping to my knees as bullets pummeled the wall right above my head. Dutch had also dropped down and he crawled over to me, half-pulling, half-dragging me to a nearby stone bench. The gunfire continued right over our heads, and with great effort Dutch pushed the bench over to give us some cover. A second later I heard the bench take several bullets, and small chunks of concrete flew up only to pepper my hair with debris.

Instinctively I covered my head and tried to make myself as small as possible while Dutch held me close. When the gunfire stopped, he whispered, "Stay here." Before I could even react, he'd moved to a crouch and darted away.

Gunfire followed after him and I wanted to cry—I was so scared for him. After a time the bullets chasing Dutch stopped, and I worried about what that meant. And then I got angry. Very, *very* angry. Footsteps through the foliage alerted me that someone was approaching the bench, slowly and cautiously, and the way they moved closer so carefully told me that it definitely wasn't Dutch. I looked down at my shaking hands and realized somewhere between the gate and the stone bench I'd dropped my pistol, but my clutch was still parked firmly under my arm.

A plan formed in my head, and after rummaging through my purse, I moved carefully onto my stomach, listening to the footsteps draw closer and closer. My heart was pounding in my chest like a jackhammer, but my brain was focused on one thing, and when I felt someone tug hard on my shoulder, I came up with all the rage of a tigress, using the edge of my palm to inflict an uppercut to the guard with one hand before zinging him good in the groin with the stun gun. He slammed to the earth with a hard thud, knocked out cold.

I sat next to him panting for a few beats, thinking my CIA trainer would've been so proud.

Quickly, however, I snapped my attention back to getting the heck out of there. I returned to the gate and looked around for something to hit the padlock with. My eyes lit on the gardeners' shack and the tools spilling out from inside. Moving quickly, I grabbed the heaviest shovel I could find among the clutter and hefted it above the lock, bringing it down hard onto the casing.

My aim was slightly off, and the shovel only half hit the metal, but to my surprise the whole lock fell apart as if it had only just been holding itself together. I threw down the shovel and tugged at the latch, then heaved the rusted metal gate open, but I didn't go through. Instead, I turned away and began moving off in the direction I'd seen Dutch go. I wasn't leaving without him.

I took two steps in his direction when I felt the cool steel of a gun in the center of my back. "Where you go, pretty girl?" I heard a heavily accented voice say.

I knew that voice and it made my blood turn to ice. I stood stock-still while I considered my options, and I knew I was definitely out of them when I felt his hand clamp down on my shoulder and spin me around. I stared right into a face I detested. A face without mercy and murderous intent. "Where Grinkov?" Yurik demanded.

"Dead."

"Good," he said, his free hand moving to the neck of my dress, and I knew he was about to rip it right off me. I closed my eyes and clenched my fists and then an explosion sounded so close to me that it knocked me backward, right out of his grip.

I fell on the ground, and in a haze, I looked up to see Dutch, standing over Yurik's dead body, seething with anger while smoke still curled from the barrel of his gun. To add to my surprise, in his other hand he held a familiar small black box and I knew what had taken him so long.

Dutch's gaze then swiveled to the soldier I'd taken out, and while

I watched, he nodded in approval. I had no time to even thank him for saving me or express how glad I was to see him, because across the lawn we heard one of the other soldiers call out for Yurik.

In the next instant Dutch had me under the arm and was lifting me to my feet. "Get through the gate!" he ordered, then turned to the unconscious guard and pulled him into the garden shack, shoving him in with all the clutter and barely managing to get the door closed.

Meanwhile I stood there staring dumbly, not wanting to leave him alone. "What about you?" I asked, seeing my stun gun in the grass and picking it up to tuck it inside my dress.

When I looked up again, I saw that Dutch wanted to toss Intuit to me, so I held out my hands and caught the device, which was much lighter than expected. He then bent over Yurik and gripped him under the arm. "Get moving!" he said again. "I'll be right behind you!"

I bolted through the gate and nearly went down amid the tangle of foliage. Somehow I managed to stay upright and behind me Dutch kept saying, "Go, go, go!" to encourage me, so I kept moving, deeper into the thick tangle, trying to pick my way quickly away from the wall. About fifteen yards into the surrounding forest, I turned back to see Dutch still struggling with Yurik's body.

"Why are you bringing him?" I whispered to Dutch. Even from here we could now hear multiple voices calling for the soldiers' leader.

"They won't stop until they find him," Dutch said, coming up to me and breathing hard. "And if they find out we've killed him, they won't stop until they hunt us down."

"We can't drag him around with us!" I protested. Yurik was at least six-two and two hundred twenty pounds.

Dutch let go of the dead man and wiped the rain out of his eyes. "We'll need to hide him."

I had an idea and shoved Intuit at him while I told him to wait there. Then I dashed back to the little shack near the wall, being careful to go quietly and keep out of sight, grabbed a shovel and a garden hoe from the ground near the shack, and pulled the iron gate closed behind me.

I picked my way back to Dutch and he actually smiled.

Wordlessly I gave him the shovel and started digging frantically at the ground with the hoe. We had to hurry because eventually the men would find the torn ivy and the broken padlock and put two and two together. Not to mention that the guard inside the shack could wake up at any moment, although I doubted he'd come to his senses anytime soon.

It didn't take long to bury the guard; much of the ground was covered by leaves and dead foliage, so we only had to dig a shallow grave and push Yurik into it before we started piling the stuff back on top.

Somewhere along that effort, however, my engagement ring slipped off and Dutch had to practically fight me to leave it and run with him when the gunfire erupted again.

Picking our way through the wet foliage and following an old path worn into the ground, we were lucky enough to discover a hunting lodge and we rushed inside to crouch down and wait for the pursuit to die down.

Dutch had taken Yurik's assault weapon, and while he stood guard, I tried to stay warm by huddling in a corner.

I was soaked through and the late afternoon was finally turning chilly. My feet were killing me, and I had no idea how I was going to run through miles of forest to the other landing strip.

To make matters worse, while I was looking at Dutch, I saw his posture stiffen. He turned silently to me and made a motion with two fingers pointing to his eyes; then he held up those same two fingers and pointed out to the right of the shack.

At least two of the soldiers had followed our trail. I felt my breath quicken. My radar was screaming at me that Dutch mustn't fire his weapon, as it would alert all the others hunting for us and they'd corner us in the shack and kill us; I was sure of it. Dutch pointed to my hand and made his fingers into a gun. I shook my head. I'd left my pistol somewhere back in Vasilii's garden. I showed him my stun gun and he frowned.

He then reached into his holster and took out Des Vries's Beretta, holding it out to me. I shook my head again vigorously, and pointed to my temple. "No shoot!" I mouthed, then cupped my ear and made a motion with my hand to indicate the others would hear.

Dutch looked at me grimly, then removed the strap of the assault weapon and laid it softly on the floor. He inched his way over to me and thrust the gun in my hand. Leaning in to whisper in my ear, he said, "I'll take care of it. You stay here."

I shook my head again—I didn't want him to leave me—but he had already turned away to retrieve the assault weapon and move to the open window on the other side of the shack. Carefully, he crept out of it and left me alone.

I took deep breaths while I huddled in the shadows, holding the gun close and waiting in the dark for something to happen. The steady drone of the rain outside prevented me from hearing the soldiers' approach, but it wasn't long before I saw the beam of a flashlight wave across the door to the shack. I was out of the glare of the light, but that didn't keep me from trying to push back deeper into the shadows.

Again my heart thundered in my chest and I tried to steady the Beretta in my hands, but the weapon was much heavier than I was used to and my hands were slick with moisture. I figured I'd have one shot in the darkened shack, and then, even if I missed, I'd have to get up and bolt out the same window Dutch had gone through.

I wondered where he was, and what was keeping him, and the beam kept getting closer and closer to the door. Someone was coming right for me.

In the next instant, the beam went out and its absence stunned me. What'd happened? Had Dutch attacked him? Did he move off in another direction? Had he dropped the flashlight?

I was shaking with fear, waiting tensely for something to happen, so when it did, I was caught off guard. A dark figure appeared in the doorway, moving stealthily in. The breath caught in my throat and I raised the gun unsteadily. I wanted to pull that trigger, I swear, but something made me pause, and in the second that I hesitated, the lone figure was tackled to the ground by someone else.

It was too dark to see who had tackled whom, but I had to assume Dutch had attacked one of the soldiers and they were now each involved in the fight of their lives. I trained the gun on them as they rolled around, trying through the din to pick out Dutch from the other man, but it was impossible.

And then I saw one of them gain the advantage and straddle the other. A hand rose up and I could see the outline of a knife in the tiny trickle of light from outside. With a hard thrust I saw the knife come down, and I cried out. I was positive Dutch hadn't been wearing a knife.

The man on the floor gave a grunt of pain and lay still, and I was so horrified by the scene that I simply crouched there, my eyes welling with tears.

The man who'd won pushed away from the figure on the ground, wiped his blade clean, and stuck it into his belt before turning to face me. I didn't know how he knew I was there, but it seemed his eyes were better than mine, and maybe he'd heard my cry.

I pointed my gun at him again, but my vision was blurred by the tears. "Dutch?" I whispered hoarsely, knowing it wasn't him.

"No," he said, and there was something about that voice. . . .

"Abigail, it's me," he said right before a shadow burst through the doorway and tackled *him* to the ground!

Alarmed, I jumped to my feet and ran over to the two figures wrestling there. "Stop!" I cried, seeing who the new assailant was. "Stop it! Dutch, please stop!"

Somehow I got the two of them apart, but not before Dutch split open Maks's lip.

For his part Maks kicked Dutch and swore at him in Russian. Dutch spat back a similar expletive and they nearly went at it again, but I forced myself between the two and insisted they calm down. When I was sure they weren't going to pummel each other, I turned to Maks and demanded, "What are you doing here?"

"I followed your map," he said, wiping his lip with his hand while glaring hard at my fiancé.

I remembered then how I'd found the map with my note to Dutch in Maks's pocket after he'd killed Mandy. "Why did you kill Mandy?" I demanded next.

Maks looked at me incredulously. "*I* didn't kill her," he said frankly. "Rick did."

It was Dutch's turn to look surprised. "*I* didn't kill her!"

"Liar!" Maks barked. "I went to your room and found her there, hanging from the door."

"Listen," Dutch said, leaning in to get in his face. "I didn't kill Mandy. The last time I saw her alive was last night right after dinner, when I left her *alive* in the room to find another place to sleep."

"You stayed in another room?" I asked, quite puzzled by the order of the events leading up to Mandy's death.

"Yeah."

"But she gave you the message to meet me in the garden this morning at six thirty, right?"

"What message?" he asked, and now I knew why he hadn't shown up.

I ignored his question and turned back to Maks. "If you didn't kill her, how did you get the map?"

Maks folded his arms across his chest defensively. "I thought you ladies were acting very suspicious, and then you called Rick 'Dutch,' and I knew something wasn't right, so I went to her room to demand she tell me what was going on, and I found her hanging there with the map still clutched in her hand. I took it and left the room, locking it behind me so that no one would discover her body until I had a chance to tell Vasilii about it. That was what I was trying to tell you when I got hit with the dart. I wanted to convince you that you were trying to protect a killer."

"He's not a killer," I said. "He's my fiancé."

Maks's eyes were large with surprise. "You and Rick are engaged?"

"No," I told him, handing Dutch the gun lest my next bit of news require him to use it to control Grinkov. "And this isn't Rick Des Vries, Maks."

Maks's gaze went back and forth between us, and I knew he was struggling to understand. "Meet Assistant Special Agent in Charge

Dutch Rivers of the United States FBI," I said, watching his reaction closely.

Maks surprised me when he stepped back and visibly relaxed. "Oh, thank God," he said. "I was worried the disk would fall into the wrong hands tonight."

It was our turn to look surprised. "Wait, what?"

Maks smiled. "You're not the only ones playing for the good guys," he said. "I was recruited by the CSIS ten years ago to run countersurveillance on organized crime here in Canada."

"*You're* a spy?" I gasped.

Maks actually laughed. "Yes, Abigail, or is your name perhaps something more exotic?"

I shook my head. "No. It's Abigail. Although everyone calls me Abby."

Maks smiled. Reaching out to take my hand, he lifted it to his lips and kissed it. "Well then, thank you, Abby, for saving my life earlier. That would have been a most excruciating death had you not given me the antidote in time."

Dutch snaked a protective arm around my middle, pulling me out of Maks's grip, and held me close while he pushed the tip of the gun into Maks's chest. "As interested in this little tea party as I am, Grinkov, I think we need to get the hell out of here."

Maks sneered at Dutch. It was clear these two weren't going to get together for hockey night if we ever made it out of here. "I've sent Eddington on ahead to the plane," he said. "He's gone to alert my pilot. We should make our way to the airstrip."

I tried to orient our position in relation to the airstrip. It had to be at least three miles through thick forest. In my current getup I'd never make it. I looked down at my feet, cursing my choice of foot attire for the hundredth time, and Dutch seemed to notice my predicament.

"Wait here," he said, handing me the gun and glaring meaningfully at Maks as if to say, "She knows how to use that," before leaving the shack.

He was back just a minute or two later with a pair of boots and a fatigue jacket. "Where'd you get that?" I asked.

Dutch stepped over the dead soldier on the floor. "The other guy was small," he said, handing me the jacket and boots.

I made a face but quickly donned the jacket and peeled my swollen and blistered feet out of the pumps, shoving them into the boots. They were several sizes too big, but I'd make them work.

We then made sure no other soldiers were nearby and left the shack. Dutch had his map and the compass, and he used his penlight to help navigate us through the woods. While we trudged through the thick forest, something kept niggling at the edge of my thoughts.

"Maks?" I said finally when I couldn't keep the bothersome thought to myself anymore.

"Yes?"

"Why did you attack me in the parking garage and steal my wallet?"

In front of me, Maks came to a halt. I stopped too and he turned to look at me. "I didn't," he said simply.

Dutch had come up short too. "What're you talking about?" he asked me.

"I found my wallet and my stun gun in the pocket of Grinkov's luggage," I said. "That's how I knew it'd been him who attacked me in the garage."

"No," Maks said, an odd look in his eyes. "As I told you the day you were attacked, we found you already unconscious. I did not strike you or take your personal items."

"But I found them in your luggage," I insisted. I was totally confused, so I focused on his energy, and sure enough I could see he was being somewhat truthful, but there was that small hint of bluff in his answer, which caused me not to completely trust him.

I looked to Dutch to gauge his reaction. He had his poker face up, but I could tell he was alarmed and the air had suddenly filled with tension. "Did you know that Abby was nearly strangled to death in Des Vries's offices?" he asked Maks.

Maks's expression turned from veiled to angry. "When?"

"The day you met with Dutch and Boklovich and insisted that I not come along," I said.

"Which left her vulnerable and alone at Des Vries's office," Dutch said, his eyes narrowing while he looked at Maks with renewed scrutiny.

Grinkov's posture stiffened. "I've been doing nothing but trying to keep her safe, Agent Rivers. Why would I wish her dead?"

"Good question," Dutch said, the muzzle of the gun back up and trained right at Maks. "And one I'd like answered when we land back in Toronto. For now, how about you walk right in front of me, huh, Maks?"

Something unreadable passed between the two men. Finally, however, Maks moved up closer to Dutch, but not before volunteering his knife, and that one gesture really bothered me. I mean, why would a guy that meant to do me harm give up a weapon I was sure Dutch didn't know he had in the first place?

Something else that bothered me was that the thief who'd stolen the drone and Intuit had clearly been at the party—the darts were evidence of that—but I still had no idea who it'd been and I felt like after all of that, we'd partly failed in our mission.

We walked on in silence for the duration of our march, and by the time we emerged from the forest at the far end of the landing strip, my legs were covered in scratches and my feet were stinging fiercely from walking sockless in boots that were way too big for me.

Still, I had on the jacket and the boots were better than the pumps, so I figured we had only one more big obstacle to overcome—getting to the plane and off the ground without incident—and we'd be home free.

As long as Dutch kept that gun trained on Maks, I knew he'd be forced to take us somewhere safe, like Victoria or Vancouver.

And I could have wept with relief when I spotted Maks's plane amid a short row of other small jets, but just as quickly my heart sank when I took in the military vehicle parked in the middle of the runway. The three of us crept close to the edge of the field to take a better look, and saw three men positioned at the top of the jeep manning a very big gun pointed right at the planes.

The message was clear—no one was getting off the ground without a fight.

And that presented Dutch and me with another terrible dilemma: He wouldn't be able to take on all three soldiers and their guns by himself, and I certainly wasn't in much of a position to help him. I mean, I now knew how to handle a gun, but I wasn't the best at killing people, as my time in the shack when the soldier had entered had already proved.

We needed Maks's help, and to get it, we'd have to trust him. Dutch sighed heavily and turned to me. "Your call, Edgar."

I knew exactly what he was thinking. I checked my radar and it suggested we'd face some sort of danger once we gained the plane. There was treachery in the ether, I was sure of it. The only other option was to turn tail and make our way back through the wilderness to the other airstrip, where we could alert the CIA that we'd been compromised, but that was nearly all the way on the other side of the island, and it was getting dark out and still raining a little.

I could feel these two choices weighing heavily on me and neither seemed good, but since we were already here at this airstrip with an awaiting plane, I decided to go with the easier choice.

So I turned to Maks and laid it all out on the table. "There's something you should know," I told him to get his attention away from the soldiers.

He seemed to know we'd be asking him for help, and when he turned to look at me, he seemed quite amused. "And that is?"

I reached over and placed a hand on Dutch's arm. "I'm hoping to marry this man in the next year or so, Maks. I love him more than I've ever loved anyone in my whole life, and if I leave this earth before I get to say 'I do,' my ghost will haunt you to the ends of the earth and I will not rest until I've driven you completely insane."

Maks's gaze never left mine and there was a mixture of emotions behind those eyes. "I know what it means to lose your true love, Abigail," he said finally, and I understood that he was referring to his late wife. "You may not trust me, but you need me. Together we can leave here. Apart we'll never make it out alive."

I nodded and motioned to Dutch. "Give him back his knife."

Reluctantly, Dutch handed Grinkov back his weapon.

"Now give him the assault rifle," I said.

Dutch hesitated.

"Don't trust *him*," I implored. "Trust *me*."

With even more reluctance Dutch handed over the big weapon.

"Now," I said, wriggling out of the jacket and lifting Maks's knife out of his hand, "what we need is a distraction." I then shucked the boots, removed my stun gun from the inside of my dress, and made a very large tear in the front of the dress with the knife. Handing the dagger back to Maks, I stepped out onto the muddy runway.

"Abby!" I heard Dutch whisper harshly. "Get the hell back here!"

I ignored him and trotted down the length of the field. The soldiers all had their backs to me, so I was able to get quite close to them before one of them spotted me. He shouted an alarm and the guns all swiveled to aim directly at me.

I swayed on my feet dramatically and began to wail, tugging at the tear in the top of my dress to expose as much cleavage as possible. "Help me!" I begged them. "Please! I've been attacked and I need help!"

The three of them eyed one another silently, and I knew they were wondering if they should shoot me or come down to investigate.

"I'm hurt!" I told them, and pulled at the dress even more. "Right here!" I added, pointing to one boob. And then I dropped to the ground in what I hoped was a believable faint, curling the stun gun into my left hand just underneath my torso.

The soldiers argued for a moment or two until one of them got down and approached me cautiously. I held perfectly still.

He said something I didn't understand as he got close, so I moaned and moved a little to show him I wasn't a threat . . . just hurt and harmless. He came close enough to hover over me and poke my hip with his boot.

The other men called to him, and he turned to reply. I used the moment to roll over and kick him in the nuts as hard as I could.

The soldier sank to his knees, clutching his groin, and I sat straight up and shocked him in the side of his neck while gunfire flew out from the surrounding foliage nearby.

By the time my stun gun ran out of juice, my target was unconscious and twitching.

Someone stepped close. "Good job, Edgar."

I looked up and grinned like I'd just received a gold star. "Thanks, cowboy."

The roar of an engine caught my attention, and I saw that Grinkov was behind the wheel of the jeep, moving it and its two dead occupants off the landing strip. Dutch dropped my borrowed jacket next to me with the boots. "Here," he said, before bending down to drag my guy off the field too.

"Don't kill him!" I told him firmly. He looked disappointed, but he didn't argue and he didn't put a bullet in the guy either, so I relaxed.

Maks got out and waved us to the plane. We ran quickly down the field only to fling ourselves back into the tall grass at the edge when one of the planes came roaring down the runway straight for us.

Dutch helped me to my feet after it'd whizzed by and lifted off. "There'll be a mad rush outta here now that the runway's clear."

We kept to the tall grass and made our way down to Grinkov's plane, which was third in line to take off.

Eddington opened the door and Dutch lifted me up. I smiled at him. "You made it out!"

"Yes, ma'am," he said, helping me while I scrambled through the door. "It was a bit tricky, but Mr. Grinkov managed to bribe a guard who allowed me the use of his jeep."

Dutch and Grinkov both made it aboard too and Maks wasted no time hurrying to the front of the plane and shouting through the cabin door, "Take us out of here, Bruce!"

"Get everybody strapped in!" the captain shouted.

I hustled over to a seat and clipped my seat belt. Dutch landed next to me, setting down the small black box that held Intuit while he secured his own belt. Meanwhile, Maks helped a trembling Eddington with the door and then motioned for him to sit down.

The plane jolted forward and my head knocked painfully against the side of the wall. Maks's poor butler hadn't yet reached his seat at the back of the plane and went tumbling head over heels right in front of me.

"Mr. Eddington!" I cried, trying to steady him as the plane bumped and jostled along.

He tried to get up and fell right over again, so I latched on to his leg and ordered him to hold still. "Just wait until we're in the air!" I commanded. "And hold on to anything you can!"

The butler reached for one of the table legs, which was bolted in place, and we bounced and jostled all the way down the rough terrain. "Come on, come on, come on!" I prayed, willing the plane to lift off.

Eddington's legs were trembling under my hand and I moved my grip to his ankle to hold him steady as we finally, blissfully began to lift into the air. I almost cheered, but something caught my eye and I let go of Eddington's ankle abruptly, all my senses alert and alarmed.

The butler hardly noticed; he was so busy getting to his feet and struggling to his seat at the back of the plane, limping as he went without his walking stick.

I felt Dutch's eyes on me. "You okay?"

I turned in my chair away from Eddington. "Look at his shoes!" I told him, discreetly pointing behind me.

Dutch gave me a quizzical look, but when he eyed Eddington's shoes, he seemed to understand exactly what I was getting at.

"I'll kill him," Dutch said, ready to confront the butler about the brand-new shoelace on his right shoe, while the well-worn lace on the other exactly matched the one left next to me on the day I was nearly strangled to death.

Before he had a chance to move, however, the door to the lavatory at the back of the plane flung open, and out came a real, live ghost wielding a most unusual-looking gun.

Chapter Sixteen

• • •

"*Mandy?*" I gasped, disbelieving my own eyes for a moment.

Her face and hands were still tinged in blue around the edges and she smiled wickedly at me. "Hey there!" she sang, pointing the muzzle my way.

I froze. I'd seen that gun in a picture back at the CIA headquarters when it had still been mounted to the drone. "Shit," Dutch swore.

Mandy's smile got even bigger. "Surprise!" she said to him. She then reached behind her with her free hand and waved a black strap with a clip attached, and as I looked more closely at her, I could see that she was strapped into a black harness hidden under her dress. The belt she appeared to have been hung by had been a prop. "I got this from the set of a TV show I worked on once. I thought someday I'd use it on Rick; you know, play dead, force him to admit how much he cared about me. But using it for this turned out so much better."

"You faked your own death?" Maks said, and I knew he was slower on the uptake than we were.

"*She* stole the drone," I said, putting so many of the puzzle pieces together. Looking at Dutch, I said, "*That's* the real reason why my radar had first pulled out Des Vries's photo back at the CIA headquarters! Remember I said he was involved but tangentially?"

Dutch nodded, and Mandy beamed at me; she looked like a woman who couldn't wait to brag about what she'd done. "Yep. Rick's a son of a bitch, but he's smart and he knew his way around weaponry. He never thought I could hold a thought in my head, so he used to let me watch him steal this or that, then resell it to the highest bidder. I learned a lot from that bastard, and when word got out that the U.S. had developed a drone that could detect a specific person's aura from half a mile up, he started looking into how to steal it. Lucky me, right around then one of Rick's bank accounts was hacked and he lost fifty thousand, and the hacker made sure to let him know who'd done it. Rick was so pissed about it that he got drunk and confessed to me that ten years ago he'd smacked an old girlfriend one too many times and she'd died, so he'd dumped her body where nobody could find it, then left Holland and never went back. He said the old girlfriend's family had dogged him for years and the hacker was her cousin, who was looking for some payback.

"That's when my idea to get rid of Rick and steal the drone really took shape. I sent an e-mail to the hacker; I told him I knew where Rick had dumped the body of his cousin, and I'd tell him where she was if he'd help me with a little mission that would make us both rich and let him get his revenge on Rick. He took the bait and we began to plot it out."

"So after you recruited Diedrich you talked Oksana into seducing the pilot," I said, working my way past Diedrich Wyngarden to the other players in her devious plot.

"I did," she admitted. "Oksana was a pretty girl, but she was super dumb. I met her in Ottawa on a modeling gig and we kept in touch here and there. When she got into trouble with the cops, she called me to see if I could help her, and I was the one that convinced Rick to get her new papers so she could sneak into the U.S. He wanted five thousand dollars for it, but I talked him down to two and told her that she'd owe me a favor someday.

"I snooped into Rick's surveillance on the pilot, and I saw that he liked to hire an escort every once in a while from the Strip. Oksana was already working for an agency and she played her role perfectly, but she was a loose end who had to be dealt with."

"Just like the pilot and Diedrich were also loose ends," I said. "So you killed them all?"

"Why leave a loose thread when it's so easy to snip it off?" she replied smartly. She was definitely proud of herself.

"How did you know Rick would get detained in Israel?" I asked her.

She laughed again. "Oh, honey," she said. "What do you take me for, an amateur?"

"Yes, actually," I told her, only now noticing the intelligence and cunning in her eyes. Why hadn't I seen that before?

Mandy seemed even more delighted by my reaction. "My whole life I've been underestimated," she said. "Everybody sees the hair and the boobs and they think dumb bimbo. Well, I learned how to use that to my advantage, didn't I? Even Rick never suspected. A few days before Rick left Jordan, I made sure to give one of my flight attendant buddies working his flight a special meal to be served to him right after takeoff. I then called ahead to the Israeli authorities and told them to watch for a first-class passenger that might be in need of medical assistance arriving on a jet out of Jordan making an emergency landing in Tel Aviv. I also told them the passenger was flying under an assumed name and that his real name was Richard Des Vries, a wanted weapons dealer.

"I knew my plan had gone off without a hitch when my friend called me in a panic and said that the meal she'd served my boyfriend must have been spoiled, because he'd been taken off the plane in Tel Aviv with a severe case of food poisoning."

Something else binged off my radar. "You murdered Kozahkov," I said knowingly.

She nodded. "I did," she said. "He and Oksana knew each other from the old country, so I used her to call him and arrange a meeting for me and Boklovich."

"But you killed him before you met with Boklovich. Why?"

Mandy shrugged. "When I walked into the penthouse and found you there, I knew something was up. So while you were in the bathroom talking to Rivers, I snooped around and found a file on Kozahkov lying on the counter. I knew you guys were about to set up a meeting with him to try to get to Boklovich before the drone went to auction, so all I had to do was send him an e-mail from Rick's laptop, which he hides in a cubby behind the couch, and which you guys obviously didn't know about, and voilà! The meeting location changed and I was able to take him out."

"But why?" I pressed. "I mean, you needed him to get to Boklovich, right?"

"I needed him to get me an in to Boklovich a little less than I needed him to lead you guys to me," she said. "Besides, I discovered that file on Rick you guys hid in the drawer, and in there I found a contact number for a friend of Rick's that you guys didn't even know about who had a connection to Vasilii, and he gave me Boklovich's number; so I called him and after I dropped Kozahkov's name and told him what I had, he agreed to meet with me and we set up the auction."

"You made those calls the day you ran away from me at Eaton Centre, right?"

Mandy smiled ear to ear. "I can't believe you fell for that. Look who's a dumb-ass now, huh?"

"Why'd you kill Sheikh Omar?" I asked her. I wanted to keep her talking so that one of us could come up with a plan, 'cause if Mandy stopped talking, I had little doubt she'd start shooting.

"Rick sold me to the sheikh for a week. After two nights I managed to escape. But I was alone in Dubai without money or ID, so I had to go back to Rick and beg him to get me out of there. If Omar hadn't been such a cheapass when Rick tried to sell him some arms, he probably would have left me there, but he used me as an excuse to drop out of the deal. That was the night I vowed to get even with Rick, and I also vowed to kill Sheikh Omar."

I eyed Maks nervously; he was staring incredulously at Mandy, like he couldn't believe she was actually capable of carrying out such an intelligent plan. "Why'd you try to kill Maks?" I asked.

"I wasn't aiming at Maks," she said, looking steadily at me.

Gulp.

"Okay," I said, still trying to keep her talking. "Then why me?"

"I don't like you," she said icily. "You were mean to me."

Double gulp.

"So what happens now, Mandy?" Dutch asked.

Mandy's eyes were exactly the kind you'd expect from a criminal genius, filled with satisfaction. "Now that I've gotten my revenge?" she asked snidely. When no one answered, she said, "Well, Agent Rivers, I guess Maks orders his pilot to fly to Hong Kong. I'm meeting with a few interested clients there, and since I'll be offering them both the prototype on the seat next to you and the disk you're carrying in your pocket, I'm pretty sure I'll be a *very* wealthy woman."

"The software on Intuit is bogus," I told her quickly, trying to bargain for our lives. "And Dutch's disk is protected by a password. It'll be useless to you, Mandy."

The gun in Mandy's hand came back to point directly at my chest. "I only need the program to work past one more demonstration," she said, "which I'm pretty sure it will do, and I'll give your fiancé exactly five seconds to give me that password, honey, or I'll pump every dart in this gun right into you, and no antidote will save you. What do you think the chances are that he'll cough it up?"

Dutch reached into his pocket and pulled out the disk, waving it at her. "Here!" he said, his voice a bit unsteady, and that broke my heart. "I'll give you the password! Just don't hurt her, okay?"

Mandy took a step toward Dutch to grab the disk, and as she did, Eddington launched himself out of his chair and tackled her to the ground. We were all so stunned that, for a moment, no one moved to help him, but Dutch finally managed to free himself from his seat belt and hurried to grab Mandy by the shoulders while Eddington pulled the gun out of her hands.

The butler then stepped back, pointed the gun at Mandy, and fired.

Something red flew right into her chest and Mandy's fingers were quick to tug out the dart and throw it on the floor.

Dutch let go of her and backed away. Looking angrily at Maks's butler, he shouted, "You jackass! I had her restrained!"

Meanwhile Mandy began shrieking. *"Where's the antidote? Some-one give me the antidote!"*

Dutch looked at me and I shook my head. He shook his too. Neither of us had our kits.

We were so distracted by Mandy that we didn't immediately notice Eddington reach down and pick up the disk. I saw too late that he was now pointing the gun at us. "William!" Maks said, getting out of his seat and stepping angrily toward his butler. "Lower your weapon!"

Eddington pocketed the CD calmly. "No."

I stood up too, absolutely furious with him. "I protected you!" I shouted at him. "When Maks was suspicious of you, I protected you!"

Eddington's eyebrows lowered dangerously. "You ratted me out," he growled, swiveling the gun to point right at my chest. "You told him all about my plans and then you attempted to blackmail me!"

My jaw dropped. *"What plans? What blackmail?"*

Eddington wasn't buying that I knew nothing of what he was talking about; I could see it in his eyes, which were seething with anger. "I'd been working on copying his paintings for years!" he yelled at me. "Quietly painting away in my room to re-create the artwork and replace it all in one night just before I left him . . . until *you* came along and told him exactly what I was plotting!"

I shook my head in disbelief. "I made all that up!" I shouted, thinking back to what I'd said, and how I'd been inspired by the creativity vibe I'd read in William's aura. "Jesus, *that's* what you were really up to?"

Eddington sneered at me. "Do not attempt to lie to me, Ms. Carter. You knew all along. And then, when we were walking out, you said that if I didn't pay you, you'd let Mr. Grinkov know!"

My eyes bulged. "I never said *that*!" I was positive I'd never told him I wanted a bribe. My brain rifled through the memories from that night, and I remembered what I'd actually said. "I told you, William, that you needed to make reparations! Not give me money!"

"Sounded like blackmail to me," he insisted.

I glanced at his shoe with the new lace. "So you came to the office and tried to kill me?"

"No," he said. "I came there to try to reason with you, cut you in for half of the fence, but then I saw you sleeping in that chair and thought it might be better to simply get you out of the way. I wanted to pummel you to death, but I'd left my walking stick in the car, and that would have been too messy anyway. Shoelaces are quite durable, and I nearly had you taken care of but you knocked me off my feet when you shoved that chair into me, and I hurt my knee even more, so I left hoping you would feel threatened by the assault and go away.

"When that didn't work, I thought I could find something out about you and use it against you instead. When Mr. Grinkov's car nearly hit you, and he sent me on ahead to see if you were all right, I had the chance to finally strike you a good blow with my walking stick and I took your wallet. But I couldn't find out anything about you or your supposed psychic abilities. It was like you never existed prior to coming into our lives."

I blinked rapidly again, trying to put the rest of the pieces together. At my feet Mandy was gripping my leg, sweating profusely and begging me to help her, which I completely ignored. "I knew you were likely working for someone else, but I wasn't sure whom," Eddington continued.

Mandy had let go of my leg and was now clinging to Dutch, begging him to help her. He was trying to disentangle himself from her, but she wasn't making it easy. Out of the corner of my eye I could see

Maks approach with his hands raised. He got up next to me and addressed his butler. "What's the plan now, William?"

"Now?" Eddington asked, never taking his angry eyes off me.

"Yes."

Eddington's gaze shifted to his employer, but the air gun stayed trained on me. "Now I finish what I started at her office," he said, and I knew in a heartbeat he was about to pull that trigger. I reacted instinctively, turning my body away from the gun at the same time that Maks shoved me hard to the floor. As I went down, I registered the click of the trigger along with a slight hiss.

I fell to my knees, gasping for air, and wondering why I didn't feel the prick of the dart. Behind me I became aware of a struggle, and I looked back to see Maks yanking the air gun out of his butler's hands, then using it to slam him hard in the head.

At the same time another struggle was taking place; Dutch was trying to disentangle his leg from Mandy's grasp. I saw her desperately flail out and hit the back of his leg right at that spot that causes your legs to buckle. Dutch lurched forward, tripped on her body, and caught the edge of the table right in his left side. There was a slight crunch and all the air went out of him. He sank to the floor clutching his side in unbearable pain. *"Dutch!"* I screamed, scrambling to my knees and crawling toward him.

But Mandy was too quick for me. In an instant her trembling fingers found his gun; yanking it from his belt, she gripped it tightly and got shakily to her feet. Then, she pointed it at his head and screamed, "Give me the fucking antidote!"

A powerful anger came over me and I launched myself at her, slamming hard into her middle. We went sailing through the air. There was a *pop, pop, pop* sound and bullets riddled the plane.

In the next instant the nose dipped and we began to descend very rapidly. Mandy flew out of my grasp, and the back of her neck hit the leg of a table. There was a terrible sound like bones breaking, and in the blink of an eye she lay still again, staring up at me with sightless eyes.

I held on to a nearby seat as the plane continued to dip lower and lower, and I could feel my stomach flutter as the plane began to pick up speed. Someone leaped over my head, and I knew it was Maks. He made it to the cockpit and yanked open the door. I looked through the opening and saw blood spattered on the windshield.

One of the bullets had hit the pilot. Maks pulled up on the wheel and the throttle and the plane stopped its rapid descent. Something bumped into me and I looked down to see that Eddington's unconscious body was sliding forward down the aisle. I shoved him away from me and prayed that Maks could stop the plummeting plane.

Still we seemed to be going down, down, down, and Eddington slid closer and closer to the front, but finally the plane leveled off and I immediately moved over to my fiancé, who was struggling to take in air. "Dutch!" I cried, smoothing back his hair. "How bad is it?"

"My . . . ribs . . . ," he gasped, his face ashen.

Mandy had broken his weakened ribs. "Maks!" I shouted. "We have to land!"

Maks didn't reply right away, and when I turned my head to look toward the cockpit, I could see him struggling to get the dead pilot out of the seat. "I'll be right back!" I promised Dutch, and moved to the front of the plane, stepping over Eddington, who was lodged against one of the front seats.

When I got to the cockpit, I helped Maks with the pilot, who'd taken a bullet to the head. We finally managed to maneuver him out of the cockpit and Maks jumped into the pilot seat to assess the situation. "Do you know how to fly the plane?" I asked.

"Somewhat," he said, his answer vague and not especially reassuring. I watched him play with some of the knobs and it was only then that I realized one of the bullets had ripped into the control panel. "We're losing altitude," he said, pulling up on the nose while watching a gauge. The plane did not seem to want to lift any higher than it was going.

"Can you land it?"

Maks looked down at the terrain. Dusk was falling, but we still had enough light to make out the ground below. I squinted through the window and saw only trees and rocks. "No, I can't land it in this," he said. "And we'll never make it to Victoria."

I looked at him and could feel all the blood drain from my face. "The plane's going to crash?"

Maks stared hard at me. "Yes."

I felt my lower lip tremble and my eyes mist over with tears. After all those close calls in the past several days, *this* was how it would end?

Maks reached over to squeeze my shoulder. "We'll have to jump," he said.

I shook my head. Was he crazy? *"Out of a moving plane?"*

Maks flipped a switch on the control panel, then got up without answering me. I followed him as he hurried past all the bodies to the back. There he opened a locker and pulled out what looked at first like a pair of backpacks and a harness with large clips by the shoulder straps. "Here," he said, handing me the harness. "Put this on and make sure the straps are secure."

He then moved over to Dutch and bent low to talk to him. I couldn't hear what they were saying, but Dutch nodded and with great effort he managed to push himself to a sitting position. Maks then placed one of the backpacks on Dutch and helped him strap in.

It finally dawned on my beleaguered brain that Maks intended to parachute out of the plane. "I can't!" I cried.

I'm not especially afraid of heights, but hurtling myself out of a plane at ten thousand feet was on my list of things I'd be happy to never try, thank you very much.

Maks didn't even look up. "There's no other choice, Abigail," he said, working Dutch's left arm through a strap. "This plane is going to crash. You either come with me, or you die."

Dutch looked up at Maks. "I can take her," he said. "I've got some jump experience."

Maks clipped the final buckle and shook his head. "If you black out, Rivers, you and she are both dead."

My jaw fell open. But before I even had a chance to speak, Dutch poked Maks in the torso. "You're the one who might black out, Grinkov," he said gruffly. "I saw you take that dart in the chest."

My eyes flew to Maks's shirt. There was a small smudge of blood just below his collar, and then I realized the man was pale and sweating. "I can make it until I have to pull the cord," Maks insisted.

"So can I," Dutch countered, but I knew better.

"I'll go with him," I told Dutch, knowing my added weight on his harness would only cause my fiancé unbearable pain, and if Maks blacked out, then I could still pull the cord, or at least I hoped I could.

Dutch tried to hold himself straight, but he was in too much pain and he kept doubling over. In that moment it was decided and I nodded to Maks. "I'm going with you," I said firmly.

He then got Dutch over to the door, and propping him upright, he gave his last set of instructions. "We're at ten thousand feet and descending," he said, holding up a gauge strapped to the parachute for Dutch to see. "You'll have about three minutes of free fall before you'll need to pull the cord. The force of the chute will probably cause further injury to your ribs, but you've got no other choice. If you're still conscious when you land, remain close to your chute. We'll do our best to find you."

Dutch was working to take in air. He coughed and some blood appeared on his lower lip. In an instant I remembered the homing device tucked into my bra, and I reached inside my dress and pulled it out, hurrying toward him to give it to my fiancé so the cavalry could find him. *"Here!"* I cried, rushing forward.

But before I could reach him, Grinkov had worked the door free, yanked Dutch forward, and pushed him by the shoulders through it.

I screamed and flew to the side of the door, but Maks stopped me and took me by both arms. "He'll live!" he snapped, his tone demanding that I get ahold of myself. "Now buckle up so that I can clip you in before we drop too low!"

I edged a little back from the door, scared to be so close to it. With shaking fingers, while the wind whipped in from the open door, I hurried into the harness. It was more complicated than I thought, but I finally figured it out and secured the last strap "Abigail!" Grinkov shouted. "We must go now!"

I turned toward him and began to edge my way to the door, trembling in fear. I was breathing so hard that little stars were staring to cloud my vision, and I just prayed that I wouldn't pass out before I reached Grinkov. In that moment where I reached out my hand to him, I remembered Intuit, and knew I couldn't leave it behind. Looking frantically about the plane, I spotted it near Eddington and held up a hand to Maks. "I have to get Intuit!" I shouted.

"Leave it!" he yelled, but I couldn't.

I reached it in four steps and hurried back toward him while shoving it into the large pocket of my oversized coat. Just as I was about to take Maks's hand, his expression changed and I paused.

The word, *What?* formed in my mind but I never got it out. In the very next instant I was hit hard from behind as someone tackled me about the waist. My feet left the ground and I shut my eyes, bracing for impact as we vaulted forward. But it never came.

Instead, the sound of the air rushing by me like a freight train coupled with the most agonized scream I'd ever heard in my life forced me to open my eyes.

Without fully comprehending what was happening, I saw the rocky terrain dotted with trees right underneath me coming closer and closer with each passing second. Someone was gripping my waist as if his life depended on it—which was incredibly ironic considering we were both plummeting to our deaths.

Looking down at my waist, I realized it was Eddington, screaming so loud it hurt. I was far too terrified to scream—in fact, I was far too terrified to do even the basic things, like breathe.

"Pull the cord!" he screamed. And he began to claw at my harness like a crazed tiger.

"I'm not wearing a parachute, you ass!" I shouted back at him, hitting him on the head several times until he understood.

He stared at me with such stunned amazement that I almost felt bad for him. And then as I watched with an almost surreal detachment, Eddington's eyes rolled up, he gasped, and he let go of me in either some sort of seizure, heart attack, or dead faint. He didn't drop away from me as much as he just moved off to the side a few yards.

Oddly, my thoughts in those seconds of free fall were all about the irony. I was about to die and all anyone would remember was that the butler did it.

Instinctively I spread my arms and legs out like you see skydivers do. My rate of descent seemed to slow just a bit, because Eddington's limp body moved down and away from me much more rapidly then. I watched the ground come up closer and closer and my mind began to race. I was falling to the rocky terrain without a parachute. There was no way I could survive. This was literally my worst nightmare, and I had a moment of clarity where I realized that my dream wasn't about my wedding to Dutch at all. It was a prophetic warning of this exact moment in time.

In my hand I still clutched the homing device, which I thought was rather silly given the situation. Somewhere below I saw a white mushroom of movement. Dutch's chute had opened. My heart broke then and there. He'd live and I wouldn't and we'd never get married. I'd never grow old with him. We'd never finish building our house together. I wouldn't see Cat, or my nephews, or Candice, or Brice, or Dave, or Milo, or our puppies, or any of the souls I loved in this world, ever again.

The finality of that was the worst thing I've ever felt in my life, and that totality pushed the abject terror right out of the way. With a heart full of regret and sadness, I turned the cap on the homing device. They'd likely find it near my body, and it would give them a reference point to find Dutch in time to save his life. It struck me that my last gift to him could be his rescue. So after twisting the cap, I tucked the pen back inside my coat. And then, something else hit me.

No . . . I mean *literally* hit me. "I've got you!" someone shouted in my ear.

I tried to twist around. "Maks!"

"Hold still!" he commanded. "And try to reach your arms back and wrap them around my waist!"

I did as he said, extending both my arms back, clutching his waist while he worked to clip us together. "I can't get it!" he yelled, and I could sense the urgency in his voice.

I could see Dutch's chute floating gently on the air. We came level to it, and I tried to see if he was still conscious, but it was impossible to tell. Then we passed him and continued to plummet. "Dammit!" Grinkov swore again, trying in vain to clip our harnesses together.

The altitude gauge on his chute was right next to me. I could see that it read eighteen hundred feet, well below where he'd told Dutch to pull his cord. I knew we were running out of room and I couldn't let both of us die. I made a decision then and there to take my chances and I let go of Maks with one arm, twisting out of his grasp while turning to face his surprised eyes. I then wrapped my legs around his waist and, before he could even react, I pulled his cord. I had just enough time to curl my fingers through his shoulder straps and brace myself before we were violently whipped upward. I was yanked so hard I thought my neck would snap.

I felt Maks's trembling form clutch me with all his waning strength just at the moment I knew I was about to drop away from him again, and somehow we managed to weather the intense force of the chute opening and we began to float downward.

"Don't let go!" he commanded.

I laid my head on his chest, breathing hard and struggling to hold my grip. My legs were shaking with effort along with my arms, and it felt like forever until we came to within a few dozen meters of the ground. "I . . . can't . . . hold . . . on!" I told him, my grip loosening.

"You've got to!" he yelled. "Abigail, we're almost there! You *must* hold on!"

My legs gave way five seconds later, and I began to slip down his body. "Hold on!" he shouted again, trying to clutch my jacket with one hand while steering the chute.

I put every single bit of effort into those final horribly long seconds. I didn't look down—I just closed my eyes, gripping him with everything I had as I tried to count to fifty.

I got to nineteen and couldn't hold one second longer. In the next instant, I was once again in free fall.

Chapter Seventeen

. . .

I hit the ground hard, and I do mean *hard*. As braced as I thought I was for impact, I was not prepared for *that*.

So much happened in that instant that it's hard to explain what I felt first. There was the bone-jarring slam of my body against the rocky terrain, which knocked all the breath right out of me, followed instantly by a lightning bolt of pain in my left shoulder that traveled all the way down my spine and radiated outward like a shock wave through my limbs.

An instant after that, my head felt like it'd just been hit with a baseball bat and then the world went dark.

When I came to, I was unbelievably dizzy and completely disoriented. I couldn't move a muscle either, but so much hurt that I didn't really want to. There was also a noise I couldn't quite figure out . . . a sort of thump, thump, thump.

Voices could be heard over this and none of them were ones I recognized. Numbers were being tossed around and terms I couldn't understand. It was like my brain couldn't decide what to overload on—pain or information.

"Stop!" I whispered, unable to do more than that.

"Patient is conscious!" someone said. "What's her name again?"

"Abigail," said a voice I did recognize. It was Maks.

"Abigail, can you hear me?" said the first man.

My eyes fluttered. "Dutch?" I croaked. Behind my lids, tears flooded my eyes. If this was the kind of shape I was in, what could have possibly happened to my fiancé?

"If you can understand me, Abigail, please squeeze my hand."

I realized then that this man was holding my hand. I squeezed and repeated my request. "Dutch?"

No one said anything and with great effort I opened my eyes. Two men in orange jumpsuits hovered over me and were sticking me with IVs. Behind them sat Maks, his expression gravely concerned in his very pale face, which was also coated in sweat. He looked barely able to sit up.

Silently I pleaded with him to tell me what had happened to Dutch. "They're searching for him," he said.

A ragged sob erupted from deep inside of me, sending a fresh wave of pain from the top of my head down to my toes, and blissfully, it was enough to send me back into the stupor of unconsciousness.

The next time I remember waking up, I was lying in a hospital bed feeling much less pain and slightly detached. The room was dim, but I could make out someone sitting in the shadows. "Dutch?"

The figure stood and stepped forward, sending my hopeful heart plummeting. It was Frost. "Hey, Cooper," he said with a smile that still looked sad. "How you feeling?"

Again my eyes welled with tears. I was so afraid for Dutch that I didn't even care what shape I was in. "Did you find him?" I gasped. "Did you find Dutch?"

Frost's eyes became pinched and he seemed to be gathering his words carefully before telling me.

"Just say it," I said, openly sobbing now, because his expression told me everything. "Just tell me what you found."

He looked at me with such sympathy then and I could feel my heart shattering into a million pieces.

The door opened before he could confess the truth, and a doctor entered. "He's out of surgery," he told Frost.

"He made it?" my handler replied, his look astonished.

The doctor nodded. "As I told you when he was brought in, I gave him only a twenty percent chance of making it through the surgery, but he's definitely a fighter and he pulled through."

"So, he'll be okay?" Frost pressed.

The doctor inhaled deeply, and I could tell he was dog-tired. "His lung was collapsed and he suffered a laceration of the liver and spleen, but we've stopped the bleeding and we've stabilized him for now. The next twenty-four hours will be crucial, and I've upgraded his chances to about sixty percent. As long as he doesn't develop a blood clot or infection, I think Agent Rivers will pull through."

Frost eyed me again; this time there was no sympathy there. Just hope.

"As for the other patient," the doctor continued.

"Grinkov," Frost said, turning back to the doctor. "Did he survive?"

I remembered Maks's pale face before I'd been pushed out of the plane and how terrible he'd looked on the helicopter that had gotten me here. "The damage from the second dose of toxins was minimal given how much of the antidote he had in his system," the doctor said. "He's sustained some kidney damage, but we think he'll be able to make a full recovery."

"Can I go see him?" I asked weakly.

Frost turned to me in surprise. "Grinkov?"

I shook my head. "Dutch."

The doctor smiled kindly and came over to check the chart hanging on the end of my bed. "You're not going anywhere, young lady," he said. "You've sustained a dislocated shoulder, broken femur, sprained wrist, fractured pelvis, and a pretty severe concussion. I don't want you even thinking about moving out of that bed for at least a week."

Again my eyes misted over. "But he needs me," I whispered. "We're getting married, Doctor," I added, as if that would make a difference and sway his decision.

The doctor laid a gentle hand on my forehead. "He needs you to get better, Ms. Cooper. And while you're getting better, we'll take good care of your fiance so that he can make it to that wedding, okay?"

Reluctantly I nodded, closed my eyes, and found myself falling asleep once again.

I'm not sure how long I slept, but it must have been a good while, because when I woke, the room was dim again, but not by quite as much, which let me know it was probably sometime late in the day.

Opening my eyes, I saw Frost once more sitting in the chair in my room, this time reading the paper.

"It was Mandy," I said to him.

He jerked a little in surprise and considered me over the top of his paper before setting it down and pulling the chair up close to my bed. "I know," he said.

"You do?"

He smiled. "You told me all about it this morning. Don't you remember?"

"No."

His eyebrows rose. "Must have been the drugs."

"What'd I tell you?"

Frost sighed. "Well, for starters you demanded hazard pay. And then you insisted we send someone to retrieve your engagement ring."

I would have laughed if I'd been able to. "I'm glad I got to the most important parts first."

Frost nodded, and sat back, but not before reaching into his shirt pocket to pull out something small and green. "It only took our guy an hour to find it after we and the CSIS raided Boklovich's estate. The cadaver dog led us right to the grave where you told us to look."

I sucked in a breath and felt my lower lip tremble. Frost handed me my engagement ring. I slipped it on and looked at it for a long time, which was how long it took me to be able to speak without crying again. "Did you find Intuit?"

Frost nodded.

"It was sticking out of the pocket of your fatigue jacket."

I smiled. "Mission accomplished," I whispered before I remembered the software Dutch had been carrying. "And the disk?" I asked Frost.

"On Agent Rivers when he was brought in."

I closed my eyes and thanked God that it had all worked out okay. "So, it's over?"

Frost shrugged. "Mostly," he said. "We're still interested in having a nice long talk with Grinkov, but he's refusing to talk to us until he gets to see you."

It was my turn to look surprised. "Why's he want to see me?"

The corners of Frost's mouth quirked up a bit. "I think because he likes you, Cooper."

I frowned. "I'm engaged," I said, holding up my left hand so he could see for himself.

Frost nodded with a sly grin. "He knows, and he likes you in spite of that."

"Let me guess: You want me to talk to him so that he'll get all chatty with you CIA boys, right?"

"We'd really appreciate it."

I tapped my finger on the metal frame of the bed. "Okay," I said.

"Yeah?"

"On two conditions."

"Oh, of course there have to be conditions," Frost mocked. "Okay, Cooper, lay 'em on me. What're your demands?"

"You arrange for me to see Dutch—today—and you boys pay for our wedding."

Frost rubbed at the scruff on his chin. He looked like he hadn't had a shower in a day or two. "Rivers is in ICU and you're not supposed to move," he began.

"Figure it out," I told him. I wasn't playin' around here. I *needed* to see my fiancé. Period.

Frost shrugged. "Okay," he conceded. "How about this? We arrange for you to be wheeled into ICU and hang out with Rivers for a while, and we pay for your honeymoon."

"Cheap bastard," I told him, but I was actually grinning.

"Blame it on budget cuts," he told me.

"Fine," I agreed. "But I wanna go somewhere *nice*, Frost. Not some Motel Six in Peoria or anything, got it?"

Frost's eyes suddenly went someplace far away. "I'll send you where I went on my honeymoon," he told me.

"Where?"

But he wouldn't tell me. "It'll be a surprise, Cooper. But don't worry, I think you two will really like it."

A few hours later, when I was rested again, Grinkov came into my room. "Hello, Abigail," he said, coming over to me and sweeping up my hand to kiss it gently on the knuckles.

"How are you?" I asked.

"I'm well," he said, his other hand moving to stroke the side of my head. "And you?"

"I'll heal."

Grinkov moved to the chair Frost had previously been holding vigil in. "I'm sorry I couldn't get the harness hooked," he said, his face fully displaying his guilt. "I didn't see William come for you until it was too late. His weight added to your rate of descent. It took me several thousand feet to make up the difference, and if you hadn't gone spread eagle like that after getting him off you, I don't think I would have made it to you in time. I'm sorry you had to fall so long and so far before I could manage to reach you."

I eyed him with incredulity. "Are you *kidding me*, Maks? You saved my life! And by my count, that was at least the third, possibly the fourth time you'd done that."

Maks shrugged that off. "You're a very special woman," he said simply. "I couldn't let anything bad happen to you."

"Thank you," I said sincerely. "And thank you also for saving Dutch."

Maks nodded. "Do you really love him?" he asked abruptly.

I looked him dead in the eyes. "With my whole heart."

Maks turned away. "You were only pretending to be attracted to me, then?"

I swallowed hard and considered lying, but then, what good would that do? "No, Maks," I said. "I really was attracted to you. And when I found out you weren't a terrible person, but someone conflicted with both good and bad elements, well, I was even more attracted. But I'm deeply in love my fiancé, and that will never change."

Maks continued to study the wall on the opposite side of the room. "The CIA would like to recruit me," he said.

"I'm sure they would."

"Do you think I should say yes?"

I considered his question for a bit before answering. "I think that the CSIS has enjoyed ruining your reputation with the bigwigs in Toronto in order to suit their own purposes, and maybe you've had enough of that. Maybe it's time you had someone else help you make a more reputable name for yourself. Of course, it'd be a tricky road with the CIA. They may like you to remain a bad guy, Maks. You should listen to the part of you that wants to be seen as a good man, a positive role model for your sons even, and decide if partnering up with them is the right way to go about doing that."

"You could mean either I should or I shouldn't with that answer," he said slyly.

I nodded. "I could."

Maks got up then and came over to stand close to me. "It was a pleasure knowing you, Abigail Carter."

I didn't bother to correct him. And I also didn't bother to push him away when he bent to kiss me on the lips. . . . I knew where my heart belonged.

The next morning I was gently transferred to a gurney and wheeled down to ICU. I'd been told that Dutch was just coming off his intubation tube, and when I got to his room, there were many nurses hovering around his bed, hooking up IV bags to both his left and right arms. None of them were happy to see me, and I had the feeling that the strings Frost had pulled to arrange this little meeting had been full of knots and tangles.

Still, after they'd tended to him, my gurney was pushed over to his side and I reached out to hold his hand. It was warm and just feeling the heat from it filled me with a happiness and relief I can't fully describe. He was still unconscious, but breathing on his own and so far showing remarkable improvement. If all went well, one of the nurses told me, he'd be out of ICU in another few days.

I was allowed only fifteen minutes with him before I'd have to leave, so I made the most of it. Holding tightly to his hand, I told him how much I loved him, how proud I was of him, and how brave I thought he was. And then I looked inside myself and knew that I couldn't deny this man anything—especially not something as insignificant as a wedding date. Looking back on my reasoning for postponing it, I realized I'd tried to make the choice all about what I wanted rather than what would be good for us.

Clanging around in my thoughts as I looked at his broken and bruised body was what the doctor had said: that Dutch had only a sixty percent chance of making it. That was better than average, yes, but it still struck a deep chord of fear in my heart.

"Dutch," I said close to his ear, "I'll make you a deal. You agree to make a full recovery and I'll marry you whenever you want. You pick the wedding date, honey, and I promise you I'll show up and say I do. No more arguments about my needing time to make it perfect. It'll be perfect just because you and I are there. If that's tomorrow, next week, or the first of November, cowboy, I will be there with bells on."

I looked down at his hand in mine and waited for a sign. I wanted him to wiggle his fingers or squeeze my hand—you know, like they show in the movies. Something to let me know that he'd heard me. But nothing happened. His hand just lay there limp and lifeless in my grasp, and I couldn't help the terrible feeling that crept over me. It's hard to explain, but an awful foreboding snaked its way down my spine, and fear wrapped itself tightly around my heart.

"Time to go," a nurse whispered too soon.

I kissed Dutch's fingers and gently laid his hand back. I was too choked up to say or do much else.

Late the next morning, when my own pain was still fairly intense and my worry over Dutch wouldn't abate, I was having a really low moment when a nurse came in. I thought it was the shift change until she told me that she was actually a nurse from the ICU. My heart began to pound hard in my chest. "What's happened?" I asked her desperately.

"It's your fiancé," she said.

My hand flew to my mouth. "No!" I said. "Please . . . God . . . *no!*"

She looked puzzled, and then she seemed to realize what I must be thinking. "He's fine," she assured me, moving quickly to my bed to hold out a folded piece of paper to me. "He woke up a little bit ago, and he asked me to give you a note."

I was too stunned to speak. My mind had gone so completely to that worst-case scenario that it took me a minute to recover from it, and in that moment the nurse smiled, tucked the note into my hand, and left me alone again.

When I could think, I unfolded the slip of paper. It was only six words long, but they were the sweetest six words I could ever remember reading. The note read:

Edgar,
   You. Me. November. Game on!